Knight Fall

ANDREW G. NELSON

HUNTZMAN
ENTERPRISES

Published by Huntzman Enterprises

Huntzman Enterprises
Edinburg, IL. 62531

First Printing: December 2016

ISBN-10: 0-9961334-9-6
ISBN-13: 978-0-9961334-9-4

Printed in the United States of America
1 3 5 7 9 10 8 6 4 2

DEDICATION

To my wife Nancy; without your love, support and constant encouragement this book would never have been possible. Thank you for always believing in me.

And to God, through whom all things are possible.

Romans 8:28

Other Titles by

Andrew G. Nelson

James Maguire Series

Perfect Pawn

Queen's Gambit

Bishop's Gate

Knight Fall

Alex Taylor Series

Small Town Secrets

Little Boy Lost

NYPD Cold Case Series

The Katherine White Murder

Non-Fiction

Uncommon Valor: Insignia of the NYPD ESU

"A knight in shining armor is a man who has never had his metal truly tested." - Author Unknown

CHAPTER ONE

Brooklyn Heights, Brooklyn, N.Y.
Saturday, December 14th, 2013 – 8:01 p.m.

Marisol Perez gazed out the windshield of the Toyota FJ Cruiser. Watching as the wipers worked diligently to scatter each new wave of snowflakes, as they hit the glass.

Up ahead, the tan granite blocks of the Brooklyn Bridge's eastern tower stood cloaked in fog; the lights from the suspension cables basking it in an eerie pallor. When the traffic light turned green she made a right onto Old Fulton Street. The wet pavement of the roadway sparkled like a field of diamonds.

The frigid streets of Brooklyn were a far cry from the warm, tropical climate of her native Puerto Rico, but it was the price she had been willing to pay for her career. A little over ten years ago, while she was a junior in college, she had been recruited by a major pharmaceutical company to be a representative. She learned early on that tight blouses and short skirts, coupled with an inviting smile, went a long way with the medical professionals she interacted with daily.

Not everyone, she corrected herself.

There were always those, generally of the female persuasion, who looked down upon her with disdain. They knew that it was all an act. A little *T&A* show to illicit a positive response from the doctors. Ironically, none of them seemed to mind when one of her chiseled-jawed, male counterparts showed up, laughing and joking with them. Not that it mattered to her.

What had started as a part-time job, to pay her college bills, had quickly turned into a full-time job and ultimately a career. Now, at thirty-one, she was the senior marketing and sales manager for the entire Tri-State area.

December was always a busy time for her, with a never ending parade of holiday parties to attend. Even the weekends were fair game, which was exactly the reason why she was out on this cold, dreary night. With the weather as bad as it was, she had thought about taking a pass on the event, but the administrator at Coney Island Hospital was an old *friend* from her rep'ing days. Back then he was known as the *hot* doctor with a great bedside manner. She had found out, when they got behind closed doors, that his bedside manner, or in this case his *desk-side* manner, extended to his office as well.

The thought of getting snowed-in at the hospital wasn't very appealing, so she bid an early goodnight and began making her way back home.

She took solace in the knowledge that in another month she would be able to make her annual escape, a three week vacation back to Puerto Rico. There she would spend her time soaking up enough sun, sand and margaritas to get her through another eleven months in the *Big Apple.*

Perez made her way along the desolate streets, driving past the old, sealed up vaults contained in the bridge's anchorage point. A hundred years ago, when this part of Brooklyn had a booming sea business, these vaults were used to store wine, among other things, because of their consistent year round temps. Now the thought of a nice glass of wine brought a smile to her face.

The bright yellow SUV made a right turn onto Henry Street and Perez immediately swerved right, pulling into a parking space just as the previous occupant pulled away.

"Yes," she exclaimed triumphantly, as she slipped into spot.

Finding a parking place so close to home was almost unheard of. In fact, if the weather hadn't been so shitty outside, she'd have walked down to the local bodega and played the lottery, to mark this momentous occasion.

Perez put the vehicle into park and shut the engine off. Then she grabbed her purse from the passenger seat and exited the

SUV. She cautiously made her way down Henry Street in her heels, slowly navigating the slush covered sidewalk, and then turned down Poplar Street. Immediately she was hit with a blast of frigid air that came in from the nearby East River. She turned her back, as she fumbled with her evening jacket, pulling the collar up and cinching the belt tight.

As she walked down the deserted street, her eyes were drawn to the gas fired lamps that lined the sidewalk. She never got tired of looking at them. They were one of the things that had originally sold her on this apartment. The lamps were like something that she envisioned in a Victorian era love story. During the nicer months she would often sit on the front stoop, gazing up at the flickering flames, and fantasize about a fairytale prince coming to whisk her away to his castle.

"Not today," she said, as she grabbed the cold metal hand rail and made her way up the slick front steps.

Inside, Perez headed up the stairs to her fourth floor apartment. Most of her visitors complained, but she'd always enjoyed it. For her it was like getting in an extra leg workout twice a day. Even though she was management now, she also knew that it didn't hurt to give the boys something nice to look at when she walked out of the room.

She unlocked the door and stepped inside. She removed her jacket and hung it on the large wooden hall tree that sat just inside the entryway. Next she headed into the kitchen, dropping her purse on the counter, and removed a bottle of merlot from the fridge. She poured herself a glass and took a sip, as she made her way down the hallway to her bedroom.

Perez sat the wine glass down on the dresser and picked up the television remote, turning it on. She removed her heels, kicking them off next to the dresser, as she watched the local news channel come on. Next she unbuttoned her blouse, letting it fall onto the bed behind her, and then slid out of her skirt, letting it fall onto the floor.

When she was done, she turned the volume up on the TV and retrieved the wine glass from the dresser. She took a sip as she headed off to the bathroom.

Perez reached into the shower, turning on the water, and closed the glass door behind her. She set the wine down on the vanity top and finished getting undressed. She paused for a moment, staring at her reflection in the mirror, and critically examined the woman who looked back at her.

While she wasn't on the *front lines* anymore, so to speak, her job was still very much *appearance* driven. The bottom line was that she sold a product, but even though the product was good, people still wanted to buy from someone who physically appealed to them.

The sales game was always about appearance. It didn't matter if you sold cars, real estate, or the cure for the common cold. Sales numbers were driven by the ability of the salesperson to connect with their customer. You could be the greatest salesperson in the world, but if you didn't have *sex appeal* you'd have to work twice as hard for the same sales numbers.

At 5'8" she was slightly taller than most women, which certainly helped her cause, but there was no easy way for someone to carve washboard abs and a firm ass, not that people didn't try. There was always this new diet, or that new fad, being hyped by a celebrity that people latched onto. It was the reason that weight loss was a fifty billion dollar industry in the United States.

The simple truth, which no one ever wanted to hear, was that it required hard work and dedication. No, there was no pill you could take for those things, if there was, she'd have sold it. The body that she had was carved out of a strict diet along with countless hours of crunches, squats and cardio. It was the reason that she spent five days a week at the gym.

Perez knew that the other women in her department talked behind her back. She had heard all the rumors of how she had *earned* her promotion on her knees. Other women might have been insulted by the snide remarks, but she wasn't. She had earned her spot through hard work and tenacity; not that she was opposed to using sex to get what she wanted. After all, this was business and you did what you needed to do to get ahead.

The women who talked behind her back were the same ones that sat in the lunchroom, eating fast food and candy-bars, while bitching about how their husbands were cheating on them. The only way they would ever go into the gym was if it they had to pass through it on the way to the lunchroom.

She remembered the poster of Arnold, posing at the Mr. Olympia contest in South Africa, which hung on the wall at the gym. It bore the saying: *'Everybody pities the weak; jealousy you have to earn.'*

No one ever pitied her, but the list of those jealous of her accomplishments grew longer every day.

Maybe one day she would make it high enough up the corporate ladder that she didn't have to invest so much energy into looking good. For now, she accepted that it was the price she had to pay in order to keep her bosses, as well as potential clients, eating out of the palm of her hand.

She picked up the glass and finished her drink, setting it back down on the vanity and headed into the shower.

The hot water felt so good, as it cascaded down her body, chasing away the cold chill that had enveloped her. She faced the wall; her hands pressing against the cold tiles, as she felt the stress slowly drain from her body. After several long minutes she reached over and grabbed the shampoo, washing her long black hair. When she was done, she added crème rinse, then grabbed the soap and began washing off her body.

She wasn't sure if it was the heat or the wine, or maybe a combination of both, but she found herself becoming aroused as her hands slid across her body.

Maybe you should have stayed in Coney Island, she thought, as she remembered the first time the good doctor had bent her over his desk.

She leaned back against the shower wall and allowed her hands to glide gently over her skin, as the vivid memory of that first encounter played out in her mind. She moaned softly, as she felt the palms of her hands brush against her hard nipples.

Perez knew exactly what she wanted. She needed more wine, a warm bed and the vibrator that waited patiently for her in her nightstand. She grudgingly repositioned her body, tilting her head slightly forward and felt the water pour down on her, as she began rinsing her hair.

When she was done, she climbed out of the shower, grabbing the towel from the heated rack, and dried her body. Then she slipped on the night shirt, which had been hanging on the back of the bathroom door, and wrapped her hair up in the towel. When she was done she grabbed the wine glass from the vanity and made her way out into the bedroom.

She had only taken a few steps toward the kitchen, when she caught movement out of the corner of her eye; a black shadow which emerged quickly from off to her right. Perez tried to turn, to get away from the threat, but it was too late. In an instant the *shadow* was upon her and she felt an incredible wave of pressure as it slammed into her, knocking her forward and onto the bed.

She struggled to fight back, but it was no use. Despite her athleticism, she was no match for the hundred pounds plus weight difference between her and her attacker.

As he straddled her body, holding her firmly in place, the man quickly secured her hands with the restraints which he had pre-positioned on the headboard rails. When the realization of what was happening finally hit her, she began to scream, but he immediately grabbed her by the back of the neck, plunging her face violently into the pillow beneath her, which instantly muffled her cries for help.

"Shut your mouth, bitch," she heard a gruff voice command, as he finished securing her wrists.

Perez began to panic, as she felt herself being suffocated. Her body thrashed about wildly, trying to dislodge herself from the man, but instinctively she knew that it was of little use. He was clearly much stronger than she was.

She felt her head jerk backward and she let out a loud gasp. Then she felt the towel being ripped forcefully from her head, and felt him tug on her hair, pulling her body violently backward.

"If you scream," he said, in a low, menacing voice, "then I am only going to hurt you more, do you understand?"

"Yes," she exclaimed, her voice cracking in fear.

"Good," the man replied, as he got up from the bed.

Behind her, she could hear him undressing, as she struggled in vain against the restraints.

Seconds ticked by slowly, as she waited, her heart beating so loudly in her chest that she thought it was going to explode. Terror gripped her as she felt the bed move under his weight. Suddenly, she felt his strong hands grip her hips, lifting her up and pulling her back against him.

She screamed as she felt him force her legs apart, pressing himself inside her. He reached around, his hand clamping down roughly over her mouth.

"I said shut up, you bitch," the man growled angrily into her ear, before he drove her face back down into the pillow, muffling her screams.

"You like to act like a slut," he said. "Well now it's time that you get treated like one."

One hand gripped the back of her head, holding it down against the pillow, as the other hand roughly pawed her body. She felt his hand grope and grab at her, playing with her breast while she felt his pelvis slamming into her ass. He grunted loudly as he thrust himself deep inside her.

She laid there defenseless, fighting to breathe, as her body was being taken against her will.

In the background, the smiling meteorologist on the television screen told the rest of the world how tomorrow was going to be a *much better day.*"

CHAPTER TWO

"You look like you could use a drink, buddy," Rich Stargold said, holding out a bottle of beer toward his friend.

"I could use the whole fucking bar, right now," James Maguire replied, as he accepted the beer and took a drink.

"It's a marriage proposal for crying out loud," Stargold said with a laugh. "I thought SEAL's were supposed to be tough."

"Don't make me do something that's gonna end with me having to hide your body, asshole," Maguire replied, draining half the beer in one gulp.

"You know, there was a time when that might have scared me, but, seeing as how you're my number two, I doubt you want to take on the additional workload that my untimely demise would bring."

"You're just lucky I love Mary and the girls," Maguire replied.

"You love *her*," Rich said, as he glanced over at Melody Anderson.

James looked over at where she stood, talking to Mary Stargold and another woman.

It seemed like only yesterday that he had first seen her at Peter Bart's charity event. He had walked into the event intent on making a brief *appearance,* but in one fateful moment his life had forever changed, when he spotted the tall, blonde haired woman across the room. Even now, she stood apart from every other lady in the world.

The sapphire blue evening dress that she was wearing clung to her body, accentuating every curve, and her long hair draped playfully over her shoulders. Melody would always complain to

9

him about how hard it was for women to get ready for a social event, while men only had to put on a suit and tie. He would just laugh because, to him, it didn't matter whether she was wearing a designer dress or old faded jeans, she always looked beautiful.

Now, nearly two years later, he couldn't imagine what his life was ever like before her.

Not that it had been all *unicorns* and *rainbows*. No, far from it, they'd shared a number of *bumps in the road* over the last nineteen months. Maguire recoiled internally, as if he had been sucker-punched by a ghost, as he recalled that night, only a few months earlier, when he had almost lost her.

He had spent a lifetime in harm's way, first as a Navy SEAL and, later, as a cop in the violence-torn seven-three precinct, in the Brooklyn North section of New York City. However, none of that experience could have ever prepared him for holding her in his arms, as he watched the life slowly drain out of her.

Even the very thought sent a cold shiver down his spine.

As if on cue, she looked over at him and smiled; a radiant smile that sent the ghosts of the past scurrying for the shadows.

"You know, you're one lucky *sonofabitch*," Rich said.

"Yes, I am," Maguire replied softly.

"Well, then you should probably go and put a ring on her finger before she comes to her senses."

Maguire looked down at his watch. It was a quarter after eight.

Besides Rich, there was only one other person that Maguire *needed* here tonight, and she was already late.

"A few more minutes," he said, as he looked back up.

"Are you getting cold feet?" Stargold asked.

"You're such an ass," Maguire replied. "No, I am not getting cold feet. It's an engagement, not a firing squad."

"Well, some would argue that they are mutually inclusive."

"Shouldn't you be doing something productive?" Maguire asked. "Like getting Mary another drink?"

"Hey, tonight I am here to support you, brother," Stargold said with a smile.

"Outstanding," Maguire replied.

Across the room, in the direction of the front door, he heard Genevieve Gordon's distinctive squeal of delight.

"I'll be right back," he replied, passing his beer to Stargold.

"See, I told you she'd be here," he replied smugly.

"Why don't you call Operations and see if they need *you* to go somewhere," Maguire replied, then turned and walked toward the front of the house.

When he arrived in the foyer, Maguire found Gen in an animated conversation with his old partner, Alex Taylor.

"You still like making an entrance, don't you?' Maguire said as he and Alex hugged each other.

"Yeah," she whispered into his ear, "but at least this time I'm not falling down drunk."

"That was quite an entrance," he said with a smile, as he pulled away to look at her.

"Yeah, it's just too bad it was at the children's Christmas party," Alex replied.

"There was that," Maguire said with a laugh.

"Then again, the night is still young," she said.

"I'm glad you made it," he said. "I was starting to get worried."

"What? You really thought I would miss the chance to see you become an *honest* man?" she said in a quiet voice. "You just better hope she says yes."

"I'm glad that you all think this is funny," he replied.

"Hey, rookie, remember that I *know* you……" Alex replied, letting the words trail off.

"Yes," he replied, staring into her eyes. "You do."

The two of them shared a bond that transcended *friendship*. It was one born out of pain and hardship; of seeing one another at not only the highest of highs, but at the lowest of lows. They'd been there for each other no matter what and they had each risked their lives for the other at times too numerous to count. Being friends was easy; being partners was something entirely different.

"Don't go and get all emotional on me, cupcake," she replied. "It's been a long ride and I could use a drink."

"It's good to see you, Alex," Maguire said.

"You too," she replied.

"Hello," a voice called out from behind her.

"Oh, I'm so sorry," Alex said sheepishly. "James, this is Peter, Peter Bates."

James looked behind Alex to see a man standing there, looking more than a bit uncomfortable. He reached his hand out, shaking Bates' hand.

"James Maguire," he said. "It's nice to meet you, Peter."

"Thank you," Bates replied, "and likewise."

"Peter is our resident doctor and medical examiner," Alex said.

"Well, hopefully we won't need either of your specialties tonight, Doctor," Maguire said with a laugh.

"Just make sure you don't screw-up your big announcement and you won't have anything to worry about," Gen said with a mischievous grin.

"Thanks for believing in me," he said sarcastically.

"Anytime," Gen replied as she waved over one of the staff, motioning toward the overnight bag that Peter was carrying.

"Please take that up to Ms. Taylor's room," she said.

Peter handed the bag over to the man.

"Now let's get you something to drink," Maguire said, "so that we can finally get this party started."

"Lead the way," Alex said.

They followed Maguire into the main room and over to where a bar had been setup.

"What's your poison this week?" he asked Alex.

"Wine is fine," she replied. "Red if you have it."

"Peter?"

"I'll have a beer," the man replied.

Maguire retrieved the two drinks from the bartender and handed them to his guests.

"Sorry that we're late," Alex said. "Today was the city hall Christmas party and I had to make an appearance to appease the board."

"Look at you doing the politic thing," Maguire said with a laugh. "Who knew?"

"Yeah, because you know just how much I *love* politics."

"Not to mention how politically *incorrect* you are," he replied.

"I prefer to think of it as having a low tolerance for bullshit," she said, taking a sip of wine. "You can't try to bend me over the barrel three hundred and sixty-four days and think on number three-sixty-five you can invite me to a party, give me some shitty spiced egg-nog and make it all better."

"Learn to play the game, Alex," Maguire replied. "It'll make your life a whole lot less stressful."

"That's what I keep telling her," Bates chimed in.

13

"Good luck with that," Maguire said. "I've been preaching that to her for years, but I haven't been able to penetrate that thick skull of hers. I'm about ready to give up."

"Nobody likes a quitter, rookie," she replied.

"She can be a tough nut to crack," Bates said.

"Easy there, *Dr. Doogie*," Alex said, glancing over her shoulder at Peter. "It's a long walk back to Penobscot."

"Well, at least I'm glad to see that country living hasn't completely stripped her of her Brooklyn North charm," Maguire replied.

"Alex!" a voice called out from behind them.

They turned and watched as Melody approached them.

"I'm so glad that you could make it tonight."

"I wouldn't have missed this for the world," she replied, as the two women hugged each other. "I was just telling James how much I love holiday parties."

"I hope you can stay for a few days," Melody said.

"Unfortunately, no, we have to head back tomorrow," Alex replied. "I have a budget meeting to go to on Monday."

"Oh, no," Melody said disappointedly. "Can't you have someone else attend for you?"

"I wish I could, but everyone in my department is local. I wouldn't put it past the board members to use that familiarity and bully them into accepting less than what we need."

"Well, I can certainly understand that," Melody replied. "It's not easy being the boss."

"Ain't that the truth," Alex said.

Melody looked over at the man standing next to Alex.

"And who is this," she asked.

"This is Dr. Peter Bates," Alex replied. "He's my designated *chaperone* for the evening."

14

"Someone needs to keep an eye on you," Maguire said softly.

"It is a pleasure to meet you, Dr. Bates," Melody replied, extending her hand toward the man.

"The pleasure is all mine," Bates replied, taking Melody's hand in his, "and please, call me Peter."

"Just ignore them, Peter," Melody said. "They are like two little kids when they get together."

Alex glanced over at Maguire and stuck her tongue out at him.

"That's very mature," he replied.

"Whatever," Alex said, taking a sip of wine.

"Enough you two," Melody said.

"Yes, dear," Maguire replied.

Melody hooked Alex's arm in hers and began to lead her away.

"We girls have some catching up to do," she said to Maguire, "and I believe you have something to say to the folks gathered here tonight."

"Break a leg, rookie," Alex said with a chuckle, as the two women walked away.

"Has Alex always been this way?" Peter asked.

"Oh, you have no idea," Maguire replied, as he watched the two women walk away.

CHAPTER THREE

Brooklyn Heights, Brooklyn, N.Y.
Saturday, December 14th, 2013 – 8:28 p.m.

Marisol Perez stared up at the man who was now on top of her. She could feel the hot sting of her tears as the man continued to assault her.

He had repositioned her so that she was now on her back and her arms were tied up behind her head. He'd stuck a pair of panties into her mouth, as a makeshift gag, ensuring that any attempt on her part to scream would be muffled.

Now he had her legs spread wide and was grunting loudly as he drove himself deep inside her. He reached down cupping her large breasts in his hands, and began playing with them roughly.

"You like that, don't you, you little fucking whore?" he hissed.

She nodded dutifully, remembering the painful sting of his hand across her ass when she refused to answer his last question.

"I know you do," he said, his voice tinged with anger. "You like dressing up like a slut, showing off your tits and ass, and now you're going to know what it's like to be treated like one."

The man pinched her nipples between his fingers, tugging on them, as his body slammed against hers.

Perez's eyes filled with tears. She wanted to scream, to make the pain stop, but all she could do was lay there and allow him to have his way with her.

Suddenly, the pace of the man's thrusts quickened and he let out a loud moan. Perez felt him erupt inside her, the man's semen filling her. She tried to resist, tried to wrest her body out of his control, but it was no use. Each spasm sent another wave deep inside her. She closed her eyes, waiting for the nightmare to end.

She felt his body collapse onto hers; felt the labored breathing of his chest against hers. Slowly she felt his erection subside and begin to slip out of her, followed by a rush of wetness as his seed drained out of her.

The man rolled off of her slowly, collapsing onto the bed next to her.

"You are one amazing slut," he said, after catching his breath.

He leaned over and slowly pulled the panties from her mouth.

"Was it as good for you as it was for me?" he asked.

"It was awesome," she replied, in a low seductive voice. Proud of the little performance she had just pulled off.

I should get an Academy Award for that performance, she thought.

"Good," he replied, as he slowly climbed up on top of her and began to untie her hands.

"Next time, try going down on me before you fuck me," she said, rubbing her sore wrists.

"Sorry, my love," the man said sheepishly. "I just got caught up in the moment and once I saw that sexy ass of yours I lost it."

"I saw that," she said with a laugh. "I hope I didn't make you wait too long. You know how doctors can just go on and on."

"Yes," he replied with a laugh. "They do tend to talk a lot. I was beginning to get a bit worried, but I had some wine while I waited."

"Speaking of which, be a dear, Ted and fetch me a glass."

"Anything for you, my love," the man said.

He leaned over and kissed her gently before getting up from the bed. She watched his naked body saunter across the room and out the door.

He was older then she normally liked, being more than twenty years her senior, and was quite out of shape. She had spent a lot of time *building him up* verbally, so that he would eventually take the *bait* that she offered him.

Still, he also had a tendency toward being a bit *quick* on the draw, but Theodore Eichenberg had other *attributes* that she found quite attractive. Namely he had a very good job, which paid quite handsomely, as well as a dull wife and family who would be devastated to learn the truth about *naughty Teddy*.

She sat up in bed and reached over, removing the pack of cigarettes from the night table. She lit one up, taking a long slow drag, as she replayed the night's fun. She liked to role-play with him. She enjoyed taking him out of his comfort zone and putting him into compromising positions.

Most recently she had made him take her over to the promenade, which overlooked the East River, and have his way with her. The cold weather had reduced the chance that they would encounter someone actually strolling along the walkway, but it did nothing to inhibit the voyeurs who peered down from the windows of the surrounding apartment. The orgasm she experienced had been incredibly intense as she gazed up at those behind the windows who were watching them.

Unfortunately, not everyone was enthused by their sexual escapades. Someone, probably an old biddy, had called the cops on them. They had barely had the chance to finish up when they saw the flashing lights approaching, in the distance, and beat a quick retreat to her apartment.

Ted had a lot to lose, personally and professionally, which added a level of risk to it, but the thought of getting *caught in the act* was like an aphrodisiac to her. The only real problem was his lack of stamina. One thing was for certain, after he left, she would have to take matters into her own hands and finish off what he had started.

"Here you are, my dear," Ted said, handing her the wine glass, as he climbed back into the bed.

"Thank you," she replied, as she took the glass from him, taking a sip.

"You really should quit," he said, taking a sip from his own glass. "You know those things are very bad for you."

"Don't lecture, Teddy," she chided him. "No one likes taking advice from reformed smokers."

"I just want you to be around for a long time," he said with a smile.

"Oh, I bet you do, *papi*," she said with an exaggerated accent. "I'm sure you want to have your way with this bad little Puerto Rican *chicka* for a very long time."

"It's what I think about every day," he said, his fingers running playfully across her breast.

"Do you, Teddy?" Perez asked, taking a drag on her cigarette and placing it in the ashtray.

The man nodded *yes,* as she leaned over, taking his flaccid manhood in her hand and began playing with it.

"Do you know what I think about?" she purred.

"No, what?" he replied, feeling him begin to stir in her hand.

"I think about you fucking me in each and every room of that Manhasset mansion you live in," she purred, squeezing him.

Eichenberg moaned as she played with him.

"You know we can't," he said.

"Sure we can," Perez replied. "Don't you want to sit at the dinner table, watching as the family enjoys their next holiday meal, knowing that you ate me on top of it?"

"Oh, God," the man exclaimed, "you are so bad."

"So send them away for a week or two," she said with a wicked laugh. "That should give me plenty of time to mark my *territory.*"

"That's reckless and you know it," he exclaimed, as he watched her hand sliding up and down his erect shaft.

"Reckless!" she said loudly, releasing her grip. "That's rich, coming from the man who enjoys *raping* his girlfriend."

"You know what I meant, Marisol," he replied defensively.

Perez got up, walked over to the closet and put on her rope cinching it closed tightly around her waist. Then she got back in bed, took a drink, and picked up the cigarette.

"Sure, I know what you meant, Ted," she replied, taking a drag on the cigarette and exhaling in his direction. "You get your rocks off here, with your slutty spic girlfriend, and then you go home to that frigid bitch of a wife, pretending to be one big happy fucking family."

"Miriam is not a frigid bitch," he said angrily.

"No?" Perez replied. "So you're going to go home and fuck her tonight?"

"That's not what I meant and you know it," Eichenberg replied.

"No, I don't know what you meant, Ted," she replied, taking a drag. "Maybe you like that, huh? Maybe you get off sticking your little dick in her, knowing that it was in me first."

"Mari!" he exclaimed. "Stop it!"

"Fuck you, Teddy," she screamed, stamping out the cigarette in the tray. "You need to go home now."

"Don't do this," he replied.

Perez got up from the bed, grabbing her wine glass, and headed toward the bathroom.

"Goodnight, Teddy," she said dismissively. "I'll call you."

She slammed the door behind her, bringing the argument to an unceremonious end. It was all an act of course, designed to make him feel bad and drive him to make it up to her, but he didn't know that.

Eichenberg closed his eyes as he tried to figure out how their night had just ended so badly. He heard the sound of the water running in the bathtub and knew it would be a long time before she would emerge.

"Fuck!"

He got up slowly, gathered up his clothing, and began getting dressed. When he was done, he walked over and knocked on the door.

"I'm going now," he said sheepishly.

"Nite," Perez called out from inside. "Give my love to Miriam and the kids."

"Fuck you!" he said angrily.

"Not for a while, Teddy," she said with a laugh, before turning on the radio and raising the volume.

Eichenberg stormed out of the bedroom, grabbing his hat and overcoat from the couch. He looked back toward the bedroom hoping that she would emerge, and stop this silliness, but she didn't.

"Cunt," he said loudly as he opened the door and stepped outside, slamming it shut behind him.

He made his way downstairs and opened the front door, pausing for a moment in the threshold, staring out into the cold night. It was sleeting now, an ugly mix of snow and freezing rain, which would wreak havoc with the long commute back to Long Island.

"That's just fucking great," he muttered, as he adjusted the collar on his overcoat.

He made his way carefully down the steps, feeling the sting on his face as the wind peppered his skin with sleet, and headed up the street to where his car was parked. As he approached the black Chevy Impala, he reached into his coat pocket and fumbled around for his keys.

"Oh, for the love of God," he exclaimed, as he began patting down his pockets for the misplaced car keys.

Eichenberg began replaying the events earlier in the night. He'd arrived here late and had been expecting her to come home soon. He'd quickly gotten ready, tossing his coat and hat onto the couch and placing the car keys....... into the basket on the hall tree next to the door.

"*Sonofabitch,*" he exclaimed.

He stood there dejectedly, staring at the locked car door that only seemed to mock him.

He was fucked.

He'd told his wife that he was going to a symposium in the Bronx, how would he explain needing her to bring his spare keys to a residential section of Brooklyn Heights?

How the hell am I going to be able to go back up there and ask for my keys back? he wondered.

Eichenberg sighed, accepting what he already knew to be true. Whether he liked it or not, he had to go back up and grovel. He knew she would laugh at him, knew how pathetic it would appear.

Perhaps Marisol would take pity on him and they would make up. Miriam didn't expect him home till after midnight and he would much rather spend the next few hours between Perez's warm thighs then in bed with his *frigid* wife.

Maybe she was right. Maybe he should send the family away for a few weeks and let Marisol have her way. That would make her happy and he liked it when she was happy.

Eichenberg turned to walk back toward the apartment and stopped dead in his tracks.

"What the fuck?" he said quizzically.

Suddenly, a shot rang out.

The .9mm projectile entered Eichenberg's skull, just above the left supraorbital foramen. It tore through the man's frontal lobe, sending a wave of bone and bullet fragments that ripped through his brain.

Eichenberg's body collapsed to the pavement in a heap. The blood pouring from the head wound steamed in the cold night air before it began to coagulate on the frozen sidewalk.

The cold wind coming off the East River kicked up, causing the edge of the overcoat to lift up and flutter in the wind, before collapsing onto the slush covered street. Above Eichenberg's body a streetlight shown down, bathing the scene in a surreal glow, and reflected off the gold, starburst shaped badge affixed to the man's belt.

CHAPTER FOUR

Southampton, Suffolk County, N.Y.
Saturday, December 14th, 2013 – 8:30 p.m.

"Can I have your attention for a minute," Maguire said as he stood next to the large Christmas tree that occupied the back portion of the room.

Next to him, Rich Stargold tapped his pen against the half empty beer bottle in his hand, making a loud clanging noise.

"Listen up, people," Rich called out.

"Thanks, buddy," Maguire said with a laugh, as the conversation in the room became hushed.

"Anytime," Stargold said with a grin.

"First, I want to thank you all for coming out on such a pleasant night," Maguire began raising his glass in a toast to the assembled group. "I want you to know that it means a lot that you would venture out to share this evening with us."

It was an eclectic group of people that had gathered in Southampton this cold December night. For all intents and purpose, it had been billed as a Christmas charity fundraiser event. NYPD chief's mingled with Fortune 500 CEO's and Navy SEAL's, who did their best to tame their salty sea-stories from their politician bosses, along with the news media folks, who always seemed to be only an elbows width away. Everyone in attendance knew the *real* reason that they were here, everyone that is except one.

The truth was that this was to be the storybook merger of the white collar princess and her blue collar prince, and no one wanted to shatter the fairytale.

"As many of you know, I have always tended to shy away from events like this," Maguire said, eliciting a laugh from those standing in front of him. "In fact, I think that was one of the main reasons my dear friend, Peter Bart, continued to harass me with invitations to his annual Spring Fling charity event. Peter understands that I am more of a blue jeans and polo shirt kind of guy, which makes it even more fun when he can force me to dress up and attend one of his little soirées."

"Well, someone has to help keep your clothes closet in the current decade," Bart called out from the back of the room.

"Will someone please get that man a piña colada," Maguire replied jokingly.

When the laughs subsided, Maguire continued.

"Thanks to your generosity we have been able to raise over one hundred thousand dollars, which will go a long way toward helping out a lot of needy families this holiday season."

A round of polite applause broke out.

The charity event had been his idea, a partnership between the NYPD and Santa's Helpers; a charitable organization which provided toys and holiday meals to poor families throughout the New York City area. It also provided a plausible cover story in order to gather everyone here tonight. The premise was that everyone in attendance had all donated to the organization and were then invited to this holiday party as a way of saying thank you.

It still amazed him that she never seemed to put two and two together, but so far she seemed to have been caught completely off guard. It also helped that most of her free time had been re-directed toward helping Gen with her baby, allowing him to plan this without interruption.

"It is at times like this, when I look out at all of you, that I am reminded of how very lucky I am," Maguire said. "It is funny to me how God brings certain people into your life, when you least expect it, something which I learned firsthand in April of 2012. I had grudgingly arrived at Peter's event intending to say hello, grab a beer, and make my way out the door as quickly as I could. I used to think that I had seen it all, but nothing could have prepared me for what would happen when I walked through the door. Melody Anderson, will you please come up here and join me?"

The room suddenly burst into a round of applause as she slowly emerged from the back of the room. Maguire watched as she made her way up to him, caught up in her beauty like a moth to the proverbial flame.

"What are you doing, James?" she said with a quizzical look, as she approached him.

"Just a slight detour, Mel," Maguire said.

She suddenly got the feeling that things weren't as they had appeared to be only a few moments earlier.

"I'm so gonna kill you later, Cowboy," she whispered in his ear.

"I'll take that chance," he said with a smile.

Maguire reached out, taking her hand in his, and then slowly dropped to one knee in front of her.

Her eyes went wide as she stared down at him.

"Melody Anderson," he began. "From the first night that I met you, I fell in love with you. That love has grown deeper with each passing day and I cannot imagine what my life would be like without you. More importantly, I don't want to imagine a life without you."

Maguire reached into his jacket pocket and slowly withdrew the box containing the engagement ring.

"I want to share this night, and all the nights to come, with you. So tonight I come before you, to ask you to be my wife."

He slowly opened the box, revealing the engagement ring. A four carat, princess cut diamond, flanked by two tanzanite stones that were set in a platinum band. It was almost as stunning as she was.

"Melody Anderson, will you marry me?" he asked.

At first she didn't say anything, completely stunned by the way this turn of events had gone, but then slowly nodded her head as the tears appeared and began to stream down her cheeks.

"Yes," she exclaimed, "Oh, God, yes, I will."

Maguire smiled, as he slowly slid the ring onto her finger.

A moment later the crowd of well-wishers began to close in around them.

CHAPTER FIVE

Brooklyn Heights, Brooklyn, N.Y.
Saturday, December 14th, 2013 – 8:46 p.m.

"Fuck, it's colder than a witches tit out there," Police Officer Shawn Lawson said, as he got back into the radio car.

"Really?" his partner Nikki Schafer asked. "So do you spend a lot of time fondling witches' tits?"

"Don't judge me," he replied, handing one of the *Dunkin' Donuts* coffee cups to Schafer. "I've been in a bit of a slump lately."

"Yeah right," she said sarcastically as she carefully peeled back the flap of the plastic lid, revealing a small hole to sip the coffee.

"Hey, it's a Saturday night and I'm here with you," he replied, taking a sip of his own coffee.

"That's not a slump, dickhead," she replied, "that's a *privilege*."

"Whatever," he said with a laugh.

The two of them had been partners in Brooklyn's 84th Precinct for the last five years.

"Look at it this way," Shaffer said, taking a sip of her coffee, "at least when the Net's game empties out, it'll be too cold for them to hang out and cause trouble."

"There is that," Lawson replied.

Cops learned to embrace brutally cold weather, which had a tendency to diminish street crimes. Of course it did little to help in the way of handling accidents, but you had to take the good with the bad.

Suddenly their banter was interrupted by series of loud, shrill beeps over their portable radios.

"Confines of the Eight-Four Precinct, report of a 10-10, shots fired," the dispatcher said. "Vicinity of 72 Poplar Street, Hicks to Henry. Units to respond?"

"*Outfuckingstanding*," Lawson said, as he reached down to grab the radio.

Shaffer learned over and activated the switch for the overhead light bar, as she dropped the shift into drive and peeled away from the curb.

"Four Adam is responding, Central."

Shaffer glanced over her shoulder, making sure no traffic was coming up behind her and dropped the car into reverse, making her way back up Court Street. When she hit the intersection, she flipped the wheel over and turned onto Joralemon Street, heading west.

"Four Adam, 10-4. Four Sergeant?"

"Sergeant in route, Central."

"Responding units, at this time, we are getting numerous calls on the shooting in the Eight-Four," the dispatcher said. "Possible man down. Notifying ESU and EMS. First unit on the scene please advise."

The RMP made its way down Joralemon, weaving in and out of the light traffic, as the vehicles siren blared. Schaffer made a right onto Hicks Street and headed north, down the narrow street, past rows of beautifully renovated brownstone apartments.

As they passed Pierrepont Street, a silver Toyota Prius slowly pulled from the curb, blocking their way and causing Shaffer to lock up the brakes.

Lawson grabbed the PA microphone.

"Move the fucking car," he screamed.

The Prius' driver panicked, the scream of the siren and the flashing lights disorienting him. He put the car back into reverse and slammed on the gas, driving the car back into the Ford F150 pickup truck that was parked behind him.

"Oh fuck," Shaffer exclaimed as the RMP accelerated past the accident.

"Serves him right," Lawson replied, as they continued up Hicks.

"I just hope we don't have to come back and handle this," she said.

The next sixty seconds was spent in silence, adrenaline coursing through their bodies, as they both anticipated what they would find when they arrived at the scene.

Was it really a confirmed shooting? Was the shooter still at the scene? Was he waiting for them?

Then they were there, making the right turn onto Poplar Street and slowing down as they pulled up, scanning the surrounding street for threats. Ahead of them, someone stood in the middle of the road, frantically waving them forward.

"Four Adam, 10-84 Central," Lawson said, as the car came to a stop. "Keep 'em coming, Central."

Schaffer put the car into park and they both jumped out, racing forward to where a group of people had gathered.

"He's a cop," a voice called out from the crowd.

Lawson pushed his way through with Shaffer in tow.

"Move out of the way," he said, as he manhandled the onlookers out of his way.

"Four Adam, confirmed shots fired," Shaffer said into her portable radio. "One confirmed victim; put a rush on the bus."

"10-4, Adam, putting a rush on the bus," the dispatcher said. "Four Sergeant, did you copy?"

"Four Sergeant, pulling up to the scene now, will advise."

Lawson knelt down, checking the man for a pulse.

Judging from the head wound, he doubted that he would find one, but this was Brooklyn North and stranger things happened here.

That wasn't the case tonight.

"Christ, Shawn, is he a fucking cop?" Nikki asked, pointing to the badge on the man's belt.

Lawson glanced over, looking at the gold starburst shield that was adorned with an eagle, oak leaves and silver stars.

"He's the fucking Chief Surgeon!" Lawson exclaimed, as he read the title on the badge.

"What do we have?" Sergeant Christina Oberti asked, as she approached the scene.

"Sarge, he's one of ours," Shaffer exclaimed.

Lawson unclipped the badge from the man's belt and handed it to the sergeant.

"Jesus Christ," she exclaimed.

"Nikki, Shawn, push these people back, give me a perimeter," she ordered.

"10-4, Sarge," Shaffer replied.

"Paul," Oberti said, turning to her driver, Police Officer Paul Sorenson, as the ambulance pulled up to the scene, "Tell those guys what we have and have them put a rush on it, he's not going to *die* in the streets."

"You got it, Boss," Sorenson said and sprinted back toward the bus.

"Four Sergeant, on the air?" the radio dispatcher asked. "Four Sergeant?"

"Four Sergeant on the air, Central," Oberti said into the radio.

"Sarge, getting reports of an MOS involved, can you confirm?"

"It's a confirmed shooting, Central. I'll 10-3 you in a moment with details, but notify the duty captain, detectives and the task force to respond forthwith."

"10-4, Sarge," the dispatcher replied.

The two EMT's approached the scene with the stretcher and quickly loaded the body, checking for any vital signs as they went along.

"He's gone," one of them said to Oberti, confirming what she already knew, as they strapped him down.

"I know," she replied. "Thank you."

She followed them back toward the waiting ambulance and watched as they loaded him up.

"What do you need, Sarge?" a voice called out from behind her.

Oberti turned and looked back, seeing another radio car team quickly approaching her.

"Escort the bus to the hospital and stay with the body," she instructed.

"10-4," came the reply as they rushed back toward their vehicle.

"Paul," Oberti said, "Have Sector Charlie block off Henry Street and tell Shaffer and Lawson to push everyone back toward Hicks. I want this entire block frozen. Have them start asking people if anyone saw or heard anything."

"Yes, ma'am," Sorenson replied.

Oberti walked back toward her RMP and sat down, reaching for the pack of cigarettes on the dashboard. As she watched the ambulance pull away from the scene, Oberti lit one up. She took a long drag as she picked up the cellphone and dialed the number for the communications dispatcher.

It was the start of what was going to be one very long night.

CHAPTER SIX

Southampton, Suffolk County, N.Y.
Saturday, December 14th, 2013 – 8:53 p.m.

"I still can't believe that he pulled it off," Alex said, as she watched Maguire and Melody mingling with the other guests.

They looked so happy together, which made it all the more difficult for her to handle.

"You think you can't believe it?" Gen replied. "I didn't know she was that gullible."

"Do you think she really figured it out and just went along?" Alex asked.

"No, she could never have kept that from me."

"That's amazing," Alex said, as she set the wine glass down onto a table. "God, I need a real drink."

"Hey, imagine how I feel," Gen said. "I'm breast feeding. The closest I get to anything with coconut in it these days is an Almond Joy bar."

"That sucks," Alex replied. "By the way, where is the baby?"

"Upstairs with daddy," Gen said.

"I was beginning to wonder where Gregor was," Alex said.

"He thought that all this would be too much for little Wolfgang," she replied. "I told him that if he was going to survive in this house, he was going to need to toughen up a bit."

"So how does motherhood suit you?"

"It's good," Gen said with a smile. "I enjoy it, although it has forced me to get my own assistant."

"No more traipsing around the country?"

"No, unfortunately, and that has really caused me some *adjustment* issues."

"I bet," Alex replied. "Although I am sure Gregor enjoys having you home."

"Yes, but it can be a battle sometimes," she said, taking a sip of her iced tea. "He hasn't come to terms with the fact that I don't have a nine-to-five job, even though I have tried to scale back my after hour calls."

"Men have a hard time coming to terms with career women," Alex said and finished the last of her wine.

"Isn't that the truth," Gen replied.

Just then, Gregor appeared next to them, holding Wolfgang close to his chest.

"Oh my God, look at him, he's so precious," Alex said.

"Thank you, Alex," Gregor said in his thick German accent, "I've missed you too."

"That's funny," Alex replied, taking a closer look at the baby, "but don't quit your day job, Mister Mom. He's gotten so big, Gen."

"Yeah, Gregor thinks he's going to grow up and play soccer, but I think he's going to be a linebacker," she said with a laugh.

"But right now he's fussy," Gregor said to Gen. "I think he's hungry."

"Dear Lord," Gen said, as she took the baby from Gregor. "I swear he takes after his father."

Gregor's faced turned beet red when he realized what she meant.

"I'll be back, Alex," Gen said as she made her way over to the private elevator with one of the security officers.

"Still got the security, huh?" Alex asked.

"*Ja,*" he replied. "No sense in taking any unnecessary risks."

"I need a real drink," she replied and headed over to the bar with Gregor.

"Still no word on that lunatic, Tatiana?"

"*Nein*," he said. "It is like she disappeared off the face of the earth."

"What can I get for you?" the bartender asked.

"I'll take a Jack & Coke on the rocks," Alex said, "with an emphasis on the Jack."

"And I'll have a *Hacker-Pschorr Weisse bier*," Gregor said.

"I can't imagine that she just packed it in," Alex said.

"No, which is the reason why we still have all the security in place," he replied.

Alex retrieved the drinks from the counter, handing the beer to Gregor.

"*Up the Irish*," Alex said and raised her glass.

"*Prosit*," Gregor replied, tapping his bottle against her glass.

Alex felt the coolness of the liquid in her throat and then the burn. It had been more than two months since her last battle with the whiskey bottle, but she felt the need tonight as she glanced back over at the happy couple. It was like she was living her worst nightmare.

Peter had found himself another doctor to chat with, which was fine with her. She didn't feel like babysitting him tonight. Hell, she didn't even know what their relationship was exactly. They'd spent one night together, and now he had some illusion that they were a couple. He was a good friend and Alex didn't want to hurt him, but she couldn't imagine it ever becoming anything more.

"So now what?" she asked, forcing her thoughts in another direction.

"Rich gave James the okay to put together a small team of detectives to start at the beginning. The thought is that she still poses a threat to a member of the NYPD, so they can claim some authority to investigate it."

"And?" Alex asked.

"Nothing," Gregor replied. "No hits at all. It's as if she simply disappeared."

"Fuck, she didn't disappear," Alex said. "She just hasn't been caught."

"That's what we believe," he replied. "She has the run of the country and she just might be making good use of that territory."

Alex finished the drink and set it on the counter, watching as the bartender picked it up and began to refill it.

"She didn't spend all that much time with Banning to be this damn good," Alex said.

"Perhaps," Gregor replied, "but then again, maybe she found something she truly enjoys."

"Or maybe she's dead."

"That possibility has been brought up, but no one really believes it."

"It certainly would be a long shot, I'll admit that," Alex said as she retrieved her glass from the counter.

"Unfortunately, we will just have to wait until she strikes again," Gregor said.

"What are you two discussing?" Maguire asked as he joined them.

"How long it's going to be until my *lady love* comes looking for her second date," Alex replied, taking a sip of her drink.

"That doesn't look like wine," Maguire said with a noticeable frown.

"I'm a big girl, rookie," she replied back with a smile. "Besides, the night is still young."

"You know, you're the reason I'm getting grey hairs," Maguire replied.

"I'm like the gift that keeps on giving," Alex said, twirling the stirrer around in her drink. "Gregor was just bringing me up to speed on our favorite psycho *femme fatale.*"

"Not much to report there," he said.

"Anything from the locals?" she asked

"*Nada,*" Maguire replied. "None of the known locations has ever been revisited."

"Do we know if they are still watching?"

"We asked them to, but if I had to stake my life on it I would say no," Maguire replied. "They don't have unlimited resources waiting on a ghost who may or may not appear."

"Ain't that the truth," she said, taking a sip of her drink. "Sounds exactly like what I'm dealing with."

"I take it that you haven't gotten any new leads on your killer kid?"

"Not since March when they found the Mercedes, which she had stolen from her mother's garage, torched in Key West."

"Maybe she decided to take a nice leisurely swim over to Havana," Maguire replied.

"Cuba already has a habit of giving refuge to cop killers," she said sarcastically. "Why not open it up to all of them."

"You think she took up residence down in Florida?"

"I spoke with the locals," Alex said, "but they didn't have anything on her. They said with the amount of tourist turnover it would be hard to pick a new face out of the crowd unless she drops anchor for a while."

"Good luck with that," Maguire said. "If she was just another dumb kid she would have been caught already."

"That's why they pay us the big bucks," Alex said with a laugh.

"So this is where the cool kids are partying, huh?" Rich asked, as he joined the three of them.

"It was," Maguire replied.

"I'm deeply hurt by your insensitivity to my feelings," Stargold replied.

"I highly doubt that, snowflake," Maguire said, "but just in case, take this as my apology."

Maguire handed Rich a beer from the bar.

"I'm better now," Rich replied. "So what deeply intellectual conversation did I interrupt now?"

"Psychotic lady killers," Alex said cheerfully.

"Awesome," he replied. "I love these cheerful chats."

The conversation was interrupted by the sound of Rich and James' cellphones going off at the same time.

Both men looked down at the devices, then back up at each other. In the background, the festive sounds of the party were interrupted by other phones going off.

"This can't be good," Maguire said, as he removed the phone from his belt and took a few steps toward a quieter part of the room.

"Maguire," he said when he answered it.

"Commissioner, this is Sergeant Aurelia from Operations," a man's voice said on the other end.

"Yeah, Sarge, what do you have?" Maguire asked.

"We've had a shooting in the eight-four, sir. The victim is Chief Eichenberg."

"The Chief Surgeon?"

"Yes, sir," the man replied. "We're still getting details, but initial reports are that he was dead at the scene. He's been removed to Brooklyn Hospital. The duty captain is heading to the scene and the duty chief is responding to the hospital."

"Is anyone in custody?"

"No, sir," the man replied. "Perp fled prior to the arrival of patrol units, ESU is conducting a search and the eight-four detectives are on the scene. I also have Brooklyn North Homicide responding."

"Are there any witnesses?" Maguire asked.

"None at the moment."

"Okay, show me responding," Maguire replied, "and notify me of any updates."

"Yes, sir."

Maguire ended the call and turned around to see Rich over in the other corner, on his cellphone, while the Chief of Department, Tony Ameche, stood next to him, talking to Sandra Barnes, the Chief of Detectives.

"Anyone know anything more than I do?" Maguire asked, as he joined the group.

"Just that Teddy took one round to the head and was DOA at the scene," Ameche replied. "The boss is on the phone with the Chief of Patrol's office right now."

"What the hell was he doing in the eight-four?" Barnes asked.

"That's a good question, Sandy," Maguire replied. "One I hope your detectives will be able to answer shortly."

A moment later Stargold joined the conversation.

"I'm sure you've all heard the same news as I have," Rich said somberly. "I just got off the phone with Carlos Hernandez; he's leaving the concert over at Rockefeller Center and heading to the scene. He'll take point till we get there."

Carlos Hernandez was the NYPD's Chief of Patrol. He'd had to miss out on tonight's party to be present for a holiday concert that was being held at the ice skating rink. Several anti-religion groups had sought permits to protest the event and been denied, due to the extreme traffic congestion normally associated with those visiting the large Christmas tree at the site. When they had been denied, they took to social media where it took on a life of its own. Hundreds of protestors had been expected, but, fortunately for them, the nasty weather had kept most of them at home.

"I'll grab a jacket and catch a ride with you," Maguire aid to Rich.

"What are you crazy?" Stargold replied. "You just got engaged."

"This takes precedence," Maguire said.

"You try and explain that to Melody," Rich said, "and this will be the shortest engagement in history. Besides, one more person, with a badge full of stars and his hands in his pockets, won't make or break things."

"Are you sure?"

"If I need you, I'll call you," Rich said, pulling Maguire to the side. "Enjoy your night, buddy, but do me a favor and try to keep Mary away from Gen's piña colada's."

"No promises," James said. "Just keep me posted."

"I will."

Maguire watched as the three of them made their way toward the front of the house and were immediately joined by a half dozen other ranking members, who would also travel back to Brooklyn.

"What the fuck was that all about?" Alex asked, as she approached Maguire. "Did you run out of the top shelf liquor already?"

"We just lost one of our people tonight," Maguire said quietly.

"Fuck," Alex exclaimed. "Who was it?"

"The Chief Surgeon," Maguire replied. "He took one to the head in the eight-four."

"Robbery?"

"Don't know. The squad is still out canvassing for witnesses."

"C'mon," she said, taking him by the hand and leading him toward the bar. "Let me buy you a drink, it's gonna be a long night."

CHAPTER SEVEN

Brooklyn Heights, Brooklyn, N.Y.
Saturday, December 14th, 2013 – 9:23 p.m.

"What do you have for me, Sam?" Captain Al Paulson asked, as he approached the group of detectives standing on the sidewalk.

Around them, members of the NYPD's Crime Scene Unit were taking photographs and setting up the 3D laser scanner, which they would use to record every detail of the scene. This type of forensic documentation allowed them to capture even the most minor detail before the site was compromised. With this digital evidence, forensic investigators would be able to examine the scene at a later date for lines of sight, bullet trajectory or blood spatter analysis. The days of hand drawn crime scene sketches were quickly becoming a thing of the past.

"Hey, Cap," Lieutenant Samantha Johnson of the Eight-Four Precinct, Detective Squad said, as the man approached her. "Aside from the obvious, I have my investigators interviewing the group of people who were on the street when patrol got to the scene. After that, I'm going to have them begin canvassing the apartments."

She hooked her thumb at the row of apartment buildings behind her.

"Have they ID'd any witnesses yet?" Paulson asked.

"No, so far everyone has indicated that they came out *after* the shooting and Chief Eichenberg was already down," she replied.

"Great, I've got the P.C. coming and I have nothing for him that he doesn't already know."

"He can't expect people to be sitting on their stoops in December."

The weather had taken a turn for the worse. The temperature had dropped and the mixed precipitation had turned to solid snow. Most crime scenes drew their fair share of ghoulish spectators who seemed to get a thrill out of watching a murder investigation. However tonight was different. With the body removed, and the weather worsening, most had retreated to the warmth of their homes.

Paulson gazed up at the windows of the apartments overlooking the scene. Dark, expressionless faces stared back at him, silent observers of the grim scene playing out on the frigid city street below.

There were always witnesses in this city, he reminded himself.

Nothing happened in the Big Apple without *someone* seeing it. The real trick was finding that someone before they faded into the background.

"He had to be here for a reason," Paulson said. "I need you to find me that reason, Sam."

"I could use a few more people."

"They are on their way," He said. "Brooklyn North Homicide was having their Christmas party down in Flatbush, so they should be here shortly."

Just then an unmarked Chevrolet Impala pulled up on the scene.

"Speak of the devil," he said.

Two men in trench coats exited the vehicle and made their way over to where Paulson and Johnson were standing.

"Glad you could join us," Paulson said. "This is Lt. Johnson from the Eight-Four PDU."

"Sorry, Boss," Detective Bill Kingston said. "There was a '53 on the BQE. Two mental midgets decided to play bumper pool and one of them overturned their ride. Highway has the entire roadway shut down."

"They do like doing that shit, don't they?" Johnson asked.

"Yeah, because they're never stuck in it," Paulson replied.

"Where do you want us to begin?" Kingston asked.

"I have my guys interviewing the witnesses on the street," Johnson said. "You guys can start on the building canvasses."

"Yes, ma'am," Kingston replied.

"If you come up with anything, let us know immediately," Paulson said. "The P.C. is in route and it would be nice to have something new to tell him."

"Understood, sir," Kingston replied, as the two men turned and headed toward the first building.

As they walked up the stoop, Kingston's partner, Detective Mike Dazi, looked back over his shoulder.

"Damn, she's easy on the eyes," he said. "How come we don't get any hot bosses like that?"

"Because we're Brooklyn North Homicide, you idiot," Kingston said. "We don't deserve nice things."

"They really should tell you that up front," Dazi said.

"What did you think they meant when they said 'it's not a job, it's an adventure'?"

Dazi reached out and opened the front door, "that's false advertising."

"Go complain to your delegate," Kingston said, as he stepped into the vestibule.

"You are my delegate."

"And your complaint is duly noted," the man replied. "Now quit your complaining, *cupcake* and get back to work."

"One day I'm gonna get a real job. Someplace where they appreciate me and treat me nice."

"Yep, and after doing a solid year of 9 to 5's you can earn a sick day and even have a whole week of vacation," Kingston said, as he examined the names on the directory. "Let me know how well that goes over."

"That would suck, wouldn't it," the man replied.

"Pick your poison," Kingston said.

"You're a helluva salesman, Bill," Dazi said. "You missed your calling."

"What, and miss out on all this *adventure*," he said with a laugh. "So what will it be? Perez or Engel?"

"What floor is Engel on?"

"First," Kingston replied.

"I'll take Engel," Dazi said.

"For the love of God, you're too young to be that lazy."

"Work smarter, not harder," Dazi replied with a grin.

Kingston pressed the doorbell and waited. A moment later a male voice came over the intercom.

"Yes?"

"It's the police, sir, can we speak to you?"

The door clicked and Kingston pushed it open. Ahead of them they saw the apartment door open and an elderly man appeared.

"Have fun chatting with Mr. Engel," he said, as he made his way toward the staircase.

"And the adventure continues," Dazi said dejectedly.

Kingston made his way up to the second floor and walked over toward the apartment door. He knocked loudly on it and waited. A moment later he heard a voice on the other side.

"Yes?"

"Police, ma'am," he said. "May I have a word with you?"

Kingston heard a click as the door unlocked and slowly opened. Immediately behind it stood a very attractive woman who was wearing a pair of grey sweatpants and matching hoodie. Despite the casual nature of the apparel, the clothing clung rather tightly to the woman, highlighting the sensual curves of her body.

Poor, Mike, he thought to himself. *He should have never taken the easy way out.*

"I'm Detective Kingston," he said, holding up his shield. "I'd like to ask you a few questions."

"What's this about?" She asked.

"I was wondering if I could speak to you about what happened outside tonight."

"I'm not sure what I can tell you," she replied.

"I promise, it will only take a few minutes, ma'am," he said. "It's rather important."

"Okay," she replied, stepping backward and allowing him to enter the apartment.

He followed her inside and watched her take a seat. She sat cross-legged on the couch and held one of the throw pillows in her lap.

In the light of the living room Kingston could tell that the woman had been crying. There was redness in her eyes and her face had a slight *puffiness* to it.

"Are you okay, ma'am?" he asked, as he sat down in the chair across from her.

"Yes, I'm okay," she replied, picking up the wine glass from the coffee table and taking a sip. "And you can call me Marisol."

"Are you sure?"

"Pre-holiday break-up," she said with a weak smile. "He's not the first, he won't be the last."

"Good attitude," Kingston said, as he removed the reporter's notepad from inside his jacket and began taking notes.

What idiot breaks up with a hottie like this? he wondered.

"So what's this about?"

"I was wondering if you may have heard or seen anything unusual tonight?"

"You mean about the shooting?" she asked.

"Yes," Kingston replied. "Was there anything that seemed odd or out of place to you?"

"I wish I could help, but I didn't know anything had happened until I heard all the sirens."

"But you knew it was a shooting?"

"My girlfriend, Rita, told me," Perez explained.

"Rita?"

"Yeah, Rita Meechum, she lives two buildings over. She called me and said someone had been shot outside."

"But you didn't personally hear anything?"

"No," Perez said. "I came home at about eight and took a hot bath."

"And you were alone?"

"Just me, some wine, and a depressing CD about everlasting love," she said with a pained look.

"Do you recall what time Ms. Meechum called you?"

Perez ran a hand through her hair as she thought about the question.

"I know that it was before nine," she said. "Maybe five or ten till?"

"Do you remember what she told you?"

"Just that someone got shot outside."

"Did you look outside?" Kingston asked.

"From my window," Perez said. "I'd just gotten out of the shower, so I was wet."

"You mean the tub?"

"Yes," she said, taking another sip of wine. "Force of habit, I guess. I meant to say tub."

"No problem," he replied. "Do you recall what you saw when you looked outside?"

"People standing around, the police cars," she said. "I saw the ambulance come and they took someone away on a stretcher."

"What time did you say you got home?"

"About eight o'clock," Perez said.

"Were you driving? Walking?" he asked.

"Driving," she replied. "I parked around the corner."

"And you didn't see anything unusual, anyone you haven't seen in the area before?"

"It's Brooklyn Heights, detective," she replied. "There's always something unusual going on, but no, nothing that I specifically recall. Honestly, it was too cold outside and wasn't really paying attention. After everything that happened today I just wanted to get inside and have a drink."

"I can certainly understand that," he said. "Is there anything at all you can remember, even something that might not have seemed important at the time?"

"No, I'm sorry," she said. "Nothing stands out."

"That's okay."

Kingston reached into his pocket and removed a business card which he handed to the woman.

"Listen, in the event that you do remember anything, please give me a call," he said.

Perez looked down at the card.

"I'll do that," she said, "*Bill.*"

There was a long pause, as the two of them stared at each other. Even though nothing was said, the message came through loud and clear. Suddenly, the moment was interrupted by a knock at the door.

"Uhm, that's probably my partner," Kingston replied sheepishly.

"Too bad," Perez said with a coy smile, as they both got up.

He followed her to the door, gazing down intently as he watched her hips swaying back and forth. He was pretty sure that she was putting on a show for him.

This shit doesn't happen to me, he thought. *Should I make an excuse to keep interviewing her?*

Perez opened the door and he saw Dazi standing outside. His partner looked at him, then at the woman, and finally back to him.

"Do you need any help, partner?" he asked, the words dripping in sarcasm.

"No, I'm done," Kingston replied, as he stood in the entryway.

He sheepishly turned away from his partner's accusatory stare, glancing around the small area just inside the doorway, but there was no place for him to hide.

"Wow, you're *quick*, Bill," Dazi said, adding to his partner's discomfort.

Kingston let the snide comment go, for now, but he'd make him pay for it soon enough.

"Thank you, Ms. Perez," he said.

"Anytime, Detective Kingston," she replied.

Suddenly, something caught his eye and he looked down into the small ornate basket that sat on the hall tree shelf.

"Oh, I do have one more question," he said.

"Sure, what is it?" Perez asked.

"Can you tell me how these got here?" he asked, holding up a set of keys attached to a black leather fob. In the center of the fob was a small, gold starburst, chief's badge.

Perez's eyes went wide as she stared at Eichenberg's car keys.

"Uhm," she began to stammer. "I don't,.... Uh,... I've never...."

"You have one chance to get your story straight, Ms. Perez," Kingston said. "I suggest you use the opportunity wisely."

Now it was her turn to be uncomfortable as the other detective entered the apartment.

"So do you want to sit down and try this again or would you like to finish this conversation at the precinct?"

"No," she replied dejectedly. "I'll tell you everything you want to know."

"Shall we?" Kingston asked, as he motioned her back toward the living room.

Perez turned, her head hung down, as she realized the truth was about to come crashing down on her.

CHAPTER EIGHT

Southampton, Suffolk County, N.Y.
Saturday, December 14th, 2013 – 10:45 p.m.

"Hey, do you remember the time we ran that red cell exercise over at Bremerton, Bubbles?" Maguire asked.

Special Agent Charles 'Bubbles' Baxter turned and shot Maguire an angry look.

Before he had been a member of Maguire's SEAL platoon, he had been a submariner. A common phrase aboard submarines was 'mind your bubble' which indicated the submarines angle, fore and aft. While he had been assigned to BUD/S school he had screwed up during PT. One of the instructors warned his swim buddy to 'mind your bubble' and the nickname stuck. The fact that Baxter was 6'5", bald, and built like a friggin' battleship only added to the overall irony of the moniker. After he'd hung up his flippers, he went to work for the Criminal Investigations Division of the Internal Revenue Service.

"That's not funny, Paddy," the man said. "Not funny at all."

"I'd have to disagree, Bubbles," Maguire said as he fought to stifle a laugh. "That was some really funny shit, but you are getting older, so maybe you just forgot."

"How could I forget," the man said. "You bastards locked me in that closet, with the base commander's yeoman, while you went and played merry marauders, sacking and pillaging everything that wasn't nailed down."

The small group of SEAL's broke into raucous laughter as they recalled the incident.

"It must have been a *big* closet," said Yonatan 'Yoni' Ashkenazi.

"No, Yoni," Bubbles roared, "it *wasn't* a big closet."

The laughter continued as Maguire wiped a tear from his eye.

"You fuckers have no idea the shit storm I had to deal with when those Navy cops finally showed up."

"I bet that poor girl is still traumatized to this day," another member of the group, Thomas 'Saint' Moore, chimed in.

"Shut the fuck up, Saint, you little needle dick bug fucker," Baxter said menacingly. "I still haven't forgiven you for that shit. I *know* you were the one who pushed me into that closet."

"Not me, buddy," the man said with a smile. "I was out boosting a set of wheels from the motor pool, unless you have proof that says otherwise."

"Uh huh," Baxter replied sarcastically. "If I had proof, you'd be shark shit right now, instead of wasting taxpayer money at that so-called job at NCIS."

"Isn't that the pot calling the kettle black, Mr. IRS?" Moore asked.

"Man, it took Mother forever to *un-fuck* that one, Bubbles," Maguire said nostalgically.

"That shit almost got me sent back to the U.S.S. *No Fuck*," Baxter replied.

"Are you serious?" Maguire asked. "Deployment would have been a blessing. By the time Mother got done sticking his size eleven boondockers up my lily white Irish ass, the damn thing resembled a friggin' porthole."

"He sure was hot, wasn't he?" Baxter asked.

"I guess we're lucky we didn't end up in the brig or worse," Moore said.

"We did have some good times," Maguire said.

"You've got a warped idea of *good times*," Baxter replied.

"Speaking of Mother, where is the old senile chief?" Moore asked. "It's not like him to miss a party with free alcohol."

Mother was the term of endearment lovingly bestowed upon Senior Chief Petty Officer (SEAL) Roy K. Gentry, US Navy – Retired, by the recalcitrant SEAL's for whom he was 'cursed to keep out of the brig, or worse, for all eternity' like some benevolent mother hen. At least that's what he repeatedly told them.

The truth was that they had given him the nickname because he was as rabid as a *mother bear* when it came to *his* tadpoles. The *Senior Chief* could tear them a new one, seven ways to Sunday, using language guaranteed to make even the most grizzled longshoreman blush, but woe to any fleet puke who dared to step on their flippers. If there was any question as to the validity behind his not so veiled threats, the combat decorations he wore, on the upper rows of his medal rack, quickly dispelled them.

After reluctantly hanging up his mask and fins, Gentry had found a new home in an *intelligence* agency whose name was not spoken and whose number appeared in no one's directory, save for the man who sat inside the office at 1600 Pennsylvania Avenue.

"He's off doing his spook shit," Maguire explained. "He called me last week to say he wasn't going to be able to make it."

"Did he say where he was going?" Baxter asked.

"Nah, just that his fun meter was red lining and that he'd have a *haji* pop in our honor," Maguire replied. "He said that he'd call when he got back."

"Sounds like he's back to picking sand out of his mess kit again," Moore said.

"Job security, baby," Baxter said, hoisting his beer up in a toast.

"Hooyah, Bubbles," Maguire replied, as he and the others raised their beers up.

"Speaking of job security," Yoni said, "can I talk to you for a minute, Paddy?"

"Sure," Maguire replied.

The two men walked over to a quite area of the room.

"What's on your mind?" Maguire asked.

"I just got word that the foreign minister is coming into town later this month," Yoni replied. "He's going to appear at the United Nations regarding the unrest in Gaza."

"I saw that they fired more Qassam rockets into Israel," Maguire replied.

"Yes, the world pressures Israel to allow humanitarian aid into Gaza and they use it as components for their rockets."

The Qassam rocket was created in 2001 and designed to allow for quick and easy construction, using common tools and components. The rocket itself consisted of a large steel tube, with stabilizer fins, and utilized a propellant that was composed of a solid mixture of sugar and potassium nitrate, a widely available fertilizer. The warhead was made up of TNT as well as another common fertilizer. The unguided rockets were far too inaccurate for use against military objectives, but they were well suited toward targeting civilian areas.

"That's one helluva ceasefire agreement you guys have."

"What do you expect when only one side is willing to uphold it?" Yoni asked rhetorically.

"How's the Iron Dome working out?" Maguire asked.

"Good, not perfect, but good," Yoni replied. "Since they first started using it in 2011 they've intercepted close to a thousand rockets."

"Well, that's better than having them fall in your backyard."

"You would think," Yoni said, "but, believe it or not, there are some politicians who complain that the cost of the rockets is too high. They question whether or not it is financially responsible to fire a thirty thousand dollar Tamir missile to take out an eight hundred dollar Qassam."

"I bet that's because they don't have family members living in the affected areas," Maguire replied.

"No, politicians like that live in their own sheltered world," Yoni replied. "Now, to make matters worse, the IDF just found another tunnel which they believe Hamas was using to smuggle people under the border fence. Now everyone is on alert for suicide bombers."

"So what do you need from me?" Maguire asked.

"After the last incident, I was wondering if you could upgrade the security detail to a presidential package?"

"Doesn't seem unreasonable under the circumstances," Maguire replied. "I'll talk to Rich about it. Where is he staying?"

"Manhattan, at the Essex House," Yoni said. "We were going to bring him out here, but, between the commute and all the unsecured area around the bay, we decided that it was best to keep things simple."

"Who's on the detail?" Maguire asked.

"Don't you mean is *she* on the detail?"

"Why can't spooks just answer a simple question?"

"Yes, Paddy," Yoni replied, "Zee will be working the detail."

"There, wasn't that easy?"

"Why do you want to open those old wounds, my friend?" Yoni asked. "You're beginning a new life, a wonderful life. Wouldn't it be better to leave the past in the past?"

"I wish I could, Yoni," Maguire replied, "but it's not in the past for me, it's still unfinished."

"I thought she said goodbye?"

"Saying goodbye and explaining why you're saying goodbye are two different things," Maguire said. "I gave her time, now I'd just like to know the truth. I don't think that is too much to ask for."

"I have learned that the truth is often very *subjective*, Paddy," Yoni replied.

"No," Maguire said, "the truth is always the truth; it is people who are subjective."

"I will let her know that you want to speak with her," Yoni said.

"Thank you."

"I am reminded of an old saying my mother used to tell me, 'What one has, one doesn't want, and what one wants, one doesn't have.' I hope that you don't lose the present while you are digging up the past."

Maguire stared across the room over at Melody. He watched as she slowly brushed a stray hair from her face. She looked so beautiful. She had a long, slender body that would have made her a natural ballerina. At first glance she appeared graceful and delicate, yet he knew that she wasn't. Beyond the beauty lay the heart of a warrior, a physical and mental toughness he had witnessed firsthand.

As if on cue, she turned to look toward him and smiled. Maguire smiled back at her and mouthed the words *I love you*. She blew him a kiss and returned back to the conversation she was having.

"No, Yoni, I'm not trying to resurrect the past; I'm just trying to give it the proper burial that it deserves."

"Then I wish you luck, but it appears that your problem with women isn't ending anytime soon," the man replied, as he motioned toward another part of the room.

Maguire looked over and saw Alex in a heated *conversation* with Peter Bates, while several other people gathered around them.

"Fuck me," Maguire said. "Hold my beer."

"*Behatslacha*," Yoni said. "Good luck, you're going to need it."

Maguire quickly made his way over toward the group, arriving just in time to catch his old partner getting into the man's face. It was a maneuver he was quite familiar with and one that he knew never ended well.

"I'm not sure who died and left you thinking you're my goddamn babysitter, but you need to back the fuck off, *capiche*?" Alex said, the words coming out more than a bit slurred

He reached in, grabbing Alex around the waist and literally spun her around toward him and away from the man. Instinctively he reached out with his left hand, catching her right hand, which was now balled into a fist, just before it could connect.

"Hey, partner," he said with a smile, as he led her away from the group.

The anger that had initially flashed across her face, in response to the perceived threat, now dissipated into one of shock.

"Oh fuck, James, I'm sorry," Alex stammered.

"I think you need a cigarette break," He said softly. "Take a walk with me."

"Yeah, sure, let me get my drink," she replied, as she tried to turn back toward the bar.

Maguire held onto her tightly, continuing to lead her toward the back of the house.

"We'll come back for that," he said.

As they made their way toward the back door, Melody came up to them.

"Is everything all right?" she asked.

"Yeah," Maguire replied, "it's all good. We're just going out for a smoke. Why don't you check up on Peter?"

"No problem," Melody said, giving Maguire a wink.

He opened the back door and led Alex out onto the back deck.

"Fuck me, it's cold out here," Alex said, fishing out the pack of cigarettes from her pocket and lighting one.

"You mind telling me what that was all about?"

"I'm too damn old to be treated like a child and told what I can and cannot do," she said, her body trembling as she took a drag on her cigarette.

Maguire knew better than to argue with her when she was like this, it was like arguing with a brick wall. They had been partners long enough for him to know when to let her calm down on her own. He also knew that Alexandria Marie Taylor had a lot of *baggage.* Hell, truth be told, the woman had a five piece, monogrammed luggage set with matching toiletry and overnight bags.

Most, if not all of her problems, stemmed from her mother, Cynthia Taylor. The woman was a grade-A certifiable, over-bearing, narcissist. Maguire had met her several times and each occasion was more painful than the one before it. He wasn't sure what bothered him more; the fact that her mother created hoops for Alex to jump through or the fact that Alex tried to actually jump through them. No matter what Alex ever accomplished in her life, it never seemed to be good enough for her mother.

Maguire couldn't begin to imagine what it must have been like for her growing up with that woman, but he knew that it had led to one major *button* that you never, ever wanted to push and that was telling Alex what to do. Unfortunately, for Peter Bates, no one seemed to have shared that particular memo with him.

"I'll be right back," Maguire said. "Try not to fall off the deck while I'm gone."

"No promises," she replied, her voice stuttering in the cold.

A few moments later Maguire returned, holding a jacket and a cup of hot coffee.

"Thanks," Alex said, as she slipped the coat on, wrapping it tightly around her.

"Here," he said, handing her the coffee. "It won't help with the hangover that's on its way, but it will keep you warm till it arrives."

"You're a riot," she replied, taking a sip of the hot liquid and lighting up another cigarette.

"So, you want to tell me what has you back chugging whiskey?" He asked. "I thought you told me you were a wine connoisseur now."

"I am," she replied, "just not today."

"What makes today any different?"

"Okay, maybe not just today," she said, taking a drag on the cigarette.

"So when did you fall off?"

"I don't need a lecture," she said coldly.

"Not lecturing you," Maguire replied. "I'm just trying to figure out what demon you're trying to drown."

"You wouldn't understand," she said.

"Try me."

Alex set the coffee cup down and leaned on the railing, staring out at the black abyss of the ocean in front of her. It seemed like the perfect metaphor for what her heart had become.

"I feel like my whole life has just been one big fuck-up, James," she said quietly. "Everything I touch seems to turn to shit."

"I thought things were going good up in Penobscot," he said. "And Peter seems like a nice enough fellow."

"Yeah, he's nice enough," Alex said with a laugh. "Peter is perfect for Penobscot."

"But not for you?"

"I really don't want to talk about this with you."

"You've never held back from me before," Maguire said. "Why start now?"

"Because now is *different*," she said angrily, as she turned to face him. "I'm different, you're different, and the whole fucking world is *different*."

"Partner's don't change, Alex."

"No, you're right, partners don't change," she said, "but we're not partners anymore, James. For Christ sake, look at us, look at where we are."

Alex motioned around her, her arms stretched out wide, as if to emphasis her point.

"Look at all of this, James, this isn't *Brooklyn-Fucking-North*," she exclaimed. "You live in a goddamn mansion now and you're the First Deputy Commissioner for Christ' sake!"

"That has no bearing on *us*, Alex," he said, his own voice now tinged with anger. "Never has, never will."

"That's easy for you to say," she said, as she turned back around to face the water. "I'm almost forty years old and what do I have to show for it? I'm the chief of a pissant little department in *Bumsfuck*, New Hampshire, who'd rather curl up on the couch with a bottle than a guy."

"That's bullshit and you know it, Alex," he replied. "So why don't you stop screwing around and tell me what this is really about?"

She reached inside, pulling out the pack of cigarettes and lit another.

It was so hard keeping up the façade. Putting on the happy face, for the whole world to see, while deep inside she did nothing but cry. Her life had become the epitome of the old Smokey Robinson song, *Tears of a Clown*.

What's the point? she wondered. *It's not like you have any real semblance of dignity left.*

"You want to know the truth, James?" she said, turning around and leaning back against the rail.

"I think you at least owe me that," he said.

"You've done everything for me," she said. "You're the only person in this world that has ever been there for me. Not my family, not my friends, no one, just you. You've seen me at my very best and my absolute worst. I've trusted you with my life too many times to even count."

"That's what partners do for one another," he replied.

"And what have I done for you, James?" she asked, standing up and walking toward him. "Besides be your anchor."

"You're not an anchor?"

"Really?" she asked. "How many times back in the Seven-Three did you get stuck on a shit detail because they were punishing me?"

"That's in the past," he replied.

"No, James," Alex said, "That's the problem, it's not my past, it's my present life. Fuck, I wouldn't even have this job if it wasn't for you; you have saved my ass so many times it's not even funny."

"You want me to stop?" he asked.

"No," she said, taking a drag on the cigarette and flipping it out onto the sand below. "I don't know what I want."

"Listen, Alex, you need to let go of the past and move-on," Maguire said.

"What, like you?" she asked.

"Yes," he said. "You deserve to be happy."

"That's easy for you to say, you have your Melody."

"And you have Peter."

"Peter is not the one I want," she replied.

"Well, who do you want?"

"You, James," Alex blurted out. "I want you."

"What?" Maguire said, his face a mix of shock and confusion.

Alex walked over, coming to a stop in front of him, then reached up, taking his face in her hands, and kissed him. Then she stepped back and looked at him.

"You wanted the truth," she said. "Now you have it."

"I don't understand, Alex," he replied.

"What's there not to understand, James, I love you," she said, finally letting go of the secret that she had kept buried deep inside her for so many years.

CHAPTER NINE

Southampton, Suffolk County, N.Y.
Sunday, December 15th, 2013 – 7:13 a.m.

"So what do we know?" Maguire asked.

"Well," Rich replied, on the other end of the phone. "It turns out that Eichenberg had been having an affair with a pharmaceutical rep for the last couple of years."

"Please tell me it had nothing to do with the job," Maguire replied.

"No, it doesn't appear so," Rich replied. "They apparently met at the hospital where he'd worked, not that it's going to matter to the media."

"So what have they been able to piece together?"

"Just that Eichenberg and the woman had been together in her apartment and got into an argument," Rich said. "He then left to go home and that was apparently when he got shot."

"But we still don't know what the root cause was, do we?" Maguire asked.

"No, nothing was taken, but no one is ruling out a robbery at this point either. So far the girlfriend has been cooperating, she gave them a list of former boyfriends and they are exploring the *jealous ex* option."

"How big is the list?"

"Big enough to be a royal pain in the ass," Rich replied. "Not to mention that it includes a number of well-to-do folks with rings on their fingers."

"Just exactly how well-to-do are we talking?"

"She wasn't a starving artist kind of girl," Rich said. "The list includes several doctors, a hospital administrator, a pharmaceutical lawyer and a federal judge."

"The little Jezebel certainly gets around, doesn't she?"

"Yeah, but it's not exactly what I would call a *who's who* list of cold-blooded killers."

"I agree, but sometimes all it takes is for someone else to start getting what you still want," Maguire replied.

"That's why they are doing discrete background checks into all of them."

"I hate to say this, but what about Ted's wife, Miriam?" Maguire asked. "Maybe he wasn't as discrete as he thought."

"Yeah, I'm having them take a peek into that as well," Rich replied.

"I hope that it is a very *cautious* peek," James said. "I don't think I need to warn you about who dear old daddy is."

Miriam Eichenberg, nee Rabinowitz, was the daughter of Moishe Rabinowitz, an extremely powerful New York City real estate magnate, philanthropist and a very influential member of the political scene. Politicians from both parties, the incumbents as well as the newcomers, sought out his blessing and endorsement, and that list wasn't limited to the locals. Even those running for the highest office in the land ended up on Rabinowitz's doorstep looking for handshake and a nod. It was said that he had the *billion dollar Rolodex* and that without his backing no political campaign could survive.

"I emphasized that point to Sandy," Stargold said. "She understands the need for absolute discretion."

"I certainly hope so," Maguire said, "because, if that discreet inquiry should go south, you won't be able to find a job working as a square badge, security guard, at a Wyoming ghost town general store."

"Aren't you just the bucket of fucking sunshine this morning," Rich replied.

"Yeah, well, I'm dealing with my own not so warm and fuzzies this morning."

"What's wrong, did Melody come to her senses and call it off?" Rich asked with a laugh.

"No, smart ass," Maguire replied, "she didn't, but I don't want to get into it on the phone."

"That sounds ominous," Rich replied.

"Still too early to tell, but we have bigger issues to contend with. When are the forensics going to be back?"

They are processing everything right now. I hope to have more answers shortly."

"Have you gone to see his family yet?" Maguire asked.

"Not yet, I'm going out there later this morning with Sandy. Right now Rabbi Morse is there, along with the C.O. of the Medical Division."

"Are you getting any pushback from City Hall?"

"Yeah, my phone has been ringing non-stop," Stargold said. "Everyone from McMasters on down."

"Let me guess, the mayor wanted answers yesterday?"

"Yeah, even before I got to the scene."

"What did you tell him?"

"That I would let him know something as soon as I knew something," Rich replied.

"That worked?"

"No, but now I'm only getting calls from his staff every half hour."

"So how are you going to play this?" Maguire asked.

"For now, as close to the vest as I can," Rich said. "There are too many people involved to keep it a complete secret, but I think it is best to play up the robbery theory until we come up with anything better."

"Just remember that Moishe Rabinowitz has his finger plugged into every nook and cranny in this city," Maguire said.

"Handle this with *due diligence*, but don't try to hide it. If word gets out that you're trying to steer the case, there are some in the media who will have a field day with it. Remember, it's not the scandal that gets people in trouble, but the cover-up."

"Wow, such wonderful choices," Rich said sarcastically. "Piss off the media or piss off Rabinowitz."

"That's why you get paid the big bucks," Maguire replied.

"You keep saying that, but I don't think it means what you think it means."

"If you say so, *Inigo*."

Behind him, Maguire heard the sound of footsteps approaching. He turned around and saw Alex coming toward him.

"I'll let you go so you can earn a few more of those dollars," Maguire said. "Call me if anything new pops up."

"I will," Rich said and ended the call.

Maguire watched as Alex walked over to the credenza and poured herself a cup of black coffee, before walking over and taking the seat across from him. She looked terrible, as if she hadn't slept at all.

"You're up early," he said.

"I like to take my beatings without an audience watching," she said, as she took a sip of coffee.

"What's that supposed to mean?"

"You know exactly what that means," Alex replied. "I was drunk, but unfortunately I wasn't drunk enough to forget what happened."

"I could act cool and say it's just water under our bridge," he replied, "but I would never minimize your feelings."

"I appreciate that," she said. "Although, to be honest, I wouldn't mind just trying to forget it ever happened."

"How long have you been holding onto it?" Maguire asked.

"Long enough," she replied.

"Why didn't you say anything before?"

"I wanted to," Alex said. "I tried."

"When?"

"The night of your party, when you got transferred to Street Crime," she said.

Maguire thought back to that night. It had been so long ago. After the party had broken up, the two of them had spent the night at his house boat, which he had previously kept moored over at the marina, on the other side of the Shinnecock Bay. They'd sat up all night on the party deck drinking and waiting for the sun to come up. He'd gone downstairs to get another bottle and when he returned, he found her curled-up asleep on the seat.

It was the last time they had been alone, at least while they were both still working for the Department. Every other occasion seemed to have been at a party or some other social function. She'd never let on that she had any feelings for him, other than the relationship which they had shared as partners.

"I never want to say anything while we worked at the Seven-Three," she explained. "Then, when you got transferred, I finally got up the nerve to tell you that I wanted something more. When you went downstairs for that bottle I decided to tell you as soon as you came back, but as I waited for you to come back I got so cold. I thought I would just lie down for a minute and get out of the breeze that was blowing. When I woke up on the couch the next morning, I realized that I had passed out. The alcohol induced bravery I had felt earlier was long gone at that point."

"Is that why you left without saying anything?" he asked.

"It had been my last chance and I let it slip away."

Maguire picked up his coffee mug and took a sip as he tried to process what she had just shared with him.

They had always been close, save for the first few days of their fledgling partnership. She'd had a massive chip on her shoulder in the beginning, which had taken a little while to knock off, but what emerged was a relationship that he had always considered to be like that of a brother and sister. That being said, it was not as if he *wasn't* attracted to her.

Alex was an incredibly attractive woman and, when she wasn't drinking, had a great personality to boot. She was also as tough as nails and, outside of his former SEAL teammates, one of the few people he would trust with his life. It was just that they had spent so many years depending on one another that he didn't want to screw it up by bringing those feelings into the mix. Obviously she had struggled with the same issues.

"I wish you would have said something," he said softly.

"Why?" she asked with a puzzled look on her face. "So I could fuck up the only good thing that has ever happened to me?"

"You don't know that."

"Don't I?" she asked. "I'm toxic, James. Everything I touch turns to shit. Whether it's work, relationships, you name it. That's one of the reasons I order take-out instead of cooking. I'm afraid I'd poison myself."

"Maybe things would have been different," he replied.

"Really?" Alex asked with a laugh. "So what, next you're gonna tell me that you have feelings for me as well?"

The question hung in the air as they sat staring at each other, lost in the thoughts that swirled through their minds, as they contemplated the next words that would be spoken. The only sound in the room was the gentle *tick* of the second hand on the large decorative clock, hanging up on the wall, which marched on without consideration to the drama unfolding just below it. With each passing second the silence answered the question.

"Oh fuck me," Alex finally muttered, as she leaned back against the couch and stared up at the ceiling.

"Who's fucking who?"

Maguire's head snapped, in the direction that the question had come from, and watched as Melody walked into the salon.

"James was just filling me in on the shooting last night," Alex said nonchalantly, as she took a sip of coffee.

"Is there anything new?" Melody asked.

"It's a really tangled web," Maguire said, as he regained his composure. "I talked to Rich this morning."

"That poor family," Melody replied, as she poured herself a cup of coffee. "Anyone else need a refill?"

"I'll take some," Alex said.

She got up from the seat and walked over to the credenza with her cup.

"How are you feeling?" Melody asked, as she refilled Alex's coffee mug.

"Like an idiot," Alex said. "I just want to apologize for the way I acted last night, I was an ass."

"There is no need to apologize, Alex," Melody said. "If I had a dollar for every time that I had one too many drinks and did something stupid I could afford a house twice as big as this one."

"Well, hopefully Peter will be as understanding."

"If he isn't then we'll have to feed him a pitcher of Gen's piña colada's and film him."

"I don't think I have ever seen him drunk," Alex said.

"Then it should make for a great video," Melody said with a laugh.

"Right now, I can't even stand the thought of someone else *drinking*," Alex said. "So I'm gonna slip outside and have a cigarette as I try to chase this headache away."

"Good luck," Melody said, as she watched Alex head out to the back deck.

"How'd you sleep, Angel?" Maguire asked.

"Like a baby," she replied. "I got worried when I didn't see you in bed."

"This shooting is a mess," he said somberly. "Ted was having an affair."

"Oh my God, seriously?"

"Yeah, they found his girlfriend. He'd been at her place when it happened."

"Do they know why he was killed?"

"No," Maguire said. "It could be anything from a robbery to a jealous ex. The big problem is that, even if it was something as simple as a robbery, there is still the affair to contend with."

"When the news finally hits it won't be good," Melody said.

"No, it won't," he said. "I just hope that there isn't any *collateral damage*."

"Collateral damage?" she asked. "You mean as in heads rolling at the Department?"

"It's a very *delicate* situation," he said.

"But why should something like this affect the police department?"

"Optics, babe," Maguire said. "Just the appearance of impropriety at the top level is enough sometimes to push that political snowball down the mountain. When it finally hits the bottom, it is often very messy."

"Have I told you how much I hate politics?" she replied.

"You and me both, but that's the nature of the world we live in."

CHAPTER TEN

1 Police Plaza, Manhattan, N.Y.
Monday, December 16th, 2013 – 10:43 a.m.

"Sorry I'm late, folks," Rich Stargold said, as he walked into the conference room and took the seat next to Maguire.

"Problem?" Maguire asked quietly.

"McMasters," Stargold replied. "We'll talk later. Please continue Sandy."

"I was just going over with Commissioner Maguire what we know so far," Sandy Barnes said. "There are no witnesses to the actual shooting and no one was observed fleeing from the scene. Given the weather at the time of the incident that isn't unusual. They pulled license plates from the surrounding area and are running down the registered owners as we speak."

"What about any camera's in the area?" Rich asked.

"Two," Barnes replied. "A residential one on Hicks and Poplar didn't pick-up any movement coming from the location. A commercial one on Henry did pick-up someone walking, but the blowing snow did a good job of obscuring any details. We've got the tech people trying to work their magic, but at this point the best we can do is a probable male."

"Do we think that's the shooter?" Rich asked.

"The camera was on Henry, facing in the direction of Poplar, but it doesn't show whether the figure emerged from that particular street," Barnes replied. "Right now they are just a *person of interest*, if we could ever identify them."

"Could whoever have done this gotten off the street without being seen?"

"Theoretically, yes," she replied.

Barnes got up and walked over to where a large map of the scene was displayed on the wall.

"There is a garden area here," she said, pointing to an area mid-block. "Someone could have jumped over the fence and made their way toward Hicks Street. Also, this area leads to the school playground. It backs up to Middagh Street."

"Is that something that you think would be feasible?" Rich asked.

"Feasible, yes," she replied, "but they checked both locations and couldn't find any trace of recent footsteps. Plus, both egresses have large metal gates which would have required a certain level of physical agility."

"Have we established the motive? Was this a robbery that went south?"

"Inventory at the scene shows that nothing was taken and there were no powder burns evident on Chief Eichenberg's body," Barnes said. "Also, there was no shell casing recovered. Whoever did this was smart enough to police his brass. At this point robbery is dropping further down the list."

"What does Ballistics have for us?" Maguire asked.

"The bullet was a .9mm hollow point," she replied. "Preliminary findings are that it entered the skull at a downward angle, so the shooter was most likely firing from a position above him."

"Above him?" Rich asked.

"Yes, probably on one of the stoops," Barnes said. "We are still waiting for word on the approximate distance to ascertain which one."

"A jealous ex is starting to sound a lot more plausible," Maguire said.

"Where are we at on those interviews?"

"Slow," Barnes replied. "For obvious reasons many of those involved didn't want to be interviewed at home, so we are having to tread carefully here; walking the fine line between investigative expediency and political awareness."

"What does your gut tell you, Sandy?" Tony Ameche asked.

"That I never should have taken the captain's test," she said.

The room broke up in laughter.

In the NYPD, civil service promotional examinations were required for supervisory rank up to captain. All promotions beyond captain, including chief, were discretionary.

"Sage advice," Ameche replied.

"Honestly, we have nine people to interview and each one is less likely than the one before," Barnes said. "That doesn't mean that one of them couldn't have done it, there are always exceptions to the rule, but none of them would be on my *short list*."

"What do we know about them?" Rich asked.

"She kept a very small circle," she replied. "All of her suitors, except for one, were in the medical industry. There is an insurance executive, several prominent hospital administrators and doctors, as well as a lawyer for a rival pharmaceutical company. The only odd man out appears to be a federal judge that she met while attending a seminar. According to her she ducked out early and met him at the bar."

"Not exactly the roster for Murder Inc.," Ameche said.

"Depends on who you talk to," Maguire said sarcastically. "Some will claim that their health insurance is killing them financially."

"That's true," Ameche replied, "but do any of those on our list have the *cojones* to pull a trigger?"

"What do you think, Sandy?" Rich asked.

Barnes looked at the others seated around the table. Her forehead furrowed as she pressed her lips tightly together, contemplating the question.

"I might be proven wrong, but my instinct says that this is a dead-end."

"How the hell do we have a three star chief murdered on the streets of New York City and we have nothing to go on?" Rich asked.

Four sets of eyes looked around the room at one another, each searching for an answer to the question that hung around their collective neck like an albatross.

"Okay, I'll be the one to ask," Maguire said. "Where are we at with the family?"

"Mrs. Eichenberg was attending her grandson Aaron's holiday recital in Great Neck," Barnes said. "It started at seven-thirty and she didn't arrive back home until after nine o'clock."

"Other family members?"

"They have an older son, Joshua, who is the grandson's father. He is also a doctor who works at Long Island Jewish. He was also at the recital. They also have two younger daughters, Bayla, who is currently doing compulsory military service in Israel, and Esther, who is a sophomore at Manhasset Secondary School."

Stargold looked over at Maguire, who just nodded and made a note of the older woman's name.

"A doctor, a soldier and a high school student," Ameche repeated. "Perhaps we can revisit that list of boyfriends?"

"We served subpoenas for their phone records," Sandy said.

"What about his other work?" Rich asked.

"We are looking into that as well," she said. "Since becoming chief surgeon, he has left most of his other positions, except for one, an associate professorship at Long Island Jewish."

"Jesus H. Christ," Ameche said. "Doctors, professors, lawyers, judges......... Can we just throw a friggin' rabbi in to round off the list?"

"I hate to break the news to you, Tony, but Moishe Rabinowitz attended rabbinical school before he went into the family real estate business," Rich said.

"Fuck it," Ameche said, tossing his pen down onto the table. "I give up."

"Alright, I think we've had enough for one day," Stargold replied. "Good work, Sandy. It was depressing as shit, from an investigative standpoint, but good work nonetheless. Let's meet back tomorrow at noon, I'll bring lunch."

As the group began gathering up their items, Maguire turned toward Rich.

"Got a minute?" he asked.

"Got all day," Stargold replied. "What do you need?"

"Coffee, Advil and a sounding board."

"Oh fuck me," Rich replied. "If you're coming to me for advice it has to be serious. Who's pregnant?"

"You're funny," Maguire said. "Wait till Sophie hits her senior year and you come crying to me."

"It's not her I'm worried about," Stargold said, "but *your* god-daughter……"

"Will learn all she needs to know about killing any boy that tries to kiss her and dispose of the evidence by the time she hits junior high."

"That's reassuring," Rich said. "Follow me; I have better coffee in my office than you do."

The two men made their way to Rich's office. Maguire sat down in one of the chairs while Stargold pour them each a cup of coffee.

"Thanks," Maguire said, as he accepted the mug.

"So what's going on with you?" Rich asked, taking the seat across from him.

Maguire took a sip of coffee and set the mug down on the edge of Rich's desk.

"It was a very interesting weekend," he said.

"Something tells me you're not referring to the engagement party," Rich replied.

"No, I'm not."

"Well, don't make me wait for it. Spit it out already."

"Saturday night, after you left, Alex, my old partner, got a bit drunk and confessed that she loves me," Maguire said.

"You just said she was drunk," Rich replied. "Drunk people say and do stupid things."

"She repeated it Sunday morning," Maguire said somberly.

"Well, there goes that theory," Rich replied. "Is she still here?"

"No, she went back to New Hampshire Sunday afternoon."

"Good," Rich replied. "Out of sight, out of mind."

"Really?" Maguire asked. "And exactly how do you propose that I push it out of my mind?"

"Well, I mean just because she said that she loved you, doesn't mean that anything changes. It's not like you love her."

"That's the problem, Rich; I can't say that I don't."

"Oh boy," Stargold replied. "You do have a problem."

"Thanks for that profound observation, Captain Obvious."

"So what are you going to do?"

"I'm still getting married," Maguire said. "If that's what you're asking. I'm just trying to process everything."

"Is it going to be a problem for you going forward?" Rich asked.

"No, and it's not just Alex. I think I am just trying to come to terms with the past, and find some closure, before I go off into the future."

"There's more?"

Maguire leaned back in the chair, closed his eyes and ran his hands through his hair.

"Oh, Christ," Stargold exclaimed. "Why do I get the feeling that I'm going to need a drink soon?"

"I never break your balls when you need to *talk* to me" Maguire said.

"You've never *not* broken my balls," Stargold said defensively. "In fact, I've often thought of getting 'suck it up, buttercup,' tattooed on my arm so I wouldn't have to bother you for your advice anymore."

"*Anyway,*" Maguire replied, ignoring Stargold's retort. "You remember Tzviya Harel?"

Stargold paused, trying to remember where he had heard that name before.

"Oh yeah," he replied. "I remember her; she was the hot Mossad chick everyone used to drool over?"

"Yeah, that was her."

Suddenly it dawned on Stargold where Maguire was going.

"No fucking way," Rich said with a smile. "You didn't, did you?"

"I'm so glad I entertain you," Maguire said sarcastically.

"No, I'm seriously in awe," Rich replied. "Every agent from here to the Anchorage field office was trying to hit that. How'd you screw that one up?"

"I didn't, smartass," Maguire said, taking a sip of coffee. "It was her father who put an end to it."

"I'm sorry, James," Stargold said. "The general was never really known for his inter-personal skills."

"No, he wasn't," Maguire replied, "and you're right, I should just let it be out of sight, out of mind, but I can't stop asking myself *what if?*"

"What if what?"

"What if I had told Alex how I felt about her back then," Maguire replied. "What if I didn't just let Zee walk away? Would it have mattered? Did I have a choice or would fate still dictate where I am today?"

"You're seriously asking me deep, existential questions?"

"I don't know what I'm asking," Maguire said. "I feel as if I should be the happiest person in the world, and yet I can't help but feel as if I am surrounded by ghosts."

"Mandy Baker," Rich said.

"Who the hell is Mandy Baker?"

"Mandy Baker is the girl I dated in college," Rich replied. "Her dad was Wayne Baker, CEO of Baker–Feldman, a major investment house that was located about eight blocks from here. We dated for about three years and I was being groomed to come into the family business."

"You were going to be an investment banker?" Maguire asked.

"*Were*, being the operative word," he replied. "One day, during my senior year, I was waiting for her in the student union. We were supposed to have lunch, but she got held up in one of her classes. So, while I was waiting, I walked into the job fair that was being held next door. I ran into a Secret Service agent and we started to talk about the job, he filled my head with all the positives. You know, protecting the leader of the free world, traveling to exotic places and living life *inside the bubble*. It sounded like the best of both worlds. I could combine my degree and travel the world doing protection. Of course he never mentioned all the God-forsaken places I was sent to."

"He must have been related to my Navy recruiter," Maguire said with a laugh.

"Bottom line is that Mandy's father threw an absolute fit. He made it clear that, in no uncertain terms, his daughter was *never* going to marry some low level civil servant. So I told Mandy that she had a choice to make. She could go with me or stay with her dad."

"So what happened?"

"She chose him," Rich replied. "Next thing I knew she was dating another guy, some pretentious little fucker named *Stefan*. I remember that he had long hair, which he kept slicked back, and drove around in one of those little British MG's. They ended up getting married and he went to work for old man Baker."

"You ever regret your decision?"

"Baker–Feldman got caught up in an SEC investigation regarding insider trading. *Stefan* cut a deal with the feds and turned witness against his father-in-law in exchange for a reduced prison sentence. He went to prison, but Baker ended up hanging himself when the Marshal's came knocking."

"Whatever happened to Mandy?" Maguire asked.

"I ran into her awhile back," Rich said. "Life hadn't been kind to her. She divorced Stefan, while he was in prison, and from the way she looked I assume that she took up drinking on a competitive level."

"Jesus Christ."

"I'm not going to say that I would have ended up in the same predicament, but I'm glad my life took another course."

"I can imagine."

"The moral of the story is that life offers you choices. When you make one, make the most of it and quit looking in the rear view mirror."

"Now who's getting all deep and philosophical?" Maguire asked.

"I have my moments," Rich said with a smile. "By the way, do you still have Tzviya Harel's phone number?"

Maguire laughed, as he got up.

He walked toward the door and paused, turning to look back at Rich.

"By the time she got done with you, there wouldn't even be enough of you left for Mary to bury."

"Ah, but what a way to go!"

"Oh, before I forget, Melody wanted me to remind you that Christmas Eve dinner is at five, so be there early."

"I know, I know," Rich said. "Mary has already warned me that the car leaves at two, with or without me."

"How'd we get so lucky?" Maguire asked.

"I don't know, but I do know that it beats being an investment banker."

CHAPTER ELEVEN

North Bellmore, Nassau County, N.Y.
Tuesday, December 17th, 2013 – 4:13 a.m.

Detective Armando Rivera sat at the kitchen table and leaned over, pulling the zipper up on the black combat boots he was wearing.

His family was sound asleep upstairs, as he prepared to head out for the overtime detail at Rockefeller Center.

Seriously, who fucking protests Christmas? he wondered.

He chided himself to quit bitching. His wife had already spent an exorbitant amount of money on Christmas gifts and the overtime would certainly help to offset those expenses.

Besides, it was a day away from the Gang Unit and the sights would be a heckuva lot nicer to look at than what he was generally accustomed to.

Rivera finished his cup of coffee and walked over to the sink. He rinsed the ceramic mug out and laid it on the counter. Next he walked into the living room and put on his gun belt, affixing the four belt keepers to hold it in place. Then he grabbed the nylon duty jacket from the couch and put it on. He picked up his hat and headed for the door, pausing a moment as he looked toward the staircase.

He thought about going upstairs to kiss his wife goodbye, but dismissed it. She had been up most of the night with their eight-year-old, who had the flu, and he didn't see the point in disturbing the remaining sleep she had left.

Rivera opened the front door and stepped out into the cold night air, feeling the tingling sensation in his chest as he took a breath. He turned around, locking the door, and then made his way toward the car parked in the driveway.

In front of him, the front lawn was covered in a thick layer of frost that shimmered like shards of broken glass under the glow of the street light. He hit the button on the key fob to unlock the door and then spotted the newspaper lying by the rear tire.

Is it too much to ask to throw the damn thing on the porch? he thought.

He reached down and picked up the soggy paper, its pages matted together in a big blob. That was almost certain to infuriate his wife, who loved reading the morning paper with her coffee. For a moment he was glad to be going to work.

"Fuck it," he said, as he turned to toss the paper in the direction of the porch.

"What the h......."

Rivera never saw muzzle flash, nor heard the sound, of the .9mm bullet that dove into his skull at a speed of around 1,300 feet per second, just beneath his right eye. The resulting trauma to the man's brain ensured that he was dead even before his body began to fall to the pavement.

CHAPTER TWELVE

Southampton, Suffolk County, N.Y.
Tuesday, December 17th, 2013 – 4:36 a.m.

Maguire heard the cellphone vibrating on the night table beside the bed. He peered over at the alarm clock and let out a sigh, as he reached for the phone.

Phone calls at this hour of the morning were never a good thing.

"Maguire."

"Commissioner, this is Police Officer Miltenberg from Operations," the female voice on the other end said. "Sorry to wake you, sir, but there's been an MOS involved shooting."

"Where?" Maguire asked, as he sat up in bed and turned on the light.

"Nassau County, sir," she replied. "A uniformed detective was shot in his driveway in North Bellmore. He was transported to Nassau County Medical Center, but it doesn't sound good."

"Has the Commissioner been notified?"

"Yes, sir, he is on his way," Miltenberg said. "Would you like me to contact your security detail to pick you up?"

"No," Maguire replied. "Have them respond directly to the hospital and I'll meet them there."

"Yes, sir."

Maguire ended the call and got out of bed.

"Bad news?" Melody asked.

"A cop was shot," Maguire replied

"Oh dear God," she replied. "Not again."

"I'm afraid so. Can you grab me some coffee to go, while I get ready?"

"Yes," Melody said, getting out of bed and putting on her robe. "I'll meet you downstairs."

"Thanks, Angel," Maguire replied as he headed off toward the bathroom

Ten minutes later he met her down by the entrance to the garage, where she stood holding a large stainless travel mug.

"Anything new?" she asked.

"Yeah, he didn't make it," Maguire said somberly.

"When does this ever end?"

"It doesn't," he said, taking the mug from her. "You just hope for the best and do your job."

"Please be careful," Melody said, as she kissed him.

"I will, I promise," Maguire said, as he opened the door to the garage and made his way over to where the unmarked Chevy Tahoe was parked.

Melody watched as the car backed out of the spot and the door began to close. Immediately her eye wandered to the vintage red Mustang that was parked in the spot next to the one that the Tahoe had just vacated.

It had been nearly two years since they had first met at Peter's party, yet it seemed like only yesterday, but in that time they had gone through so much. The memories came flooding back to her and her body physically shuddered as she closed the door. There had been the most amazing of highs and yet, just like now, there had also been incredible lows.

Melody looked over at the clock on the wall and realized that she was not going to be able to go back to sleep. She made her way back into the kitchen and got a cup of coffee, then returned to the salon. She sat down on one of the sofas and stared out the window. She could make out the pearlescent glow of the white-caps in the moonlight, as the waves crested off in the distance. It was so beautiful, so majestic, and for all that she had, it made her feel so small and insignificant.

"You're up early."

Melody turned around to see Gen approaching her, cradling Wolfgang in her arms.

"James," she replied softly. "There was another officer killed."

"Oh, no," Gen said. "Not again."

"That's what I said," Melody replied, "but I am afraid so."

Gen sat down on the couch across from Melody, as the baby continued to nurse.

"Never in a million years did I ever think that this would be something we would ever be dealing with," Gen said.

"I think the thing that gets to me is that I can't do anything," Melody replied. "I think about those poor families and I feel so utterly useless."

"There's never a good time to lose someone, but right before Christmas? That seems so unbelievably cruel."

"I know," Melody said. "There are days when I wish I didn't talk him into taking this job. I kind of liked living in my own little fantasy world, secluded from the evil in the world."

"Things certainly have changed," Gen replied.

"Changing subjects," Melody said. "I need to ask you a question."

Gen sensed the subtle change in Melody's tone. The two women had been friends for so long that they had become like twins, often finishing each other's sentences or, in a case like this, sensing when something wasn't right.

"What's wrong?" Gen asked.

"Nothing," Melody said. "At least nothing that I can pin down. More like a weird feeling I have."

"About what?"

"Did you get any vibe when Alex was here?"

"Alex?" Gen asked with a quizzical look. "No, why?"

"I just got the feeling that I was interrupting something."

"Interrupting who?"

"Her and James."

"Oh, don't be silly, Mel," Gen said.

"I know," Melody said. "It's just me. I came down Sunday morning and felt as if I walked into something private."

"What was going on?"

"That's it, nothing was going on," Melody said. "They were talking about the other shooting."

"Mel, you need to remember that they were partners," Gen said. "They do have a bond, but it's no different than you and I."

"I know," Melody said. "I'm just being stupid."

"No, you're not being stupid, you're being jealous."

"No, I'm not," Melody said defensively. "Am I?"

"Yes, you are," Gen said with a laugh, "but it is okay."

"I really don't want to be that way," Melody said.

"Do you trust James?"

"Yes, of course," Melody replied.

"Then what are you really worried about?" Gen asked.

Melody looked back out the window as she thought about the question. Now, instead of seeing the majesty in the breaking waves, she saw nothing but blackness and despair.

"Losing him," she said softly.

For the majority of her adult life, Melody had been in charge. It was something that she was accustomed to doing. If a decision needed to be made, she was the one with the final say. They were not always easy to make, but she never shied away from them. It was how she had built her company into the global powerhouse that it was today. It didn't matter whether the financial forecast was calm or stormy, she was always on the proverbial bridge, the good captain giving direct orders to her subordinates and maintaining control. Now she realized that she was no longer in that position. She had become some rear echelon admiral, sitting behind her comfy desk hearing about what was going on.

Since James had taken the job working for Rich, she had altered her life to accommodate his. It had made sense in the beginning and she had the luxury of delegating some of the tasks that she normally performed to Gen or other senior managers within her company. But now it felt as if she was somehow disconnected, out of touch with herself and everything that she knew. James was doing well, but most days she just sat around waiting for him to come home and it was finally getting to her.

It dawned on her that she wasn't afraid of losing him so much as she was afraid that she was losing herself.

"Those gears are spinning," Gen said as she lifted Wolfgang up and slowly began patting his back.

"I'm sick and tired of sitting around this house," Melody said. "It's time for a drastic change, Chicky."

"Ooh," Gen said with a giddy tone. "What country are we going to invade?"

"Eventually, D.C.," Melody said. "It's about time to shake things up on the Hill and get them to pull the trigger on *Dragon's Breath*, but first I need to blow off some steam."

"Cabo?" Gen asked excitedly.

"Montana," Melody replied.

"Oh, you mean that you really need to blow off some steam."

"Call the head of R&D and let them know I'll be stopping by for a little R&R. If it fires bullets or blows things up I want it available."

"What about, James?" Gen asked. "You know he won't be thrilled about you going."

"He'll just have to get over that," Melody replied. "He put a ring on it, not a collar. I need to get out of my dresses and into some faded jeans and do something productive."

"I hear you," Gen said, as she watched Melody get up. "Hey, not to change the subject, but speaking of dresses, do you know what you're wearing for Christmas dinner?"

"Ugh, after what I went through the other day trying to pick out a dress for the party I'm ready to throw out everything I have."

"You?" Gen said with a laugh. "Try having a kid and see what wonders that does to your body."

"At least you can get rid of the weight," Melody replied. "I'm not as lucky."

Gen frowned, realizing that her friend was talking about the scars from being shot.

"They're not that noticeable," Gen said.

"Your right," Melody replied. "Just as long as I wear dresses that go up to my neck."

"Sweetie, James doesn't care about any of that."

"I know he doesn't, but I do. It's not the physical scars that bother me so much, Gen, but the mental ones. I try to suppress them, but it's a bit hard when you are constantly living with reminders."

"Do you think you should talk to someone?"

"Maybe," Melody replied. "I'll think about it."

"I can make some calls if you'd like, find someone discreet."

"I'll let you, but for now, I just want to take out my anger by being on the other side of the gun."

CHAPTER THIRTEEN

Jones Beach, Nassau County, N.Y.
Tuesday, December 17th, 2013 – 5:11 a.m.

The young man sat atop the boardwalk railing and stared out at the ocean as he mindless stroked the edges of his goatee. His long blond hair was blown about playfully by the wind coming off the water.

He enjoyed coming out here, especially in the late evening or early morning hours. There was never anyone around, no human interruptions of his private moments. The beach was someplace where he could clear his mind of all of life's problems; the minutia that always seemed to be trying to derail his plans.

He had thought that, by growing up in the rugged mountains of Montana, he had learned everything there was to finding inner peace and tranquility among nature. He had grown up on the outskirts of Troy, near the Kootenay River. He would often hike up into the mountains just to sit and watch nature's majesty unfold around him, but here, near the ocean, things were different.

It was true that the mountains were majestic, but the ocean was both majestic and *powerful*. Mountains were stationary, the water wasn't. It went where it wanted to and if a mountain happened to be in its way, it wore the mountain down.

As a kid he had always strived to be the mountain, but now that he had become an adult, and had tasted the world's injustices, he decided that he needed to be the water. To him, the world had become the mountain, majestic, but at the same time cold and unforgiving. What he needed to be was the water, both majestic *and* powerful. Powerful enough to cut through the mountain, erode it, undermine it, and then watch as it crumbled under the pressure from his relentless power.

Yes, he would become the water.

He took a final drag on his cigarette and flicked it off into the sand below. Then he climbed down from the railing and made his way to the lone car parked in the lot.

It was a short drive from Jones Beach to the 2nd floor apartment he rented in one of the cookie-cutter homes in Levittown.

The town had received its name from its builder, the firm of Levitt & Sons, Inc. which was founded by Abraham Levitt. Prior to WWII the company had designed upper middle class homes on Long Island. During the war, William 'Bill' Levitt, one of Abraham Levitt's sons, had been a lieutenant in the Seabees, the U.S. Army's Construction Battalion. During his time he had developed expertise in the mass-production building of military housing using uniform and interchangeable parts. After the war, Bill Levitt saw a need for affordable housing for returning veterans. America's post-war prosperity and baby boom had created a crisis of affordable housing. The company purchased one thousand acres of potato farmland and he persuaded his father, along with his architect-brother, Alfred, to embrace the utilitarian system of construction that he had learned in the service.

The result was the first truly mass-produced suburb in America. The small homes were built on concrete slabs and featured one finished floor along with an unfinished attic, which some turned into an apartment that was rented out to returning GIs and their young families.

While many of the current owners had improved on Levitt's design, this particular section seemed to be stuck in the past, with all the homes retaining the same exterior design as when they were originally constructed. He pulled up to the curb in front of the house and grabbed the large black *Pelican* travel case from the passenger seat. He then made his way to the separate entrance in the back yard and climbed the staircase. Once inside the apartment, he locked the door behind him and set the case down next to the bathroom door. Then he walked into the living room / kitchenette area, hanging his coat up on the hook and proceeded to open the refrigerator. He examined its contents, making a mental note to go to the grocery store. He removed the remaining half of the roast beef hero, which he had gotten for dinner the day before, and grabbed a Coke.

He walked over to the couch and sat down, turning the television on as he began to eat. At 6:00 a.m. the top news stories re-cycled and he watched the local news anchor report that an off-duty New York City cop had been killed in Bellmore. A moment later they cut to a live shot of a reporter outside Nassau County Medical Center. He continued to eat as the reporter talked. Finally the segment ended and the news anchor transitioned to the weatherman who talked about the latest weather pattern that was coming into the tri-state area.

When he was finished eating he gathered up the wrapper, along with the empty Coke can, and threw them away. He then made his way toward the bedroom, picking up the case as he went. He unlocked the bedroom door and stepped inside, locking it behind him. His landlord seemed like a lovely, but slightly nosey, older woman.

The few times he had seen her, she tried to engage him in a conversation. He'd always managed to bow out graciously, but he began to pay the rent by slipping the money under the door, so as to limit his contact with her. He didn't think that she would snoop around his apartment, but if she did, she would be restricted to the other room.

The large room was effectively divided into two-parts by an old chimney that came up through the middle of it. On one side was a single bed and on the other was a small work desk. He set the case down and turned on the light over the desk. He reached over and picked up a pair of latex gloves, slipping them on his hands. He sat down and opened the latches on the case, carefully removing the matte-black body of the unmanned aerial vehicle, then set it down on the desk in front of him.

The UAV was comprised of the main body which attached to eight skeletal arms, making it appear like some spider out of a sci-fi movie. To the naked eye it appeared to be such a fragile looking device, but looks could be very deceiving and, in this case, very deadly.

It had started its life out as just another high-end commercial drone, but it was the aftermarket additions which set it apart from the rest.

In addition to the upgraded avionics system and a hi-def video system, there was a small, rectangular housing unit that was contained on the underbody of the UAV. It was the components that were encased inside this unit that provided the truly terrifying aspects of this particular UAV.

He turned the drone over and removed a small screwdriver from the desk drawer. He then opened the main door for the housing unit. Inside was a secondary door which he also opened and then removed a small USB drive that he sat on the desk, next to his laptop. The drive contained the data that was most precious to him; video confirmation of his latest achievement.

When he was done, he turned his attention back to the primary unit. He removed four large hex-head bolts and opened the case. He retracted a braided metal spring and guide rod, which he set down on the desk. Then he focused his attention on the ten inch long cylindrical tube inside.

This had been the trickiest part of the whole assembly, as it required to him to combine two separate items within one unit. The first four and a half inches of the tube were done in a 1:10

twist and were then pinned to the remaining eight inch tube, which was baffled and ported. This particular style that he was using was referred to as a *wet can* because it used a small quantity of water in the expansion chambers to cool propellant gases, thereby reducing their volume. While the coolant lasted only a few uses, before it had to be replenished, his design never called for more than one use.

Once he had removed the tube from the housing unit, he grabbed a pair of plyers and removed the small brass casing from inside it. He held it up to the light, inspecting it closely, as an art aficionado would do with a Rembrandt or Monet.

When he was done admiring his work he reached over and grabbed a small plastic jar. He opened it and dropped the casing inside, listening to the sound of the metallic *clink* as it hit the one already inside.

He set the pliers down on the desk, removed the gloves and rubbed his eyes. It had been a long night and he needed to get some rest. The files on the USB could wait till later, when he was well rested and could evaluate them.

Outside, the sun was just beginning to rise, painting the interior of the room with the first streams of light. He picked up the red sharpie pen and drew a large X through one of the images that hung above the desk. It was a bit melodramatic, but it served to identify the goals accomplished from the ones that remained.

He turned off the desk lamp and made his way over to the bed.

Two down and so many more to go, he thought, as he began to undress. When he was done, he lay down on the bed and reached over, pulling the tie-back from the black-out curtain. He yawned and then closed his eyes, drifting off into a well-deserved sleep.

CHAPTER FOURTEEN

1 Police Plaza, Manhattan, N.Y.
Tuesday, December 17ᵗʰ, 2013 – 1:25 p.m.

Maguire clasped his hands on top of his head, closed his eyes and leaned back in the chair, as he listened to Rich talk with Sandy Barnes.

"I have two dead members of this Department and you're telling me that the *greatest detectives in the world* have nothing for me?"

"I wish I had something else to give you, sir," Barnes said with a tone of exasperation.

The three of them sat in Maguire's conference room as they tried to piece together what had taken place over the last few days.

The Eichenberg investigation was barely treading water as one by one the list of potential suspects had been whittled down. Even Miriam Eichenberg's cellphone records hadn't produced anything, other than a borderline unhealthy need to call her sister, Ruth, two to three times a day.

"I'm sorry, Sandy," Rich said, sitting down in the chair next to Maguire. "It's not your fault."

"There are no red-flag financial issues and Eichenberg had no apparent problems with anyone, either socially or through work," Barnes said. "In fact, the only thing we have to focus on is his extramarital relationship with Marisol Perez and, to be quiet honest, that is leading us nowhere fast."

"So we have a dead chief and we have absolutely nothing to go on?" Maguire asked.

"At this point, all that we *definitively* know is that he was killed by a bullet," she replied, "and we cannot rule out that this was simply a street robbery that went bad."

"You think he got made?" Rich asked.

"He was wearing his shield on his belt," Barnes replied. "It's possible that when he reached for his wallet the perp saw it and panicked."

"Let's change our course for a moment," Maguire said. "What do we actually know about the Rivera murder?"

"Not much," Sandy said. "Thirty-four year's old, been a member of the Department for eleven years. Made detective in 2011 and was assigned to the Gang Unit. We can't rule out a revenge killing so I have them pulling his arrest records."

"How many are we talking about?" Maguire asked.

"He was a pretty active cop," Sandy said. "I think it's around the five hundred plus range. We'll focus on the felonies, as well as if there were any *frequent fliers*, folks he arrested more than once, who might have had a grudge."

"Have we come up with any witnesses?" Rich asked.

"None to the actual shooting," Sandy replied. "His neighbor, Bryce Harper, was leaving for work when he spotted him lying in the driveway. The Nassau County EMT, that worked on Rivera, said that he hadn't been gone that long when they transported him to the hospital, but the witness said that he didn't hear any noise and that he'd been outside a few minutes earlier getting his newspaper."

"What about the wife?" Stargold asked.

"She was sleeping when it happened," Barnes explained. "She didn't wake up until she heard the neighbor pounding on the door."

Rich remembered seeing the young, brown haired woman at the hospital earlier this morning. She looked up at him, with reddened eyes and tear stained cheeks, when he walked into the room. Her eyes pleaded with him, looking for something that would make sense of the tragedy that had come crashing down on her. There was nothing to prepare a person for that. There were no words that he could muster which would provide her any measure of solace. He couldn't do it for the families of William Maldonado and Thomas Dixon, or for Miriam Eichenberg, and he couldn't do it for her.

This was the part of the job that no one had warned him about. It made sense in a way. How could you begin to tell someone how to console a person who had just lost their loved one in the line of duty?

"On behalf of a grateful city."

Stargold recalled the words he had said, when he had presented the flag to Maldonado's mother. At the time he had believed it, but now he knew that it was a lie. The city wasn't at all grateful, nor did it really even care. They were *heroes*, as long as their name was in the headlines, but once another story broke they became nothing more than an anecdotal footnote in the city's history, another name to be added to the cold, black granite memorial wall down in Battery Park City.

There were nights when he would leave 1PP to go home and he would have the security detail drive him over to the memorial. There he would walk along and read the names of the fallen, determined never to let their memories pass. It was the least that the living could do.

He got up and walked around the room. It was moments like this that he regretted taking the job. Not that it was too difficult for him, but that he felt like a caged lion. Deep inside he just wanted to be out there, in the field, beating the bushes and following the clues.

Men like him and Maguire weren't made for this type of role; they were *doers* not *tellers*. It was the ultimate of ironies. You worked hard, proved your worth out on the street, and then someone rewarded you by taking you away from the job that you were good at and chained you to a desk.

"You alright, Buddy?" Maguire asked.

Stargold looked back at him quizzically.

"Yeah," he replied hesitantly. "I'm just trying to process all of this, hoping to figure out how to put all the pieces of this puzzle together."

"Is there any chance that we might be able to find some video?" Maguire asked.

"We're still canvassing," Barnes said, "but it's slim. The house itself is located in the middle of a residential area which is bordered by several major roads with commercial establishments. These locations might have surveillance cameras, but there are several smaller roads which allow access and egress as well."

"If I was planning on killing a cop, or anyone else for that matter, I'd try and lessen my exposure anyway I could," Rich said.

"That's the general consensus, but we could get lucky," she replied.

"You know I'm not a big fan of coincidences," Maguire said. "Is there any chance that these two cases might be related?"

"There isn't anything that ties them together that I can see," Barnes said, "neither in their personal or professional lives."

"I'm just thinking out loud," Maguire said. "I can't help but think that we are missing something."

"The only potential link, if you can call it that, is that no shell casings have been found as of yet."

"That's unusual," Rich said.

"Yes and no," Barnes replied. "Until we establish where the shooter was, we won't know. If it came from the roadway, there's a chance it was fired from within a car."

"Or maybe we just have a smart shooter," Rich replied.

"Another coincidence...." Maguire said.

"Okay, I think we have done enough damage for one afternoon," Rich said. "Let's hope our detectives have a lot better luck uncovering the clues then us three. We'll reconvene here tomorrow morning at eleven for an update."

"Got a minute?" Rich said to Maguire as Barnes gathered up her papers and walked out of the conference room.

"Yeah, what's on your mind?"

"I feel like I'm losing it," Stargold said.

"Why?" Maguire asked, a look of concern on his face.

"I've been in office for less than a year and I've already lost four of my people," Rich said. "I'm questioning whether or not I'm really cut out for this job."

"None of these deaths are your fault," Maguire said.

"Yeah, but it's my Department," Stargold said. "Ultimately I'm responsible for it."

"You're no more responsible for this then one of your predecessors was responsible for the twenty-three officers we lost on September 11th."

"Stop throwing logic into the argument."

"You have heart, Rich," Maguire said. "That's why it bothers you. If it didn't than you'd have a problem."

"Maybe if someone else was sitting in the seat things would be different."

"They might be different, but it wouldn't be better," Maguire said, "but you already know that. So what's really bothering you?"

"I don't know," Stargold said. "I feel like I have become a spectator in my own game."

"It's not easy going from being the player to the coach."

"That's exactly it," Stargold exclaimed. "I feel like they made me the team's coach and now we aren't wining anymore. I just want to run out on the field and get things moving in the right direction, but I can't."

"No, you can't," Maguire said. "So stop trying to lift the world up on your shoulders. That's not your job anymore. You're the leader now and it's *your job* to motivate your people to get *their job* done."

"You make it sound so easy," Rich said with a laugh.

"Hell, I show up here every day and work for you," Maguire said. "If you could convince me to do that, you can convince anyone."

"Actually, I think it was Melody who did that."

"She can be very persuasive," Maguire said, as he got up from his chair, "but I still would have said no if it was anyone other than you."

Stargold nodded.

"Then it's time to get back to work, Mister *Commissioner.*"

CHAPTER FIFTEEN

Penobscot, New Hampshire
Tuesday, December 17th, 2013 – 5:16 p.m.

"Are you okay, Boss?"

Alex turned her gaze away from the window to the doorway, where Police Officer Abby Simpson stood.

"Huh?" she asked.

"Check your watch," Simpson said. "You're on your own time now."

"I guess I just got a bunch of stuff on my mind," Alex replied.

"Doctor Hunk?" Simpson asked, referring to Peter Bates.

"Why does it always have to be about men?"

"Because men are always the problem," Abby said.

"Can't really argue that point," Alex replied, "but no, it's not Peter."

"Ooh," Simpson said with a smile, "a mystery man."

Alex removed a cigarette, from the pack on her desk, and lit one up. She knew that there was no point in trying to lie to her. When it came to gossip, Abby could be as tenacious as the most grizzled veteran detective. Besides that, the two of them had developed a friendship that went beyond the job and right now she desperately needed another woman's opinion.

"Pull up a seat," Alex said.

Abby walked into the office, closing the door behind her, and grabbed the pack of cigarettes from the desk.

"You're doing a really bad job of quitting," Alex said.

"I blame you," Abby said, as she lit the cigarette. "You're a bad influence."

"Yeah, that's why I can smoke your ass on the treadmill."

"Actually, bodybuilders don't recognize cardio as a legitimate exercise."

"Whatever," Alex said dismissively.

"So, is he from around here?"

"No," Alex replied.

"Oh fuck," Abby said. "It is another man."

"If you say *anything*, to *anyone*, I will kill you."

"Yeah, yeah, who is it?"

Alex took a long drag on the cigarette as she pondered what she was about to share. She'd had this bottled up inside her for so long, that it was still difficult for her to put into words.

"It's my old partner, James, from New York," Alex said.

"Is it serious?"

"Nothing ever happened," Alex replied. "I never worked up the courage to tell him and now it's too late."

"It's never too late," Abby said. "If you still care about him, tell him."

"He's getting married."

"Wait, you mean the party that you went to this weekend?"

"Yep," Alex said. "One in the same."

"Oh wow," Abby replied, "that really sucks. Does he know how you feel?"

"He didn't," Alex exclaimed, "but he does now."

"What happened?"

"I got into a battle with a fifth of Jack and I lost."

"Wait, you told him when you were drunk?"

"Yep," she replied. "It seemed like the reasonable thing to do at the moment, although, in retrospect, I recall that I sobered up, fairly quickly, after the words came out."

"I bet that set off some fireworks."

"Not really," Alex said. "I said it to him in private; right after he broke up the argument Peter and I were having?"

"Whoa, back up a minute," Abby said. "What the hell happened with Peter?"

"He tried to play the part of referee in my drinking game and I didn't take it very well."

"Okay, so let me get this straight," Abby said. "You got into a fight with Peter, which was broken up by your old partner, whom you then proceeded to tell that you loved him, at his engagement party?"

"That about sums it up?"

Abby let out a long, slow whistle. "I think I need to go to more parties with you."

"I certainly do know how to liven things up," Alex said.

"So where exactly does that leave things with you and James?"

"I honestly don't know."

"I imagine that it would be hard," Abby said. "Having an unrequited love for someone could be tough."

"That's the problem, Abs," Alex replied. "I don't know if it is unrequited."

Abby looked at Alex, a quizzically look on her face as she tried to process what she had just been told.

"But, he's getting married."

"Yeah," Alex said, as she crushed her cigarette out in the ashtray. "Sometimes life can be a bit *complicated*."

CHAPTER SIXTEEN

Little Neck, Queens, N.Y.
Wednesday, December 18th, 2013 – 5:57 a.m.

Detective Leticia Palmer sat behind the wheel of the Black Chevy Tahoe, outside the home of Winston St. Clair, the NYPD's Deputy Commissioner of Training.

St. Clair was one of the lucky ones who had survived the *deck re-shuffling* when the new administration had come in. It had worked out well for her, because she had been able to maintain her position as St. Clair's driver. The idea of actually having to go back to teaching social science courses, at the Police Academy, wasn't very appealing to her.

Not that she actually believed that St. Clair would let that happen to her.

She had been with him since he had first gotten the position several years prior. St. Clair had been a uniformed member of the service, rising up to the rank of lieutenant. His last assignment had been as a social science instructor at the academy, many years ago. After he retired, he had taken a position as a professor at Fordham University. Then, when St. Clair's old partner from Manhattan North had become deputy commissioner of training, he was brought in as the man's assistant. Then the DCT got the job running the *Federal Law Enforcement Training Center* in Glynco, Georgia and they gave St. Claire the job running the Training Bureau.

Palmer had originally gotten the job as his driver through a hook, a well-connected friend in the fraternal organization which she and St. Clair both belonged to, but she had kept the job because of her *other* qualifications. Over time, St. Clair had begun to share a lot during their daily rides to and from the academy. It soon became clearly obvious that Mrs. St. Clair was more interested in *her* social needs then in taking the time to meet *his* needs. At a seminar held in Boston, on establishing protocols for police sensitivity training in dealing with inner-city youths, they had shared a couple of drinks at the hotel bar. By the time they made it back to their respective rooms, she had offered him an alternative method for having his needs met, and he had taken it.

For as complicated a man as St. Clair was, his needs were surprisingly simple. In fact, she had actually begun to get bored by his *vanilla* routine and she had made it her mission to spice up his sex life. It didn't take all too long before he was eating out of her hand.

It was exactly the kind of job *insurance* that had gotten her a nice shiny detective's badge and kept her secure in the knowledge that her recruit teaching days where long gone.

She glanced out the window at the large, two-story, tan brick home, with the terra cotta roof and wooden double doors. The second floor bedrooms, which faced the street, had matching balconies with wrought iron railings that flanked either side of a large picture window. She'd been in the house a couple of times, while Mrs. St. Clair was out of town with the children, and she couldn't help but be a little bit jealous. It was a far cry from the house that she had in Cambria Heights, just a few miles drive south of here, on the Cross Island Parkway.

One day, she thought.

It had just begun to snow outside, and she adjusted the SUV's windshield wipers, watching as it scattered the powdery flakes that had begun to accumulate. It was almost time for him to come out, so she adjusted the radio station, from the hip-hop one which she preferred, and selected the pre-set one for the jazz station which he insisted on. As if on cue, she saw the foyer light come on inside the house. A moment later St. Clair emerged from the house, locking the door behind him.

Palmer reached down, setting the Styrofoam coffee container into the cup holder, and then unlocked the door. She got out of the vehicle, and began to make her way around to the passenger side.

She might have been in-charge in the bedroom, but when it came to the *real world*, there were still protocols that had to be followed and opening the door for the *boss* was one of them. It was all part of the *pomp and circumstance* of being an important person.

As she rounded the back of the car she heard a muffled *crack*.

It was an unusual sound, something which sounded only vaguely familiar. Like the muffled sound of a 2x4 being struck against something hard, far off in the distance. She glanced around, trying to place the sound she had heard, but didn't observe anything out of the ordinary.

As Palmer made her way around the SUV, she expected to see St. Clair approaching the vehicle, but he was not there. She was positive that she had seen him come out.

Did he go back inside? she wondered.

She cautiously traversed the slick sidewalk, keeping an eye on the front door.

"Commissioner?" she called out.

When she didn't hear a reply, she made her way up the staircase. As she turned a corner, she saw the body of Winston St. Clair crumbled on the granite walkway in front of her.

Her first thought was that he'd had a heart attack, but then she saw the blood begin streaming down the staircase in front of her and she let out a scream.

CHAPTER SEVENTEEN

Long Island Jewish Hospital, Little Neck, Queens, N.Y.
Wednesday, December 18th, 2013 – 7:23 a.m.

"What the fuck is happening?" Stargold asked, as he paced around the table in the hospital's conference room.

"Like the man said, 'once is happenstance, twice is coincidence, three times is enemy action,'" Maguire replied ominously.

"So you think we are being targeted?"

"You have a better theory?" Maguire asked, taking a sip of coffee.

Stargold paused his pacing to stare back at his friend. James could see the weariness in the man's face, the toll that the last few months had taken on him.

It was a far cry from their days of doing dignitary protection. Back then they were responsible for themselves and their individual assignments, but they were just one part of the overall protection detail, which was overseen by higher-ups in the organizational chart. As long as everything went as planned, the bosses got the accolades and they remained the unseen cogs in the machinery. Unfortunately, now *they* were the bosses and things were most certainly not going as planned.

"No," Rich replied, as he collapsed into one of the chairs.

His voice sounded just as tired as he appeared.

Maguire honestly felt bad for Rich. As much as they were partners in this, Rich still sat in the number one seat. No matter what happened, everything was going to get laid at his doorstep.

It was a far cry from Maguire's military days.

Back then, if they had been targeted by an enemy, they would respond with extreme prejudice. Today, there was no one to strike back against. It was as if they were being targeted by a ghost.

"We need to put a face on this," Maguire said.

"Sandy's people are working on that," Rich replied. "I even got a call from Dan Bridges over at the Bureau offering their resources."

"Maybe we need a new set of eyes," Maguire said.

"Who do you have in mind?" Rich asked.

"You remember Detective Angelo Antonucci?"

Stargold thought for a moment. "Yeah, he was the guy that broke the Ripper case."

"Yeah, that's him," Maguire replied. "I was going to have him take a look at this. See if he can find some other *dots* for us to connect."

"Make the call," Rich said.

As Maguire reached for his cellphone there was a knock at the door.

"Come in," Rich called out.

The door opened and one of the officers from his security detail peered into the room.

"Commissioner, the mayor just arrived," the man said. "They are going to do the press conference downstairs."

"Okay, I'm coming," Stargold said.

"Go on," Maguire said to him, "I've got this."

"Okay, you heading back to the office?"

"Yeah, but I'm going to head over to the crime scene first and take a look."

"Alright, I'll call you when I am leaving here," Stargold said. "Wish me luck."

In another time and another place Maguire would have shot him a smartass reply. It was something they had done to one another for as long as both men could remember, but today was not the day for that.

Maguire nodded somberly, "you'll be fine."

As he watched Rich leave the room he wondered if that was the truth or if he was telling him a convenient lie.

Did it really matter? he wondered.

"Hello?" he heard a low voice say.

Maguire turned his attention back to the cellphone.

"Sandy, I'm so sorry," he said into the phone. "I didn't even realize I had hit your number."

"Don't feel bad, Commissioner," she replied. "My alarm clock went off this morning and I picked up my cellphone to answer it. I think we are all running on empty."

"I just wonder if they'll let us shut the department down for a few days of some much needed R&R after we find out who's doing this."

"You really want me to answer that?" she asked.

"Not really," he replied. "We all have a right to our delusional fantasies."

"How are things at the hospital?"

"The Boss is doing a presser with the mayor in a few minutes," Maguire replied. "How are things on your end?"

"They are doing canvasses, but nothing new so far," Sandy replied. "The best witness is still his driver, but the only thing she could tell us was that she *heard* something."

"Have we been able to qualify exactly what that was?"

"Nope, just something *muffled.*"

"Could it have been a silencer?" he asked.

"That's my thought," Barnes replied, "but that still doesn't explain how she didn't see anyone."

"And she is positive that she was outside the vehicle?"

"Yes, she said that she saw St. Clair come out of the house and got out to open the passenger door for him. By the time she walked around, he was down."

"I'm coming down to the scene," he replied. "I need to see it for myself."

"I'll be here," she said.

"Oh, I almost forgot," Maguire said. "I'm stealing one of your people again."

"Who?" Barnes asked.

"Antonucci," he replied, "from Cold Case."

"You know, at this point you should just trade me outright for him," she said. "Give me a white shield, who is good with a computer, and a future draft pick to be agreed on later."

"You want two for one, huh?" Maguire asked.

"Well, he does do good work."

"Deal," Maguire said with a laugh. "I'll be over there in a little while."

"I'll be waiting," Barnes replied.

Maguire ended the call and then selected another number, listening to it ring. A moment later he heard a voice answer on the other end.

"Angelo, it's Commissioner Maguire," he said. "Are you in the office?"

"No, sir," the man replied. "I'm just watching life pass me by on the L.I.E."

"What exit?"

"I've been staring at the sign for exit 36 for the last fifteen minutes."

"Get off and meet me over at this address," Maguire said, reading off the location.

"What's going on?" Antonucci asked.

"Deputy Commissioner St. Clair was killed last night."

"I'll be there in five minutes," Antonucci said.

CHAPTER EIGHTEEN

Little Neck, Queens, N.Y.
Wednesday, December 18th, 2013 – 8:11 a.m.

Detective Antonucci stood in front of the late Winston St. Clair's home, taking in the scene.

The street was blocked off fifty feet away on either end. Despite the cold temps, groups of on-lookers gathered behind the yellow crime scene tape as Crime Scene Unit technicians went about the task of recording every detail.

He had already gotten the *bumper sticker* version of what had transpired, from the Chief of Detectives, and was trying to make sense of everything.

Aside from the police activity, it appeared to be a quiet, albeit very affluent, residential street. In this area of the city, real estate price tags easily topped the seven figure range. It wasn't exactly the type of location that one would expect a murder to take place, let alone the murder of a police official in front of an armed officer.

Antonucci opened the door and peered inside the unmarked black Chevy Tahoe, which sat at the curb, in front of the residence. The soothing strains of a saxophone played softly on the radio while a container of coffee sat idly in the cup holder.

"Why didn't they take her out first?" Antonucci asked, as he stared into the vehicle compartment.

Why did you assume it was a they? he wondered rhetorically.

"Ang."

Antonucci turned around to see Maguire walking toward him with a member of his security detail.

"I'd say good morning, sir, but it doesn't seem appropriate."

"You're right about that," Maguire replied. "So what are your first thoughts?"

"Confused," Antonucci said.

"About?"

"Everything," he said somberly.

"Join the club," Maguire replied. "We've got three dead members of the service and there seems to be a lot more questions than there are answers."

"I'd like to say that I have kept up to date on things, but I've been running several other cases," Antonucci said. "What particulars can you give me about each of the shootings?"

"The Chief Surgeon was shot outside his girlfriend's home in Brooklyn," Maguire said. "Our detective was heading in for a detail when he was killed in his driveway in North Bellmore, and Commissioner St. Clair was killed as he walked out of his house and toward his car."

"Different ranks, different locations, different situations," Antonucci remarked.

"Now the question is whether there were different killers?"

"It's possible," Antonucci replied, "but if you really believed that I don't think you would have called me."

"You're right," Maguire replied. "I want you to take a look at this and see if there is anything we are missing. Sometimes you need a fresh set of eyes that haven't been *influenced* by the facts as we know them."

"I'll need access to the current case folders," Antonucci said. "As well as the personnel folders for each of the victims and a place to sort through it all,"

"Chief Barnes will get you copies of everything that we have so far and you can work out of my conference room," Maguire replied. "Just let me know whatever you need."

"I'll get to work on it immediately," he said.

CHAPTER NINETEEN

Southampton, Suffolk County, N.Y.
Wednesday, December 18th, 2013 – 10:12 a.m.

"Are you sure about this?" Genevieve asked, as her and Melody walked toward the Gulfstream G550, which sat waiting on the tarmac at Francis S. Gabreski Airport in Westhampton Beach.

"I need to get away, Gen," Melody replied. "Just for a few days."

"Listen, I understand," Gen said. "If I didn't have to worry about nursing, I'd be flying out with you."

"Who'd have ever *thunk* you'd be the responsible one?"

"I have my moments."

"Uh huh," Melody said with a laugh. "You just keep telling yourself that."

"Haters gonna hate," Gen said dismissively. "*Anyway*, when do you think you'll be back?"

"Friday night," Melody replied, "Saturday the latest. I just have to blow off some steam and I can't think of a more expedient way than with high explosives."

"Well, I've set up the meeting at GDL for Monday at ten a.m., so you have to be back by then."

"Oh don't worry, I'll be back," Melody said. "I just need to get a first-hand demo before we have to start hitting the hallowed halls of Congress. I can read all the reports in the world, but it helps to be able to visualize it. I also want to find out what is holding up the tests, that they said they were going to schedule, for Dragon's Breath at China Lake."

"Good luck," Gen said, "Last I heard there was a pissing match going on in the Senate Armed Services Committee in regards to sequestration."

"Yeah, they'll drag their feet on this, but they'll buy a dozen cargo planes and then put them right into moth balls," she said angrily. "I bet *someone* is holding up the testing, because someone else won't co-sponsor a funding bill for *their* district."

"Washington, D.C., 'you will never find a more wretched hive of scum and villainy,'" Gen said with a laugh. "Don't forget to blow something up for me."

"I will, Chicky," Melody replied. "Remember to keep the boys on a short leash."

Melody walked up the steps, followed by a member of her security detail.

"Good morning, Ms. Anderson," Captain Katrina Mann said, as Melody entered the plane.

"Morning, Kat," Melody replied. "How is everything?"

"I'm getting paid to fly and no one's trying to shoot me out of the sky," the former Air Force pilot said, as she closed the plane's door. "Life can't get much better."

"I'm always happy when I can add so much personal fulfillment to your life," Melody replied, as she peered into the cockpit. "Morning, Renee."

"Morning, Ms. Anderson," Renee Ashcroft said from the co-pilot's chair.

"Renee and I were just sitting here wondering if cowboys were still *in season* in Montana." Mann said.

"I believe they are," Melody said with a laugh. "Just remember not to get caught *poaching*. I'm pretty sure the locals shoot back."

"It's probably better off to stay on the ranch then and just play liar's poker."

"You bring the alcohol and I'll bring the money," Melody said.

"It's a deal," said Ashcroft.

"Well then let's fire up this beast and get this show on the road."

CHAPTER TWENTY

1 Police Plaza, Manhattan, N.Y.
Wednesday, December 18ᵗʰ, 2013 – 3:41 p.m.

"So where are we at with all of this?" Rich asked.

"Sandy has her people working on it, and I brought in my guy to take a look from the sidelines," Maguire said. "He's reviewing the case folders in my conference room."

"What are your thoughts on that?"

"He's good at thinking outside the box," Maguire said. "At the end of the day he might come up with the same conclusions, but, then again he might not. Right now we need to utilize every tool in our shed."

"We really need to catch a break."

"Something will give," Maguire replied. "Whoever is behind this will eventually fuck up."

"I know that," Stargold said. "The only problem is whether or not that comes before they can strike again."

"We don't know that they will."

"The reality is that we don't know much of anything," Rich replied in frustration. "Have you seen any of the newspaper coverage? I got a call from a friend over at the News. Apparently tomorrow's headline is *NYPDazed*. The editorial asks how we can protect the city if we can't protect ourselves."

"Newspapers, and the media in general, make money by telling stories. The stories don't have to be real; they just have to be salacious. Pointing fingers and casting baseless accusations isn't news, it's a witch hunt."

"Yeah, well I hate to break the news to you, but I think some of those folks in city hall believe the stuff they read," Rich said. "You might want to take a look outside because I think they are erecting a pole over there to burn someone at the stake."

Maguire picked up his coffee mug and took a sip.

"Wouldn't matter to me if they were," Maguire replied. "The truth is that we are doing everything we can. If we weren't then they would have something to bitch about, but we are."

"Tell that to the folks across the street," Stargold said.

"Rich, you and I are not politicians. There is always going to be a political crisis and always something new that we are going to get trashed on by the media. A spike in murders in the two-eight, robberies in the one-oh-three; someone is always going to have something to bitch about. Yet the more effective we are the more people begin asking 'why do we need so many cops?' It's the nature of the beast; damned if you do and damned if you don't."

"I hate this fucking job."

"No you don't," Maguire said. "You just hate the game."

"Whatever," Rich replied. "That still doesn't help with what we are going to do about this."

"We're gonna be cops," Maguire said. "We are going to do the job we were hired to do and not worry about trying to keep it. The worst that can happen is McMaster's fires us, but we are going to focus on catching whoever is doing this and not give a flying fuck about pleasing the media or the politicians."

"Well, speaking of politicians, I just got word that Eliza Cook is coming into town after the first of the year to announce her candidacy for president."

"Sure, why not," Maguire said. "It's not as if we don't have anything else going on."

"I know," he said. "It's a shitty time, but she has apparently had this set up for a while. I worked with the guy who is heading up her security detail. He was on the Presidential Protection Detail before he retired and went into private security. I told him you would give him a call and iron out the details."

"What's his name?"

"Bob Paine," Rich replied, writing a number down on a piece of paper and handing it to Maguire.

"I'll call him and get things squared away," Maguire said. "After her last performance, when she bitch slapped the president on national television, I can't wait to see what she pulls out of her hat."

"The only consolation is that while she is here making the announcement, she's also going to be attending a 9/11 healthcare event earlier in the day, so at least the media will be forced to cover it."

"Well, if it takes a visit from the *queen of mean* to bring attention to the fact that Congress has been dragging their collective heals on providing money for long term medical care for our people, so be it," Maguire said. "The only time those fuckers seem willing to spend exorbitant amounts of money is on their own pay raises and health insurance."

"Politicians," Rich replied.

The phone on Rich's desk buzzed. He looked down and saw the call was from his secretary. He put the call on speaker.

"Yes?" Stargold said.

"Commissioner, Chief Barnes is here to see you."

"Thanks, Maggie, send her in."

A moment later the door opened and Sandy Barnes walked in.

"Sorry to interrupt, sirs, but I figured you would want to hear this news."

"Good or bad?" Rich asked.

"We just got the ballistics back from the Eichenberg and Rivera shootings."

"And?"

"They're a match," Sandy said, as she took a seat.

"Well, now we have our answer," Maguire said.

"Just waiting for the results from the St. Claire shooting," she said. "They are also running it through *IBIS*. It's a longshot, but who knows, maybe we will catch a break."

IBIS stood for the Integrated Ballistics Information System, a program run by the Bureau of Alcohol, Tobacco and Firearms, which allowed for comparison checks to be made against bullet and shell casings in the system's data base.

"So someone targeted them," Rich said.

"It would seem so," Maguire said. "The question now is who and why."

"Let's hope we figure that out soon."

CHAPTER TWENTY-ONE

Southampton, Suffolk County, N.Y.
Wednesday, December 18th, 2013 – 9:53 p.m.

Maguire laid the case folder, that he'd been reading, on the bed next to him and picked up his cellphone. He hit the number and listened to it ring.

"Hey, how are you feeling?" Melody asked.

"Tired," Maguire said.

"I bet you are," she replied. "Is there anything new?"

"Yeah, it looks as if the shootings are related. They got a ballistics match on the first two."

"Oh my God," she said softly. "I'm so sorry, James."

"Well, at least it gives us a better direction to look in," he replied. "So how are things in God's country?"

"Amazing," she said. "I'm staring out the window and everything is covered in snow. It looks so clean and peaceful. Like the world has left this part pristine and untouched."

"You're making me jealous," Maguire said.

"You could always come out here," she replied. "I'd let you play with all the toys that I have."

"I wish I could," he said. "God knows I could use a break."

"But you can't, right?"

"Nope, not with everything going on here."

"I knew that," she said. "I guess I was just trying to be a little selfish."

"Our lives are a bit hectic, aren't they?" he asked.

"To put it mildly," she said with a sigh.

"Then on top of everything going on with the shootings, we just got word the former secretary of state is coming in to announce her candidacy for president."

"You know, I had a feeling it was coming soon," Melody said. "I just got an email the other day from one of her former staffers. I think they are trying to make sure they have their donors lined up."

"You're a donor?"

"Does that surprise you?"

"A bit," he said.

"It's just business," Melody said. "I think you would find that my address book is a bit *eclectic*."

"Yeah, and mine is a bit *eccentric*."

"There's nothing wrong with having a *diverse* group of friends," she replied.

"Yeah, that's what my friends are, diverse," James said with a laugh.

"Well, if all you do is surround yourself with the same like-minded folks, you find yourself leaving in a vacuum and that's never a good thing."

"Still, Eliza Cook doesn't seem like your typical candidate," Maguire said.

"I'm torn," she replied. "Our political positions don't exactly line up in sync, but she does have a pair of brass balls and I can certainly respect that."

"After the tongue lashing she gave *POTUS* on live television I'd say they were more like titanium balls."

"It was pretty intense," Melody said.

"I'm not a big fan of the public berating, but I have to say it was a long time in coming," Maguire replied. "Our friends are dropping like flies, while our enemies just keep laughing their asses off at what passes for foreign policy these days."

"Which is the reason I'm torn," she said. "Maybe we need someone with a bit of passion. Someone who will push back instead of apologize."

"So you think you'll back her, even if you don't agree with her?"

"I don't know," Melody said. "I've never spoken to her directly, but I have had some business discussions with a few folks that are close to her. I'm not exactly sure just how *married* she is to her positions. I get the feeling that she might just be in a *relationship* with them until something better comes along."

"I'm not sure what bothers me more, her political positions or the fact that she might not actually have any."

"When I first started off in business I naively believed that folks in D.C. had a belief system, sadly, those days are long gone," she said. "I learned that politics is just another form of business. Once you get elected to it you don't want to get fired from it. It's too lucrative. The easiest way to ensure that is to make sure your re-election coffers are filled so that you can easily defend yourself."

"And it doesn't bother you to be a part of that system?"

"Sure it does," she said, "but what would you suggest I do?"

"I thought you were the one who said you hated politics," Maguire said.

"I do, but this is the world that we created. If I don't play in it someone else will and at least I know where *my* moral compass points."

"Well now that I am thoroughly depressed," he replied.

"I'm sorry if I crushed your utopian world view, Cowboy," Melody said with a laugh. "Would you like me to get you the name of a good therapist?"

"Oh boy, someone's a bit feisty tonight."

"Maybe a bit," Melody said, "but some whiskey will do that."

"Rough day at the office?"

"Fun day at the office," she replied. "I think I found a replacement for your Suburban."

"Oh yeah?" Maguire replied. "I can't wait to hear this one."

"Well, you ever see those SUV's with the machine guns mounted on top?"

"Yeah, you have one?"

"I have a *better* one," she said with a cocky tone. "Those others expose the gunner, the one I was in today lets you shoot from within the vehicle, through a remote weapons system. It has a big cushy chair and it even has a cup holder. You know, in case you want to have a *mocha chai latte* while disposing of threats."

"Oh, that'll make rush hour traffic more interesting."

"We just need to keep Gen out of it," Melody said. "You know how she is with road rage."

"That scenario is going to give me nightmares."

"But enough about me," she replied. "What is happening with your investigation?"

"To be honest, I'd rather just talk about what you are doing," he said. "I need a break from thinking about it."

"I'm sorry. I wish I was there to make it better."

"No, as much as I didn't want you to go, I knew that you needed to get out of here. I'm surprised you didn't do it sooner."

"The only reason I did was that I'm going to have to start making some of those aforementioned politicians pay up for the money I've given them over the years, but I need to know first-hand what I am talking about."

"And do you now?"

"Mostly," she replied. "I had a chance to go over the technical data. Today I got to see some of the hardware and tomorrow I'm going to see an actual test of the system."

"Then what?"

"Then Gen and I will do a full-on blitz on the Hill," she replied. "The whole government sequestration nonsense has screwed everything over, but there is still money to be spent. We just need to make sure that they spend it on the right projects and not some crap, just because it happens to be in some connected prick's district."

"See, just talking to you about your world makes mine almost seem more *palatable*."

"Glad I could help."

In the background Maguire could hear noise.

"What's that?" he asked.

"Oh, Kat and Renee just got here," Melody replied. "It's girls' poker night."

"Seriously?"

"What? You think just because we're girls that we can't have some fun?"

"I didn't say that," Maguire replied. "But you are staying indoors though, aren't you?"

"Yes, dear," she said.

"Okay, just wasn't sure if I should contact the local P.D. and put them on standby."

"Don't worry, I can cover my own bail money," she said. "Now if you'll excuse me, I'm about to show these two hooligans why I'm the boss."

"Pictures or it never happened."

"In your dreams, Cowboy," she said with a laugh.

"Love ya, Mel."

"Love you too."

Maguire ended the call and laid the phone on the night table. He looked over at the alarm clock and then turned the light off. Morning would be here soon and he had no idea what the new day would bring.

CHAPTER TWENTY-TWO

Levittown, Nassau County, N.Y.
Thursday, December 19th, 2013 – 2:14 a.m.

The man laid the soldering iron down in the cradle and leaned back in his chair, rubbing his eyes.

The UAV had nicked the wall of the home, as he flew it back, causing one of the protective engine guides to impinge on one of the blades. Had it been a four motor vehicle, which required all of its engines to maintain flight control, it would have been a disaster. It was exactly the reason why he had built this platform to be as robust as it was.

The eight engines provided him with enough power to accommodate its modified design. Even though there was no recycling of a slide involved, like on a proper semi-automatic firearm, there was still enough recoil that the extra engine power allowed him to compensate for that.

Unfortunately he hadn't expected the other cop to get out of the car so quickly and he'd gotten nervous; clipping the house as he piloted the UAV back to him.

You'd have thought you'd have gotten your nerves under control after so many years, he thought.

He checked the weld, making sure that it was good, and then wiped the device down before loading the vehicle back into its protective case. When it was secured, he removed his gloves and opened the book on the desk. He began re-reading the most recent entries.

It would have been nice to have someone that could do the intelligence gathering work, but that would have been an unnecessary risk. At least this way he was relying on his own observations and not the recollections of a third party. After all, he knew firsthand how things like that didn't always end up well.

Today's target would be a bit different. For starters, it would have to take place in a much more open area. He'd been concerned about the first one, but the terrible weather had pretty much negated the risk of being seen. Targets two and three were pretty much a walk in the park, considering their local, but this one would be unique.

He never considered his targets by name. It wasn't that he had any reservations, but he had found that it was easier to think of them as *objects* and not living people.

He stared up at the photos on the board above the desk. Three were already crossed out and he took a moment to examine the face of target four. He memorized the facial features, the individual characteristics that made each one unique. It helped to know them intimately well, so that when you saw them appear in the display you would not hesitate. To him it was no different than a driver memorizing the map of his route.

His observations had determined that target four would potentially be the most difficult. He had actually intended to take out this target first, but, as he did his reconnaissance, he had decided to push back this operation.

Target four actually resided in a gated apartment complex. He had done several walking tours of the area, trying to identify a weakness, but there was none that he could see.

Entry into the compound was through a gated thoroughfare. In addition to it being manned twenty-four / seven, there were also security cameras which scanned the interior as well as the exterior of the fence line.

If he was conducting a personal attack against the target, he could have slipped in between their defenses undetected, but that was not his specialty. There were others who preferred their work to be *up close and personal*, but he much preferred the detached approach.

He'd managed to find a location where he could do observations of the apartment and determined that someone else resided there as well. After determining that the attack would have to take place at a secondary location, he began to conduct surveillance. Target four was boring. When they were not at work, they were at home. In fact, the only deviation was the frequent morning stop at a coffee shop, several blocks from the apartment.

While target four was a creature of habit, that habit did not provide him any window of easier opportunity. The coffee shop sat just off a busy intersection. While he could find a quiet, off-street location to operate from, the UAV could be exposed. The time of the morning was the truly difficult part. It was that in-between time, where traffic was unpredictable. Some days there were several vehicles arriving within moments of each other, while at other times there was no one else around.

Target four would be the most exposed as they exited and re-entered the vehicle, he would just have to play it by ear and hope for the best. If anything happened, at least he knew that he would be able to get away.

The thought of losing the UAV was a concern to him, but it was a calculated risk. Obviously they would know his modus operandi, but little more. The device was his own design; created using widely available commercial parts. There were no serial numbers on the device, nothing which could be traced directly backed to him.

He was also particularly methodically when it came to the handling of the vehicle. From the time it came out of the case, until the time it went back in, no part of it ever touched his bare hands. If it ever did fall into the wrong hands, there would be nothing linking him to it.

The man looked down at his watch. He had a little less than two hours before he would have to leave. He turned off the desk light and got up, making his way out to the kitchen. He poured himself a glass of milk and looked out the window, at the street below.

It was a quiet neighborhood and he rarely saw anyone outside. It was one of the things that had attracted him to this place. People just came and went, oblivious to anything else around them. He had moved in this past August; just before the start of the school year. He began watching the rhythm, learning the ebb and flow. Adults left early for work and school buses came and went. Later on the process was reversed. It was all a well-choreographed movement. He came and went without seeing anyone. More importantly, he moved about without anyone seeing him. He was a ghost; someone who would never be remembered.

He finished his milk and rinsed the glass out, laying it on the counter. He made his way back to the bedroom and laid down. He had a long day ahead of him and he needed to take a quick power nap.

CHAPTER TWENTY-THREE

Bayside, Queens, N.Y.
Thursday, December 19th, 2013 – 6:04 a.m.

Inspector Josephine Kennedy came to a stop, at the exit for the apartment complex, and nudged the nose of the unmarked car forward, just beyond the gate, to get a better look at the oncoming traffic. The car physically shuddered, as it was battered by the winds coming off the East River.

It was generally quiet at this time of the morning, but there was no point in being careless. It wouldn't be a good example for the commanding officer of the Police Academy's Recruit Training Section to get into an accident with a department vehicle. Not after all the lecturers and training that new officers had to undergo regarding driver safety.

Besides which, 'I really needed my caffeine fix,' was never considered a justifiable reason.

Kennedy turned right onto the service road of the Cross Island Parkway. It was only a few blocks until it turned into Bell Boulevard and a dozen more till she reached the Dunkin' Donut coffee shop that had just recently opened. She liked this new location much better as it had a parking lot. Finding a spot to park the car around the corner wasn't much of an issue in the summer, but on a cold winter day such as this it really mattered.

Fortunately, the parking lot was empty. Kennedy pulled the car into the spot closest to the front door and then ran inside. On a day like today, the extra-large container of coffee served as much to beat away the chill as it did to awaken the senses. The toasted coconut donut in the bag was a reward for having not taken the day off to begin with.

When Kennedy got back into the car, she set the container on the dashboard, and then reached into the bag to retrieve the donut.

"Aw, crap," Kennedy said, as she felt her fingers slide against the still warm glazing.

"See, that's what you get for being a friggin' *gavone*," she chided herself, as she pulled her fingers from the bag, licking the pieces of shredded coconut from them.

She set the bag down on the passenger seat next to her and leaned over, to grab a napkin from the glove box, just as the driver's side window erupted in a shower of glass.

Kennedy's body slammed into the dashboard, as the bullet struck her in the back of the head.

A car had pulled in next to her, just as the window had exploded. The vehicles occupant walked around cautiously and peered into the unmarked police car, seeing the body slumped over.

The man froze, staring at the blood that poured out from the back of the woman's head. Then he heard the voices over the radio. He reached in cautiously and lifted the microphone off the hook. He held it to his mouth and depressed the transmit button.

"Uhm, hello," he said nervously.

"Transmitting unit please identify yourself," the female voice of the dispatcher said over the radio.

"There's a police officer shot," the man said.

"All units, clear the air," the dispatcher said. "What is the location of the officer shot?"

"At the Dunkin' Donuts on Bell Boulevard," the man said. "Near 36th."

Immediately a series of high pitched beeps came over the radio.

"Confines of the 111th Precinct, report of a 10-13, officer shot," the dispatcher said, as she repeated the location.

In the background, other dispatchers began to take action. Alerts went out over the local division, as well as the ones handling specialized units such as the Aviation Unit, Emergency Service Unit and Highway Patrol. In addition, a message was sent to the FDNY dispatcher handling EMS calls for that area of Queens to have a bus respond.

"Please hurry," the man said. "There's a lot of blood."

"Units are on the way," the dispatcher replied. "Just stay with me. Did you see anyone?"

"No, no one," he said, his voice frantic. "Please hurry."

In the background the man heard the sound of sirens as radio cars converged on the scene to save their fallen comrade.

CHAPTER TWENTY-FOUR

Jones Beach, Nassau County, N.Y.
Tuesday, December 17th, 2013 – 6:43 a.m.

"Fuck!"

The man screamed out, as he angrily paced along the deserted stretch of boardwalk. Despite the cold wind coming off the ocean he could still feel the perspiration soaking through the shirt he was wearing under his jacket.

His mind was racing, as he replayed the morning's operation out in his head. Instinctively he knew something had gone wrong the moment that he had pressed the *fire* button.

The weather conditions had been less than optimal, but it had been a calculated risk. There had been no way to *improve* the odds, unless he wanted to postpone the operation till the spring. Still, the wind had been a concern to him, but, when the opportunity presented itself, he'd taken the shot anyway.

Unfortunately, just as his finger had hit the button, he'd seen her move. In that fleeting moment, he'd watched the *sure kill* disappear, replaced by a lingering question mark. The side window erupted in a spray of shattered glass and her body had slumped forward, but he *knew* that something had gone wrong. The window of opportunity for this kill had been small to begin with, even under the best of conditions, and now he was left wondering if he had committed a fatal error.

Dead people told no tales, but he could not say for certain whether she was dead or not.

There were too many lingering questions, but the biggest one right now was had she seen anything? Anonymity and fear were his trademarks. People couldn't fight against an unknown enemy, let alone protect themselves, and what they couldn't fight against caused them to live in fear.

Fear of the next attack, fear of being the next target.

Had he lost that? he wondered.

The thought sent a chill through him. For the first time in his life it was he who felt fear clutching at his throat.

How long do I have?

CHAPTER TWENTY-FIVE

1 Police Plaza, Manhattan, N.Y.
Thursday, December 19th, 2013 – 11:57 a.m.

"Please tell me that you have something for me, Ang?" Maguire asked, as he walked into the conference room, followed by Stargold and Barnes.

"I do," the man said. "At least I think I do."

"Well let's hear it, son," Rich said, taking a seat, "because we really need a break right now."

There were five blackboards setup in the room, and the large conference table was filled from one end to the other with case folders. It was apparent from the discarded coffee cups, which littered the room, that the man had not taken a break in the last twenty-four hours.

"At first I looked into the different cases," Antonucci said. "Looking for any type of similarity, but there really isn't any, aside from the fact that all three were killed; although the angle of entry on the bullets is a bit perplexing."

"How so?" Rich asked.

"On the Eichenberg shooting ballistics estimated that the shot came from about three feet above, so it was assumed the shooter was on the stoop," Antonucci replied. "Similar, but not exact, angles on both the Rivera and St. Clair shooting, but there were no high ground available in those instances to explain it."

"What does that tell you?" Barnes asked.

"Either our killer is close to nine feet tall, a ninja, or we are missing something."

"I hate fucking riddles," Rich said. "Do we have anything concrete to work with?"

"Well, I began looking at the killer, or killers, but at this point the details are just too vague to give us any real clues."

"I don't mean to be rude, Detective," Barnes said, "but we already know all this."

"Yes, ma'am, and I appreciate your concern," Antonucci replied. "So I stopped going down the same track as everyone else was going down and began looking at this as three individual cold cases."

"What do you mean?" Rich asked.

"Well, Commissioner, I turned my attention to the victims, looking at their past rather than their present," Antonucci said.

"So what did you find out, Ang?" Maguire asked.

"Okay, well, first I looked at Chief Eichenberg," he said. "He's been a department surgeon for the last thirty-three years, starting off as a district surgeon back in 1990. Back in 2005 he started participating in the applicant medical screening process and then in 2010 he was selected to be the new Supervising Chief Surgeon. His selection was a bit controversial, because of his ties to the former mayor, but under the last regime that became pretty much standard operating procedure. There really wasn't a whole lot more in his folder, not that I thought there would be."

"From there I began looking into our detective. He has a bit more in his folder. Armando Rivera came on the job in 1998. After he graduated from the academy and did his field training he was assigned to the Four-Four. He was an active cop, racking up a pretty healthy arrest record. Then in 2006, he put in for a transfer to the Applicant Processing Division. In 2011, there was a complaint filed against him for sexual harassment. He ended up getting bounced out of APD and sent to the One-Thirteen. While the case was founded, but there must have been more to the story because, after about a year of *penance*, he was transferred to the Gang Unit."

"You think it was a bullshit charge?" Maguire asked.

"I think so," Antonucci said. "I haven't seen the particulars, but he never lost his shield. I think this was a slap on the wrist, go behave, and then they quietly put him in a decent command."

"Any problems while he was in Gang?" Rich asked.

"None," Antonucci said. "Again, he was an active guy with solid evaluations."

"What about St. Clair?" Barnes asked.

"He is an odd one," Antonucci said. "He retired from the job as a lieutenant and went into the academic world, but he came back as an assistant after his old partner, Robinson Carter, was made the Deputy Commissioner of Training. When he left to take over the job at *FLETC*, they promoted St. Claire to the top spot. It was at this point that I took a step back and looked at the big picture."

"And what did you see," Rich asked.

"They have all been part of the applicant process," Antonucci said. "I believe that the killer is targeting members because they were involved in the investigatory phase, medical review, or training. The attack on Inspector Kennedy just solidifies that for me."

Rich looked at Maguire, then at Barnes.

"How the fuck did we miss this?" Stargold asked.

"Does it matter at this point?" Maguire asked. "What we need to do now is figure out exactly how they are linked."

"We need to examine things from the period they are all linked. The common denominator in all this seems to be Rivera, and he didn't begin in APD until 2006 and he was out in 2011. So realistically we are only looking at a window of roughly five years."

"What do you need, Ang?"

"All of Rivera's investigatory folders from APD."

Maguire picked up the phone and pressed a button.

"Chief of Personnel, Officer Callahan, how may I help you?" the voice on the other end said.

"This is Commissioner Maguire, I need to speak to Chief Hall," he said.

"Please hold, sir."

A moment later Maguire heard the call get transferred.

"Yes, Commissioner, what do you need?" Hall asked, when he came on the line.

"Nathan, I need you to have APD pull all of the applicant folders that Detective Armando Rivera investigated, from 2006 to 2011 while he was assigned there, and have them delivered to Detective Antonucci in my office forthwith, and by forthwith I mean thirty minutes ago."

"Yes, sir," Hall said. "Understood."

Maguire hung up the phone.

"You'll get your files, Ang," he said. "I just need you to find the killer in them."

"I'll do my best, sir."

CHAPTER TWENTY-SIX

1 Police Plaza, Manhattan, N.Y.
Friday, December 20th, 2013 – 12:53 a.m.

"I think I may have found something," Antonucci said.

Maguire looked up from the folder he had been reading. He had decided to act as a second set of eyes for Antonucci, perusing each folder as the man had completed his review.

There had been over a thousand case folders delivered, so they had broken them down into two groups: current active members of the department and applicants who had been rejected. They had decided to look at the rejected ones first, seeing as they were the ones who most likely would have had a grudge.

The conference room was filled with the pungent smell of Chinese take-out and coffee that had been *cooking* in the pot for too long. They had been at it for over twelve hours now and the strain was beginning to take its toll.

"What do you have?" Maguire asked.

"Gerald F. Spangler, Jr.," Antonucci replied.

"Okay, why is he interesting?"

"Because Rivera indicated he should not be hired and he was over ruled," Antonucci replied.

"By who?"

"Police Commissioner Ray Kellenberg," the man replied.

"Kellenberg?" Maguire asked. "Are you sure?"

Antonucci pulled a sheet of paper from the folder and handed it to him.

Maguire examined the document. It was a standard report known as a UF49, from the former police commissioner to Captain Brenda Melodia, the former C.O. of the Applicant Processing Division, on the Kellenberg's personal stationary. The only thing that made this unusual was the hand-written note on the bottom.

Brenda, contents noted. Proceed with processing as expeditiously as possible. I want Spangler in the next recruit class.

"What the fuck?" Maguire said with a quizzical look on his face. "You have the original report this references?"

Antonucci hand him another piece of paper.

It was another UF49, from Melodia to Kellenberg, identifying those potential recruits who were deemed to be ineligible. Halfway down the list was Gerald F. Spangler, Jr., with a notation that the ineligibility was due to psychological reasons.

"There are a lot of folks on this list, Ang," Maguire said. "What makes you think it's him?"

"Because of this," he said, sliding over another UF49 from Rivera to Melodia.

This report detailed Rivera's investigation of Spangler, including a notation that he had failed the psychological evaluation and was ineligible. On the bottom was an endorsement indicating that the finding was over-ruled by the police commissioner.

"Why would you over rule an ineligibility based on a pysch failure?"

"I don't know, Boss," Antonucci said, "but I've often wondered about some of the decisions you folks in 1PP have made in the past."

"You and me both," Maguire said. "If Kellenberg said to push him through, then why is Spangler's file in the rejected pile?"

Antonucci scrolled through the paperwork and pulled out another piece of paper.

"Because Melodia didn't let it go," he said. "She sent a 2nd report, this time through channels, outlining the psych issues with Spangler."

"That must have pissed off Kellenberg," Maguire said.

"It's probably why she is no longer the C.O. of APD anymore."

The term, *through channels*, meant that the report went to the police commissioner, but it went through the chain of command. Meaning a lot more people saw the report, including the Chief of Personnel and Chief of Department, and had to sign off on it. It was a way for Melodia to cover her ass, should anything go wrong.

"There has to be more," Maguire said. "Keep looking through the file. Rivera would have covered his ass as well.

"I really need a cigarette," Antonucci said, getting up from the desk.

A while back he had limited himself to six a day. It was after midnight and he still had five to go.

"The smoking lamp is lit," Maguire said, as he slid one of the half empty coffee cups across the table.

"I thought that was against the rules," Antonucci said.

"It is," Maguire said, "but I make the rules."

"Are you sure, Boss?"

"My old Navy chief smoked and he used to say 'as long as you get the job done, don't question the means'. He had a long track record of success and no one said boo to him. Find me my answer and you can smoke anywhere in this damn building."

Antonucci lit up the cigarette, feeling like a kid in a bathroom stall, at a Catholic school, waiting for the principal to come through the door.

He took a long drag and sat back down at the desk. He removed all the paperwork out of the folder, flipped them upside down, and began going through them from the beginning. Twenty minutes later he held up a paper.

"You were in the military," Antonucci said. "What's an MOS?"

"It stands for military occupational specialty code," Maguire said. "Why?"

"You know what a 15W is?"

"That's used by the *ground pounders*," Maguire replied. "It's the Army designator for a UAV operator."

"You mean the guys who pilot the drones?"

"Yeah," Maguire said. "Why?"

"Well, maybe that would explain why no one *saw* a perp," Antonucci said. "And why the shots came from above the victims.

"*Sonofabitch*," Maguire said. "Is there any paperwork back from the military?"

Antonucci flipped through the papers until he found a document.

"I got this," he said, sliding the paper across the desk.

Maguire picked it up and looked at it.

"This is a DD 214 form," he said. "Basically it's a verification of military service."

"So he was legitimately in the Army?"

"Yes, but this is interesting," Maguire said. "He got out under a *general discharge.*"

"And this means?"

"Well, there are a couple of ways of getting out," Maguire explained. "Honorable discharge is what everyone wants, but not everyone gets it. Dishonorable is when you really screw the pooch, but there are a few others, including a general discharge. A general discharge has two caveats. One is under honorable conditions and the other is under less than honorable conditions. His was a UHC discharge, but we need to find out why."

"Why, what's the difference?" Antonucci asked.

"To receive a general discharge from the military there has to be some form of non-judicial punishment to correct unacceptable military behavior or failure to meet military standards," Maguire explained. "The discharging officer must give the reason for the discharge in writing. So there should be something on file."

Antonucci continued to look through the file, sifting through the paperwork to find something related to Spangler's military service.

"Wait a minute," he said, as he began reading a handwritten note. "Looks like Rivera talked to someone about this."

"What does it say?" Maguire asked.

"Rivera talked to Sergeant 1st Class Cecilia Gomez regarding Spangler's discharge. He notes that the conversation was completely off the record and Gomez informed him that she could not provide any details. However, she advised him that Spangler had some *issues* while in the military and that *we* should request his entire personnel record to see the extent of the issues. She added that if he were applying for a law enforcement position that it was in our best interests to *strongly* reject him."

"What the fuck?" Maguire replied. "There's nothing else?"

Antonucci flipped over the last few pages.

"He sent a request, but there was no official reply to it."

"Why in God's name would Kellenberg even consider going against something like this?"

"I guess that's the million dollar question."

"Then I guess it's time to knock on Mr. Spangler's door and ask him a few questions."

CHAPTER TWENTY-SEVEN

Levittown, Nassau County, N.Y.
Friday, December 20ᵗʰ, 2013 – 2:47 p.m.

The Brooklyn residence that was listed in Spangler's APD folder was an old one. Under the pretense of doing a follow-up background check, investigators reached out to the landlord who informed them that Spangler had moved out several months back and had not left any forwarding address. He described him as being quiet and very respectful, during the handful of times they had spoken, but that he was a very private person who mostly kept to himself.

It had taken the combined efforts of the NYPD's Intelligence, Counter Terrorism and Detective Bureau's several hours of intensive investigation, but by midday they had finally traced Gerald Spangler back to the house on Eden Lane.

In the end, his undoing had been a change of address form which he had filled out for the Department of Veterans Affairs. The mail was sent to a post office box in Levittown. Detectives and special agents from the FBI's Joint Terrorism Task Force had gone to the post office and interviewed the Post Master, as well as several of the workers. During the course of one interview, the postal worker had recognized the applicant photo of Spangler and recalled that he had picked-up a package, which needed to be signed for, on Monday.

Outside, they noticed that the small strip mall, where the post office was located in, had several surveillance cameras positioned around the parking lot.

They reviewed the video for Monday and spotted the man getting out of his car. The registration on the vehicle came back to an abandoned lot in Brooklyn, but a review of the license plate number had determined that it had received a ticket from the Nassau County Police Department, for parking on the wrong side of the street, on Eden Lane.

Over the course of the last two hours members of the FBI's Special Surveillance Group began to stream into the area, discretely monitoring the residence and keeping it under constant observation. In addition, snipers from the Bureau's SWAT team had set up an *over-watch* position in the houses that overlooked all four sides of the target residence.

There had been a bit of inter-agency squabbling as to who would take the lead with Deputy Chief Julie Preston, the C.O. of the NYPD's Emergency Service Unit, arguing that since it was NYPD officers who had been targeted, ESU should do the entry. However, since they were operating in Nassau County, and this was being viewed as a potential act of domestic terrorism, it was decided that, for the sake of continuity, the FBI should run the entire operation; from surveillance to take-down.

To the average viewer, nothing appeared out of the ordinary. Two delivery trucks came and went, a jogger made his way down the street while two women walked by with their dog, and several houses down a man worked on his car in the driveway. At the far end of the block a LILCO *crew* sat inside their warm work tent, frustrating unknowing residents with the occasional power *outage* that would keep them resetting the clocks on their microwaves. It was all part of a well-choreographed ballet of *deception*.

From the command vehicle two blocks away, Maguire, along with Rich Stargold and Special Agent's Kurt Silverman, the head of the JTTF, and Frank Selvaggio, the SWAT team leader, watched the live camera feed from the USPS truck as it pulled onto the block and stopped in front of the residence where the car had received the ticket.

"Target vehicle is not in sight," the voice said, over the encrypted radio channel. "I say again, target vehicle is not in sight. I'm proceeding to the residence."

That was to be expected.

Since arriving, no one had spotted Spangler's car, either on Eden Lane or on any of the surrounding streets.

Maguire watched as the man disappeared into the back and returned a moment later carrying a priority package. On another camera feed, this one from the LILCO work tent, he watched the *postal employee* approach the residence and then disappear from view, cut off from the camera eye by the bay window that protrude out from the front of the house.

"Yes?" an elderly woman's voice was heard on the audio channel.

"Good afternoon, ma'am," the FBI agent said. "I have a delivery for a Gerald Spangler."

"Jerry lives upstairs," the woman replied, "but I don't think he's home."

"Are you sure?" the man asked.

"Well, I don't see his car," she replied, "and he always parks it out front."

"Do you know when he will be back?"

"I'm sorry, I don't," she said. "He left early this morning."

"Cardinal base copy," he said. "Redbird has flown the coop."

"Base copy," Selvaggio said. "SAM Leader, all teams move in."

"Are you okay?" they heard the woman ask, a hint of concern in her voice.

"Ma'am, listen to me, this is very important," the man said. "My name is FBI Special Agent Williamson, is there anyone else in the house?"

"No, why?" she asked.

"I need you to come with me now."

As the woman watched, a large black Lenco Bearcat armored vehicle pulled into the driveway, while several black Chevy Suburban's converged on the street in front. Agents clad in tactical gear, and carrying automatic weapons, stood on the running boards, clinging to the rails that ran along the vehicles roof.

There were four operators per side and when the SUV's came to a stop, they quickly dismounted. A few of them took up positions around the perimeter, their weapons leveled at the exposed windows, while several more launched ladders up to the garage and the western side of the house, where large windows were located. The rest made their way toward the entrance in the back of the house.

"I don't understand," she said, her voice quivering with fear.

"It's okay, I'll explain everything."

The agent quickly ushered her to the rear of the Bearcat and, once she was safely inside, the vehicle pulled away.

"Target residence is clear," Williamson said.

Inside the command vehicle Selvaggio looked over at Silverman, waiting for confirmation.

"You have a green light," Silverman said with a nod.

"SAM leader to SAM 32, you have a green light on entry, repeat you have a green light."

"SAM 32, copy, green light," a voice said over the radio. "SAM 32 to all SAM Unit's, breaching on Three, Two, One...."

The first man held the storm door open while the second man, known as the *breacher*, brought the one man ram down onto the exterior door, shattering it free from the jamb in a shower of wooden splinters. At the same time, those members on the ladders shattered the windows and tossed in flashbangs. The small, black diversionary devices weighed just over eight ounces, but emitted an intensely loud *bang*, in excess of one hundred and seventy decibels, along with a blinding flash of light. The objective was to disorient and confuse any occupants of the location while entry was being made.

The team made its way up the narrow, confined staircase, knowing the extreme danger they were in, as they quickly approached the second floor door. It was a typical interior door, constructed of nothing more than two thin sheets of wood veneer which were affixed over a simple honeycomb center. It would give way very quickly once they hit it, but they also knew that, if the target was still inside, they were in a kill-zone until they did so.

The breacher hit the interior door, a second and a half after the flashbangs went off inside. The ram sent it exploding inwards, and the team entered the apartment in a well synchronized drill.

It took less than ten seconds for the team to clear the two rooms and confirm that Gerald Spangler was indeed long gone.

"SAM 32 to SAM Leader, location is clear," the man said with a hint of frustration in his voice. "I repeat, the location is clear."

Selvaggio looked over at Silverman, "It's all yours, Kurt."

"Thanks, Frank," Silverman replied.

"Let's go see if he left us any clues," Rich said, as the three men left the command vehicle.

CHAPTER TWENTY-EIGHT

Levittown, Nassau County, N.Y.
Friday, December 20th, 2013 – 3:07 p.m.

While Spangler hadn't left them any clues to pursue, he certainly hadn't left the apartment barren either.

The JTTF investigators had torn the place apart, going so far as to remove the drywall from around the chimney enclosure and the knee walls, to search for anything that might help them find Spangler.

In the end, it was all for naught.

The refrigerator and cabinets were still stocked with an ample supply of food. Investigators also found a number of articles of clothing still hung up in the closet and the bed was unmade, as if Spangler had simply gone out for the day. What struck them as odd was the lack of anything tangible. There were no papers, no mail, and no personal effects, nothing that would have said that Gerald Spangler had ever personally occupied this space.

However, the most disturbing thing that they had found was also a good indicator that he wasn't returning anytime soon. Above the empty desk in the bedroom was a series of photos, with large X's though them, along with a taunting, hand scribbled note that read: *If you're reading this, you're too late. There's more to come.*

According to the woman who owned the home, Spangler had also paid the rent in advance till February.

Clearly something hadn't gone as planned.

"What do you make of this?" Rich asked Maguire.

"Kennedy survived," Maguire replied. "I think he knew he screwed up and left quickly, just to be on the safe-side."

"Why not take everything?"

"Perhaps he was waiting to see if we pieced it all together," Maguire replied. "Maybe he parked his ass in one of those restaurants on Wantagh Ave and waited to see if anyone showed up."

"We have an APB out for his plate," Silverman said. "He'll turn up eventually."

"Have them check around the malls, the larger restaurants," Maguire replied. "Especially those with large parking garages. Odds are that he's already dumped the car, but at least we can go through it and see if he slipped up and left anything behind."

"You sound like you've given this some thought," Silverman said.

"It's what I would have done," Maguire replied. "Safe houses, safe cars, it's all *standard operating procedure*. You don't have a primary without having a secondary. If you're really smart you have a tertiary or more."

"This prick is like a fucking ghost," Rich said angrily.

"No, he's not," Maguire replied. "If he were, we wouldn't have a name. We know who he is, but he is still good."

"Any suggestions?" Rich asked.

"Yeah, we need to find out what's in his military jacket," Maguire said. "We need to know what we are really dealing with."

"Well, they rejected the first request," Rich said. "Can you back channel it?"

"I'll make some calls," Maguire replied. "Someone should be able to shed some light on him."

"Well, let's make it quick," Stargold replied. "Because according to him, there's still *more to come*."

CHAPTER TWENTY-NINE

FOB Chapman - Khost, Afghanistan
Saturday, December 21st, 2013 – 5:33 a.m. *(E.S.T. +9 ½ hrs)*

Roy Gentry glanced over at the screen on the cellphone, which sat vibrating on the night table, then down at the Casio G-Force watch on his wrist.

"I didn't want to sleep in anyway," he mumbled, as he reached for the phone.

"*Sahr pikheyr*," Maguire said, in passable Pashtu, when Gentry answered the phone.

"It might be *morning*, but if you're calling me it isn't *good*."

On the other end of the phone Maguire smiled.

Gentry hadn't told him where he had been going; just that his fun meter was red-lining and that he'd have a *haji pop* in honor of Maguire's engagement. Most assumed that he was back in the sandbox, military slang for Iraq, but he knew that Mother was also a master of deception and *misdirection*. In the current unstable global climate it could be a toss-up.

It was true that Iraq had been experiencing a rash of bombings lately, but that wasn't really all that *unusual*. The fact was that the majority of those attacks were sectarian violence, pitting Shia against Sunni civilians, or against Iraqi government officials.

On the other hand, the U.S. Army had just lost six soldiers when their UH-60 Blackhawk helicopter was taken down in the Shahjoi district of Afghanistan's Zabul province. This attack was being credited to a resurgent Taliban. What was more concerning was this was only the latest in a string of incidents with helicopters. It was a problem that had hit the SEAL community particular hard. Two years earlier, the Taliban had taken out a CH-47D Chinook helicopter, Call sign: *Extortion 17*, killing all thirty-eight on board, including seventeen Navy SEAL's, fifteen of which were from Team Six. It was the worst loss of American lives, in a single incident in the Afghanistan campaign, surpassing *Operation Red Wings* in 2005.

Extortion 17 was also heavily shrouded in controversy with many believing that the helicopter was intentionally lured into a Taliban hot zone and questions as to why several *unidentified* Afghan Commandos were allowed to board the helicopter just before takeoff.

So it wasn't exactly hard for him to surmise where Mother was calling home these days.

"Hey, I gave you a whole extra three minutes of rack time, Mother," Maguire said. "I heard that old people didn't need as much sleep."

"I just got to bed two hours ago," Gentry said gruffly.

"You used to tell me sleep deprivation builds character."

"I've already got enough character to last two lifetimes," Gentry replied, "but I don't think you called me to discuss my glowing attributes."

"I need to get access to a military personnel folder that the military might not want to release," Maguire said.

"And I'm sure you have a good reason for such a nefarious deed...."

"Three dead cops, a fourth in the hospital, and the promise of more to come."

Gentry sat up in bed and turned on the light.

"You think your shooters a soldier?"

"We think he's pulling the trigger by *proxy*," Maguire said. "His MOS was a drone operator. Applied to the department, but got rejected for psych reasons. His investigator, who is one of my dead cops, had an *off-the-record* conversation with an Army E-7 that he had some *issues* and that he should review his personnel folder. That request was officially rejected."

"What's your suspect's name?" Gentry asked, picking up the pad and pen on the nightstand.

"Spangler, Gerald F., Jr." Maguire replied. "I just sent you a copy of his DD 214 by text message."

"Give it a minute," Gentry said. "It's gotta wade through some water and hike a few hills to get to me."

"I really hate to bother you," Maguire said, "but time is of the essence on this one. Our boy has bugged out of his cave and is in the wind, but he left us a note saying he isn't done yet."

Gentry heard the ping, indicating that he'd received a new text message.

"Hold on, I think I just got your love letter."

He selected the icon and pulled up the message, glancing over the scanned document.

"Fuck if that name doesn't sound familiar," Gentry said.

"Don't worry, you're old," Maguire replied. "They say your memory is the first thing to go."

"It'll come to me in a few hours, and you can be sure that I'll return the *o'dark thirty* phone call to let you know," Gentry said. "For now, let me make a few calls and I'll get back to you as soon as I can."

"Thanks, Mother," Maguire said. "Sorry for waking you."

"Don't worry about it, Paddy," Mother replied. "On the other hand, my new friend, who's sitting in a steel box next door, might not be too happy with my dour countenance when we have our little chat later on."

"It's gonna suck to be him."

"Play stupid games, win stupid prizes."

"I'll send him a condolence card and a nice plant when you're done with him," Maguire said.

"Where that boys heading there ain't gonna be no sunlight for a plant to grow," Gentry said. "I'll call you back as soon as I know more."

"Hooyah," Maguire said and ended the call.

CHAPTER THIRTY

Southampton, Suffolk County, N.Y.
Saturday, December 21st, 2013 – 11:17 a.m.

"Hello?" Maguire said, as he answered the cellphone.

"Commissioner Maguire, this is Senator Mays," the man said on the other end. "I understand that you would like to take a look at some documents."

"I would indeed, but I feel bad that you had to get involved in such a fairly simple request, sir."

"Well, you need to remember that this is Washington and nothing is ever really *simple*," Mays said. "I think things are kept overly complicated in order to ensure job security."

"You're probably right about that," Maguire replied.

"However, in this particular instance, appearance might be a bit deceiving."

"How so?"

"Let's just say it's a bit *complicated*," Mays replied.

"Why am I not surprised about that?"

"That's because you're a smart man, Commissioner."

"Sometimes I really wonder about that," Maguire said. "If I were truly smart I should be sitting on a beach somewhere sipping drinks with little umbrellas in them."

"Nonsense," Mays replied. "People like you and me are old warriors. We're not good at walking away from trouble."

"That's putting a nice *spin* on it," Maguire said.

"Well, I am a politician after all," Mays said with a laugh. "Spinning bullshit is what I do."

"So what can you tell me about my former soldier?"

"The person you're interested in wasn't exactly your run of the mill grunt."

"Why do you say that?" Maguire asked.

"Not on the phone," Mays replied conspiratorially. "How soon can you get down here?"

Maguire looked down at his watch.

"If I can scrounge up a bird and a crew I should be able to get there by two."

"I'll text you the address," Mays said, "and I'll have my wife break out another MRE for dinner."

"I've always been partial to the Chili Mac," Maguire said with a laugh.

"I'll see what we can do."

Maguire ended the call and then selected a number, listening as the phone rang.

"Operations, Sergeant Naples."

"Sarge, this is Commissioner Maguire."

"Yes, Commissioner, what can I do for you?"

"Notify the C.O. of Aviation that I need a bird to pick me up at my home for a flight down to D.C. as soon as he can arrange it."

"Yes, sir," the man said. "I'll notify him immediately."

"Okay, have someone call me back when they are airborne."

"Will do."

Maguire ended the call and headed upstairs to change. On his way, he stopped off on the second floor and peaked into Genevieve's office.

"Working on a Saturday?" he said.

Gen looked up from the laptop screen.

"The baby is taking his nap," she said. "Either I do it now or it won't get done."

"All the stuff they never tell you about, huh?"

"I love him to death, but he can be so draining."

"That's funny, Mel says the same thing about me," he said with a laugh.

"Must be a *boy* thing," Gen replied. "Gregor has the same effect on me at times."

"Where is Gregor?"

"He headed over to Peter's," she said. "They got a new guy on the security detail so Gregor wanted to have a chat with him to let him know what his role was and what was expected of him."

"He can't let go, can he?"

"No, and honestly I don't want him to," Gen said. "It's too much of who he is. He's never going to be a *house dad*."

"Hey, you never know, you just might like him with a *dad bod*," Maguire said with a laugh.

"That's *never* going to happen," she said with a smirk.

"Sleep deprivation is making someone cranky."

"No, he made me get back into the gym right after giving birth so he isn't gonna be slacking off anytime soon."

"And we all know how much you love the gym."

"Did I miss the memo? Is this pick on Gen day or did you actually need something?"

"Actually I do," Maguire said. "I'm flying down to D.C."

"Now?"

"Yeah, they're sending a helicopter to pick me up and we'll be landing at the South Capitol Street Heliport at Buzzard Point. Normally I'd have the D.C. cops give me a lift, but this meeting is off the record and I'm not looking to raise any eyebrows."

"No problem, I'll have GDL Security pick you up," Gen replied.

"What time do you think you'll get in?"

"Flight time to D.C. is about an hour and a half from here."

"I'll have them leave when you get picked up," she said, "just to be on the safe side. Where are you going?"

"Just across the Potomac," he replied, "in Falls Church."

"When are you coming back?"

"Tonight, but I doubt I'll be home before Mel gets back."

"That's fine, we actually have a lot of things to go over so I can use a few hours of one on one time. Does she know?"

"No," he replied. "I tried to call on the way up, but it went straight to voicemail."

"I talked to her this morning and she mentioned that they were going to be doing one more test this morning before she flew back," Gen said. "The reception is shoddy out there. She was going to call me from the plane, so I'll let her know then."

"Okay, thanks," Maguire replied. "I have to go get ready."

"Happy flying!" Gen said, giving him a thumbs up.

"I much prefer the happy landings," he said with a laugh and head back out into the hallway.

He rode the elevator up to the third floor and made his way toward the bedroom. Inside he pulled out the cellphone and called Rich, as he sat down on the end of the bed, looking out the window at the ocean.

"Tell me you have good news," Stargold said when he answered.

"Not sure," Maguire replied. "I'm having a meeting this afternoon with someone who supposedly has answers."

"That sounds sinister."

"Yeah, apparently our Mr. Spangler is *complicated*."

"Has anyone ever told you that you're a shit magnet?"

"It's been mentioned a time or two," Maguire said, stifling a chuckle.

"A time or two my ass," Rich replied. "You're like a walking black cloud."

"You hired me," Maguire said.

"That's what happens when I listen to Mary," Stargold replied. "But I don't think you called to resign so what do you need?"

"Gas money."

"Gas money? For what?"

"For the helicopter that Aviation is sending to pick me up?"

"Aviation? Where the hell is this meeting?"

"D.C."

"Jesus H. Christ, you don't do anything *small* do you?" Rich asked.

"Like I said, it's *complicated*."

"Hey, all kidding aside, what do you think is going on with this Spangler?"

"I don't think there is any question that the military is trying to hide something," Maguire said. "The only real question is why are they trying to hide it."

"You think this meeting is gonna clarify that?"

"If this guy doesn't know the answer then we are truly fucked."

"Well, have a happy flight," Rich said. "You need any logistical help on the other end? Transportation?"

"Nah, I've got all that covered," Maguire replied. "This is all off the record. I'm slipping in and out like a thief in the night."

"Oh good, I was afraid for a moment something might go wrong...."

"Oh ye of little faith."

"At least you're not going to another foreign country so I don't have to worry about an international incident."

"You keep it up and I'm going to have Melody double your rent."

"Just get us some answers," Rich said somberly. "At this point I really don't care how you do it or who you have to do it to. Until we put an end to this, we all have targets on our back."

"I'll take care, buddy."

"I know you will," Rich replied and ended the call.

Maguire got up and walked over to the door that led to the deck. He opened it up and stepped outside. Immediately he could smell the saltiness in the air as he stared out at the ocean in front of him. He watched as the blue waves began to form in the distance, the swells rising up in the air as they raced toward the shoreline at breakneck speeds. At the last moment they broke up violently in a tumultuous spray of white foam that raced forward for a moment longer before quickly receding backward.

His memories drew him back to the sandy beaches of Coronado, California. He remembered the *surf torture*, lying with the rest of his BUD/S classmates in the swash zone and feeling the incoming waves buffeting their bodies with frigid water. They laid there for what seemed like an eternity, their arms interlocked with one another's as they shivered violently. Despite the clothing they wore, gritty sand managed to find its way inside, chafing their body as the wet material rubbed it against their skin. If that wasn't enough, the instructors would have them crawl back up into the sand, turning them into living, breathing *sugar cookies*.

Despite the physical intensity and mental brutality of the training, he looked back on that time with fond memories.

Within the special operation's community, each branch was quick to tell you why their training was the toughest, but the truth was that they were all equally tough. Special operators, whether PJ's, SF, Recon or SEAL's, all trained in a manner that not only pushed their physical and mental capabilities to the breaking point, but then went beyond. To be part of such an elite society you had to learn that 'I Can't' was no longer part of your vocabulary.

"The only easy day was yesterday," he said softly, as he watched the wave's crash below him.

The cellphone rang, pulling him from his memories.

"Maguire," he said, as he answered.

"Commissioner, this is Sgt. Naples," the man replied. "I wanted to let you know that Aviation just went wheel's up. They should be there shortly."

"Thank you, Sarge."

Maguire ended the call and then went to get changed.

CHAPTER THIRTY-ONE

Washington, D.C.
Saturday, December 21ˢᵗ, 2013 – 1:33 p.m.

Maguire stared out the window of the Agusta A119 as the helicopter followed the Anacostia River, passing over the Navy Yard, and slowly began making its descent toward the South Capitol Street Heliport.

Off in the distance, the dome of the U.S. Capitol stood out against the clear blue winter sky. No matter how many times one saw it, it was still an impressive sight.

Washington, D.C. was a dichotomy. It was a city that was home to the most powerful man in the world and to some of the poorest in the nation. It was, to quote Dickens, *A Tale of Two Cities.*

While the wealth in D.C. grew continually for its more affluent residents the same could not be said for those living east of the Anacostia. Improvements had begun to take place in the area, especially along the river, but it was in the form of a benign sounding word called *gentrification.*

Gentrification was the name given to the acquisition of undervalued land, whether commercial or residential, by the wealthy who then transformed it into desirable real estate. Cities were generally happy for the metamorphosis, because increased value translated into increased tax revenues, but the cost was often borne on the shoulders of lower income residents who were displaced.

Maguire had seen it first hand in Brooklyn North where dilapidated brown stone buildings were scooped up for a fraction of the price of Manhattan ones. The buildings, which unscrupulous landlords had ignored for decades, were then renovated and sold for exorbitant profit. The trend had started in Brooklyn Heights and was spreading east, block by block, pushing low income residents into ever constricting neighborhoods. This resulted in increased animus, by those who had been displaced, toward those they viewed as invaders. As always, the cops were the ones who were caught in the middle.

In his headset Maguire could hear the pilot talking to a member of the Metropolitan Police's Aviation Unit as they came in to land. A moment later he watched as the large 'H' of the helipad came into view. The pilot brought the helicopter in, hovering for a moment as he aligned the ship and then set it down.

"Welcome to D.C., Commissioner," Sergeant John O'Hara said over the headset as he powered down the helicopter. "Don't forget to lock the doors on your way out."

"Roger that, John," Maguire replied. "Wish I could give you an ETA for my return, but I'm not sure how long this will last."

"No problem, sir," O'Hara replied. "The MPD guys are good to us and we're on the clock. Just give us a heads up when you're on your way back and we'll have the rotors up and running."

"Sounds good, I'll see you boys soon."

Maguire exited the helicopter and made his way over toward the waiting Suburban. A man in a dark blue suit exited the front passenger seat and held the rear door open.

"Good afternoon, sir," the man said when Maguire got close. "I'm Mike Moliske, head of GDL security."

"Pleasure to meet you, Mr. Moliske," Maguire said, shaking the man's hand. "I'm sorry to screw-up your Saturday. I hope that I am not taking you away from anything important."

The man had a cool, firm grip and Maguire could feel the strength behind it.

"No, sir," he replied, as Maguire got into the SUV. "Besides, it's always nice to get out from behind my desk."

The man shut the door and climbed inside. The vehicle made its way past the chain link security fence, navigating its way through the commercial area, before finally turning onto South Capitol Street SW and headed north toward the highway.

"First time in D.C., sir?"

"No, I've been here a few times," Maguire replied.

"Then I assume we can dispense with the typical drive-bys?" Moliske asked.

"Yeah, unless they're making burgers in the White House Mess, we can take a pass.

"Personally I prefer the beef fajita salad," Moliske replied.

"I take it you've spent time there?" Maguire asked.

"I did four years on the Presidential Protective Detail," the man replied.

"You don't look old enough to be retired from the Service."

"I saw the handwriting on the wall, so to speak," the man said. "The agency was changing and I wasn't exactly ecstatic about the course it was heading in. I had twenty-one years in when a friend recommended me for the GDL position. I interviewed and they made me an offer I couldn't refuse."

"Smart man," Maguire said. "So do you know my boss, Rich Stargold?"

"Oh yes," Moliske said. "He's one of the most honorable men I know. I worked with him a handful of times over the course of my career."

"Well, we'll just keep that between us," Maguire said with a laugh. "I don't need him getting a big head."

The SUV made its way over the Arland D. Williams, Jr. Memorial Bridge, which spanned the Potomac River, and crossed into Virginia. A few moments later it turned north onto Jefferson Davis Highway, passing the Pentagon, as it headed toward Falls Church.

Twenty minutes later the Suburban pulled into the driveway of the split level, contemporary home on Waterway Place. The vehicle made its way down the long, tree lined, sloping road until it pulled up in front of the house. Moliske exited the vehicle and opened the rear passenger door.

"I'll try not to make this too long," Maguire said.

"No need to worry, Commissioner," Moliske replied. "We don't turn into pumpkins until midnight."

"Mike, if I'm not home in bed by midnight, your boss will have my head on a pike," Maguire said with a laugh.

He made his way down the stone walkway and rang the doorbell. A moment later a tall, slender woman, wearing a blue silk blouse and dark pants, answered the door.

The woman had short, perfectly coiffed, salt and pepper hair, and bright green eyes and what could only be described as a proud, patrician face. She was older, perhaps in her early 60's, but she had an athletic appearance.

Probably a runner, he thought.

"Commissioner Maguire?" the woman asked.

"Yes, ma'am," he replied, "but please, call me James."

"I'm Penelope," the woman replied, extending her hand toward him. "Please come inside."

Maguire stepped into the foyer and removed his coat, hanging it on the coat rack, just inside the doorway.

"Vernon is waiting for you in the conservatory," she said. "Follow me."

She led him through the hallway and down a series of several steps. The home was the perfect meld between modern and rustic. Sharp, angled walls were paired with stone tile flooring and wood ceilings. The walls were tastefully decorated with artwork along with several statues that sat atop granite pillars. Most of which were in keeping with the *wilderness* theme of Mays' home state.

A moment later she led Maguire into a large, bright room with floor to ceiling windows. Beyond the windows was a magnificent waterfront view of Lake Barcroft.

Senator Vernon Mays sat on the far side of the room, in a dark mahogany colored leather, wingback chair, reading over some documents. Just behind him, in the large stone fireplace, flames danced across the oak logs sitting on the grate.

"Dear, Commissioner Maguire is here," she said.

Mays looked up from the papers, and then set them down on the oak side table, next to his chair.

"James, please come in," he said, as he stood up.

He extended his hand out toward Maguire and the two men shook.

"Please, have a seat."

The man motioned toward the chair next to his.

"Can I get you two anything?" Penelope Mays asked.

"I'll take a refill, Penny," Mays said, handing his wife the empty glass tumbler. "James?"

"I'll take a whiskey, if you have it."

"Coming right up," she replied.

The two men watched as she left the room, closing the door behind her.

"Sorry to drag you down here on your day off, James," the man said, "but under the circumstances I am sure you will understand."

"My definition of *day off* has gotten a little skewed lately, Senator," Maguire replied.

Mays held up the stack of papers he had been reading when Maguire arrived.

"I'll be fine as soon as I figure out how to get those twenty extra hours into the work day," he replied. "Sadly, this is the only place I actually seem to get *any* work done. When I'm at my office, the phone is ringing, constituents are stopping by, or I'm in some damn meeting. So I bring this home to see just what the hell I'm voting on."

"At least you read it," Maguire said.

"You ever have problems sleeping at night, let me know. I'll package a bunch of appropriations and send them to you. You start on page one of the Coastal Salmon Recovery Fund and I guarantee you'll be asleep before page two."

"Do I want to know the price tag on that?" Maguire asked.

"No, you don't," Mays said somberly, "but what's even worse is when my *esteemed* constituents submit requests for funding that agencies don't even want."

"Are you serious?"

"As a heart attack," Mays said. "I've got one right now for ninety million dollars to upgrade the M1 Abrams. That's getting jammed through while the Army Chief of Staff is protesting that they already have enough tanks, including two thousand that are currently serving as *cactus pots* in the California desert."

"Why?"

"Because suppliers for the upgrades are spread out across any number of congressional districts," Mays replied. "Those suppliers have workers, union workers to be exact, and those workers vote. Unemployed union workers are not inclined to re-elect the folks who gave them their pink slips."

"I hate to say it, but I really hate D.C."

"You and me both," Mays said, "and I don't think this is going to do anything to reverse those feelings."

Maguire watched as Mays reached down, removing a brown file folder from the open briefcase at his feet, and handed it to

Maguire. The cover bore the legend 'Military Personnel Records Jacket – United States Army.'

"Spangler's folder?"

"What there is of it," Mays replied.

Just then the door opened and Penelope Mays walked into the room carrying two glasses. She walked over and sat them down on the table next to each man.

"Commissioner, are you staying for dinner?" she asked.

"I don't want to be an imposition," Maguire said.

"No imposition at all," she replied, "and there is enough for your men."

"Well, thank you, ma'am," he said. "In that case I would love to."

"We'll eat at four," she replied. "If that's all, then I will leave you two alone."

"Thank you, my dear," Mays said, as his wife walked out of the room.

Maguire went back to reviewing the folder.

Most of the information in the folder was pedigree stuff. In addition to his DD214 there was additional background information on Spangler, specifically his qualification sheet, what military specialty schools he attended, training certificates, rank and pay records, etc.

Spangler had enlisted in the Army in 2003 and attained the rank of sergeant. In 2008 he applied for the Army's

Unmanned Aircraft Systems Operator (15W) program and was accepted.

It was all pretty much vanilla stuff. That was until he got up to an almost completely redacted, eight page report from the Judge Advocate General to the Secretary of the Army.

"What the....." Maguire said softly, as he flipped through the blackened pages.

"And that is why you are sitting here this afternoon, James," Mays replied.

"Tell me you know what's behind the magic marker."

"I do," Mays said, "but it goes without saying that everything we are about to discuss is off the record."

"Understood, sir," Maguire replied.

Mays picked up his drink and took a sip, then set it back down on the table.

"The story isn't as much about Spangler, as it is about his uncle."

"And that would be?"

"Colonel Maximillian Spangler, United States Marine Corps, retired."

"Wait, his uncle is *Mad Max*?"

"One in the same," Mays replied.

Maximillian 'Mad Max' Spangler was a legend in the Marine Corps. After Saddam Hussein had invaded Kuwait, then Captain

Spangler had deployed as the commanding officer of a Light Armored Infantry Battalion and participated in Task Force Archangel.

In the opening days of Operation Desert Storm, an Iraqi mechanized division counter-attacked the command element of the FIRST Marine Division in Southeastern Kuwait. Fires from a nearby oil field, previously set ablaze by a retreating Iraqi Army, shrouded the battlefield in dense black smoke. In the ensuing chaos, an Iraqi mechanized brigade punched forward, mounting their counter-attack, which threatened to cut off the Marine Command Post forces. An intense twelve hour battle raged, during which time Captain Spangler maneuvered his Light Armored Vehicle Company into harm's way.

When the LAV-25 command vehicle he was in sustained severe damage, he commandeered another and continued to direct his forces, skillfully integrating his company's weapons in the assault by reinforcing TOW missile positions and AH-1W Attack Helicopters. Spangler's hard charging attack kept him at the forefront of the fight, leading quick violent attacks. Several times during the battle he stood in the hatch, directing his troops and exposing himself to heavy enemy fire. It was during this battle that he earned the moniker *Mad Max*.

His mastery of the battlefield dynamics allowed him to obtain a decisive defeat against the vastly larger Iraqi forces. In the end, Spangler's assault led to the destruction of more than fifty enemy Armored Personnel Carriers and resulted in the capture of over two hundred Iraqi soldiers. Those who managed to evade escape delivered a shocking tale to their compatriots of the maniacal Marine commander who directed the withering assault upon them.

For his courage, in the face of heavy enemy fire and utmost devotion to duty, Captain Spangler was awarded the Navy Cross, the Nation's second highest decoration for valor. Before returning to the United States he would also be awarded the Bronze Star with Valor device and the Purple Heart.

After he left the Marine Corps, Spangler formed Aequitas LLC, a defense lobbying firm with Robert Grant, the former House Majority Whip. Spangler's military *bona fides*, coupled with Grant's access, made them the go to firm to push defense issues. They represented some of the biggest entities in the industry and they had access to the most intimate of inner circles, including those of the West Wing as well as the E-ring of the Pentagon.

"So how does *Mad Max* figure into this?" Maguire asked.

"Well, you have to go back a number of years," Mays said. "Spangler's mother died of a cerebral embolism before he could even walk. His father, Gerald F. Spangler, Sr., was killed in a car accident when junior was ten. So right off the bat the kids a bit fucked up. Uncle Max was divorced, with no kids of his own, so he stepped up to the plate, providing a father figure for the young man. He took junior along to all the command events and showed him the *fun* side of military service. As the story goes, young Gerald grew up more enamored with his uncle's military exploits than his own dad."

"It's not hard to understand why," Maguire said. "All kids want to play soldier and here you have a real live hero to emulate."

"Exactly," Mays replied. "So when junior hit eighteen, he marched himself off to the nearest Marine Corps recruiter and tried to enlist."

"Tried?"

"Let's just say that he wasn't Corps material."

"Then how'd he get into the Army?"

"Max *knew* some people," Mays replied. "He figured he could find a nice home for the kid to do his time, get him a couple of *breathing* medals, maybe a few campaign or service ribbons, and then pull him into the lobbying firm."

"So what happened?"

"Junior didn't get the memo," Mays said. "Ironically, the kid actually excelled in the Army. Seems he was perfect GI materially. He took to boot camp like a duck to water. Word was that they were eyeing him for the Army Marksmanship Unit. I guess he wasn't satisfied with playing the part of the *office commando* that Max had set him up in, so he applied for the drone operator program and got selected. Apparently all those years playing video games actually paid off and he became an accomplished MQ-1C operator."

The MQ-1C *Gray Eagle* was the United States Army's medium-altitude, long-endurance, unmanned aircraft system. The UAV is capable of operating for thirty-six hours at altitudes up to 25,000 feet and has an operating range of 200 nautical miles. Inside the aircraft's nose fairing is a synthetic aperture radar/ground moving target indicator (SAR/GMTI) system. Its sensors can fuse infrared imagery and use the SAR to scan and detect changes in terrain like tire tracks, footprints, and buried improvised explosive devices.

The UAV was outfitted with an AN/AAS-52 Multi-spectral Targeting System (MTS) under the nose. It was also capable of being armed with weapons, such as AGM-114 Hellfire missiles and GBU-44/B Viper Strike guided bombs. In addition to its overt weapons system, the Gray Eagle was also capable of carrying the Army's Networked Electronic Warfare, Remotely Operated (NERO) system, for jamming enemy communications.

"Where did he end up?" Maguire asked.

"Afghanistan," Mays said. "He was assigned to Task Force ODIN. At first he was doing primarily observation flights, identifying insurgent troop movements so that they could be dealt with by the spec ops folks on the ground, but then they began arming and using them for *direct action* missions."

"It sounds like he had a solid career going for him."

"He did," Mays replied. "Right up until he sent a Hellfire missile through the window of a school house; in a little village just outside Hesa Awaal Behsood in Wardak Province."

"Holy shit," Maguire said.

"That's putting it mildly," Mays said, taking a drink. "Truth be told, it wasn't the kids fault. He was just acting on the intelligence that was provided to him."

"So why did he draw the short stick?"

"Politics," Mays said curtly. "What else."

"Sounds like the guy who gave the order fucked up," Maguire said. "Why didn't they just hang his ass out to dry?"

"Because they were operating off the so-called military intelligence that one of the local goat fucker's was running," Mays replied. "He claimed that the Taliban were using the location as cover for an IED manufacturing site. Unfortunately, if they had been operating there in the past, they'd moved on and the kids had moved back in. All total they lost sixteen children and their teacher in the explosion."

"What a cluster fuck," Maguire said softly, as he reached down, picked up his glass, and took a drink.

"That it was."

"So why'd the shit role downhill onto Spangler?" Maguire asked. "Why didn't they fry whoever it was that supplied the Intel?"

"Because the guy who ran the intel program, Rafeeq al-Wardak, is related to General Ali-Mohammed Alim Fidayi, the head of the local police."

"Is there anyone there who isn't related?"

"No, not really," Mays said. "It's a cloudy gene pool."

"So where is al-Wardak now?"

"That's a good question," Mays said. "They sent some folks to have a *chat* with him. But, at the last minute, he rolled up his bedroll and made like the wind."

"Sounds like an admission of guilt to me," Maguire said.

"His guilt isn't in question," Mays replied. "The question ultimately came down to *why*. It seems that they've been having an on-going internal war between the Hazara and Kuchi tribes over land ownership. The district is predominantly Hazara, but the Kuchi use the land for grazing. The Hazara claim that the Kuchi are being armed by the Taliban."

"They're fighting a war over feeding rights?"

"It got so bad that, at one point, the U.N. even got involved."

"I'm sure that led to an amicable resolution," Maguire said sarcastically.

"I think they signed an agreement and then promptly proceeded to burn down some homes."

"Sounds like your typical U.N. *success* story," Maguire said, "but why tag a school?"

"The working theory is that al-Wardak got paid off to tip the bad intel because the school was teaching female students," Mays replied. "Taliban must have figured it would be a win-win for them. Get rid of the school and give us a black eye at the same time."

"Wouldn't that be even more reason to lay the blame at the foot of the rat who fed us the bad intel?"

"You would think, wouldn't you?" Mays replied, "but then that wouldn't be Afghanistan would it? It seems that Hamid Karzai was beating the anti-coalition drum again so the locals were off-limits."

"Well if it was a local fucking other locals, why didn't they just let *them* handle it?"

"Because they weren't the ones who pitched the fit," Mays replied. "Remember I told you that the kid's teacher was also killed?"

"I remember."

"Well, she wasn't just your run of the mill teacher," Mays said. "Her name was Jillian Mitchell."

"Should that ring a bell?" Maguire asked.

"Not unless you happen to be well versed in Chicago politics," Mays said.

"I can barely keep up with New York politics let alone what's happening out there."

"Well Jillian Mitchell was the only child of Aubry Mitchell," Mays replied. "Mitchell doesn't run the party in Chicago, but he sure as hell finances it."

"So this was some sort of eye for an eye thing?" Maguire asked.

"To be honest, yes," Mays replied. "Mitchell called POTUS and Spangler's fate, so far as his career was concerned, was effectively sealed."

"So the President crucified some poor E-5, who was just acting on orders, to satisfy someone's need for revenge?"

"Tried to," Mays said. "My understanding is that originally they toyed with the idea of going after him criminally."

"You've got to be kidding me."

"I wish I was. Things looked bleak until Mad Max got involved. He made a few phone calls of his own, and the re-election coffers of the folks he reached out to weren't tied to Chicago. Ultimately they worked out the deal for the general discharge, but by then it was too late. Between being labeled a child killer and then being screwed over by the service, the kid's head was already scrambled."

"It would have been nice to know up front, when he applied to us," Maguire said. "I'm sure that being told he was in and then being rejected was probably the straw the broke the proverbial camel's back."

Mays frowned and shrugged his shoulders.

"The world's not fair, James," he replied. "You know that. One side was trying to hang the kid while the other side was trying to cut him down. Max did everything he could to keep his nephew, and his future, from getting fucked over. We'd all do it."

"Except that his nephew turned into a goddamn cop-killing sociopath," Maguire replied angrily.

"I wish I could give you a better answer," Mays said, "but that's what you're dealing with, in a nutshell."

"I know, Senator, and thank you," Maguire said, as he rubbed his weary eyes. "I really appreciate your help and didn't mean to snap at you. The last few days have been a bit difficult."

"I won't even pretend to know what you and your department are going through, James. I just wish I could do more."

"No, you've done enough," Maguire replied. "At least this gives us a better idea as to who we are going up against."

"If it's any consolation, what's happening in New York hasn't fallen on deaf ears down here. There are a lot of folks that are a bit *rattled* by all this, including the ones who were all too eager to make Spangler a sacrificial lamb."

"Honestly, it serves them right," Maguire replied. "It seems to me that there are a lot of people down here that like to treat the military as if they're some sort of disposable lap dog. They're all too eager to toss them into harm's way, to do their bidding, and then hang them out to dry when it goes against their polling numbers."

"It is a nasty business."

"Too nasty for most," Maguire said tersely. "Seems like most politicians view wearing the uniform of this country as being beneath them, present company excluded."

Mays picked up his drink and got up from the chair. He walked over to the window and stared out across the snow covered back lawn that led to the water's edge.

"Did you know that I was a *mustang*, James?"

"I did," Maguire replied.

Mustang was slang for an officer who had entered military service as an enlisted member. The use of the term dated back to World War II and referred to an officer who had earned a battlefield commission, such as Medal of Honor recipient, Audie Murphy. They were usually older and more experienced than their peers, who entered the military via commissioning from one of the service academies.

The term was often used as a pejorative by *ring-knocker's*, those officers who had graduated from an academy and possessed a class ring, to note the difference between the two, like a class system. Mustangs were generally viewed as being wild and unpredictable. In truth, their practical time, spent in the lower ranks, often served them much better than their compatriot's theoretical one.

After their last meeting he had checked into Mays' Navy career. He didn't make a habit of trusting many politicians, or officers for that matter. But Mays had struck him as being *different* than the ones he had previously come to know. He'd had a very distinguished naval career, but that was not unusual for someone who had risen to the rank of rear admiral. What had been most important to Maguire were the opinions of those who had worked under Mays.

Mays' last command had been as the Commander, Carrier Strike Group Eight. He had made some inquiries through the SEAL community and had been put in touch with a retired senior chief who had been the command's senior enlisted when Mays was the C.O. According to the chief, "Mays put the best interests of his crew before anything else, including his own career." It was enough for Maguire to count the man as an asset and not an adversary.

"Back when I was an enlisted puke I thought I could change the naval world by becoming an officer," Mays said. "So I played my cards right and I got a shot at OCS. Then, when I became an officer, I thought that the higher I went the more influence I could wield. Then I learned that nothing ever really changes, just the faces."

Mays laughed and took a drink.

"You know, my father was one of those old hard chargers," Mays continued. "God was he an honest-to-goodness, tough as nails *sonofabitch*. Gruff, cantankerous, politically incorrect, but when he talked, you had better listen. He had the biggest hands that I'd ever seen and I swear he could bend a piece of steel without blinking an eye."

"They don't make them like that anymore," Maguire said.

"If they did, they'd imprison them by the end of the first day for hurting everyone's *feelings*," Mays scoffed. "I remember when I graduated OCS and got my *butter bars*. I thought I was such hot-shit; walking around as if Jesus Christ himself had anointed me. Then my father showed up at graduation in his senior chief's uniform. It wasn't the first time I had seen him in uniform, but it was the first time I had really *seen* him for who he was. God what a spectacle it was. He looked like one of those Russian general's with all of his medals glistening on his chest. I swear they sounded like a goddamn glockenspiel with every step he took. He walks up to me, looks me straight in the eye, and hooks his thumb over at a group of enlisted standing off to the side Then he says, 'don't ever forget where you came from, junior. The only difference between you and them now is that when you fuck up, they may die. So don't fuck up.'"

"What did you say?"

"Hooyah, Chief!" Mays replied. "What the hell else could I say? I was scared shitless. He was the only man I knew who could make the rank of *ensign* sound like a four-letter word. I swear I felt like the family black sheep for years."

Maguire laughed knowingly.

Men like Mays' father and Roy Gentry were an entirely different breed. Some called them old-school, but it was more than that. It was a warrior's mindset. You knew the minute one of them walked into the room. They commanded respect, both from below their pay grade as well as above. Once in their presence you immediately knew there was something to be cautious about. They did not suffer fools easily and were quick to point out the folly of some educated officer's plan. In fact, it was not uncommon for some senior officers to seek out the counsel of the old chief, knowing they would get a real *no-shitter.*

"The sad thing is that so many of those who sit behind desks nowadays *have* forgotten about the ones they send into harm's way. They just worry about playing things safe, saying the right things, ticking the correct boxes, just to ensure the continued upward mobility of their careers. I got sick and tired of my fellow *officers* treating everyone beneath them as if they were expendable pieces on a game board."

"So is that why you left the Navy?" Maguire asked.

"In a way, yes," Mays replied, turning around to face Maguire. "I left to run for office. I guess I still hadn't learned my lesson. I thought that by going into Congress I could have a better chance at fixing things."

"Sometimes reality can be a tough pill to swallow."

"Isn't that the truth," Mays said, raising his glass in a mock toast. "So what made you go back?"

"Half a bottle of tequila and a crappy poker hand," Maguire replied.

"Guess neither of us learned our lesson."

Just then the door opened and Penelope Mays entered the room.

"You boys will have to shelve your discussion for the moment," she said. "It's time for dinner."

With that the two men followed her out of the room.

CHAPTER THIRTY-TWO

Point Pleasant, New Jersey
Saturday, December 21st, 2013 – 5:18 p.m.

Spangler sat in the shabby leather chair watching the evening news.

Something wasn't right.

It had been more than twenty-four hours and still there had been no news coverage of the raid. He knew they knew; he had seen them respond to the house on Eden Lane from his vantage point in the parking lot on Wantagh Avenue.

It might have seemed reckless to some, but it was a calculated risk. By the time he'd pulled into the parking lot he had already swapped vehicles and his long blonde hair was gone. He now sported a bald head along with a dark brown goatee which gave him the appearance of a younger version of *Heisenberg*.

As he sat drinking his coffee, he watched as a parade of vehicles had passed by him. They weren't overt, at least not to the untrained eye, but they screamed *police* to someone who knew what to look for.

Prior to conducting the first operation, Spangler had *watched* his new home. He took the time to learn the rhythm, to see the things that were normal. On any given day one or maybe two things would be different, but on this day there was a whole lot of different. That could only mean that they figured it out, knew that it was him.

Whoever had put the pieces together was good, he thought.

Now the remaining question was: *what would they do?*

He had fully expected them to flood the airways with bulletins, alerting the public as to who they were searching for. So far, that had not been the case and that concerned him.

What are you up to? he wondered, as he leaned back in the chair and examined his current accommodations.

The motel had certainly seen its better days, but it served his purpose. Namely it had a bed, shower and a television. Aside from those basics, it lacked anything that would even remotely qualify as an amenity. In today's modern society, any potential guest would have been put off by the lack of Wi-Fi or even a hardline internet service, but for him it was not a requirement, because he made sure to never leave an electronic footprint.

At one time this place might have been a jewel of the Point Pleasant beach community, but that time was now measured in decades past. At the present, it stood like a white-washed hulk along the shoreline; an eyesore waiting for a larger fish to come along and gobble it up for the land rights.

It was probably owned by an older couple, he thought. *Hell bent on holding out till the bitter end.*

While most would happily pass it by, seeking out the more modern accommodations and their amenities, this place suited him just fine.

It sat on the main road with its back facing the ocean. This being the off-season, the clerk had offered him a room with a view of the beach, which he promptly declined. He'd selected a second floor room that faced the street so that he could monitor any activity. He knew that if *they* came for him that they'd do it through the front door and not by the water.

Spangler got up from his chair and walked over toward the window. He pulled the blind to the side and peered out at the deserted street below.

The cold wind coming off the Atlantic ensured that even the most seasoned residents were inside their homes staying warm. He scanned the cars that were parked along the roadway looking for *tells*. Inclement weather was always good for that. In the cold you could look for exhaust coming out of tailpipes. During rain or, as in the case tonight, snow you could check for the occasional *wave* of wiper blades, as they fought to keep the windshield clear.

Much to his relief, all was quiet outside.

He walked over to the table and opened the bag that was sitting on top of it. He reached in and withdrew a tan plastic pouch.

"Chili Mac," he said, as he read the label on the MRE. "Awesome."

It was one of the more edible choices and his personal favorite. He removed the knife from his belt and slit the top open, dumping the contents onto the table.

Spangler prepared the entrée, placing the chili mac package, along with the jalapeno cheese spread packet, into the flameless heater and added water. While that began to cook he sorted through the other *goodies*.

He took the package of crackers and smashed them up with his hand and set them off to the side. Spangler smiled at the sight of the Skittles, their colorful candy wrapper looking so out of place among the other drab packages. He slipped the *kippered beef* packet into his jacket pocket. It was always a nice treat to have some jerky on hand when you needed something quickly.

Spangler let out a groan as he examined the desert packet. This evening he would be *treated* to the amazing vanilla pudding. When prepared properly it had the consistency and taste of joint compound. When prepared poorly it had the consistency of runny join compound. He set the package to the side as he debated just how hungry he really was.

He looked over at the lemon-lime *carbo electro* drink packet. This was the military's attempt at a beverage to replenish electrolytes. What it tasted like was a cross between Mountain Dew and asparagus infused pee. He opted to pass, preferring the motel's coffee pot instead.

When the meal was done cooking, he removed it from its package, and began doctoring it up. He poured the melted cheese spread over the chili mac and added the crushed crackers. When he was done, he poured himself a cup of coffee and took his *dinner* over to the chair and continued watching the news.

Spangler reached the spoon inside and took a bite.

Just like old times, he thought.

CHAPTER THIRTY-THREE

Falls Church, Virginia
Saturday, December 21st, 2013 – 6:43 p.m.

"Thank you so much for a wonderful dinner, ma'am," Maguire said, as he slipped on his coat.

"Well you're quite welcome," Penelope Mays replied. "It was so very nice to meet you. If you ever find yourself back in Virginia I certainly hope that you will stop in and see us."

"I will do that," he replied.

"I'll walk you out to your car," Senator Mays said, putting on his own jacket and opening the front door.

"Good night, Mrs. Mays," Maguire said, as he walked outside, "and thanks again for your hospitality."

"Good night," she said and closed the door behind them.

"I appreciate your help, Senator," Maguire said, as they walked toward the waiting SUV.

"I'm glad I could help, James," the man said. "I heard that Eliza Cook is heading up to your neck of the woods."

"Yeah, she's announcing her candidacy for president."

"I know," Mays said.

"You don't seem too shocked."

"Let's just say that you're the *second* visitor to come out here this week."

"Is that a good thing or a bad thing?" Maguire asked.

Mays' face contorted slightly, as if he was honestly searching for the right answer.

"I don't know," he said after a moment. "It seems like it was more of a probing mission."

"You think she was looking to see if you were going to support her?"

"Eliza Cook is one tough lady," he said. "She has a keen intellect and can play ruthless party politics like no one else.

"Good thing you guys are on the same team."

"I've known Eliza since her days in the Senate," Mays said. "In fact we met before I was ever elected. I had to appear before her budget committee. By the time I left the hearing I knew what a shish-kebab felt like."

"Ouch."

"It certainly wasn't fun. She's ruthless, but she's also fair. The folks over at the Pentagon were trying to put one over on her and it didn't work."

"You sound like you're a supporter," Maguire said.

"I'm torn," Mays said. "I'm not sure how long we can continue with the division in Washington and I think my colleagues on the other side of the aisle will dig their heels in against her. On the other hand we need someone with a pair of brass balls and I think she has the biggest balls of anyone who is going to run."

"If you don't mind me asking, sir, why are you telling me all this?"

"I guess I'm just talking out loud," he said. "I like you, James. I've liked you from the moment I first met you. You strike me as real straight shooter; someone who would have made a fine Navy chief."

"That's very kind of you to say, sir."

"More importantly, you're an outsider," Mays said. "You live down here long enough and you forget what it is like to talk to someone outside the *bubble*. Everyone here tells you what you want to hear, instead of what you *need* to hear."

"Before dinner you asked me what made me go back," Maguire said. "The truth is that, like you, it's who I am. The Navy, the Senate, the NYPD, it really doesn't matter what the '*it*' is, what matters is who *we* are."

"And you were willing to give up a very lucrative security consulting business to become a public servant again," Mays said.

Maguire smiled. Obviously he hadn't been the only one to do a little snooping into someone's background.

"Sir, people like us serve because we want to make things better, not to get ourselves ahead. We're both well-acquainted with taking orders, as well as giving them, but we also want to make things better for those under us. At the end of the day, that is what truly drives us."

"You're pretty smart for a 2nd class petty officer."

"I'd ask you to pass that information along to Senior Chief Gentry, but he'd just remind you that I was an idiot before he managed to hammer me into a proper sailor."

"God bless Navy chiefs," Mays said with a smile.

"Hooyah," Maguire replied, as he shook the man's hand and walked toward the SUV.

Mike Moliske exited the front seat and opened the back door to let him in.

Maguire stopped before getting in.

"Oh, Senator," he said, looking back at Mays.

"Yes, Commissioner?"

"In case you wanted an answer, I'd advise you to say yes to any offer," Maguire said. "One man, with the right attitude, *can* make a difference."

"I'll keep that in mind," Mays said.

"Good night, sir."

"Good night, James," Mays replied and headed back toward the house.

Maguire got into the Suburban as Moliske closed the door and then climbed into the front seat.

"All good, sir?"

"Yes," Maguire replied. "I'm sorry to have kept you so long."

"It's all good, sir," Moliske said. "Is there anywhere else that you need to go or should we head back to the helo?"

"No, I think I've done enough damage for one day, Mike. We can head back now."

Maguire removed his cellphone and sent a text to O'Hara, notifying him that he was on his way back and then phoned Rich.

"Well, how bad is it?" Stargold asked when he answered the call.

"I'll give you the play-by-play when I get back home, Maguire replied, "but let's just say that I understand now why he probably went off the deep end."

"So you're telling me that he's really not wrapped to tight?"

"He got screwed over royally by DOD, enough so that it probably pushed him to the precipice. When the job bounced him it was probably enough to send him over."

"Awesome," Rich replied. "Just fucking awesome. Do they have any suggestions?"

"Actually, they are just as worried about Spangler as we are," Maguire replied. "I think the feeling is that he might just head south when he's finished with us."

"That might not be a *bad* thing," Stargold said with a tone of contempt. "So are they going to help us?"

"Judging from the redacted folder I was shown, I think the only thing they will openly admit to is that Spangler *was* a soldier at one time."

On the other end of the phone, Stargold let out a sigh, as he leaned back in his chair and stared out the window. Off in the distance he could see the Statue of Liberty, her torch lit up brightly against the darkness of the night.

He'd spent over two decades in law enforcement, the majority of that with the United States Secret Service. While he had held a number of supervisory positions during that time, there had always been someone above his pay grade to make the final decisions. Now he was *it*, the top dog of the Nation's largest police department and there was no one else to turn to.

"Well, maybe it's time we let the cat out of the bag," he said.

"What do you want to do?" Maguire asked.

"I'm going to have the Deputy Commissioner of Public Information schedule a press conference for Monday morning," Rich said. "Let's ID Spangler as a *person of interest* and see what kind of shit storm that stirs up."

"Are you going to run with the full story?"

"I'm not going to play all the cards, but I'm also not going to cover DOD's ass," Rich said. "They have a public information officer just like us. Maybe it's time for them to field some questions as well."

"Sounds like a plan."

"You want me to stop by before I head home? Maguire asked. "I can have them stop off at the South Street Heliport and catch a ride over to you."

"No," Rich said, "you've already done enough. Go home and get some rest. Try and enjoy what's left of the weekend. We'll talk tomorrow and finalize what we want to say Monday."

"You're the boss," Maguire said.

"Don't I feel special," Rich said with a laugh. "Oh, before I forget, I got a call from the hospital. They changed Joe Kennedy's medical status from critical to serious, but stable. She's not out of the woods, but at least she's on the right path."

"Thank God for that," Maguire replied.

"Okay, go have fun and I'll talk to you tomorrow."

"Give my love to Mary and the girls," Maguire said and ended the call.

CHAPTER THIRTY-FOUR

1 Police Plaza, Manhattan, N.Y.
Monday, December 23rd, 2013 – 10:03 a.m.

Stargold walked into the small auditorium with Maguire in tow. Following them were Tony Ameche and Sandra Barnes, as well as the Deputy Commissioner of Public Information, Tom Cleary. Each of their faces reflected a somber appearance which seemed perfectly appropriate under the circumstances.

The room was filled with reporters, both from the local newspapers as well as those from the local and cable news networks. Rich made his way to the podium and set his leather portfolio down on top of it, opening it to the pre-written statement.

"Thank you for coming on such short notice," he began. "As you are all aware, this Department has been rocked recently by a series of attacks targeting both our sworn and civilian members. At first these attacks seemed to be random in nature, but though hard work and perseverance, by the members of the Detective Bureau, we believe that we have linked each of the killings back to a single individual."

Maguire nodded to an officer from D.C.P.I., who began handing out informational sheets to the assemblage of reporters.

"At this time, the NYPD is identifying Gerald Spangler, Jr. as a person of interest in the murders of Deputy Commissioner of Training Winston St. Clair, Chief Surgeon Theodore Eichenberg, Detective Armando Rivera, and the attempted murder of Inspector Josephine Kennedy."

Immediately the room broke up into loud shouts, as each of the reporters tried to call out questions.

"Please," Rich said, holding up his hands, "I know you all have questions, but one at a time."

Commissioner Cleary stepped up next to the podium and began pointing toward individual reporters.

"Commissioner, I'm John Talbot, from the Daily Eagle, has Spangler been directly linked to the murders?"

"At this time, Mr. Spangler is only a person of interest," Rich said. "We believe that the attacks were committed by a single individual and we want to speak to him regarding that."

Cleary pointed toward another reporter.

"Commissioner Stargold, I'm Andrea Kohl, CBN," the woman said. "I have a two part question. First, do you believe that this individual is still in the metro area and second, do you believe that he poses a threat?"

"Well, obviously we are concerned for the safety of the public," Rich said. "If someone is brash enough to target law enforcement, then they certainly pose a risk to the civilian population. We would ask that if they see Mr. Spangler to just report it to their local police agency or 911. Likewise, we would ask that Mr. Spangler contact us directly so that we can speak with him regarding this."

Cleary nodded to another reporter in the front row.

"Malcom Smith from the Globe, Commissioner," the man said. "Attacking police officers in this type of ambush style, seems to speak of calculation and capability beyond what we are used to seeing. Is there anything about this person that would indicate that they have some type of specialized training?"

"We know that Mr. Spangler is a military veteran who served with the United States Army," Rich replied. "However, any question pertaining to his military career, or what specific type of training he was given, is a question that is best directed to the Department of Defense. As I said, we only wish to speak with him at this time."

As Rich watched, the collective group of reporters began removing their cellphones, shooting off emails and texts to those back at their office; instructing them to reach out to the DOD and get a response regarding Spangler. He smiled inwardly as he imagined the nightmare that was about to descend upon them. Perhaps they'd be more inclined to share information, now that they had a vested interest in covering their asses.

"One more question," he said.

"Commissioner Stargold, I'm Katie Storm from AP, do you know why each of the officers were targeted?"

"We believe that there is a direct link between each of the officers, but we are not going to go into the details at this time. Again, thank you very much for your time and if anyone needs additional clarification, Commissioner Cleary will be happy to talk with you."

Tom Cleary approached the podium as Rich and the others began walking out of the room.

"Well?" Rich asked Maguire when they were out of earshot.

"I think the phone line at the Department of Defense just melted," Maguire said sarcastically, "but otherwise I think it went really well. I assume we should get a call before the end of the day."

"You really think so?"

"At the very minimum I expect that we will hear from his uncle or his representative," Maguire said.

"Let's hope you're right," Rich said.

"Putting a face out there should at least knock him out of his rhythm," Maguire replied. "He isn't going to like having the target on his back for a change."

"Yeah, but what if he disappears?"

"He won't," Maguire said.

"You sound confident," Rich said, as the two men and their security detail entered the private elevator.

"Spangler's on a personal crusade," Maguire replied, as the elevator began to ascend. "He perceives that he has been wronged by a lot of people, not just by us, but we are apparently first on the list."

"So you don't think he's going to pack up and go somewhere else?"

"No," Maguire said, "I don't. He started here and he'll end here, at least the part that deals with the Department, before he moves on."

"What makes you say that?"

"He's not worried about being caught," Maguire said. "He doesn't think we can stop him. Call it narcissism, over-confidence, or arrogance, but he knows he is good at what he does and he is going to prove it to us all. If he was worried, he would have taken steps to mask his attacks, but he did them one after the other, taunting us to figure it out."

"Well isn't that just a cheery little fucking picture," Rich said, as the elevator doors opened.

"You know that we don't live in a *rose colored glasses* kind of world, buddy."

"I don't know what world we live in anymore," Rich replied. "I just wish this whole *peace on Earth, good will to man* stuff would kick in already."

"Its job security, baby."

"Oh, before I forget, do you need us to bring anything for Christmas Eve?"

"Hell no," Maguire said. "The White House doesn't put out a spread like the one she has planned. I'm going to have to work out twice a day through the New Year just to fit into my clothes."

"Do what I do," Rich replied, "just buy bigger suits."

"Did you forget that we have a gym downstairs?" Maguire asked with a laugh. "You really should lead by example."

"Christ, I'm so out of shape right now that the only thing I'd be leading is a charge to the E.R. to get oxygen."

Maguire hooked a thumb in the direction of the two detectives from the security detail.

"January 2, buddy, me and you are gonna show these kids how it's done."

"Oh, that's wonderful," Rich said, as he turned and walked toward his office. "I'm just gonna go and update my life insurance beneficiary now. I'll talk to you later."

"Have fun while you can, slacker."

CHAPTER THIRTY-FIVE

Point Pleasant, New Jersey
Monday, December 23rd, 2013 – 4:53 p.m.

Spangler carefully removed the MRE packet from the heater and dumped the contents, listed on the package as pork sausage in cream gravy, onto the paper plate. Clearly the *truth in advertising* standards did not apply to the Department of Defense.

He picked up the plate, along with the cup of coffee he had poured himself, and sat down in front of the television.

After four days, holed up inside the motel room, he was nearing the end of his emergency provisions. He knew that he would have to leave by tomorrow. He had a cache of weapons and other supplies stashed in a long term storage place in Trenton.

In his pre-planning phase it had seemed like the perfect spot. The location was busy enough that it would not attract any attention, yet was close to the highway so that he could jump off and re-supply when it came time to head south for the second part of his plan.

At the present moment he was having a hard time processing the lack of information on the news. Knowing that they had identified the residence in Levittown, he'd expected that this would be plastered all over the news.

Maybe they haven't figured out who you are yet, he thought.

It seemed implausible, but he couldn't rule it out either. Maybe someone on the block had called about a suspicious person, and they had responded to that, without knowing who he actually was.

His landlady was a sweet old lady, but she wasn't exactly sharp. He was pretty sure that her vision was so bad that there was no way she could identify him; even if he was standing directly in front of her. It was one of the reasons that the location was so attractive to him.

He picked at the *pork sausage* with his fork, just as the opening scroll for the five o'clock news came on. A moment later a very stern looking male reporter and a rather ditzy looking, but well endowed, female reporter, introduced themselves to the viewing audience. He wondered if there was a focus group that said this particular coupling appealed to the widest viewership.

Spangler stabbed at one of the pieces of meat as the male reporter began with the lead story. The anonymity he had enjoyed came to a crashing halt as he saw the photograph of himself appear on the screen along with his name.

"Fuck me," he said softly, as he lowered the fork down onto the plate.

"Police in New York City announced today that they are looking to speak to a *person of interest* in the recent string of shootings; which have claimed the lives of three members of the NYPD and left another in critical condition," the male reporter said. "The individual, identified as Gerald F. Spangler, Jr., is a former member of the United States Army who had served in Afghanistan. Police did not link him directly to the killings, but said that they believe he might have information concerning them. Given Mr. Spangler's previous military training, people are being cautioned against approaching him. Anyone with information on the whereabouts of Gerald Spangler is asked to contact the NYPD or their local law enforcement agency."

Spangler picked up the remote from the table and turned the television off. He closed his eyes and leaned back in the chair, letting out a sigh, as he began to replay what the reporter had said.

Obviously they knew his name, but what was most interesting was how they were only referring to him as a *person of interest*. Actually, in a way, it was quiet infuriating and he found himself getting angry.

Why hadn't they identified him as the suspect? he wondered.

They'd found the apartment and they knew who he was. They must have found the taunting message he had left them, yet they were not calling him a suspect. It was as if they were purposefully denying him his due; refusing to give him the credit.

Things had changed now. The game had entered a new phase and he had to plan accordingly. He no longer looked the same as the person in the photo, but there was no need to tempt fate. If someone had the chance to look at him long enough they might make the connection. He needed to get to a safe place where he could think things through. Nothing would alter his plans to get even, but smart people thought tactically, not emotionally.

He had no *obligation* to speak with the police, since he wasn't *technically* being identified as a suspect, but he still wanted to know what they had. However, he wasn't an idiot and he had no intention of just waltzing into any police facility to find out. There was another *option*, but that one might be as equally dangerous.

Spangler finished his *dinner* and got up. He walked over to the closet where he removed the two black *bugout* bags and set them on the bed. One contained clothing, while the other contained weapons, food rations and other tactical / survival gear. From the clothing bag he removed the last pair of clean undergarments, as well as a pair of mil-spec cargo pants and a clean combat shirt.

He stripped down, depositing the old clothes into the bag and headed off to the shower. Once he got to the storage locker he'd swap out the bags, getting a new supply of clothes. He'd leave the old bag behind as a souvenir for the facility owner when they finally clipped the lock.

Heck, maybe it would wind up on one of those storage unit television shows where they bid for the contents, he thought.

Spangler laughed at the image of them opening the bag to find his old, dirty clothing.

He walked into the bathroom and turned on the shower. He'd slept most of the day so he felt refreshed, but he needed to take a shower now, while he still had the chance. He'd been holed up too long in this motel room and his body was feeling the effects of it. He didn't know what the next few hours, or days for that matter, held for him. Either way, the long, hot shower would feel good and give him a chance to decide what to do next.

CHAPTER THIRTY-SIX

Southampton, Suffolk County, N.Y.
Monday, December 23rd, 2013 – 6:42 p.m.

"More to the left," Melody said.

"Angel, I love you, but it's an ornament for the love of God," Maguire said, as he tried to balance himself on the ladder while leaning over precariously. "Can't I just hang it here?"

"My ornament, my tree, my way," she said sternly.

"No fighting in front of the children," Gen said, as her and Gregor watched the last of the interior decorating.

"In case any of you have forgotten, we already have a tree in the other room," he replied. "I don't see why we need another one in the entry way?"

"Because this year is *special*," she said. "It's Wolfgang's first Christmas plus Mary and the girls will be here as well. I want it to be memorable, so I'm not sure why one more little tree is too much to ask for."

Maguire looked up at the top of the tree which easily extended another five feet over his head.

"Sweetheart, I've seen redwoods in California that were smaller than this Christmas tree."

"Fine," she said with a tone of exasperation. "Leave it right there."

Maguire attached the last ornament to the tree and then made his way down the ladder. He walked over and stood next to Melody, draping his arm over her shoulder.

"It looks beautiful, Angel," he said.

"You're not just saying that, are you?"

"No, I mean it," Maguire said. "The house looks lovely."

"I just want everything to be perfect this Christmas," she said. "We have so much to be thankful for and I just wanted to celebrate."

Maguire turned to look at her, taking her face gently in his hands and kissing her.

"You've done an amazing job decorating," he said, "both inside and out. The fact that the electric company called and asked if we wanted to get on a *payment plan* should be of no concern to you."

"Well at least I don't have to worry about the girls opening up their presents under that garish *Charlie Brown* tree you had on the boat."

"Heh, that's a *vintage* piece," he said with a laugh.

"Just because something's *old*, doesn't mean it's not junk."

"I'm deeply hurt," Maguire said, crossing his hands over his chest.

"Suck it up, Popeye," Gen said, handing him a glass of eggnog.

Maguire took a sip and smiled. "Ah, now I know why you're so feisty."

"Momma needs some R&R," Gen said with a laugh.

The four of them made their way back into the salon and sat down in front of the fireplace.

"Can anyone think of anything that I might have missed?" Melody asked.

"Eleven pipers piping, ten lords a leaping,…" Maguire replied.

"Hush, I'm being serious."

"I know you are, babe, but you really need to stop and take a breather. There's really nothing more for you to do except to enjoy it all."

Melody closed her eyes and leaned back, feeling her body collapse into the leather cushions.

"You're right," she said.

"The sad part is that you put in all this work decorating and then in a few days, poof, it's all gone."

"Not in my world," she replied. "I'll stretch it out till the bitter end."

"What? Like those homes that have the broken holiday lights hanging from the gutters in July?" Maguire asked.

"Maybe I will," Melody said with a laugh. "Maybe I'll keep the decorations up year round, turn this place into the North Pole of Southampton."

"I'm pretty sure there's an ordinance against that," Gen said.

"Then I'll have to buy a politician or two and get that ordinance changed."

"Rich people problems," Maguire scoffed.

"Don't be hateful," Melody chided him.

Maguire felt the vibration of the cellphone. He unclipped it from his belt and looked at the number.

"I've gotta take this," he said, as he slowly got up from the couch.

"Don't be too long," Melody said.

"I won't," Maguire replied. "I promise.

"And bring me a refill," she called after him, as he walked out of the room.

"Took you long enough," Maguire said when he answered the phone.

"Do you have any idea of the shit storm you've unleashed, tadpole?" Mother replied.

"No, but I am sure you're going to tell me."

"I've fielded about two dozen calls from everyone but Mad Max himself, although at least half were probably at his direction."

"I guess outing junior touched a nerve."

"You know how *we* are, Paddy," Mother said cautiously. "We protect family, even when they go off the reservation."

"Well, Chief Max's *lil injun* done went rogue and now he's hunting in my reservation," Maguire said with a tinge of anger, as he opened the door and walked down the steps, into the garage. "I have every intention of doing whatever is necessary to take care of my family."

"You don't have to explain yourself to me," Mother replied. "You're my family and you know I'll go to war with you."

Maguire sat down at the work bench.

"I'm sorry," he said. "I didn't mean it that way. I guess I'm just wearing a bit thin."

"I know you didn't," Mother replied. "I was just saying that right or wrong, Max's is gonna try to help out his dysfunctional kin."

"What are his surrogates asking?"

"The usual," Mother replied. "Just how serious of a suspect is he? Whether or not you have the wrong guy? What kind of operator are you?"

Maguire laughed at the last part. More important than guilt or innocence, everyone wanted to know exactly who they were dealing with.

"What did you tell them?"

"I said that if you ran him to ground, then they should probably get ready to hire a damn good attorney."

"Are they asking for anything?"

"Just information at this point," Mother replied. "Although I suspect that you might get a direct call from Max, or one of his surrogates, shortly."

"It makes me wonder if he's even heard from the kid yet."

"The kid's a computer dweeb, not an operator," Mother said. "Killing someone from behind a video screen is one thing, but when you feel the heat on your own neck things are going to get dicey. You've gone and put his face up for the entire world to see now, at some point he will have to go running back home for help."

"When the time comes, do you think Uncle Max will give the kid up?" Maguire asked.

"I guess that will depend on just how serious he thinks your case is," Mother replied. "Right or wrong, he is blood. Max will do his best to save him, even if that means saving him from himself."

"If they ask, let them know I'm coming for him," Maguire said. "How it ends is entirely up to them."

"Roger that, Paddy," Mother replied. "Watch your six and keep your powder dry."

"Hooyah," Maguire said and ended the call.

He waited a moment and then placed a call, listening as the phone rang.

"Whatcha got for me?" Rich asked, when he came on the line.

"It looks like we poked the hornet's nest pretty good."

"Yeah, but do you think we poked it hard enough to make Spangler call his uncle?"

"That's the real question, isn't it?"

"Judge Potts seemed a bit hesitant on the warrant to conduct a wiretap on the uncle's phones, but he finally acquiesced after Kurt pressed him on the domestic terrorism angle and Spangler's note that there would be more."

"That's mighty nice of him," Maguire said sarcastically. "I wonder if he would have been more obliging if Spangler had popped a judge or two."

"To be fair, I think they are getting a lot of pressure from the folks on the left about all the rubber stamp warrants they are reporting in the media."

"Everyone loves to bitch until the wolf is at *their* door."

"It's the same old song and dance we play every day," Rich replied.

"Just because I play it, doesn't mean I have to like it."

"Then you'll like this even less," Rich said. "Potts only gave us two weeks on the phones. He wants an update before he will extend it."

Maguire let out a sigh as he leaned back in the chair.

In a way he understood the reluctance from the courts. One would expect that someone, who had spent his entire adult life in the military and law enforcement, would be an avid supporter of the Patriot Act, but Maguire had often found himself at odds with it.

What had started off, after the September 11th attacks, as a desire to keep America safe from further terrorist attacks had somehow morphed into a judicial free-for-all. He'd watched as the investigating agencies had pushed the boundaries of keeping the *homeland* safe; well beyond what the intended act's purpose had been, swinging the pendulum far to the right.

Warrants that had once been based on solid probable cause, arrived at through good old fashioned police work, were now being handed out like free government checks. Many of the provisions of the act, which many erroneously believed only targeted foreign terrorists, routinely interchanged the terms terror investigations and criminal investigations. An inconsequential thing to most, but it was a matter of extreme seriousness to those involved in investigations as well as those who found themselves at the center of such investigations.

On one hand, most people agreed that the government should have the tools available to track down terrorists who intended to harm the homeland, but, on the other hand, what happened when those tools were used improperly on American citizens?

Maguire recalled a recent report he had read about a couple's entire bank account being seized by the Internal Revenue Service. They were never charged with a crime and never saw the inside of a court. In fact, the sole reason their money was confiscated was that investigators felt their bank deposits were *questionable.*

In the end, it seemed to him that the increased protection all came at the cost of individual rights. People shrugged their shoulders meekly and accepted that it was *just the way things are now.* Meanwhile, the government continued to grow bigger and exercised even more control for the greater good.

The Founding Fathers, in their infinite wisdom, had established an ingenious system of *checks and balances* within the three branches of government so that power could not be concentrated within any one branch. Political chicanery and party politics had blurred the lines between the duties of the executive and legislative branches. Now the judicial seemed willing to abdicate their role as well, all for the ever elusive *greater good* of course.

Well, maybe not all of them, he thought, as he recalled Rich's comment about Judge Potts hesitation.

Perhaps the pendulum was swinging back in the other direction, but was the damage already done?

"Honestly, if he doesn't make contact in the next few days he probably won't," Maguire said.

"I agree," Rich replied, "but at least this will give us a better direction. If he contacts the uncle he might be looking for a way out."

"I hope you're right. Just tell them to monitor the calls very carefully. There might only be a word or two between them, so we will have to be ready to act. Also look for any incoming calls on brand new phones. I'm pretty sure that if Spangler does reach out to his uncle it will be on a burner phone."

"Hey, I'm not a rookie at this," Rich said with a laugh. "I did manage to keep the President safe when you weren't around."

"Well, you are getting older now, so I don't want to take any chances with your failing memory."

"Old my ass," Rich replied.

"Just remember to bring my present when you come out for Christmas."

"My presence will be all the present you need," Rich said with a laugh. "I'll call you if I hear anything."

Before he could reply, Stargold ended the call.

"Damn, he's getting quicker," Maguire said with a chuckle, as he stared at the cellphone.

He laid the phone down on the bench and glanced over at the red Mustang parked in the next bay over, sandwiched between the black Tahoe and Melody's silver Mercedes G63.

How long had it been since he'd driven it? he wondered.

So much had changed in the last twenty months. The majority had been for the good. He loved Melody and was glad to be back in the Department, despite the good natured ribbing he gave Rich. But, that being said, there was still a part of him that missed the old days. He'd given up his own security consulting business to go back to the NYPD, given up the bachelor life for the soon-to-be-married one, and traded in his beloved houseboat for a mansion.

In a way, you never really appreciated true autonomy until it was gone.

"Rich people problems," he muttered to himself, as he got up and headed back inside.

CHAPTER THIRTY-SEVEN

Trenton, New Jersey
Monday, December 23rd, 2013 – 10:21 p.m.

The caked-on muck, which clung to the high pressure sodium security lights, created an eerie pall that hung over the deserted rows of storage lockers.

Spangler navigated the dark blue, late model Honda CRV, down the rows, *sans* headlights, until he reached the right locker. He glanced around, scanning the area for potential targets, before exiting the vehicle. He thrust his left hand into his jacket pocket, feeling the rough, stippled grips of the small semi-automatic against his skin.

In *this* neighborhood and at this time of night, he wasn't as much concerned with running into a witness, as he was common thieves. Despite the facilities claim to be safe and secure, he saw a number of areas in the shadows where the concertina wire, which ran along the fence tops, had been removed. He was actually surprised to see the locker intact.

After taking another quick look around, he unlocked the door and opened it. He didn't bother to turn on the unit's light, as he already knew exactly where everything was. He also didn't want to send out a signal to anyone that might be looking for an easy score.

He made his way to the back and opened up the two black garbage bags. Inside each one was a duffel bag containing food, clothing, additional ammo, a couple of pre-paid *burner* cellphones, and other supplies. He had just used the plastic bags to keep out any unwanted creepy-crawlers along with the elements.

When he was done, he carried them out to the vehicle and placed them into the back, removing one of the phones which he put into his jacket pocket. Then he grabbed the used bag, containing his old clothing, and tossed it back into the locker. He shut the door and relocked it.

A moment later he pulled out of the storage facility and made his way toward the waterfront.

Spangler glanced out the side window at the dilapidated homes of the inner city. Occasionally he would see someone sitting on a front stoop, smoking a cigarette, eying him warily.

Everyone looks for threats out here, he thought.

The cold weather had driven most of the residents inside, but he wondered how it was in the summer time.

Trenton, like most urban inner cities, had a history of violence. Its decline, like many U.S. cities, began back in the 1950's when an exodus of the middle class population began in earnest. The 1968 riots all but sealed the city's fate.

But the city wasn't always like that. In addition to a number of politicians and professional sports players, it was also the birthplace of Supreme Court Justices Antonin Scalia and Samuel Alito, as well as Medal of Honor recipients Frank William Crilley and William J. Johnston, Sr.

In fact, Trenton had once been the capital of the United States. It was also the site of General George Washington's pivotal Revolutionary War victory, when he crossed the Delaware River and defeated the Hessian troops encamped in Trenton. Granted that was over two hundred years ago, but in a city with such negative headlines you took the positives where you found them.

As Spangler made his way down Lalor Street, he noticed a Trenton Police car stopped in the parking lot outside a Dunkin' Donuts.

Immediately he looked down at the speedometer, checking his speed. He subconsciously held his breath, even as he felt his heart begin to race. He knew that there was no way the cop could know who he was, but that didn't stop the fear from creeping in. He glanced over cautiously, as he passed the police vehicle, and then waited, for what seemed like eternity, for the emergency lights to come.

They didn't.

Half a block later Spangler breathed a sigh of relief. A few minutes later he turned onto Route 29 and made his way south, toward I-295.

The steady flow of traffic served to reduce the stress he had felt inside the city. Red lights and stop signs made him feel uneasy, as if people had a chance to see him. Moving along at highway speed seemed to grant him an enhanced sense of anonymity.

Traffic on the highway was much lighter than he had thought it would be and he made decent time as he drove south. The Christmas songs playing on the radio seemed so out of place to him and he had to remind himself that tomorrow was Christmas Eve.

Being so narrowly focused on the mission at hand had caused him to lose track of time, not that there was any reason for him to be interested in the holiday. He had no family waiting for him around the tree, no *special someone* to exchange presents with.

Could it have been different? he wondered.

There was a time when Spangler had believed it would be. He'd held onto to the childish dreams of having both a family and a career, but at every turn it had been thwarted and not through any fault of his own. He'd been a good soldier, dedicated, thoughtful, and hard-working. He had given his all to the Army and what had he gotten in return for it? A knife in the back.

Spangler recalled being brought into the interrogation room by the two special agents from the Army's Criminal Investigation Command. They had struck him as an odd pair. The senior special agent, a man named Charlie Peterman, was an older, grizzled looking, bald-headed guy, whose rumpled suit looked as if he had just rolled out of bed in it. In a way it sort of matched his demeanor. Spangler recalled that he had horrible bad breath, a mix of coffee and stale cigarettes. On the other hand, his partner, Agent Kimberly Ross, was a young and very attractive looking woman. She had auburn hair and bright blue eyes. Ross didn't say much, which was okay, because Peterman said enough for both of them.

Obviously Peterman viewed himself as the senior investigator of the two. For his part, Spangler spent most of the interrogation wondering just how she managed to fit her rather ample breasts inside the snug blouse she wore.

Peterman tried to break him, tried to fuck with him psychologically, blaming him for the murders. He remembered the bald-headed little prick telling him how he was going to be charged with murder and shipped off to the military's maximum security prison at Fort Leavenworth, Kansas. When Peterman had *unexpectedly* gotten called out of the room, Ross took over, gently telling him how things would go so much easier on him in court if he just admitted that he had made a mistake.

It was classic good cop / bad cop.

They knew the truth, that he'd been operating under intelligence provided to him, but they tried to get him to confess to screwing up, as if he was the one that had provided the original faulty intel to begin with.

That was the military way, wasn't it?

A higher up screwed the pooch and just let the blame roll downhill until it finally stuck to some poor E-4 or E-5 schmuck. Grunts were a dime a dozen, but officers were expensive.

At least they gave him the wonderful opportunity to mentally undress her while she interrogated him.

Spangler had thought he'd put all that bullshit behind him when he had applied for the NYPD, but he was wrong. They were nothing more than institutional bullies. They made a regular habit of fucking with the lives of people who they deemed as being unimportant or who were politically unconnected. Once again they thought they could push him around, but not anymore. This time the little man was standing up and soon they would all pay.

He took a deep breath, letting it out slowly, and smiled at the face looking back at him in the rearview mirror.

He was alone in the world and he was okay with that.

Well, not quite alone, he thought.

Uncle Max had always been there for him. He was the only one who had never turned his back on him, even after Spangler had threw a wrench into his plans and put in for the drone operator program. Hell, Spangler knew that he might very well have ended up in Leavenworth if it wasn't for his uncle, which only made what he had to do next even that much harder.

CHAPTER THIRTY-EIGHT

Bowie, Maryland
Monday, December 23rd, 2013 – 11:58 p.m.

Max Spangler glanced down at the cellphone vibrating on his desk and swallowed hard.

It wasn't his normal cellphone, which made the call even more disturbing. There was only one person who had this number and he'd been awaiting the call ever since he'd been told about the news conference in New York City, but waiting for it and *getting* it were two entirely different things.

Spangler felt his jaw clench instinctively and he drummed his fingers angrily on the desktop before picking the phone up.

"Is it true?" he asked gruffly.

There was a moment's hesitation before he heard a meek, "Yes."

"Jesus H. Christ," he said softly, as he stared out into the darkness beyond the French windows of his home office.

"I...,"

"Don't say another word," Spangler said angrily. "Just get your ass to the shack and await my instructions, do I make myself clear?"

"Yes, sir."

Spangler ended the call and tossed the cellphone back onto the desk.

"Sonofabitch!"

The man got up and walked over to the window, gazing out into the night sky. Outside, the snow had begun to fall in earnest, briefly lit up by the spotlights in the garden, before falling to the ground.

The majority of people would be happy to have a white Christmas, but it didn't matter to him. He had a company to run and he didn't allow himself such luxuries as holidays. Holidays were for people without drive, without ambition. They stayed at home and pissed away the opportunities; opportunities that he was more than happy to seize upon. It was how he had gotten here and, more importantly, how he planned to stay here.

He turned his attention back to the matter at hand. He had been dreading the call, not for what he heard, but for what he had already known in his heart.

No one wanted to believe it, but he knew that his nephew was guilty. He sensed it in the way any leader senses things. Jerry was a good kid at heart, but he'd always had *issues*. Max had patiently waited, hoping that his nephew would *mature*, but he never really did.

Spangler had thought that the military would help him, straighten him out so-to-speak, so he facilitated things to get him into a nice, cushy Army job, but he had been wrong. His nephew's immaturity, coupled with a desire for *grander* things, landed him in a world of trouble, one that had nearly caused Spangler to use up every ace card he'd been holding just to get him out of it. Now his nephew had gone from being the Army's scapegoat to a bona fide killer and once again he would have to clean up the mess.

He turned and walked back over to the desk. He picked up the phone and hit the speed dial button. After a few rings he heard the groggy voice of Winston DuPont answer.

"Hello?"

"I need you to reach out to them and see what they've got," Spangler said.

"Do you know what time it is?"

"Does that really matter?"

"For Christ's sake, Max, it's after midnight," the man replied. "It's Christmas Eve tomorrow."

"I don't give a shit if it's the end of the world," Spangler said angrily, "and God knows I pay you enough that you shouldn't care either."

"I can't promise you anything, but I'll do my best."

"I'm not *asking* you to promise me anything, Winston. I'm telling you to find out what they've got. If you can't do that, then you're not the man for this job."

"You know that they're going to want to speak with him," DuPont said.

"It's Christmas, Winston, tell them to put it on their *Santa wish list*," Spangler said sarcastically. "Call me as soon as you know something."

He ended the call and set the phone on the desk. Then he walked over to the wet bar and poured himself a scotch on the rocks.

Why was it so hard to find people who didn't question, but just acted?

Marines didn't ask why you wanted something killed; they just killed it with extreme prejudice. Tell a Marine to attack a position and the only thing you'd hear was an enthusiastic *Ooh-Rah*. There were never any questions about *why it needed to be attacked* or *who was inside it.*

God how he wished he could go back in time.

He looked up at the photos on the wall, an entire career encapsulated in a series of eight by ten photos. There were crisp, clear pictures of him with presidents, prime ministers, an assortment of other dignitaries and politicians. They were your typical D.C. circle-jerk photos; everyone looking to kiss some ass and rise up the food chain. His eyes moved along the photographs until he got to the grainy ones. They lacked the notoriety and prestige of the former, but they were the ones that meant the most to him.

Most of the photos were taken in the Iraqi desert and were of him with his beloved *Devil Dogs* after combat operations. A few were taken in later years, some at his promotions and a few others at command ceremonies, but it was always the old warrior ones that called to him.

How many are still left? he wondered.

"Semper-Fi, boys," Spangler said quietly, hosting his glass in a toast before taking a sip.

He let the moment pass, then turned around and headed back to his desk.

Spangler sat down and glanced up at the clock on the wall. It was just after one o'clock in the afternoon Tokyo time. Christmas didn't matter to the business minded Japanese people. At least he could get something accomplished while the rest of America sat on its collective ass and racked up mountains of credit card debt.

It wasn't that he was against celebrating the baby Jesus' birth; it was just that Americans had managed to lose sight of what they were actually celebrating. They'd commercialized the hell out of the holiday and managed to drag it well into the New Year, like drunken sailors who just didn't know when to quit. In a few more years they'd be playing *Jingle Bells* in June.

He picked up the cellphone, selecting a number from the contact list and listened as it rang. A moment later he heard the call connect.

"*Kon'nichiwa*, Yoshimoto," Spangler said, putting his nephew troubles on the back-burner for a moment.

CHAPTER THIRTY-NINE

Southampton, Suffolk County, N.Y.
Tuesday, December 24th, 2013 – 3:23 p.m.

"Excuse me, sir."

Maguire looked up from the book he was reading to see Oliver Bell, the security director, standing just outside the entry way.

"Yes, Oliver," Maguire replied.

"Just got word they are in-bound, sir," the man said. "They should be wheel's down in five minutes. I have a car waiting down at the helipad."

"Okay, thank you very much. How are we doing on staffing?"

"As per Ms. Anderson's request, we've scaled everything back to just the necessary personnel," he replied. "

"I know Melody wanted as many people to be with their families as possible," Maguire said.

"I understand, but that still doesn't leave a lot of security," he replied. "There are only three of us tonight and then down to only two per shift until the 26th."

"Under any other circumstances I'd agree with you, Oliver," Maguire said, setting the book down on the couch, "but this battle was lost, even before it began. We'll just have to double lock the doors and windows for the next few days."

"Aye-aye, sir," Oliver said.

Maguire smiled as the man left the room.

Melody had worked closely with Gen to ensure that everyone would be here early enough that all the non-essential folks could go home and be with their families. She even arranged it that Rich, Mary and the girls would be picked up at the downtown heliport, so that his security detail didn't have to drive them out to Southampton.

She knew that she couldn't let everyone off for the holidays, but that didn't mean she wouldn't try. It was just one of the many reasons why people liked to work for her.

Just then he heard the elevator chime softly and watched as she got off with Gen in tow.

"Do we know where they are at?" Melody asked, as she walked into the salon. "Shouldn't they be here by now?"

"Just about," Maguire said, getting up from the couch. "Oliver said they were on approach."

"I've been sitting upstairs hitting refresh on the weather map," she replied. "The storm is getting worse. Now they are predicting up to a foot of snow."

"Which means we'll probably get 1-2 inches," Maguire said with a laugh.

"I just want everyone here so I can stop worrying."

"Relax, Angel. They'll be here soon."

Just then Gen appeared carrying two mugs.

"Here," she said, handing one to Melody. "You need something to calm your nerves."

"I do," Melody replied eagerly, as she accepted the mug and took a sip.

"Oh my God," she said. "This is amazing. What is it?"

"Coconut Rum Spiked S'more Hot Chocolate," Gen said, sipping from her mug. "You might want to plan on adding an extra five miles to your morning run."

"It'll be worth it."

"Where's Gregor?" Maguire asked.

"Upstairs, with Wolfgang, watching his beloved FCK play Berlin," Gen said.

"They play soccer on Christmas Eve?"

"No, he missed the game the other night because he had a personnel meeting with Peter," Gen explained. "Ernst recorded it for him and now he's afraid that if he doesn't watch it, someone back home will spoil it for him."

"He does take his soccer seriously," Maguire said.

"Go *Teufel's*," Gen said with a laugh, as she thrust her fist in the air.

"I wonder how long it will be before he packs up Wolfie and takes him to his first home game?"

"He's already started," Gen replied. "He wants to go to Germany next fall to show us off to the family. I'm sure he will use it as a ruse to slip in a game or two."

Just then the front door opened and in rushed Emily Stargold.

"Aunt Melody," Emily cried out, as she dropped her backpack and came barreling into the salon.

"Emmie," Melody said, setting her mug on the table just as the young girl launched herself into Melody's arms.

"Oh my goodness, you're getting so big," Melody said, as she hugged her. "Pretty soon you'll be driving too."

"Don't even start, Mel," Mary Stargold said, as she walked in.

"What good is a license if you can't even drive?" Sophie Stargold said tersely.

"Oh, I think I hear Rich calling me about the luggage," Maguire said, tussling Emily's hair as Melody set her down. "I'd better go help."

"Little chicken shit," Mary whispered in his ear, as he stopped and hugged her.

"I love you too," Maguire replied, and then slowly slipped away.

"No driving?" Melody asked, as Sophie collapsed melodramatically on the couch.

"No," she said. "Dad doesn't think I need to drive since we live in Manhattan."

"He does have a point," Melody said. "You don't know anguish till you've sat in New York City traffic."

"It's not fair."

"Life's not fair," Mary said, "get used to it."

"Can I go to the game room?" Sophie asked.

"Yes," Melody said. "Go have fun."

Sophie got up from the couch and headed toward the elevator.

"Can I go too?" Emily asked.

"Yes," Mary replied, "but please don't bug your sister."

"I promise," Emily said, before scampering off after her sister.

"Here, you look like you could use some help," Gen said, handing Mary a mug.

"If it has alcohol, I'd rather you just mainline it."

"Just imagine if you had to drive out here," Melody said, sitting down on the couch.

"One of us wouldn't have made it here."

"I'm so glad I had a boy," Gen said.

"Well you're here now," Melody said, "so sit down and relax. You'll be a hero again by the morning."

"I hope you're right," Mary replied. "I can't imagine going back to Manhattan with *Sad-Sack Sophie*."

"You guys are staying all week, right?" Melody asked.

"Yes, as long as you can stand the three of us," Mary replied. "I'm assuming the boys will make some excuse to go back to work early."

"Not my boy," Gen said. "He already knows he has babysitting duty this week. I was a good girl for nine months, now its momma's turn to unwind."

"Maybe the girls can help him," Mary said with a particularly evil grin.

"God save poor Gregor," Melody said.

"Oh he'll be just fine," Gen said. "He's dealt with terrorists before, what difficulty could he possibly have dealing with a teenage girl, a pre-teen girl and a newborn....."

The three women paused, glancing back and forth at one another conspiratorially, before bursting out in uncontrollable laughter.

"What's so funny?" Maguire asked, as he and Rich walked into the room.

"Nothing," Melody replied. "We were just discussing the activities for the week.

"Well, we're just going to run these bags up to the bedrooms," Maguire said, "and have ourselves a little chat about Department business."

"Take your time," Melody said. "Dinner's not for another hour."

CHAPTER FORTY

Edgewater, Maryland
Tuesday, December 24th, 2013 – 4:13 p.m.

The *Shack* was a non-descript cabin that sat on fifteen acres of land along the western shoreline of the Rhode River in Edgewater. Spangler had purchased it more than two decades ago when he thought he would just retire and take up fishing. The only problem was that Spangler hated fishing almost as much as he hated the thought of retirement.

Even though he no longer used it, he kept the property as a tax deduction, allowing colleagues and clients to use it when they were in town and needed a break from urban life. Big city people seemed to like the idea of getting *back to nature*, as long as there were amenities to go along with it. When Spangler felt the need to get back to nature he went to the two hundred acre ranch he owned, in the rugged western part of Montana, with nothing more than a *Kabar* knife, his rifle and a few MRE's to sustain him.

There was no actual driveway that led up to the shack, just a discreet marker off the main road, which only Spangler and a few close associates knew about. As he approached it, he glanced in his rearview mirror, making sure that he was not being followed. The road he was on was long and quite narrow, with heavy forest lining either side of the roadway. Spangler had intentionally picked this time, knowing that sunset would have forced anyone following him to use their headlights and thereby giving themselves away.

It was possible that they could have used FLIR capable aerial surveillance, but they would have most likely had to rely on the county police aviation unit and he already had a solid source who would have alerted him.

He slowed the black Jeep Cherokee to a crawl, as he approached the marker, then took a hard left, plunging through the overgrowth and down what could only *loosely* be described as a pathway.

A few moments later he emerged into the clearing. Ahead of him was the old wooden cabin. The outside timber was weathered to the point of being almost *silverish* in color. To the casual observer it would almost appear to be abandoned, but that was intentional. Once inside, it became immediately apparent that the exterior did not match its well-appointed interior.

Spangler pulled up directly behind the car, which was covered in a camo tarp, parked next to the cabin. He scanned the area, looking for anything that didn't seem right, before getting out of the vehicle. He walked around to the passenger side, grabbing the box of food from the seat next to him, and then headed toward the front door.

The cabin's shutters were closed tightly, making it impossible for anyone to look inside, but that didn't mean that his arrival went unnoticed. There were remote sensors around the property that alerted occupants to any movement along the grounds. Additionally, discretely placed cameras, with night-vision capability, provided twenty-four / seven visual monitoring.

The ground sensors and cameras could also be accessed remotely, which meant that Spangler had been keeping tabs on his wayward nephew since he had arrived at the location last night.

He knocked on the door and waited for it to open. A moment later he heard the latch unlock and the door open cautiously.

Spangler walked inside without saying a word to his nephew; as he assessed the interior of the dimly lit room. The discarded remains of an MRE and a half-finished mug of coffee sat on the table. A crumpled blanket and pillow lay on the couch while a TV news anchor droned on about NASA confirming that astronauts aboard the International Space Station had successfully completed repairs on a cooling pump. What concerned him the most was what he *didn't* see, which meant that any firearms his nephew had were most likely on him or hidden away. Spangler didn't like unknowns, especially when it concerned deadly weapons.

He set the box down on the small kitchen table as he heard the sound of the door being locked. He removed the brown leather aviator jacket he was wearing and turned around to face his nephew.

The boy he had raised was long gone, replaced by a man who seemed ill at ease with himself. He'd thought the military would change the boy, mold him into a man, and, truth be told, it had. However, those changes had been like fragile seeds, sewn into difficult soil and they had been ripped away before they could properly take root. Perhaps he should have pushed to get him into the Corps. Chances are he would have died early in his first deployment, but there was honor in death.

Jerry's clothing seemed baggy, hanging off his lanky frame. He'd never been a big kid, even growing up, but now it appeared as if the sum of his recent activities had taken a significant physical toll on him.

"For Christ's sake, Jerry, what have you done?"

"I had no choice."

"The hell you didn't," Max said angrily. "This isn't war; you killed those cops in cold blood."

"They were my enemies just as much as the Taliban were in Afghanistan."

"Are you serious?" Max asked, as he sat down in one of the chairs. "Please explain to me how? Why?"

"They knew what they doing," Jerry said. "They were all complicit."

"Who?"

"The cops, the military," the young man said angrily. "They were working together to fuck me over. The Army wasn't happy that they couldn't get me for their screw-up in Afghanistan so they used those cops to fuck with me."

"Jesus Christ, Jerry," Max said, his voice a mix of annoyance and pity. "I could have fixed this if you had just given me more time. "

"You knew they were wrong Uncle Max, you had to fight for me with the Army and they were going to make you fight again."

"Yes, and I would have done it. Police Commissioners come and go, but they are political animals. Just because one caved in to pressure didn't mean the next one would have. I could have still made a deal if you had just let me do it my way."

"I took an oath to defend against all enemies, both foreign and domestic."

"This is not a war, Jerry," Max screamed. "You don't get to go out and shoot up the streets of New York City because they didn't give you a goddamn job."

"I'm not going to be pushed around anymore," Jerry replied, his voice cool and menacing. "Not by anyone."

Just then Max's cellphone began ringing. He removed it from his pocket, glancing at the display and held his finger up, silencing his nephew.

"What do you have for me?"

"They want to speak with him," Winston DuPont replied.

"You'd better have more than that."

"I spoke Angela Washington this afternoon. She's the NYPD's Deputy Commissioner of Legal Matters; we also went to Stanford together. It sounds like they have a majority of the pieces, but they haven't put the puzzle together enough to arrest him."

"Will they?"

"If they speak with him, yes," DuPont replied.

"Then it's your job to make sure they don't."

"I'll need a plausible excuse."

"He's suffering from combat related PTSD," Max replied. "He's been sent to a residential treatment facility."

Jerry began to protest, but the look his uncle shot him ended the conversation before it even began.

"When? Where?" DuPont asked dubiously.

"Three days before the first shooting, you don't need to know where," Spangler said.

"They'll eventually want a name."

"Don't worry," Spangler replied. "When the time comes they'll get their name and the in-take records will corroborate what you tell them."

"I've requested a meeting with the police commissioner on Thursday," DuPont said. "I should have more to go on after that."

"Okay," Spangler said. "Enjoy your holiday."

"What's left of it," DuPont replied.

Spangler ended the call; he had nothing more to say.

He didn't particularly like DuPont, but he certainly respected his capabilities. DuPont had been his personal attorney for nearly a decade and in that time he had earned every penny of his rather sizeable salary, but that didn't mean they were going to become friends. Spangler's military career had taught him that it was best not to get close to people. He evaluated everyone for what they brought to the table; nothing more, nothing less. If they were capable, he used them to the best of their abilities. When they stopped being useful, he cut them off and moved on. He should have done that with Jerry long ago, but he was blood and you had to respect that.

"There's nothing *wrong* with me," Jerry protested, "and I'm not going to any treatment facility."

"You'll go where I tell you, when I tell you," Max replied. "That is unless you prefer the accommodations of a six by nine foot cell on death row."

"I'm not going to jail," Jerry said defiantly.

"You will, if you don't do exactly as you're told," Max replied.

The two men stared at each other, the younger Spangler barely containing the rage that seethed beneath his skin, while the older just stared back with the confidence born from routinely making life and death decisions.

Despite the age difference, Max was clearly the one who should not be trifled with. In fact, everything about his uncle seemed to exude strength. The close-cropped hair was a bit greyer then Jerry had remembered, but the dangerous blue eyes were still the same. And if that alone wasn't enough to intimidate, then the lean muscles of the man's biceps, which stretched the material of the black USMC polo shirt that he wore, would dissuade any further argument.

In the end it was Jerry who blinked, lowering his head submissively.

Max slowly rose up from his seat and walked toward his nephew. He wrapped his arms around Jerry, hugging him. He could almost feel the young man's body slump, as he affectionately ran his hand slowly up and down his back.

"Everything that has happened, is in the past," he whispered in the young man's ear. "We don't look backward, that's not where we are heading. Understood?"

"Yes, sir," Jerry replied softly.

"Good," Max said. "Stay put, I'll be in touch when I know more."

"Merry Christmas, Uncle."

"Yeah" Max replied, "you too, Jerry."

Max opened the front door and headed toward the Jeep. He got inside and stared back at the shack. His mind began racing, images of his nephew, as a young boy, full of life and energy, flooding his thoughts. Then he shuddered, as he recalled the feel of the semi-automatic handgun, hidden in the small of the back, as he was hugging his nephew goodbye.

"How'd we get here, Jerry?" he said softly.

A second later the moment was gone and he started the vehicle.

"This is why you have a dog," Spangler chided himself, as he made his way down the path and back onto the roadway.

Dogs were faithful, people were not.

CHAPTER FORTY-ONE

Southampton, Suffolk County, N.Y.
Tuesday, December 24th, 2013 – 4:16 p.m.

"You didn't need my help carrying these bags up here," Maguire said, as he sat the luggage down on top of the bed. "So what did you want to tell me?"

"I got a call from Angie just before we left."

"What did she want?"

"She said that a guy named Winston DuPont had reached out to her claiming that he represented Gerald Spangler."

"Is the guy legit?" Maguire asked, taking a seat in one of the empty chairs in the adjacent sitting room.

"Angie said yes," Rich replied, choosing the chair across from him. "She went to law school with the guy, said he is general counsel to Spangler's uncle."

"What did he want to know?" Maguire asked.

"The usual, why we were interested in talking to him, what we had on him."

"What did Angie say?"

"Not much," Rich said. "She told him that we wanted to speak with him regarding his whereabouts at the time of the shooting, but that she was not at liberty to discuss the particulars of the case."

"What did he say?"

"He asked for a meeting with us to discuss his client."

"When?"

"This Thursday," Rich said. "I hate to cut into the holidays, but I thought we should strike while the iron is hot."

"Absolutely," Maguire replied. "Fuck, I'd fly down there now if it meant getting our hands on that little cock sucker."

"We don't have to fly anywhere, DuPont is coming to us."

"Of course he is," Maguire said with a laugh. "He is going to do his best to keep as much distance as possible between us and his client."

"You don't think Spangler's in the area anymore?"

"No, I don't," Maguire said. "I take him at his word that he's not finished, but I think he hit the road for now."

"You think he's down in Maryland, with his uncle?" Rich asked.

"It's possible, but I doubt it. Max is too much of a player to be directly connected to the kid. He might keep him close, but he is going to establish some wall to insulate himself."

"DuPont?"

"What better way than with lawyer / client confidentiality."

"How do you want to play it?"

"Close to the vest," Maguire said. "The truth is, that with an attorney involved, our odds of speaking with him have dropped exponentially."

"That's what I was afraid you'd say," Rich said.

"It is what it is," Maguire replied. "Might not be the answer we wanted, but we have Spangler on his heels for the moment and maybe we can build on that."

"What are you thinking?"

"DuPont is a criminal attorney," Maguire said. "He is comfortable with bending the law to suit his needs. What happens if we take that card away from him?"

"He still won't give us Spangler."

"He might not, but the chatter may," Maguire replied. "We know DuPont is working for Max. If we rile him up bad enough, I bet he calls the old man within ten seconds of leaving 1PP."

"And what's the point of that?"

"If we can rattle DuPont enough that he calls Spangler right away, then I'm inclined to believe that Max will reach out to his nephew."

"He hasn't so far," Rich replied. "I spoke to Kurt earlier and they haven't gotten anything yet on Max's phones."

"Perhaps they are monitoring the wrong phones."

"Then what's the point?" Rich asked. "If Max has a number we don't know about, we still aren't going to get anything from the wiretap."

"You leave that up to me," Maguire said with a smile.

"Why do I worry when you say it like that?"

"Don't sweat the small stuff. Besides, you don't want to be police commissioner forever."

"Can I ask if it's illegal?"

"Why do you have to break things down into black and white all the time? Why can't you just be happy with shades of grey?"

"Because when you start dealing in *shades of grey*, I'm the one who usually gets whipped."

"It's not *technically* illegal," Maguire replied.

"Technically?"

"If you don't know that something exists,...."

"What doesn't exist?"

Both men turned to see Melody standing in the doorway.

"Uhm,..... Santa?" Maguire said sheepishly.

"You'd better rethink that notion before Mrs. Claus hears you and sends your gifts to someone more appreciative."

"You're little elf is trying to convince me to swim in murky waters again."

"My little elf is going to get his ass bitten one day, if he doesn't stay out of those ponds."

"Fortunately for me I have a tough ass," Maguire said with a laugh. "Tough, but oh so cute."

"Yeah, well unfortunately for me, after some of my latest meetings over at City Hall, I have almost no ass left. Can we stick with the traditional for the moment? See what the Bureau guys come up with?"

"You're the boss," Maguire said.

"I hate you," Rich replied.

"It's my great ass isn't it?" Maguire said with a laugh. "I told you that you should spend more time in the gym."

"Honestly, I want to catch this piece of shit so bad I can taste it and I don't want that to cloud my judgment. I don't want his attorney ripping the heart out of our case because we didn't cross a T or dot and I."

"Okay, we'll play it your way, Mr. Spit and Polish, but if Kurt's crew can't come up with anything after our little meeting with DuPont, at least hear me out."

"Deal," Rich replied.

"Now that you two have averted a crisis, would you mind closing the book on work for the next twenty-four hours and allow us to have a cop free Christmas?"

Maguire got up and walked over to Melody, then wrapped his arm around her, hugging her tightly. "You've got a deal, Mrs. Claus."

"Good, because after tomorrow, when Sophie gets her new car, all this is gonna seem like a Sunday walk in the park for you two."

"God, please don't remind me," Rich replied. "I'm so not ready for this."

"She's gonna need a car when she goes off to college," Melody said. "She might as well get acclimated to it slowly."

"I'm just not sure I'll ever get acclimated to it," Rich replied. "It seems like only yesterday I was bottle feeding her and now my little girl is going away to college."

"Don't be so melodramatic," Maguire said. "She's going to Stony Brook, not UCLA. Besides, I hear that going prematurely bald is an *in* thing now."

"Have I told you how much I hate you?" Rich asked, as he got up from the chair.

"Only on those days ending in Y," Maguire said with a laugh. "Come on, I'll help you drown your parental sorrows in some egg-nog."

"You're never gonna have kids are you?"

Maguire wrapped his arm over his friends shoulder and pulled him close.

"We get to have all the fun with Sophie and Emily, then send them home to you. Why should we mess with a good thing?"

Melody heard Rich sigh audibly, as the two men walked away. Then she felt a little twinge inside her, as Maguire's words replayed in her head.

Should we mess with a good thing? she wondered.

CHAPTER FORTY-TWO

Edgewater, Maryland
Wednesday, December 25th, 2013 – 6:17 a.m.

"You'll go where I tell you, when I tell you. That is unless you prefer the accommodations of a six by nine foot cell on death row."

His uncle's words replaying in his head for what seemed like the millionth time.

He slid the rod with the bronze bore cleaning brush down the barrel of the Glock 19, feeling it glide slowly against the Tenifer treated steel. On the coffee table in front of him lay the remaining pieces of the handgun.

There was no mechanical reason to clean the weapon, as Spangler kept it as clean as the first day he had taken it out of the box, but was more of a psychological activity. When it came to his weapon, he knew every part intimately. Each pin, each spring, was cared for lovingly. When he pulled the trigger, there was no question as to whether the gun would fire. It never failed him.

"You'll go where I tell you, when I tell you. That is unless you prefer the accommodations of a six by nine foot cell on death row."

Spangler closed his eyes, clenching them tightly as he willed the words to go away. He loved his uncle, but the man didn't understand. He was *Mad Max* Spangler, the war hero, and no one would dare mess with him.

Maybe that's why they mess with you, because they can't mess with him.

"Shut up," Spangler said angrily.

He hated the voices, but that didn't mean they were wrong. Sometimes they made some very valid points, even if they were unpleasant to hear at times.

In a way it made sense to him. His uncle was a Marine Corps hero and the Army would certainly have a grudge to settle. Stories of inter-service animosity were legendary. Spangler recalled reading one such story, coined the 'Battle of the Smiths,' in which a Marine Corps general relieved an Army general of his command during the invasion of Saipan, during World War II. As the story went, the Marine general felt the Army troops were lagging behind, costing casualties to his men. Unfortunately, he had never observed the landscape and was unaware that the soldiers had to make their way through a valley which was surrounded by hills and cliffs under Japanese control, turning the open terrain into a killing field.

Had his fate been sealed because someone held a grudge?

Spangler felt the anger welling up inside him. It bothered him that he had no one else to turn to. Sure he had his uncle, but he didn't really understand. After all, he was just his nephew. A poor child whom his uncle felt obligated to take under his wing after his drunkard brother killed himself.

That really is my legacy, isn't it? he thought.

He was nothing more than the son of a common drunk who couldn't even avoid hitting a truck.

Spangler picked up the gun's slide and slid the barrel back into place. Then he slid the slide onto the gun's frame and cycled it several times, ensuring that the action moved smoothly, before putting the magazine in and chambering a round. Then he sat it down on the coffee table and picked up the manila folder lying next to it.

Inside were a series of photos he had taken during his reconnaissance missions. It had taken him awhile to capture them all, every person whom he deemed responsible for his fall. The photos included the CID agents, his commanding officer, the Army attorney, and the NYPD investigator, everyone who'd had a hand in fucking with him. There were some ceremonial figures included as well, but he didn't think he could actually get close enough to kill someone like the Secretary of Defense or the President, but it was nice to have goals.

Many of the photos contained pertinent information on the target, including their home and work addresses, the vehicles they used, as well as any routines he had uncovered as a result of his observations. Some were still blank, which meant that he hadn't been able to track them down, at least as of yet.

Spangler got up and walked into the kitchen. He poured himself another cup of coffee and opened the shutter, peering out into the darkness beyond the window. Off in the distance the horizon was just beginning to lighten, signaling the coming dawn.

He envisioned families, across the world, awaking to share a Christmas morning. Exuberant children tore away at the brightly colored wrapping paper which shrouded the baubles that they had lusted for all year, while their parents fought to stay awake on the couch.

It was equivalent to a drug rush. A brief moment of utter bliss followed by a crash, as items once dreamt of as being indispensable now lay discarded beneath the tree as their new owners look to the future and begin the process anew.

Spangler glanced back at the folder on the coffee table.

Which of them new it would be their last? he wondered.

He looked back toward the horizon as the reddish hue of the sun began to grow in the eastern sky.

Like the toys under the tree, they thought they could just discard him, but they were wrong. Now he would show them what they had really created. Now they would all pay.

●●●

Emily Stargold sat in the center of the room surrounded by a growing pile of wrapping paper, as her newly acquired robotic puppy kept a vigilant eye out.

"Here, Ems, this one is from me," Maguire said, handing her the large box.

Emily shook the box gently before tearing into the paper.

"What did you do?" Melody said, her eyes squinting accusatorily.

"I saw it on the way home, couldn't resist."

"It's a gun!" Emily announced loudly as she opened the box to reveal a brightly colored plastic gun with eighteen soft-foam bullets.

"I swear, you can't be trusted," Melody replied.

Maguire smiled mischievously, as he took a sip of his coffee.

"Do not shoot that toward anyone," Mary said sternly, "and that goes double for your sister."

"I won't," replied Emily.

"Unless it's Uncle James, then shoot him all you want," Rich said tiredly, as he lay on the couch next to Mary.

"Nice," Maguire, tossing one of the throw pillows at Rich.

"*Children*, behave," Melody admonished.

"Is that it?" Gen asked.

"Let me look," Melody replied, as she searched beneath the tree.

"See if there's any coal under there for your fiancée," Rich said.

"Behave," Mary said, nudging him with her elbow.

"Actually, there is one more," Melody called out, emerging from under the tree with a small box. "It's for Sophie, from Mom and Dad."

Sophie looked up from the CD case she had been reading and took the box from Melody's hand. She began tearing the paper off to reveal a non-descript, white rectangular box. She looked over at her parents with a curious look, but only received passive looks in response. She then opened the box to reveal a small die-cast car.

"*Surprise*," Rich called out.

"Very funny, dad," she said, dropping the box into her lap.

"What? You said you wanted a car."

"You know what I meant," Sophie replied.

"Maybe you should take a closer look at it," Mary said with a smile.

Sophie picked up the box again, removing the car, and began examining it. Her eyes went wide when she turned it over she saw the key taped to the bottom.

"No way," she said incredulously.

"Yes way," Mary replied, "see, we're not really evil parents."

"Oh my God," she cried out, leaping to her feet and wrapping her arms tightly around Mary's neck. "Thank you so much."

"Hey don't I get any of this?" Rich asked.

Sophie leaned over and hugged her dad.

"I guess you want to see it?" Mary asked.

"It's here?"

"Yep, it's in the garage, but you'd better ask Aunt Melody."

Sophie turned around to look at Melody who nodded lovingly.

She immediately took off for the garage.

"Stay away from the Mustang," Maguire called out.

"You ever gonna give that car up?" Rich asked.

"Not in this lifetime."

"Boys and their toys," Melody said.

Suddenly they heard an engine roar to life.

"Girl's and theirs," Maguire said with a chuckle.

"You better go rein your daughter in before she fills the garage with carbon monoxide or we end up owing Melody a new garage door," Mary said.

"As you wish, my love," Rich said.

"I'll come with you," James said. "We'll teach her to do donuts in the courtyard."

"And you'll be out there with a toothbrush getting the rubber off the cobblestone," Melody called out.

"Go ahead, Gregor," Gen said. "I know you want to."

"I love you, *Mausi*," he said, kissing her gently on the forehead.

"Ah, the post-Christmas hush," Melody said, as she sank down into the couch.

"Coffee refills?" Gen asked.

"Oh God yes," Melody said, offering up her cup.

"Can I have some?" Emily asked.

"No, baby, not for another twelve years," Gen said with a smile. "But you can go get some milk or juice if you want."

"Okay," Emily replied, then scampered off toward the kitchen.

"Thank you, Mel," Mary said. "This really meant a lot to us, to the girls."

"Don't thank me, Mary," Melody said, taking a sip of her coffee. "I wanted this. I wanted to know what it felt like to have a house full of family."

"And?"

"I can't think of anything more rewarding," Melody replied, "or anywhere else I would rather be."

"To family," Gen said, holding up her mug.

"To family," Mary and Melody repeated, as they tapped each other's glass.

CHAPTER FORTY-THREE

Penobscot, New Hampshire
Wednesday, December 25th, 2013 – 1:13 p.m.

Alex sat on the couch, nursing a glass of wine, as she stared serenely at the flames, flickering off the logs, in the fireplace. Inside her head was an entirely different story.

For the past ten days she had been unable to focus on anything but the conversation she'd had with Maguire. The fact that they had not spoken since was beginning to drive her nuts.

Not talking for ten days was not all that unusual, they had gone longer, but not talking after you'd professed your love for someone was never a good sign. She tried to assuage her fears by telling herself that he was just busy with the shootings. It lasted for a little while, but eventually the fear that she had lost him for good would come creeping back in.

Alex kept replaying the last conversation they'd had in her mind. He never actually said the words, but he had certainly alluded to having feelings for her.

So why the fuck haven't you called?

She set the wine glass down on the coffee table and lit up a cigarette. She so wanted to trade the wine in for whiskey and she almost had, on several occasions, but fought through the urge. Now, as the days of silence progressed, she began wondering what the purpose of fighting that urge was serving.

Peter had stopped by her house twice since they'd returned to Penobscot. The first time he'd come over to say how sorry he was for what happened and to say he understood. She didn't have the desire to rekindle the argument, by telling him just how much he didn't know, so she just smiled and let him be magnanimous.

It bothered her that she was having to fight to have feelings for him. He didn't deserve that. He deserved a lot more than she was able to give him now.

Would that ever change? she wondered. *Perhaps the real question was would she ever change?*

She'd wished she had never gone to the party. She could have kept her feelings for James bottled up inside her and perhaps she would have *learned* to love Peter.

It had been so easy living with her secret, something that was safely hidden away deep inside her. Now that the cat was out of the bag, what would happen? That's what really bothered her, the not knowing just how deeply this was going to impact their relationship. She didn't think she could handle not having him in her life.

Which brought her back to Peter.

How do you build a relationship with one person, while you desire another? she wondered.

The second time he'd shown up was last night, appearing on her doorstep with a bottle of wine, a dozen roses and her Christmas *present*. She pawned off her very *un*-Christmas like attitude on a severe migraine. After a few drinks Peter took the hint, gave her a kiss on her forehead and left; telling her that if she felt better that he would love for her to come to Christmas dinner at his house. The idea of being paraded around, in front of his family, seemed absurd under the current circumstances.

Alex took a final drag on the cigarette then crushed it out in the ashtray. She got up and put another log on the fire, then went into the kitchen to get a refill of her drink. She'd just put the cork back in the bottle when the doorbell rang.

She groaned audibly at the intrusion, letting her body melodramatically collapse onto the counter as she waited.

The doorbell rang again, this time accompanied by a series of urgent sounding knocks.

"Fuck, fuck and double fuck," Alex muttered.

She grabbed her glass and walked to the door, peering through the peephole before grudgingly opening the door.

Standing on the porch was Abby Simpson, wearing a bright red bubble jacket, with an equally bright green scarf, along with a pair of reindeer antlers with little brass bells on the tip.

"Jesus H. Christ, let me get my gun and put you out of your misery."

"Merry Christmas to you too," Abby exclaimed. "I come bearing gifts."

Abby held up the brightly colored Mylar gift bag.

"Bah Humbug," Alex replied. "Now, go away."

Abby brushed past Alex and headed toward the kitchen.

"You don't listen very well."

"You didn't mean it," Abby said, as she grabbed a wine glass from the cabinet and poured herself a drink.

"How do you know?"

"Because if you really meant it you wouldn't have opened the door," Abby replied.

"Don't you have someplace else to haunt on Christmas?" Alex asked.

"Nope, everyone has a charity case to save on Christmas and you're mine."

"Outstanding," Alex said sarcastically, as she made her way back to the couch. "Don't expect anything more from me, than this."

"Grinch much?" Abby asked, sitting down in the chair next to the couch.

"Excuse me, but I didn't ask you to save me, *Cindy Lou Who*."

"What's wrong? Hasn't Dr. *Hunk* paid you a holiday house call yet?"

"Don't start," Alex said, lighting up another cigarette.

"Or are you still kicking yourself for opening Pandora's Box?"

"You're ruining my holiday buzz," Alex said.

"You need to just let it go," Abby said. "What's done is done and you can't take it back."

"That's easy for you to say."

"What, you think I never screwed up romantically with a guy before?"

Alex thought about that for a moment. In the eighteen months she had known Abby, she had never heard her mention or even seen her with a man before. In fact, she'd begun to think that Abby might not have held an interest in the opposite sex, not that it mattered to her. Alex tended to judge people based on their capabilities and not what they did behind closed doors.

"Yeah, yeah, I know, I don't date much, but that's by choice," Abby said, as if she'd read Alex's mind. "It's bad enough that this job makes it tough to meet the right person, but add to that the world of bodybuilding and the pool to draw from becomes exponentially smaller."

"What about other bodybuilders?" Alex asked. "I'd imagine that they'd be more accepting."

"Oh they are, but I have a hard enough time managing my own eating and supplement schedule, without needing to take on someone else's routine."

"I never really thought about it that way before."

"Besides, I'm not sharing my mirrors with anyone," Abby said with a laugh.

"No, God forbid you made room for anyone else to 'mire themselves in the mirror."

"I mean is it too much to ask for a normal guy?"

"I'd offer you Peter."

"You don't mean that," Abby said. "You like him."

"I do," Alex replied. "I just don't know if it's ever going to move beyond *like*."

"You could do a lot worse than Peter Bates to have as a *friend with benefits*."

"That's the problem," Alex said, tapping the end of her cigarette into the ashtray. "Peter wants to be more than friends and I'm not sure I can ever commit beyond that."

"I know that you're still freaked about the party," Abby replied. "Give it some time. Things will settle down."

"The problem is all I have is time."

"Have you talked to him about it?"

"Nope, not since I left New York."

Abby reached down and picked up Alex's pack of cigarettes and lit one.

"That sucks," she said, taking a drag.

"Yeah, that's what is getting to me, the not knowing."

"I don't know him, but I know you," she said. "He's not going to just ignore you. From what you told me it sounds like he's grappling with some issues himself."

"That's what I keep telling myself" Alex said. "I just hope that I'm not lying to myself."

"You're not, just give it some more time. It'll work itself out, you'll see."

"From your lips to God's ears, Abby."

"So for now, here we sit," Abby said, hoisting her wine glass up in a mock toast. "Two amazing women, all alone on Christmas."

"*Fa la fucking la.....*" Alex replied, tapping her glass against Abby's. "So what's in the bag?"

"Two bottles of wine, some chocolate, a bag of popcorn and a movie."

"That doesn't sound too bad. What's the movie?"

"*Love Actually.*"

"*Awesome,*" Alex replied, rolling her eyes and taking a sip of wine.

CHAPTER FORTY-FOUR

1 Police Plaza, Manhattan, N.Y.
Thursday, December 26th, 2013 – 10:23 a.m.

"You've got nothing," Winston DuPont said.

"Then let us speak to him," Rich replied.

"Why?" the man asked. "What useful purpose would it serve?"

"Perhaps it would clear him," Maguire said.

"With all due respect, Commissioner Maguire, I'm not in the habit of allowing my clients to make the authorities case for them."

"Your client was identified as renting an apartment in which photos of our dead officers were found along with a note saying there would be more."

"My client is a sick young man who suffers from post-traumatic stress disorder, brought about by authorities who attempted to railroad him for doing his job," DuPont said. "An alleged crime for which he was ultimately found not guilty."

"With all due respect, Mr. DuPont, there is a big difference between being found not guilty and not being guilty."

DuPont looked over at Maguire and smiled smugly.

"Maybe there is in the court of public opinion, but, fortunately for us, not in a court of law. Gerald is sick and is obtaining help. If your case hinges on a piece of paper, I will show you a half dozen others where innocent people admitted to crimes for the sole purpose of obtaining notoriety."

"Listen, we are just looking for answers to stop a killer," Rich said.

"And I empathize with you, Commissioner Stargold, but Gerald Spangler is not your man."

"How do you know that?"

"Because he is in a mental health facility receiving treatment for his combat related PTSD."

"When did he go in for treatment?

DuPont opened the folder in front of him.

"December 11th," DuPont said, closing the folder.

Next to Maguire, Angelo Antonucci began going through his case folder, looking for a particular document.

"Do you have a name for this facility?" Rich asked.

"Yes," DuPont replied smugly, "and before you ask, no, I won't give it to you. My client has the right to receive the treatment he deserves without being drawn deeper into the witch hunt that caused him to be there in the first place."

"Witch hunt?" Rich asked. "Is that what you think this is?"

"Isn't it?" DuPont replied. "My client was railroaded by the Army, made to be a scapegoat for doing his job. Then, when they couldn't get him, they put undue influence on the prior police commissioner who did their bidding and rescinded his application."

"And that, coupled with what we found in *his* apartment, doesn't make you wonder?" Rich asked.

"I wonder about a lot of things, Commissioner Stargold."

Antonucci nudged Maguire and pointed down to the paper. Maguire leaned over and began reading the entry, as DuPont watched them casually, but curiously.

"You said that your client has been in a treatment facility since the 11th," Maguire asked, looking up from the document.

"Yes," DuPont said stoically. "Why do you ask?"

Maguire slid the document out of the folder and across the table toward DuPont.

"Because we have a witness statement from his landlord that says he was at his residence on the morning of the 20th."

DuPont fished the eyeglass case from his jacket pocket. He put on his reading glasses and began scanning the report. A moment later he laid it on the table.

"This is what you're hanging your case on? The testimony of a seventy-two year old woman?"

"Are you saying she's wrong?"

"I'm saying that it's useless," DuPont replied. "For crying out loud, she's an old woman. As earnest as she might be, by the time this would go to trial I'd have her recalling that the last time she saw my client it was July 20th and he was going to the beach. You're going to have to do more than that."

"I get that this might be a game to you, Mr. DuPont, but you're not burying your people."

DuPont removed the glasses, placing them back in the case, and returned them to the inner jacket pocket.

"Commissioner Stargold, I am truly sorry for what you and your department have had to go through," the man replied. "I am a huge supporter of law enforcement and I cannot imagine how difficult this must be, but I won't abrogate my responsibility to my client just to satisfy your desire to find him guilty without doing your job properly."

"He's going to kill again," Rich said.

"Then I suggest that you work harder to identify the killer before that happens," DuPont replied coldly.

"Gerald Spangler isn't paying your retainer," Maguire said. "So you might want to inform whoever it is that the next time we knock it'll be with a federal warrant."

"And why would it be a federal warrant?"

"Because this case is being investigated jointly by the NYPD and the FBI for links to domestic terrorism," Maguire replied.

"Domestic terrorism?" DuPont scoffed. "That's a bit of a stretch isn't it?"

"A military trained operative targeting members of a police organization with weaponized aerial equipment. No, I don't think that's much of a stretch at all."

"Then I think our conversation is through here," DuPont said, as he rose from his seat. "Angela, it was good to see you again, even if you're on the wrong side."

"I'm sure we'll be in touch," Washington replied coolly.

The four of them watched as the man walked out of the conference room.

"Well that went well," Rich said, breaking the ice, as Maguire picked up the phone and dialed a number.

"Kurt, its Maguire, tell your people to amp it up. DuPont just left here."

Maguire listened for a moment as the man talked.

"Okay, great, keep me posted."

"What did Kurt say?" Rich asked.

"They've got a stingray deployed."

"What's a stingray?" Washington asked curiously.

"Stingray is IMSI-catcher," Maguire replied. "Basically it is a portable spy device that is able to track cellphone signals inside vehicles, homes and buildings. It acts as fake cell towers, which in turn allows us to pinpoint the location of a targeted device by sucking up its data, text messages, emails and cell-site information."

"Is that even legal?"

"Let's just say that it is *complicated*."

"How do they limit it to just Spangler's phone," she asked.

"They don't," Maguire replied. "They can't. As long as the stingray is active, it will intercept data off any other cellphone users in the area."

"Jesus, do you realize the implications in terms of the Fourth Amendment?"

Maguire shrugged his shoulders.

Yes, he was well aware of the implications, but at this moment all he could focus on was catching Spangler. He wasn't interested in anyone else's calls or texts, but that didn't mean others weren't. He knew for a fact that nothing was *secret* anymore. Technology had increased to the point that extraordinary measures now had to be taken to keep pace with it, and they didn't always operate within the framework of the law or the Constitution for that matter. If the private sector did it, it was a crime; if the government did it, it was for national security.

Would it eventually blow up? he thought. *Probably, the pendulum always swings back.*

If he thought about it too long it almost became a sci-fi scenario. Would there eventually be a utopian world; where the police no longer existed? Could you be arrested and charged with a crime, before it happened, just because you had *thought* about it?

If you said that to people most would laugh dismissively, but he also recalled laughing when he'd first read *1984* back in high school. Now, whenever he watched the evening news it made him think that some people had used Orwell's ominous novel as a *how-to-guide* instead of the warning it was intended to be. It always seemed that the innocent pursuit of the utopian *fairytale* inevitably led to the dystopian *nightmare*.

One thing was for certain, the future was going to be a minefield in terms of navigating the razor's edge between security and personal liberty.

"I guess that's why we have lawyers, Angie," Maguire said somberly.

"You and I both know they aren't the answer either," she replied. "Ethics are a hindrance when it comes to convictions or acquittals, depending on what side of the aisle you sit on."

"Case in point, DuPont is lying," Maguire replied.

"How do you know?" she asked.

"The surveillance video from the post office puts Spangler in Levittown on the 16th."

"You may be right, but he'll eat that up and spit it out," Washington said. "DuPont's right about dragging this out until everyone's memory is foggy. At the very least I would get someone out to that post office and document every step of that interaction; including how they positively identified Spangler. If they just got a signature without any actual ID DuPont will get it tossed out or have Spangler's *twin* appear in court."

"He's an only child," Rich said.

"So you say," Washington replied, "but I've seen Winston at work. If he needs to I'm sure he'd find a way to resurrect Spangler's father from the grave just to testify that his son has a twin."

"So now what?" Rich asked.

"Now we watch the phones," Maguire said, "and hope we turn up Spangler."

"Don't move to quickly on him," Washington said. "You're not going to get a chance to interrogate him, not with DuPont representing him. If you ask him anything more than his name and if he wants a cup of coffee, Winston will scream bloody murder to get it tossed."

"You have any suggestions?" Rich asked.

"DuPont has a lot to deal with, but it's not insurmountable. If you want to put this prick behind bars, you're better get something tangible to link him to the crimes, like the murder weapon."

"Why didn't I think of that," Rich said sarcastically.

"Hey, buddy, if it were easy, everyone would do it," Maguire said.

"Is it too much to ask to just catch a break on one case?" Rich asked.

"Ang, I want you to head back out to the post office and re-interview everyone involved. Dot the I's and cross the T's. I want the entire process they used to identify Spangler documented. Show them his photo and get a 100% ID on him. Reach out to JTTF before you go, have them send one of the postal inspectors with you, just in case the post master in Levittown starts getting cold feet."

"Yes, sir," Antonucci replied.

"While you're out there, stop by the apartment and do the same thing with the landlord. Lock her in on the last time she saw him and any other time after the 11th."

"I'll let you know what I find out," Antonucci said, as he got up and headed for the door.

"Do you need me for anything else, Commissioner?" Washington asked.

"No, Angie," Rich replied. "Thanks for everything."

"You're welcome," the woman replied.

A moment later Maguire and Rich stared at each other across the conference table.

"And then there were two," Maguire said with a laugh, as he checked his cellphone.

"You waiting on a call?" Rich asked.

"Actually, I've been trying to get in touch with Alex for the last couple of days, but it just keeps going to voice mail."

"You think she's dodging you after what happened?"

"No, I don't think so," Maguire replied. "Alex isn't like that."

"You try texting her? Maybe she doesn't feel like talking."

"Tried, but it said that it *failed*."

"Maybe they're having line problems up there. I mean it is New Hampshire and it is winter."

"I'm sure it's nothing," Maguire replied. "I'll give a call to the P.D. to double check; they'll know where their boss is."

"You ever miss being at the bottom of the food chain?" Rich asked. "No worries; just do your thing and go home?"

"Yeah, of course I do," Maguire replied. "There's something to be said about finishing up your set and swinging out for a few days of R&R without having the phone ring."

"I miss it too. I wonder when do we get it back?"

"We don't, Rich," Maguire said. "Unfortunately, we crossed that particular bridge the day we took this job and now we can't go back."

Rich got up and walked around the room, looking at the photos that adorned the walls. It was a photographic account of the history of New York City, both the good and the bad.

What would his legacy be? he wondered.

"It's the waiting I hate," he said softly. "Politicians wait, bureaucrats wait, they sit around while someone else does the work and they wait."

"You wanna work?" Maguire asked. "Come on, let's go."

"Where?"

"Times Square," Maguire replied. "I'm hungry; let's go get something to eat and we can go on some radio runs, maybe even do a car stop."

"You're not serious, are you?"

"Absolutely," Maguire said. "You want to be proactive, let's go be proactive."

"Can we do that?" Rich asked quizzically.

"You're the police commissioner; you can do anything you want. You might give the patrol supervisor a heart attack, but what's life without a little excitement."

"Let me get my coat."

Maguire chuckled. "That's the spirit."

CHAPTER FORTY-FIVE

Southampton, Suffolk County, N.Y.
Thursday, December 26th, 2013 – 6:41 p.m.

"You should have seen the poor sergeant's face when he realized that Rich was standing next to him," Maguire said, laughing as he recalled the incident.

They had just left Del Frisco's in midtown when a report of a 10-85, officer needs assistance, came over the radio at 5th Avenue and West 50th Street, just outside St. Patrick's Cathedral. A foot post had attempted to apprehend a purse-snatcher who'd decided he would rather fight than get arrested. Since they were only a block away, they had been the first car on the scene and had assisted the rookie officer in getting the suspect handcuffed. A moment later the rest of the cavalry, including the officer's sergeant, had arrived.

"Have you lost your mind," Mary said angrily.

"What?" Rich protested. "I'm the police commissioner, I was, uhm,… policing."

"Well, I'm the wife of the police commissioner and if you ever do that again I'm going to be the ex-wife," she said. "Do I make myself clear?"

"And what exactly were you doing while all this was going on?" Melody asked.

"Me?" Maguire said sheepishly, "oh, I was just happy that guy didn't try and run. I had too much steak for lunch."

"Uh huh," Melody said, clearly annoyed.

"Looks like someone's in trouble," Gen said with a snicker.

"*You have no idea*," Mary and Melody said simultaneously.

"Seriously, haven't you two grown up yet?" Mary asked. "Or are you going backward?"

"We're fine," Rich said, taking her hand in his. "I'm fine, don't worry."

"You have a family for crying out loud," Mary said.

"So do the rest of those guys out there, babe," Rich replied. "And everyone went home, safe and sound."

"Please don't do that again."

"I promise," Rich replied, leaning over and kissing Mary.

"See, all better," Maguire chimed in.

"I don't think so, Cowboy," Melody said. "We'll talk later, when there are no witnesses to *complicate* things."

"Seeing as how you are so keen to go out get *involved* in things, I think as punishment you need to go for a little ride with Ms. Sophie," Mary said.

"Not that, anything but that," Rich said.

"You should have thought about that before. Besides, she only has a few more days till we go back home."

"Fine, fine," Rich said, as he got up off the couch.

"That's the spirit, Rich," Maguire replied.

"I'm glad you think so, you're going with me."

"What? No, no," Maguire said defensively. "I wish I could help, but I got a ton of work to do."

"You're there for the crime, you're there for the time," Rich replied.

Maguire looked at Melody, then Mary, but got the same silent, smirking response.

"That's the last time I try and cheer you up, buddy," Maguire replied.

"Come on, it'll be fun," Rich said. "I'll get you some hot chocolate."

"I've seen Sophie drive; you'd better make it an Irish coffee."

"You boys have fun," Melody called out, as the two men left the room.

"You gave in too easy," Maguire said, as they made their way to the garage.

"I had an idea I wanted to discuss with you."

"Aren't we in enough trouble?"

"This is about Spangler."

"What are you thinking?"

"Kurt said the phones have been quiet at the Uncle's place, which means that Spangler is laying low. So what if we were to do something to draw him out?"

"Like what?" Maguire asked.

"Remember talking about doing the hiring program aimed at veterans?"

"Yeah."

"Well, I was thinking about doing an announcement tomorrow to that effect," Rich said. "We say that, in an effort to make the NYPD the most modern and capable police agency in the nation, we are looking at hiring returning vets with a wide range of skills, including protecting the skies of New York City from aerial threats."

"That's bound to hit a nerve, but I'm not sure how you think that will draw him out."

"By making it personal," Rich said. "We have Tom Cleary alert the media that we plan on holding a major press conference Monday at the new police academy construction site. Tell them that not only will the academy be state-of-the-art, but so will our recruit training. By giving military veterans special preference, it will give us the advantage we need in fighting the threats we face as a city. I'll even go on some of the weekend news shows and give them a tease."

"You think by giving him a target he's gonna bite?"

"Make it a big enough target,......."

"You?"

"And you," Rich replied. "Along with Tony Ameche and Nathan Hall."

"Do we get to bring the band with us?" Maguire asked. "You know, just in case we all go down with the ship?"

"We won't need a band," Rich said. "Besides I thought you liked fighting?"

"I like *winning*, there's a difference," Maguire replied. "Plus I don't like to fight fair."

"Neither do I," Rich said. "I know we deploy counter measures at the White House, to protect against any UAV's. I'm pretty sure that the guys over at the Technical Security Division also have some portable tricks they might be willing to share with us."

"It has to be foolproof," Maguire said.

"I agree, we control the environment," Rich replied. "We limit exactly how and where Spangler can approach from. Once we have him it will be game over. DuPont won't have a snowballs chance in hell of getting him off if we catch him in the act."

"I'll make some calls tonight and have ESU start working on a protection plan," Maguire said. "We'll do the standard presidential package with counter-snipers. If the Secret Service is willing to share their UAV counter-measures, I'll have our people fly down this weekend for a briefing."

"Sounds like we have a working plan," Rich replied.

"A *working* plan," Maguire said cautiously. "From now until the conference we had better iron out all the bugs or a working plan is all that it will be."

"I feel better doing something, even if it is just *planning*. It beats the hell out of sitting back waiting for someone else to dictate the time and place."

"Who's dictating what?"

Maguire and Stargold turned abruptly to see Sophie walking down the stairs.

"Me," Rich replied. "I'm dictating where we drive and how long we go for."

"Whatever, dad," Sophie said, as she brushed past him and made her way to the driver's side.

"Perhaps we have been looking at this all the wrong way," Maguire said, opening the rear passenger door.

"How do you figure?" Rich asked, as he got into the front passenger seat.

"Well, it gets us away from the ladies, and we have our very own designated driver."

Behind them the garage door began to open, revealing the lights of the black Suburban that was waiting in the courtyard.

"Really? They're coming too?" Sophie asked, as she put the car into reverse.

"Hey, I've seen you drive," Rich replied. "They're here in case I need a ride back from the ditch you get stuck in."

"That's so funny," Sophie said. "I'm a *great* driver."

She hit the gas a bit too hard, causing the car to lurch backward. Maguire and Rich felt their bodies slam forward; the motion arrested a split second later by their seatbelts.

Sophie let out a scream, as she hit the break and brought the car to a jerking halt.

"Better make that a double Irish coffee," Maguire said softly from the back seat, "and go very light on the coffee."

"Look at it this way," Rich said, as Sophie recovered and began backing out of the garage. "After tonight, everything else is going to look like a walk in the park."

"*Awesome*," Maguire said, glancing back at the relative safety of the Suburban following them.

So close, and yet so far away, he thought.

CHAPTER FORTY-SIX

Edgewater, Maryland
Saturday, December 28th, 2013 – 12:13 p.m.

Spangler carefully picked at the *food* on his plate the way a young child typically did, as they searched for the one *decent* morsel, among the sea of vegetables, which their mother had put in front of them.

He'd hit the wall in terms of creative MRE *cuisine* and was now longing for something substantive, like a juicy steak or even a real slice of pizza. It didn't help matters that he felt like a caged rat, jumping every time he heard an unusual *sound*. He pushed the plate away and got up from the table. Spangler sat down on the couch and picked up the remote, turning on the television set. He began scrolling through the channels, searching for something to occupy his time. It amazed him that, with so many networks available, there was rarely anything decent to watch.

He watched somberly as one station after the other seemed to play another *reality* show focused on the antics of a narcissistic *pseudo-celebrity*, whose only real claim to fame revolved around their adoring, almost cult-like, social media following. It seemed as if the current generation was willing to make anyone a star, as long as they were willing to post incessant *selfies* of themselves.

No wonder they refer to the television as an idiot box, he thought.

He was just about to turn it off when he spotted a familiar face being interviewed on one of the cable news channel weekend shows.

"New York City has always been considered to be one of the toughest proving grounds for anyone," Eric Bollen said, "but being police commissioner has to be at the top of the list."

"Well, I think the mayor has a tougher job, keeping all the pieces together, but I'll concede that it's probably in the top three," Stargold replied.

"Fair enough, but you've had to overcome some pretty significant hurdles over the last few months," the reporter said. "You've managed to thwart not one, but two terror attacks, within your first year."

"The real credit for that belongs to the Department as a whole," Rich replied. "I have the honor of being the commissioner of the greatest police department in the world, but the praise belongs to my people who do amazing work in a normally thankless job."

"I imagine that recent events must be taking a heavy toll."

"Police work has never been an easy job, Eric, and no one fully understands this better than the men and women of the NYPD. You don't do it for the accolades and you certainly don't do it for the outstanding salary."

"Yet a lot of people like to claim that police work doesn't rank high up on the list of deadly jobs when you compare it to others."

"That is true, especially when you compare it to the other industries like logging, commercial fishing, aviation or construction, but the difference is that in many instances the fatalities in those trades are accidental. In police work you have a target on your back from the moment you put on that uniform. You intentionally put yourself into harm's way knowing full-well that there is a chance you might not go home at the end of your shift."

"This last year has been particularly deadly for the NYPD," Bollen said, as he read from a sheet of paper on the desk in front of him. "You've lost five members, three this month alone."

"It is never easy losing someone, yet we take some margin of comfort in knowing that Inspector Kennedy continues to improve from her shooting each day."

"Inspector Kennedy was the last officer shot, correct?"

"Yes," Rich replied. "I just got word last night that she was transferred out of the intensive care unit."

"That is a gift we can all be thankful for this Christmas," Bollen said.

Spangler sat staring impassively at the television, even as the anger raged inside him.

What the hell did he know about being thankful? What hell had he been put through in his life that qualified him to speak on this subject?

"Are you any closer to finding the killer?" Bollen asked.

"It's been particularly frustrating, mostly due to the lack of any witnesses," Stargold replied, "but thanks to some very diligent police work we are narrowing our focus and hope to bring closure to this investigation shortly."

"You previously identified a man named Gerald Spangler as a person of interest, is he still the focus of the investigation?"

"Because this is an on-going investigation, which is actually very fluid at this moment, all I can say is that we are hoping to speak with Mr. Spangler soon regarding some information he might have."

Spangler hit the rewind button and replayed Rich's comment.

Fluid? he thought. *What could be fluid?*

In the Army he was taught that combat was frequently described as a fluid situation, meaning that conditions were highly unpredictable and likely to change from one moment to the next.

He wasn't in New York, so why were they hoping to speak with him soon?

The only thing that had changed was that his uncle had him holed up here while his attorney had gone to talk to *them*.

What had they talked about?

Spangler felt his stomach becoming queasy, as a wave of panic gripped him.

Had the attorney given him up?

Spangler had never liked attorneys, not after what they did to him. It didn't matter whether they were prosecutors or defense attorneys; they were all in it for themselves. His attorney knew the military had been lying and where had it gotten him?

Royally fucked, he thought.

"You're getting ready to open a new state-of-the-art training facility in Queens," Bollen said.

"Yes, we designed it with an emphasis in policing for the 21st century," Rich replied. "As you know, after the September 11th attacks, policing underwent a crash course in dealing with terrorism. Things which hadn't been on the radar of local police departments were now front and center. The most recent attempt earlier this year proved that we must take the training initiative."

"And you think military veterans are the answer?"

"I do," Rich replied. "In fact, I'm holding a press conference on Monday morning, at the site of the new police academy, where I will be making a big announcement concerning hiring plans for 2014."

"I gotta ask, Commissioner, can I get a sneak preview?"

"I don't want to get into to many details, but we are going to be looking at emphasizing hiring for returning veterans."

"Some would argue that it sounds like you're trying to militarize the police department."

"The truth is that police agencies have always been para-military organizations," Rich replied. "That's not a direful assessment, but a factually correct one. We have organizational structure, tactics, and training, which parallel our military in many ways. I believe veterans are a perfect fit for law enforcement."

"And you think that's necessary?"

"New York City remains the target of choice for many of the hardcore terror groups. We see their tactics being reworked and new threats emerging which are specifically focused on us. Who better to help us deal with these escalating threats than those who have served on the front lines? I believe that the deployment experience veterans bring to the table is something which cannot be replicated and will serve the citizens of this great city, should the need arise."

"Police Commissioner Stargold, it's always a pleasure talking to you," Bollen replied, extending his hand across the desk to shake Rich's. "Good luck and I look forward to hearing more of your ideas at Monday's press conference."

"Thank you, Eric."

"Next up, I talk to Federal Reserve Board Chairman......"

Spangler pressed the off button and watched the screen fade to black.

The queasiness was gone, as was the panic, replaced by anger. It was as if they were all mocking him. No one took him seriously, not the Army, not the NYPD, not even his uncle. He looked around the interior of the small cabin. He didn't doubt that his uncle loved him, but he was always trying to *think* things though. He had a tactician's mind, always probing for weakness, exploiting situations using surgical strikes.

Sometimes you just need a really big hammer, he thought.

Spangler was done waiting for the knock at the door. He'd rather be a hunted prey than a caged rat.

He picked up the Glock from the coffee table and went to pack his bags.

It was time to remind them again of who they were dealing with.

CHAPTER FORTY-SEVEN

Southampton, Suffolk County, N.Y.
Saturday, December 28th, 2013 – 9:22 p.m.

"So give me some good news, Julie," Maguire said into his cellphone, as he spoke to Deputy Chief Julie Preston, the commanding officer of the NYPD's Emergency Service Unit.

"I've got a crew at the Secret Service's facility in Beltsville," she replied. "After the Commissioner's phone call they were more than happy to help us out."

"Can it be done?"

"According to them, yes," she said. "They are going over the details with our people right now and will outfit them with the same military grade, very high dollar stuff they are using at the White House."

"Give me the bumper sticker version," Maguire replied.

"We will have several pieces of equipment in place that will give us virtually 360 degrees of protection," she replied. "Our backs will be exposed, because of the proximity of LaGuardia Airport, but since we will have the building behind us I don't envision that being a problem. The devices the Secret Service are loaning us utilize both traditional radar as well as audio technology that can *listen* for drones."

"What's the effective range?" Maguire asked.

"It's around three thousand meters for the radar component, and about a thousand for the audio."

"So that puts it well beyond what we could expect to see for a shot taken from a drone based platform?"

"Considerably beyond," Preston replied.

"Okay, so once we know it's coming, what do we do?"

"The units are equipped with video tracking that will give the operator the capability to see the object in real-time. In addition, it will also conduct a digital tracking analysis. Realistically speaking, with the ranges we are going to be dealing with we should be able to immediately pinpoint where the device took off from and scoop up our perp before he knows what's happening."

"Sounds pretty impressive," Maguire said, "but what do we do when we know it's in bound?

"The devices are also equipped with an RF disruption capability which will allow us to drop it out of the sky before it ever gets close enough to taking a shot," she replied. "They tell us these devices are 99.9% effective."

"Indulge me a bit, but what happens *if* we don't detect it till it is on top of us?"

"We are going to have rings of physical security in place out to three hundred feet from the dais," she replied. "The odds of someone getting into the secure area with a device are highly unlikely. But, just in case, we will also have computer countermeasures deployed which the Service tells us will jam any signals coming from the operating unit to the drone, rendering it inoperable."

"As much as I hate to admit it, I think we are turning a corner into the world of emerging threats."

"It scares me too," Preston replied. "We're dealing with one homicidal nut-job right now, but what happens when these things become more common place? Can we ever feel safe?"

Maguire picked up the glass of whiskey from his desk and took a sip, as he contemplated the grim overtones of her statement.

Could they ever feel safe again?

There was a paradigm shift occurring and everyone was trying to play catch-up; hoping that they could, before something terrible happened.

Crime had gone from a personal attack to a faceless one almost overnight. The implications of a lone wolf terrorist, sitting in a midtown hotel room, flying an explosives laden drone into Rockefeller Center during the tree lighting ceremony were staggering. Even worse, what if one was used to transport a weaponized WMD?

While most people acknowledged that commercially available drones had limited range and flight time, that didn't exactly bring out the *warm and fuzzies,* especially when you stopped to consider that you were on an island, with over a million inhabitants, that was less than two and a half miles at its widest point. An experienced operator could cover a lot of distance in under a half hour zipping through the skies.

Could any area truly be considered secure anymore?

You could control access on the streets, but how could you control the air immediately above it?

"When the dust settles, we are going to have to sit down and begin to brainstorm how we are going to protect ourselves in the future," he said. "The ramifications of this threat are staggering."

"I agree," she said. "I've been sitting here wondering what would happen if one of these things were used to drop weapons into Riker's Island."

"Or fly one with some explosives into the engine of a jet taking off from JFK."

"I think it's time we retire."

"I'll admit that the idea does sound good," he replied. "Call me tomorrow and update me on any new developments."

"I will," Preston said. "Have a good night."

"You too, Julie," Maguire said, as he ended the call.

He closed his eyes and leaned back in his chair, trying to shut off the alarm bells ringing in his head.

"Penny for your thoughts," he heard Melody say softly.

"You don't want to buy these thoughts," he replied.

Melody walked over to the desk and sat down on his lap, feeling his arms wrap around her waist. She picked up the glass and took a sip.

"Is it really that bad?" she asked.

"Theoretically, no," he replied.

"You've never been very good with theory," she replied.

"Theory never factors in the inevitable appearance by *Mr. Murphy*," Maguire replied.

"Maybe he won't show."

"That little fucker always shows up," Maguire said sarcastically.

"Can you just cancel?"

Maguire frowned, as he considered her suggestion. It wasn't that he hadn't thought about it, but he just couldn't come up with a viable option. They had been on defense up to this point and it was getting them nowhere. They had to do something that would give them an edge, or at least push Spangler back on his heels enough that he made a mistake.

"No," he said dejectedly.

"So what are you going to do?" she asked.

"The Secret Service is going to hook us up with the countermeasures they use at the White House," Maguire replied.

"Well, if it's good enough for the President," Melody said.

"I know what you're gonna say," he replied, "and you're right. If they're comfortable with it, we should be. I guess I'm just nit-picking shit."

"It's what you do," she said, kissing his cheek. "It's what makes you good at your job."

Maguire laughed.

"What's so funny?"

"I was just thinking about how different things were when I was in the teams."

"How so?" Melody asked.

"You ever see those boxes in the hallways that had the fire hose and axe, the ones that say 'in case of fire, break glass'?" he asked.

"Yeah, we have them at GDL."

"Well we were like the hose and the axe, but instead of *fire* it said *war*," Maguire replied. "We were *unleashed* on the problems and no one questioned the methods we used to get the job done. I can't do that now."

"If you could, what would you do?"

"Spangler would be lying on a steel table at the Morgue."

Melody sighed softly.

It was hard sometimes reconciling the man she loved. The best definition of Maguire was that he was a living dichotomy. On one hand he was a kind, warm-hearted, and gentle person who was great with children and made her heart skip a beat whenever he kissed her, but on the other hand she knew there was a darker side to him, one that had seen and done so many terrible things.

He didn't talk about it, but she knew that he had killed before. What bothered her more than anything was that it didn't really bother her. She loved him and would do anything for him. She rationalized that if he needed to kill someone, then they probably had it coming. Whatever he was, he was hers, and she had no intention of letting him go.

There was something overtly erotic about being with someone who was that dangerous. Something which appealed to her on a very deep, primal level.

She reached over, picking up the glass, and finished off the last of the whiskey. Then she repositioned herself on his lap, so that her legs straddled his, and wrapped her arms around his neck.

"Mrs. Claus has been very good and very patient," she said in a low, seductive voice. "Do what you *have* to do Monday, but do what you *need* to do tonight."

Maguire smiled and then stood up, holding onto her, as he felt her legs wrap around his waist. He felt her warm lips on his neck, kissing him, as he walked toward the waiting bed.

There would be plenty of time for thinking and re-thinking plans tomorrow, but for tonight there was only one thing that was on both of their minds.

CHAPTER FORTY-EIGHT

Bowie, Maryland
Sunday, December 29th, 2013 – 12:37 a.m.

Spangler crept slowly along the dense tree line, keeping his body low to the ground. He was like a predator stalking his unsuspecting prey, the landscape in front of him bathed in the eerie greenish hue of the night-vision goggles he was wearing.

He made his way up the embankment and took up a position behind a rocky outcropping, about a hundred feet west of where the surveillance van sat along an isolated access road. He moved aside one of the rocks and peered through the stone wall.

To the untrained eye, the vehicle was innocuous enough. It was just another utility company *eyesore* that littered the daily landscape. In this case, a telecomm company whose brightly colored decals, displayed prominently along its sides, might have been enough for the casual observer to dismiss it as being *harmless*, but, to the trained observer, the signs that this vehicle was anything but benign were readily apparent.

Theoretically, they could have been monitoring any of the dozen or so homes in this rural area, but only one residence had direct links to him, which made the occupants of the vehicle direct threats.

His first thought had been to dispatch the vehicles occupants, but he was unsure as to what he was going up against. He'd taken steps to minimize any heat signature his body was giving off, and he was fairly confident that his current snow-covered position afforded him protection from any technology-assisted prying eyes, but if they were using IR thermal imaging equipment, he'd never be able get close enough to the vehicle without being detected. Even if he was successful at eliminating the occupants, all it would take was one radio message to bring everything crashing down on him.

Spangler grudgingly conceded that, in this case, discretion was the better part of valor and began to slowly make his way back down the embankment. When he was sure that he was out of sight, he headed south through the woods, following the familiar stream that meandered through his uncle's property. Fifteen minutes later he found himself gazing at the home's stone façade, the light from his uncle's office burning brightly through the goggles.

He turned off the night vision device, placing it into his backpack, and allowed his eyes to re-acclimate the darkness. It was a strange feeling, losing his ability to see through the darkness, and it felt as if he had instantly gone from the predator to the prey. Spangler got up and began walking toward the rear patio. Inside the brightly lit office he could see his uncle sitting at his desk. It amazed him at just how little sleep the older man needed.

He began to approach the house slowly, ticking off in his mind the steps he had memorized by heart. Even as his foot touched the ground, beyond the invisible boundary, he knew that the motion sensors were setting off alarms inside the house. As if on cue, he saw his uncle react, hitting the button which locked the doors into the office and closed the drapes behind him. It effectively cut-off any potential entry into the now hardened location and removed any ability to see inside. Had the potential threat decided to just fire through the windows, spraying the interior with bullets, they would have found the same type of armored glass used at the White House.

At the same time, halogen lights came on, illuminating the grounds, and bathing the exterior of the home in brilliant light. Had he still been wearing the NV goggles, he would have been blinded by the intense lights, which was exactly their purpose.

Spangler walked over to the patio, setting his backpack on the ground and took a seat on one of the benches. Inside, he knew that his uncle would be scanning the video feeds to identify the threats. A moment later the majority of the lights began to turn off, until only the ones illuminating the patio remained on. A minute later he watched as one of the patio doors opened and his uncle stepped outside.

"What are you doing here, Jerry?" Max asked.

"I've come to say goodbye, uncle."

"What the hell are you talking about?" the man asked. "Where do you think you're going to?"

"I can't stay here. They're going to come for me and I can't be in that cabin waiting to be taken."

"Who's going to come for you, Jerry? No one knows you're here."

"They *know*," the young man said sarcastically. "That's why I didn't call. They're sitting right down the road tracing all your calls."

"Jesus H. Christ," Max said angrily. "Don't you think I already knew that? You may think you're smart, Jerry, but don't ever think for one moment that you're smarter than me."

"But if they're monitoring your calls, then they know...."

"Those federal boys hear what I *want* them to hear and nothing more. Your problem is that you spent so much time working *in* the system, that you actually believe that the system creates all the technological toys you enjoy. If government had to depend on itself to design something superior, we'd still be fighting wars with swords."

"I don't understand."

"Of course you don't, Jerry, and that's precisely the problem," Max said, as he turned and headed back into his office.

Jerry got up, grabbing his backpack, and obediently followed his uncle. Once inside the room he watched as the man hit the reset button on his desk and the drapes began to open back up. Then he walked over to the wet bar and poured himself a drink before sitting down on one of the couches, across from his desk.

In many ways, this was his uncle's personal *Oval Office*. The style and furnishings intentionally mimicked the office at 1600 Pennsylvania Avenue, as did the security features. The sound-proof walls were specially designed to prevent eavesdropping from the outside and there was even a secret door which led to a hard room and escape tunnel, although he had never been able to determine where on the grounds it opened at.

The older man loved the trappings of power and who better to emulate than the leader of the free world. In fact, the only major difference between the two offices was that, where the President had his presidential seal rug, Uncle Max had a USMC eagle, globe and anchor rug.

The young man took a seat on the couch, across from his uncle, and patiently waited for him to speak.

"Tell me something, Jerry," Max finally said. "What is more important, the light bulb or the light switch?"

"The bulb," the young man replied quickly.

"Why?"

"Because without the bulb you couldn't see."

"You can't see during the daytime?"

"Well, yeah, but…"

"Can you sleep with the lights on?" Max asked, taking a drink.

"Not really."

"What if you were trying to move undetected, would you prefer the lights on or off?"

"Off," the man said softly, realizing how he'd been misled into answering too quickly.

"So you admit the light switch has at least an equal position of importance in the grand scheme of things."

"Yes, sir."

"Granted, the technology in that van parked down the road is cutting edge," Max said, "but that doesn't mean that it can't be *tamed* if someone had the proper switch. That's where the real power lies. Not in the technology, but in the ability to control the technology."

"So our conversations can't be detected?"

"Their IMSI's work by being the bigger cell tower," Max said, "causing unsuspecting cellphones to connect to their stronger signal. The designers of the technology understood that, like all things, it would eventually be misused and put safeguards, a *switch* if you will, into place to protect their conversations. Let's just say that they also have a vested interest in keeping my conversations discrete as well."

"Won't that look suspicious?"

"It would, which is why I still allow them to listen in on certain conversations. For all intents and purposes I am just a concerned uncle looking to help my wayward nephew."

"So they don't know I'm here?"

"No, I was very specific in my conversations with DuPont that I was just trying to establish that you were represented by counsel early-on, so that if they did find you they couldn't question you without him being there."

"I can't stay in that cabin anymore, I'm going stir crazy."

"I don't think you fully appreciate the seriousness of this, Jerry. Either you follow orders or there are only two outcomes. One, you end up in jail or two, you end up dead. Neither of which works out well for either of us."

"I'm not afraid to die," the young man said, his voice laced with indignation.

"*Goddamnit*, you little shit, this isn't about you or your stupid little game of vendetta," Max yelled. "Do you honestly think that anyone gives a rat's ass about you? I have multi-billion dollar projects in the works and I'll be damned if I'm going to let you fuck up one red cent of that, which is exactly why you need to disappear."

"I'm not going back to the shack," Jerry protested. "I can't breathe in there."

"You're not going back there," Max replied, finishing his drink and setting it down on the coffee table.

Jerry watched as his uncle got up and walked over to the desk. He tapped some keys on the laptop computer and then began writing on a notepad. When he was done he tore the paper off the pad, then reached into one of the desk drawers and removed a manila envelope. He got up and walked back over, handing them to his nephew.

"What's this?"

"It's your new home," the man replied. "Those are the coordinates to fifteen hundred acres of rugged country living just northwest of Creighton, South Dakota."

"They'll trace it," Jerry said. "They'll find me. Eventually they'll begin digging through your records and show up."

"That's the beauty of this," Max replied. "It doesn't belong to me. It's courtesy of a client of mine from Saudi Arabia. My understanding is there isn't much to it, just a primitive cabin, but it beats the inside of a jail cell. Inside the envelope are the keys to an olive drab green Hummer parked in a lot in Greenbelt, the location is written down on a paper inside. In the back is a steel security locker with two-hundred and fifty thousand in cash along with new ID. There's also a suppressed SR-25 rifle that should help you catch your dinner if the money runs out."

"You don't get it," Jerry said. "I can't leave, I'm on a mission."

"Your mission is *over*," Max said dangerously. "Either you make the decision to end it now, and walk away, or I will."

Anger flashed across the young man's face, but it was no match for the cold lethality that stared back at him. There was no actual choice in his uncle's words. He knew all too well what his uncle was capable of and he also knew that the man never bluffed.

"Fine," he replied dejectedly.

Max smiled, easing the tension that had gripped the room a moment earlier.

"That's my boy," he said warmly. "Trust me, you're gonna love the *Cornhusker* state. It'll be just like going home."

"It's still not fair."

"For Christ's sake, Jerry, you've made your point already," Max said, as he got up from the couch and headed back over to the bar to refill his drink. "Believe me when I say that I'm saving you from yourself. If you kept this little game of yours going you were going to end up in a body bag. The cops don't have enough to charge you *now*, so let it go and fade into obscurity."

Max lowered the bottle to the glass tumbler just as the .9mm *Hydra-Shok* round entered his lower back, the force slamming his body into the wet bar. The small projectile struck between the T11 and T12 vertebrae, severing his spinal cord and leaving him paralyzed from the waist down.

Some would call it a cowards attack, shooting a man in the back, but Jerry would argue that it was the ultimate compliment. His uncle was an incredibly dangerous man, armed or not, and Jerry knew that his only chance was to catch him at a moment of vulnerability. He had no intention of halting his mission for anyone, but he also knew that he could not continue it if he had to constantly look over his shoulder for his uncle. There could be only one survivor in this particular game and he knew that his shot had to be perfect.

Jerry got up and walked across the room toward the man.

His face had gone pale and his breathing was raspy, as he struggled to pull his lifeless lower-half along the floor, leaving a trail of blood through his beloved Marine Corps rug. The hard-as-nails demeanor was gone and he didn't seem as threatening now.

Perhaps that's the shock, he thought.

Even severely wounded he knew the old man was trying to make his way toward the desk where he kept his Colt .45 pistol.

"Always the warrior," Jerry said softly. "I hope you understand that it wasn't personal. I truly believe you would have stopped me from completing my mission and I just couldn't allow that."

The man stopped and looked up at his nephew. He coughed and bright red, frothy blood gushed from his mouth.

"Semper Fi, Uncle Max," as he leveled the pistol, taking aim at the man's head, and fired a shot to end his suffering.

CHAPTER FORTY-NINE

Greenbelt, Maryland
Sunday, December 29th, 2013 – 4:11 a.m.

Spangler sat in his car, at the far end of the metro parking lot, keeping the Hummer under observation. When he was sure that no one else had an interest in the vehicle, he exited his car, grabbing his bags and made his way over to it.

Fifteen minutes later he was in a desolate part of the Beltway Plaza Mall parking lot running a diagnostic check for any tracking devices. Once he was sure that the vehicle was clean, he inspected the contents of the security box in the back. True to his word, his uncle had secured him all new identification to go along with the cash he had mentioned. He glanced around; making sure no one was looking, and then removed the SR-25 rifle.

Spangler popped the protective covers and took a quick glimpse down the scope. A moment later he had the cross-hair reticle placed on the head a middle-aged man pumping gas into his Prius at the gas station about a half a mile away.

"Good morning," he whispered quietly.

The gun was a hybrid sniper / assault rifle that took a match grade barrel 7.62 NATO and mounted it on a semi-automatic, high-capacity magazine receiver. He closed the scope covers and placed the rifle back in the box. Then he inspected the silencer and the magazines.

The rifle would certainly come in handy for hunting prey of both the four and two leg varieties.

Spangler closed the back door and got into the vehicle. He still had a lot of things to consider and he was quickly running out of time.

CHAPTER FIFTY

College Point, Queens, N.Y.

Monday, December 30th, 2013 – 12:32 p.m.

The caravan of Suburban's pulled onto 28th Avenue where they were quickly ushered past the security checkpoint and into the construction site.

Maguire glanced out the passenger window at the throng of reporters and cameras set-up in front of the makeshift dais.

"Looks like it's show time," he heard Rich say.

"I'm just glad you're the one who's *starring* in this little production," Maguire said sarcastically.

"No guts, no glory," Rich replied, as the vehicles came to a stop.

Maguire bit his tongue, as he opened passenger door and stepped outside.

The sun shone brilliantly in the afternoon sky, making it feel much warmer than the actual temperature. He watched as Detective Amanda Massi, a member of his security detail, walked toward him.

"How are we looking, Amanda?"

"Everything is locked down," she replied. "Communications sent down one of their big temporary headquarters vehicles. Chief Preston is waiting for you there."

"Thanks," he replied. "Any problems so far?"

"No, everything has been running smooth. DCPI got the media folks squared away. The construction foreman gave his people an early lunch and told them to go home."

"At least we don't have to worry about jackhammers going off during the P.C.'s little speech."

"That wouldn't be good."

"Where's Mike?" he asked, referring to Massi's partner, Detective Mike Torres.

"He's with the car," she replied, pointing toward the SUV parked behind the construction trailer.

"Well, we better go see what the folks from ESU have to say."

Maguire walked over to the THV and stepped inside the trailer. There was a flurry of activity as the officers inside coordinated security with the posts assigned around the academy complex. In the far corner, Julie Preston sat talking to an ESU captain.

"What do you have for me, Julie," Maguire asked, as he took a seat at the table.

"Everything's in place," she replied. "The countermeasures we spoke about the other day are deployed and have been tested."

"And?"

"100% detection," Preston said. "We tested them three times."

"How close did it get?" Maguire asked.

"I had them go out to the northbound service road of the Whitestone. Even with all the ambient noise from the expressway, we still got a hit the moment the drone went active."

"Did it disable it?"

"It did," she replied. "I also had them run a test north and south of here, same results."

"What about our backdoor?"

"That's where we set up the computer countermeasures."

"What happens if we do manage to lock onto one?"

"I have the A-Team pre-positioned south of us on 32nd Avenue and Truck's 9 and 10 will cover the northern part, west and east of the Whitestone respectively," Preston replied. "As soon as we get a location, they'll move in."

"I know you have, but I'm going to ask anyway, what about a flesh and blood shooter?"

"Typical presidential package," she replied. "We have counter-sniper teams providing over-watch and a counter-assault team in the wings. The press has been vetted, patrol is covering the surrounding rooftops and the folks from Intel are watching everyone."

"Guess there's not much more we can do, but cross our fingers."

"I'd say we are as close to golden as we can get."

Maguire looked down at his watch.

"Remind me how golden we are in thirty-five minutes."

"All we can do is plan for everything and then do the best we can."

"Like the man said, 'the only easy day was yesterday.'"

"Sounds like a wise man."

"You don't know the half of it, Julie," Maguire said, as he got up from the table. "I'll catch up with you later."

He made his way back outside and cautiously eyed the scene. His eyes darted back and forth from the rooftops of the nearby commercial buildings to the high-rise apartments on the other side of the expressway. It was something he'd done hundreds of times before when he'd worked in Intel, looking for the one thing that seemed *out of place*. Unfortunately, he only had two eyes and there were countless potential threats. It was for that reason he despised outdoor events.

His weighty thoughts were scattered by the sound of a ship's bell calling from Flushing Bay, about a block to the west of where he was standing. It was a familiar sound that brought back memories of another time and place. Almost immediately he was thrown back in time, to the *grinder* at the Naval Special Warfare Training Center in Coronado, California, where he had gone through BUD/S.

The grinder was the legendary concrete and asphalt courtyard, just outside the quarterdeck doors, where potential SEAL's performed their calisthenics. Just off to the edge of the grinder hung a shiny, brass ship's bell. Everyone who'd gone through BUD/S had an intimate relationship with *the Bell*. It wasn't particularly imposing at first, but it soon became one of the most dreaded aspects of SEAL training, hanging there silently taunting the recruits who were pushed far beyond their breaking point.

The Bell was affixed to one of the support columns by a braided rope. First-phase BUD/S classmen had the responsibility to make sure that bell was kept clean and shiny to the point that it reflected like a mirror. At one point, everyone in the class had touched it so that each and every one of them understood its importance and significance. At the end of their training, each candidate would ring the Bell to signify that he had *made it*, but ringing the bell before the end of training had an equally powerful, but much more gloomy meaning.

Drop on Request, or DOR, meant that you'd had enough and were done. If you reached the point where you couldn't take it, when the training just became too brutal, all you had to do was walk up to the Bell and ring it three times. That was it. It was a one-way street straight out of BUD/S. It was the promise of hot food, cold beer and a warm bed. It ended the pain, it ended the cold, it ended the sleepless nights, and it ended your chance to become a Navy SEAL.

As a reminder to those who remained, the green training helmets of each candidate who quit, their names stenciled in white across the front, lined the edge of the grinder. The line grew longer with each passing day. By the time *Hell Week* hit there were over a hundred helmets staring back at him.

Most people think SEAL's possess some super-human physical strength that allows them to make it through BUD/S, but the truth is that ninety percent is about mental strength. Candidates just decide that they are too cold, too sandy, too sore or too wet to go on. It's the mind that gives up first, not the body. Hell Week was designed to weed out the candidates who couldn't cut it. It was five and a half days of cold, wet brutally tough operational training on less than four hours of sleep. It tested the limits of physical toughness and mental endurance, but above all it tested your determination and desire.

For those that endured, and fought the urge to ring the Bell, there was no mercy, no reward. Maguire remembered one night while they were doing *log PT*, an innocuous name for a particularly cruel training evolution that required seven cold and saltwater soaked men to carry a hundred and fifty pound log over their heads, while running up and down the beach. As the hours ticked by the log only became heavier, until, in the middle of the evolution, one of their boat crew DOR'd, scrambling up the sand dune to ring the bell. For the rest of them, there was no replacement crew member, no additional time to recover, just the cold admonition of Instructor Gray who simply said: *'He's dead; you're still alive, keep moving.'*

That was a pivotal moment for the rest of his team and it became their silent mantra that helped them get through Hell Week: *We're not dead, we can't quit.*

"You okay, Boss?"

Maguire shook off the memory and glanced over at Amanda Massi who was standing next to him.

"What? Oh, yeah," Maguire replied, "I'm fine. I was just taking a little mental walk down memory lane."

"They're getting ready to start the press conference."

"Okay, stay sharp," he said, as he made his way toward the dais."

CHAPTER FIFTY-ONE

College Point, Queens, N.Y.
Monday, December 30th, 2013 – 1:03 p.m.

The key to not getting caught was to always have a fluid offensive. If your opponent couldn't anticipate what your next move would be, then they were kept to a perpetual game of defense.

The sleek black rifle sat atop the dining room table, its stock resting comfortably on the polished mahogany wood, while its barrel was held aloft by the adjustable metal bipod legs.

From its vantage point in the 11th floor apartment, it held a commanding view of the construction site on the opposite side of the expressway.

From a place you cannot see, comes a sound you will never hear.

Most people looked down on sniping as some detached form of killing, but the truth was that it was the most intimate of kills; at least for the one who pulled the trigger. It was like a well-choreographed, lethal ballet.

Long before a sniper ever takes a shot, there are countless variables that must be factored in. Range to the target, wind speed and wind direction, target movement, light source, even temperature, as well as barometric pressure, factor into the equation. So many variables had to be considered, long before the finger ever squeezed the trigger.

Preparing to take the shot required an intense amount of mental and physical preparation, a fact which was completely lost on the elderly couple laying dead on the floor behind the table.

Oh well, not every performance could have an audience.

Slowly the stock rose up, coming to rest in the shoulder pocket.

Looking through the rifle's scope put everything in its proper perspective. There was only the target reticle and the target; nothing more, nothing less.

Breathe in, breathe out.

With all the mental preparation done, the crosshairs slowly lined up on the target which was just less than eight hundred meters away.

Slowly, the finger began to tighten on the trigger.

Breathe in, breathe out, and hold.

●●●

"Ladies and gentlemen, I want to thank you all for taking the time to brave the elements and stand out here in the cold with me," Rich said to the throng of reporters gathered in front of him, "while I offer you the vision for the NYPD going forward."

It was an even bigger turnout than he had actually expected. Not only were all the local print and television outlets in attendance, but so were most of the major cable stations as well. Unfortunately, well attended didn't mean that it was friendly.

Upon arriving, his Deputy Commissioner of Public Information, Tom Cleary, had quickly pulled him to the side to prepare him for the fact that many were lining up hardball questions concerning the militarization of the police.

There had been several incidents around the country, involving law enforcement, which had sparked protests. Images of heavily armed men in tactical gear and riding in armored vehicles had been exploited by the media. It presented a chilling, if not entirely accurate, image of the police which community activists, and many in the *social justice community*, were quick to exploit.

While there was certainly merit to many of the complex issues facing the country, many of the *peaceful* protests were being co-opted by outside factions, whose sole purpose was to foment violent altercations with the police.

Inevitably the protests spiraled out of control, often as the result of local government officials wishing to give the protestors their *space*. Molotov cocktails were routinely hurled at law enforcement before being unleashed on commercial establishments, which were often looted before they burned to the ground. Most of these incidents occurred in the poorest neighborhoods, which were already facing an extremely difficult financial burden.

When the sun finally rose, and the damage was fully assessed, the socio-economic situation only became bleaker.

Despite exercising an amazing amount of restraint, the police were quickly labeled as being the aggressors. It didn't matter that they were the target of bottles, bricks, and worse, all that mattered to the media was the image of heavily armed men in their tactical gear squaring off against the impoverished masses.

In the world of journalism, tragedy always sold better than joy.

"As you are all very well aware of, the world we live in is a dangerous place. Something I don't think any of us envision changing anytime soon. As much as I, and everyone gathered here with me today, would like it to be different, the truth is we have a responsibility to the citizens of this great city to do everything in our power to protect them. Just as the threats we face have evolved, so must our officers and their training."

As Rich continued his speech, Maguire scanned the horizon, just beyond the group of people in front of them, his eyes darting back and forth, searching for the glint of metal against the clear blue December sky.

His years of doing dignitary protection had taught him to always look for the one thing that was *out of place*. It could be something as overt as a jacket on a warm day or as innocuous as a dispassionate glance at an otherwise festive event. He'd spent countless hours walking rope lines with politicians, willing to put himself into harm's way if needed. When you were up-close and personal, you always wanted to see the hands, but this was a different animal altogether.

"New York City has never been a stranger to terrorism," Rich continued. "Whether it was the Wall Street bombing in the 1920's, the *Mad Bomber* in the 1940's, domestic terrorism in the 70's or Islamic terrorists today, this city has always had a target on it. As the threat evolves, so must we. Those who are inclined to attack us only have to be right once, while we have to be right one hundred percent of the time."

"As police commissioner I have to explore every option available to me to keep this city safe, which is why I directed Chief of Personnel, Nathan Hall, to establish a new hiring program that will focus on recruiting members of our armed services to help us deal with these evolving threats."

Almost immediately the gathering of reporters erupted into a chorus of questions.

"Yes, Arnold," Rich said, pointing to a man off to his left.

"Commissioner Stargold are you aware of the recent report by Doctor Claude Richmond of UC Berkley which took exception to the practice of hiring returning vets, stating, and I quote 'it is unconscionable for us to expect that soldiers, trained to be combat killers, can be trusted to demonstrate the restraint required of law enforcement officials."

"Arnold, that's a pretty inflammatory statement and one that I would happily take exception with," Rich replied. "Over the course of my law enforcement career I have had the opportunity to work with a number of veterans, including Commissioner Maguire, who are some of the finest officers I have ever known. I would suggest that Doctor Richmond leave his theoretical world from time to time and see what the rest of us are doing in the real one."

Rich selected another reporter from the crowd.

"Commissioner, Paul Ellis, from the Times. What would you say to the people who argue that this is just the latest escalation in the militarization of the police," the man said asked.

"I'd say that, like Dr. Richmond, they are woefully ill-informed on the subject," Rich replied. "Honestly, it often amazes me how people can make such baseless accusations and you folks in the media seem happy to parrot them."

"To be fair, Commissioner, I'm just pointing out the concerns...."

"The concerns of *whom*, Paul?" Rich asked with a tinge of annoyance. "The self-proclaimed experts in academia and politics? The ones who have never worn a uniform, but know exactly how things should be done? I often find myself amazed by this phenomenon, but then I am reminded that this type of ignorance is not new. My esteemed predecessor, Theodore Roosevelt, gave a speech which contained a passage that became known as the *man in the arena*. I would highly suggest that you should all read it. The truth is, that throughout history, law enforcement has always been forced to evolve. It wasn't an unprovoked escalation on the part of the police, but a direct response to the threats they faced. I wonder if the same folks, pointing their fingers at the police, would like the fire department to go back to using buckets?"

"Yes, but you have to admit that there seems to be a growing disproportional use of force...."

"Paul," Rich replied, cutting the man off, "you know what's really disproportional? I'll tell you, lack of personal responsibility. Everywhere we turn we see someone making excuses for why something happened. A violent mob burns down a store; *they're just frustrated they can't find a job*. The same mob loots a store; *they're just venting their frustrations at the system*. We have some people that have turned excuses for bad behavior into a cottage industry. Maybe, just maybe, if the parents of some of these *disaffected* youth actually started taking a more proactive role in raising responsible children, instead of letting them act like marauding thugs, we wouldn't need to worry about equipping our police to deal with them."

Maguire raised his hand to his face, as if to rub his chin, and softly whispered: "*easy there, tiger*."

Rich turned away from the man and pointed toward a blonde-haired woman in the front row.

"Last question, please."

"Commissioner, Janice Edwards, from CNN. Are the recent deaths within your department one of the reasons you are adopting this policy?"

"No, those shooting are under investigation and we are exploring a variety of different things, but they do underscore the need for us to take a more proactive role in the future. Crime will always continue to evolve and we must do everything we can to not only keep up with it, but to do our best to stay ahead of it and that is precisely the reason why I believe we need to focus on hiring our veterans. Thank you all for coming out and Commissioner Cleary will respond to any additional questions you might have."

"Well that went well," Maguire said with a laugh, as they walked off the dais and headed toward the waiting SUV.

Falling in silently behind them were Amanda Massi and Sergeant David Walcott, the head of Rich's security detail.

"I hate the fucking press," Rich said. "Every one of those *sonsofbitches* should have to spend a week in a radio car before they are allowed to report a story on the police."

"Yeah, good luck with that," Maguire said. "For now you might want to change your cellphone to an unlisted number or at least block the city hall extensions."

"Fuck it, it was worth it just to wipe that smug look off his face," Rich replied. "No one wants to talk about personal responsibility when it's so much easier to pin the blame on the cop."

"Hey, you're preaching to the choir, brother, but on a side note, no Spangler."

"Jesus, I got so caught up with them that I'd completely forgotten why we were here," Rich said. "I'm not sure whether I should be elated or disappointed."

"Well, I guess we go back to the old drawing board."

"You want to ride back with me?" Rich asked.

"No, you go ahead, I need to talk to Julie," Maguire said. "Plus I have a two o'clock meeting with Matt Pagano over at Port Authority to discuss Eliza Cook's arrival."

"Okay, you go have fun," Rich said, as his security man opened the Suburban's door.

"I'll talk to you later, buddy,"

"Hey," Rich called out.

Maguire turned around to see his friend smiling broadly.

"I told you that we didn't need a band."

As Maguire formulated his sarcastic response, he watched as the center of his friend's chest erupted.

CHAPTER FIFTY-TWO

Flushing, Queens, N.Y.
Monday, December 30th, 2013 – 2:23 p.m.

Maguire sat in the small, windowless office inside New York Hospital staring blankly into the Styrofoam coffee cup in his hands.

Across from him, Massi sat silently, keeping a watchful eye on him, while Torres guarded the door. In the corridors outside the room, a phalanx of cops had gathered which threatened to shut down the hospital's emergency operations. Even now, non-life threatening cases were being re-directed to other area medical facilities.

No matter what he did to try and will away the surreal images in his mind, they returned, making him feel like some helpless character in a horror movie who could escape the villain.

In the blink of an eye, the mischievous smile had vanished from Rich's face, replaced by one of pain and confusion, as his body slumped forward. In an instant he felt the familiar reaction, the so called *fight or flight* response, begin to kick in. Even before the security team could react, Maguire was racing forward, reaching Rich just as his body hit the hard, dirt road.

The physical damage was extensive, a fact clearly borne out by the man's now crimson colored shirt. He took his friend up in his arms, holding him tightly, as the protection detail closed in around them.

"Rich, Rich!" he screamed, as he watched his friends eyes roll backward.

The scene around him erupted as Torres pulled the Suburban ahead of them, providing cover as several ESU tactical medics arrived to render aid to their fallen boss.

"Commissioner, we have to go," Massi said, tugging at Maguire's arm.

He started to protest, until one of the medics forcefully said, "You need to go *now*, sir."

Maguire conceded that he was only in the way. He could do nothing more for his friend than what the medics were already doing. He lowered his friend to the ground and got up, feeling Massi guiding him to the waiting SUV with urgency. Torres already had the door opened and she pushed him inside, climbing into the seat next to him. A moment later he felt the vehicle lurch forward as it sped out of the lot.

"What the fuck just happened?" Torres said, as the SUV barreled down Ullmer Street. "Where are we going?"

"Head to the One-Oh-Nine," Amanda replied. "Are you all right, sir?"

"Yeah," Maguire said, wiping his bloody hands on his shirt. "Yeah, I'm fine."

Massi reached over and grabbed the radio mic. "Car 2 to Central, emergency transmission."

"Go ahead with transmission Car 2."

"Show us responding to the One-Oh-Nine, Central, and have them secure the perimeter."

"10-4, Car 2, notifying them now."

Moments later the SUV sped past the RMP's, which blocked off the surrounding streets, and pulled into the precinct's parking lot.

Massi ushered Maguire through the command's back door where a somber looking lieutenant met them and led them to the C.O.'s office.

"Give me a few minutes, will you Amanda," Maguire said, as he settled down behind the desk.

"I'll be right outside, if you need anything."

"Just find out what hospital they are taking him to and tell Chief Ameche I want an update in five minutes."

"Yes, sir," she replied, closing the door behind her, as she left the room.

Maguire pulled the cellphone from his pocket and placed the call, listening as it rang.

"Hey, Cowboy, how'd it go?" Melody said cheerfully.

"Mel, Rich has been shot," Maguire said.

Almost immediately he heard her let out a loud gasp.

"Oh my God," she exclaimed, "what happened? Are you okay?"

"I'm okay, I don't know," he replied. "We were done with the press conference and he got shot. I don't have anything else."

"Is he going to be okay?"

Maguire stared at the oversized precinct map, which hung on the wall across from him, as he contemplated the answer.

"I don't know."

Silence gripped the phone line as they both dealt with the emptiness of his answer.

"Does Mary know?" Melody asked.

"It just happened," Maguire replied.

"Do you want me to come?"

"I don't even know where they have taken him. They brought me to the One-Oh-Nine in Flushing and I'm waiting for an update. As soon as I know something more I'll let you know."

Just then there was a knock at the door.

"Babe, I have to go."

"I love you," she said.

"Love you too," he said and ended the call. "Come in."

The door opened and Massi stepped inside.

"The ambulance is on its way to New York Hospital and Chief Ameche is holding for you on line two," she said, pointing toward the desktop phone.

Maguire picked up the handset and hit the blinking button.

"Tony, what the hell happened out there?" Maguire asked. "How'd we miss it?"

"According to ESU we didn't," Ameche said. "None of the countermeasures detected anything."

"How is that possible?"

"It looks like the shot came from one of the apartment buildings," the man replied. "They got a hit off one of their *ShotSpotter* devices and they are hitting the building now."

"Fuck," Maguire said angrily. "Listen, I really need you to handle this. I'm heading over to the hospital now."

"You do what you have to do," Tony said. "I'll take care of things out here and keep you updated."

"Thank you," Maguire replied. "I'll talk to you later."

"Commissioner, I just spoke to the mayor's detail. He's still on vacation, but they are making arrangements with Aviation to pick him up and bring him back to the city."

"What about Commissioner Stargold's wife?"

"She's been notified," Amanda said. "Monsignor O'Connor went over with the security detail to pick her up and bring her to the hospital."

Maguire swallowed hard, then got up and headed toward the door.

"Get in touch with Inspector Martin. Have him notify Luke and Pete to make arrangements to pick-up Melody and bring her to the hospital."

"I already took care of it, Boss," she said. "They're on their way."

"What would I ever do without you, Amanda?"

He was brought back to the present moment by the cellphone ringing on the coffee table in front of him.

"Maguire," he said.

"I just heard about the shooting," Kurt Silverman said. "Is he okay?"

"I don't know, Kurt," Maguire replied. "He's in surgery right now."

"*Unfuckingreal*," Silverman said. "What happened?"

"We'd just finished up the press conference and were getting ready to leave when he got shot."

"You think it was Spangler?"

"He's at the top of the list," Maguire replied. "Have your people knock on the uncle's door and advise him that it would be in his nephew's best interest to speak with us."

"You know he's going to push back, tell us to speak to his attorney."

"Then you have them pass on a personal message to him, from me," Maguire replied. "Tell him that he either brings him in on his own or that he can start picking out the suit that he wants to bury him in."

"I'll let them know," Kurt replied.

He understood the anger and frustration.

"Is there anything else I can do?" he asked.

"Pray," Maguire said somberly.

"I will," Silverman replied, "and if there is anything you need, you have the entire New York field office at your disposal."

"Thank you, Kurt. Call me when you hear something."

"Will do."

Maguire ended the call and laid the phone back on the table.

"God, I need coffee."

"I'll get it for you," Amanda said.

"No, I need to do something," Maguire replied. "Sitting here isn't helping."

"Then I'll go for a walk with you," she said.

Once outside the room, it seemed as if he was walking through a gauntlet.

There were upward of a hundred uniformed and plainclothes officers lining the hallway. Every eye turned to look at him, a mix of confusion, empathy, anger and sadness on their faces. He understood it all, had lived it himself, but now they were looking to him as the one who was supposed to have the answers, to make sense of the senseless, and he didn't.

Just then there was a flurry of activity as the emergency room doors opened and mass of people came rushing through. They paused for a moment, getting their bearings. In the middle of the throng, Maguire spotted Mary. She was incredibly pale and appeared to just be hanging on by a thread.

She spotted Maguire and immediately broke from the group, rushing toward him. He ran to her, catching her just as she collapsed in his arms.

For a moment the sound of the otherwise hectic emergency room was silent, except for the sound of Mary's grief stricken sobbing.

CHAPTER FIFTY-THREE

Bowie, Maryland
Monday, December 30th, 2013 – 3:11 p.m.

FBI Investigative Specialist Mark Szabo sat in the back of the surveillance van as his partner diligently monitored the exotic, and extremely expensive, audio equipment.

This was the side of surveillance that no one ever saw. Hollywood never made movies about the countless hours of mind-numbingly boring surveillances that failed to produce anything more substantive than hash brown casserole recipes, cheating spouse gossip, or little Johnny's failing grades. Most of the time it was a strain to just remain alert coupled with not ingesting enough caffeine to cause any serious health consequences.

They had been conducting the current observation for the past four days and up till now had very little to show for it. He just hoped that something happened soon, as he had a much needed tropical vacation coming up in three weeks.

He felt the vibration of the cellphone in his pocket and took it out, examining the screen for the caller ID information.

"Hey, heads up, it's the office," he said, as he answered the call. "Szabo."

"Hey, Mark, it's Dom," the voice on the other end said. "You guys have any activity there?"

Dom was Assistant Special Agent in Charge Dominick Corey, their boss in the Special Surveillance Group.

"No, it's been dead on this end since we took over."

"Is Spangler home?" the man asked.

"According to Dominguez and Richardson he is," Szabo replied. "They said he arrived home at 10 o'clock last night. No one has come or gone since. Why?"

"We got a request from the NYPD to have a word with him."

"That sounds grim."

"Someone shot their police commissioner," Corey replied.

"What do they want us to tell him?" Szabo asked.

"I think they want us to rattle his cage a bit. Convince him it is in the best interest of his nephew's long-term health to turn himself in."

"Lucky us,"

"Just keep monitoring the lines," Corey said, "I have a team in route to speak with him, let me know if he leaves before they arrive or if he makes any calls after they are gone."

"Roger that,' Szabo replied, ending the call.

"What was that all about?"

Szabo turned in his chair to look at his partner, Frank Boone.

"Boss wanted to know if Spangler was home. He's sending some agents down to have a chat with him."

"About what?"

"Someone shot the NYPD commissioner."

"Jesus Christ, are you serious?"

"Yep," Szabo replied. "I think things are about to get a whole lot more interesting."

CHAPTER FIFTY-FOUR

New York Hospital, Flushing, Queens, N.Y.
Monday, December 30th, 2013 – 3:59 p.m.

The only sound, in the small, private surgical waiting room, was the clock hanging on the wall, which dutifully marked the passing of each second, as the room's occupants silently dealt with their emotions.

The hospital had worked diligently to accommodate the growing police presence while also trying to restore the operating capability of the emergency room.

Maguire sat on the couch, drinking a cup of coffee, while Mary leaned against him, her arms wrapped tightly around his left arm, as if trying to draw support from him. They had given her something to calm her down, but he could still feel her body trembling against his.

He'd mentally gone through the list of things to say, the hollow assurances that everything was going to be alright, but he could not bring himself to say them. They were empty platitudes which well-intentioned people said when they didn't know what else to say. He'd been here before and, as kind as those words were, they didn't bring any sense of relief. In the end, the only assurances that really mattered were the ones that came from the doctors and right now they weren't saying anything.

There was a soft knock on the door. Maguire glanced up, watching as Torres opened it and peeked out. A moment later he watched as the man opened it wider and Melody stepped inside, followed by the other two members of his security team.

Melody walked over and kissed him, then knelt down in front of Mary. He felt her release his arm and immediately wrap them around Melody.

"I've got ya, hon," Melody said softly, as Mary sobbed.

"I need to get an update," Maguire said.

Melody looked over at him and nodded.

"Do what you have to do," she replied. "I'll take care of her."

Maguire leaned over, kissing her head softly, then got up and walked over to where the security team stood talking.

"Follow me," he said and led them out into the hallway.

"First things first," he said. "Where are the kids?"

"They are with Ms. Gordon," Luke replied.

"Do they know what happened?"

"Just that there was a shooting," the man said. "It's all over the news."

"Okay, Pete, you take security on the door," Maguire said. "Luke, reach out to Chief Ameche and see if they have any updates."

"Yes, sir," both men replied.

Maguire looked over at Massi and Torres.

"You guys need a break."

"We're fine, sir," Massi said.

"None of us are fine, Amanda," Maguire replied. "Go take a break. Get yourself some coffee and something to eat. When you're done then come and find me."

Massi began to object, but he raised a finger, silencing her before she could protest.

"That's an order," he said gently. "None of us know what the next few hours or days are going to hold. Take the down time when you can get it. If I need you I will call, I promise."

The two detectives grudgingly accepted his instruction and headed down the hallway.

Maguire smiled as he watched them walk away. It was the greatest compliment they could give him, not wanting to leave his side. Most cops would have taken off *running* down the hallway after being told to take a break, especially after what they had all been through. The fact that they wanted to stay spoke volumes as to their feelings for him.

"Boss?"

Maguire turned around to see Jackson standing behind him holding up a cellphone.

"Yeah, Luke?"

"I've got Chief Ameche on the line."

"Thanks," Maguire said, as he took the phone from him. "Tony, what do you have for me?"

"They located the apartment the shot came from," Ameche said. "Inside they found the bodies of the two elderly residents. Both had been killed by a single shot to the head and then propped up on the couch; as if they were *watching* the whole thing."

"Jesus," Maguire replied, as he leaned against the wall.

"They found a single spent casing sitting upright on the dining room table. Crime scene is going over the apartment with a fine-tooth comb as we speak."

"This fucker is taunting us," Maguire said. "Once the media starts reporting, that the folks with guns can't even protect themselves, then the city is going to come apart at the seams."

"I'm afraid to say it, but I'm out of ideas," Ameche said. "If every cop is worried they have a target on their back, how the hell are we going to do our job? This goes well beyond the *normal* police response."

"Reach out to Intel and let them know I want security details on everyone that was involved with Spangler's processing. Angelo Antonucci over at Cold Case was doing a work-up on Spangler; he should have a list of all the names."

"But the P.C. wasn't even here when Spangler was being investigated by Applicant Processing," Ameche said. "How do we know he hasn't *modified* his list?"

"Call it a hunch," Maguire replied. "Rich is the titular head of the Department and he probably made it personal with Spangler when he announced the hiring plan. I don't imagine it would take much to set off this psychotic little fucker. That being said, I'd have Operations reach out to the former P.C. and let him know he probably has a rather large bull's-eye on his back as well."

"Last I heard he was out of the country working as an advisor to some sheik in the Middle East, but I'll have them track him down," Ameche said. "Is there any word on the Boss yet?"

"No, nothing yet," Maguire said. "He's still in the operating room."

Silence momentarily gripped the phone line.

"Is there anything else you need me to do?"

"Just hold things down out there," Maguire said, "and let me know if anything else turns up."

"Will do," the man said.

"Thanks, Tony. I'll call you back if I hear anything on this end."

Maguire ended the call and handed the cellphone back to Jackson. He glanced over at the uniformed cop who stood outside the waiting room door. The tall, gangly looking officer wore an ill-fitting uniform, which gave the impression that its wearer had stolen it from his big brother's closet.

God, he looks so young, he thought.

Maguire had the benefit of coming into the Department after having first serving in the Navy. It made his transition a whole lot easier, especially considering what he'd already been exposed to, but he had felt bad for some of his fellow classmates who struggled with the challenges of switching from civilian life to police officer. It wasn't an easy thing to do.

One day you were flipping burgers, shoveling ditches, stocking shelves, or maybe attending college classes. As a civilian you lived in an insular environment, one in which your world view was wholly dependent upon what the news brought to you or what you were taught in school.

Then on another day you woke up, raised your hand and swore an oath. After a few months in the police academy you were put out on the streets to uphold the law and man was that ever an eye opener. Suddenly you were an outcast, a pariah among your friends, someone who they could no longer have *fun* with because of the badge in your pocket.

Soon they stopped calling, but it was okay. After each passing day you began to realize that you had less and less in common with them. They viewed the world through rose colored glasses, while you had a front row seat to man's inhumanity to man. Every day you bore witness to the good, the bad and the ugly of the city.

At twenty-one-years-old you were given the responsibility to bring law and order to every call you were assigned to. Everyone looked to you to know what to do in every situation, whether it was a routine call or a life and death struggle. You had the power to arrest people or, even worse, write them a summons. Unlike fireman, people never wanted to see *you*. Cops often found themselves withdrawing into their own little world, surrounded by other cops, because none of their former friends could ever understand what it was like to watch someone die in their arms. It took a special kind of person to run from one emergency call to another, dealing with heartache and tragedy as a daily routine.

Most twenty-one-year-olds worried about what movie they were going to see or panicked over what grade they were going to get. Very few ever had to deal with the stark reality of a gun fight, in some dingy back alley, at three o'clock in the morning.

"You look like you could use this."

Maguire looked over to see Luke Jackson standing there holding a Styrofoam coffee cup.

"I could use something a helluva lot stronger right about now, Luke," Maguire said, as he accepted the cup, "but thanks for thinking about me."

"Anything new?"

"They found two more people murdered in the apartment that the killer took the shot from."

"This guy is one sick fuck," Jackson said.

"Yeah, he is," Maguire replied. "Let's just hope we catch a break, and put an end to his little reign of terror, before he adds someone else to his list of victims."

Maguire glanced over as the door to the operating room opened up and a weary looking man, dressed in sweat-stained scrubs, emerged.

"Any news, Doc?" Maguire asked.

"Right now it's still touch and go," Dr. Marcus DuBois, the Chief of Trauma and Emergency Surgery. "Commissioner Stargold has suffered severe damage."

"But he's going to be alright?" Maguire asked. "Isn't he?"

"All I can say right now is that we are doing everything in our power to help him."

"I appreciate that, Doc. When do you think you'll know more?"

The man frowned and shrugged his shoulders. "We're still too *deep* in the woods to say."

"Is there anything we can do?" Maguire asked.

"Pray," the man replied. "Hard."

CHAPTER FIFTY-FIVE

Bowie, Maryland
Monday, December 30th, 2013 – 4:02 p.m.

"Didn't they say this guy was home?" FBI Special Agent Sheila Mason asked, as she stood in front of the ornamental wrought iron gate and pressed the buzzer.

"That's what the SSG guys said," her partner, Agent Larry Wilson, replied. "They said Spangler came home at ten last night and no one's left the property since."

"Well, unless the buzzer is broken, or the man went deaf, I don't know what to do."

Wilson stepped back and looked at the six foot high stone wall that lined the perimeter of the property.

"Tell me you're not thinking what I think you're thinking."

"Dom said it was really important that we get through to this guy, you want to tell him that you left without even trying to talk to the man?"

"This is private property."

"SSG said they didn't see him leave, Sheila. What if there's a medical emergency inside?"

"That's a helluva stretch," Mason replied.

"Well, maybe he's fallen and he can't get up."

"So you're going to rely on an old, late night TV commercial for your justification?"

"You gonna let me go alone, partner?"

"Do not pull that shit with me, Larry."

"I'm just saying we do a quick sneak and peak, if everything looks buttoned up we leave and let Dom know the SSG folks fucked up. Then it's on them."

"I'm not dressed for this," Mason protested, pointing to the business suit she was wearing.

"I'll give you a boost."

"I rip anything, you're paying for it."

Wilson leaned down against the wall, cupping his hands in front of him, and looked over at his partner. "Deal."

"Stand your silly ass up, Larry," the woman said indignantly, as she walked over toward the wall. "It hasn't been all *that* long since the academy."

Wilson watched as his partner jumped up, grabbing the top of the stone wall and lifted herself up and over. A moment later he joined her on the other side, dusting off the snow from his hands on the sides of his overcoat.

"This is all your show," Mason said, motioning up the driveway. "Lead the way."

Wilson headed up the winding driveway, toward the imposing mansion that sat atop the hill.

"What's the story with this guy?" Mason asked.

"Former Marine," Wilson replied. "Now he's a defense lobbyist."

"War may be hell, but it does seem to pay well," she said as she looked around the expansive property.

"Everything pays well," her partner replied. "Everything, that is, except law enforcement."

"Ain't that the truth," Mason grumbled.

A moment later they stood in front of a large wood front door.

Wilson knocked hard on the ornate door then peeked inside through the glass panel on the side.

"Maybe this one works," Mason said, as she rang the doorbell.

Inside they heard a loud series of low to high pitched chimes, announcing their presence.

"Damn, that would wake the dead," Wilson said.

"Look at the size of this place, Larry," Mason replied. "You've got to have them that loud in order to hear it ring on the other end of the house."

"You could fit five of my houses inside this place and still have room left over."

Mason stepped back and peered upward at the windows on the second floor.

"I think the SSG folks fucked up."

"Maybe," Wilson said, as he walked away from the front door and headed around the back of the house.

"Where the hell are you going?"

"Just seeing how the other half lives," he called back over his shoulder, as he continued walking.

"You want to get transferred to the Fairbanks field office?"

"Maybe he's just out back planning his Spring garden."

Mason looked back toward the car, then back at her partner, watching as he disappeared behind the house.

"You just can't leave well enough alone, can you, Larry?" she said, her voiced filled with exasperation.

Mason liked her partner, but there were times when she wished he wasn't so anal about things. All they had to say was that there was no answer at the door, let the SSG guys explain to Dom how they'd fucked up. Or maybe the guy was inside whacking off and just didn't want to be disturbed. But no, her partner had to go and be *Dudley-Do-Right.*

"Fuck me," she said angrily, as she grudgingly set off down the snow covered path made by her partner.

Moments later she found him peering through a large window that overlooked the back yard.

"You find *anything,*" she asked.

Wilson looked over at her.

"Yeah, the SSG guys were right, he didn't leave," Wilson replied.

"Yeah, why is that?"

"Because I was right, Sheila, he's fallen, but I don't think he's going to be getting up anytime soon."

350

Mason looked at him curiously, then walked over to the window and peered inside, seeing the body splayed out on the floor.

"*Sonofabitch!*"

CHAPTER FIFTY-SIX

New York Hospital, Flushing, Queens, N.Y.
Monday, December 30ᵗʰ, 2013 – 5:13 p.m.

Maguire sat in the corner of the room, cradling the cup of lukewarm coffee, as he stared over at Melody who was holding Mary in her arms, rocking her gently. Monsignor O'Connor sat on the chair next to them reading his Bible.

It was quite again, at least for the moment.

Over the last half hour a steady procession of people had stopped by to speak with Mary. Everyone from the Mayor, who was holding an emergency meeting of his advisors two doors down, to Cardinal Rinaldi, the Archbishop of New York City, who was a close friend of O'Connor.

She smiled through it all, graciously accepting their well wishes and prayers, as she fought back tears. Once the *important* people had stopped in, Maguire had instructed Peter May to politely inform anyone else that she wasn't to be disturbed.

Now the only sounds were the muffled conversations and footfalls in the hallway outside, along with the sound of the second hand ticking away on the clock hanging up on the wall.

It was moments like this that were his personal kryptonite. No matter how many times he went through it, he never was able to find the words to bring any comfort to others.

How could you? he thought. *How could anyone be comforted in light of something so senseless?*

The truth was that life simply was not fair. The accidents and the *intentionals* happened to both the good and bad alike. As a result, some people lived and some people died. Like most things in police work, it became the topic of dark humor.

Maguire had seen more than his fair share of shootings and the one thing you learned early on was to never assume anything. He recalled one robbery incident where the shop owner had suffered a minor graze wound and was transported to the hospital. When they had finished up with their report, he and Alex had gone over to get additional information from the man, only to find out that he had died. Apparently the shooting had thrown him into cardiac arrest.

On the other hand, it became a running joke that the bad guys, who'd take half a dozen rounds to the chest and were still popping off at the mouth in the E.R., would be *treated and released*. The common belief among cops was that the majority of them were just too stupid to go into shock.

It was always easy to laugh about things which didn't impact you directly, but there was nothing humorous about it now. He had no words to take away the pain and hurt. Not for himself and not for those around him.

The vibration of the cell phone startled him, pulling him away from his thoughts. He removed it from his pocket, staring at the name on the screen before answering it.

"Hold on for a minute, Kurt," he said.

"I've got to take this," he said to Melody.

"Go ahead, we'll be okay," she said.

Maguire got up and walked out of the room.

"What have you got for me?" he said, once he was in the hallway.

"You're not gonna be happy," Silverman said.

"Spangler wouldn't talk?" Maguire asked.

"Spangler can't talk," Silverman replied. "Courtesy of the bullets inside him?"

"Are you fucking kidding me?"

"I wish I was," Silverman replied. "The Baltimore field office sent two agents down to have that little chat you requested and found him dead in his office."

"You said bullets. I take it this wasn't an accident or a suicide."

"Unless it was one of those special *Dallas* bullets," Silverman replied. "You know the ones that go into the body, leave the body, and go back in."

"How many?"

"One to the back, one to the head."

Maguire thought about that for a moment. It had to be his nephew; it was the only thing that made sense. Mad Max wouldn't have turned his back to someone he didn't know and what better way to take the fight out of someone than with a well-placed shot to the back. The nephew would have understood that, even wounded, Max would pose a lethal threat so a kill shot would have been necessary.

"I could be wrong, but I don't think there is going to be any question as to who the shooter was in this case," Maguire replied. "Any idea when?"

"Won't know definitively, until the autopsy results come in, but they say it looks like he's been dead for a while. The SSG guys on the scene said there was no unaccounted for traffic, in or out, since early last night."

"So the killer didn't drive up?"

"No, but the place is littered with security cameras, inside and out," Silverman said. "We have the Evidence Response Team in route. I'm sure we will have our answer soon enough."

"Okay, let me know as soon as they come up with anything."

"Will do," Silverman said. "How's the Commissioner doing?"

"Still touch and go," Maguire replied.

"We're all praying for him."

"Thank you, Kurt," Maguire said. "I'll talk to you later."

When he ended the call he selected another number. Three rings later he heard the voice on the other end answer.

"Do you ever get tired of bothering me?" Mother asked.

"Where are you at?" Maguire asked, walking down to a deserted area of the hallway.

"Getting ready to land at Andrews, why?"

"We've got problems."

"What do you mean *we*?"

"I mean Spangler just declared war on *everyone*," Maguire replied. "He shot my friend this morning and he put a bullet into his uncle."

"Mad Max is dead?"

"According to the FBI he is," Maguire said. "They're sitting in his office, with the body, as we speak. Their evidence guys are in route to begin picking the place apart."

"Jesus Christ," Mother said. "That's not gonna work out for us."

Maguire understood that the *us* had nothing to do with him, but that didn't mean he still couldn't leverage that to his needs. The agency Mother worked for had its frying pans in a lot of kitchens, most of them were official, but a few were very *un-official*.

"I didn't think it would," Maguire replied, as he sat down on a bench. "I hear the Bureau's case load is getting backed up, perhaps they could use a break."

"Hold on for a minute," Mother said.

Maguire heard the phone go silent. He stared up at the acoustic ceiling tiles as he waited patiently. A few minutes later Mother came back on the line.

"I have a team in route," Mother said. "I'll be wheels down in about five minutes and I'll head over there. What makes you think it's your guy?"

"I don't know, call it a gut feeling," Maguire replied. "I just think he's settling scores. According to the Bureau guys the place has a ton of cameras in place, so it shouldn't be too hard to positively ID the shooter. "

"I'll handle things on this end."

"Let me know if you find anything," Maguire said. "I want this bastard. It's personal now."

"How's your friend?"

"He's bad," Maguire said. "It could go either way."

"I'll say a prayer for him."

"Thanks," Maguire said, as he watched the operating room doors open again and several people stepped out into the hallway. "Hey look, I have to go. I'll talk to you later."

"I'll call you as soon as I know something."

Maguire hung up the phone and walked over toward them.

CHAPTER FIFTY-SEVEN

Interstate 76, Pennsylvania
Monday, December 30th, 2013 – 5:22 p.m.

Spangler exited onto the westbound Pennsylvania Turnpike, cautiously eyeing the state police car that sat off on the side of the road as he passed through the toll plaza. It wasn't until he had gotten about a quarter of a mile down the road that he realized he'd been holding his breath.

He glanced up occasionally, looking into the rearview mirror, searching for the flashing lights. Soon he began to feel a sense of calmness return, as he put more distance between him and the cruiser.

There was no reason to be alarmed, but he guessed that anyone guilty of doing what he had would always feel a twinge of panic when they saw the police. He accepted that his uncle truly did have his best interests at heart, so there was no reason to believe that he would have set him up. Max Spangler was many things, but stupid was not one of them, and he was right when he said that his arrest would be bad for both of them.

In fact, he had grudgingly accepted that his recent activities were becoming problematic. It wasn't that he felt the need to stop, but he began to realize that he had too much to do. By targeting just one enemy, he was making himself predictable. He'd had a good run and now it was time to disappear off the radar.

With the body count he had racked up in New York, everyone would be focusing their attention to stopping the next attack, while he would turn his attention toward other *interests*. Unfortunately, before he could begin this next phase of his mission, he needed to rest and do some research.

Spangler couldn't wait to see the look on Special Agent Charlie Peterman's face when the time came. He had made it personal between the two of them and Spangler was more than willing to repay the *kindness*.

As for Agent Kimberly Ross, well Spangler had something extra *special* in store for her. She wasn't innocent, but she certainly wasn't the prick that Peterman was. There was also the fact that she was young and attractive. If the South Dakota winters were anything like the ones in Montana, he could use the distraction. One thing was for certain, Agent Ross would learn that there could be worse things than death.

Then again, maybe she'd enjoy it, he thought.

After all, she didn't seem too concerned about using her *assets* to try and gain a confession from him. Perhaps she would put forth the same effort into staying alive.

Spangler knew that he would have to proceed a bit more cautiously with this latest endeavor. While cops were equally dangerous, they didn't seem to recognize the danger they faced until they were actually working. Too often they were lax in their own personal security, especially when in familiar surroundings. The prey he would be hunting now would be soldiers, like himself, who were always on guard.

He would of course have to head back east at some point, but he would do it at his choosing. No one could maintain their purposeful vigilance 24/7. Eventually things broke down. Bumps in the night, which drew a quick response in the beginning, became nothing more than an annoyance as the weeks dragged into months. He would let them fall back into a state of complacency and then *bang*, another enemy to add to the list.

Up ahead the green and white highway sign indicated the mileage until Harrisburg. His travels would take him another twelve hundred miles beyond that; more than enough time for him to come up with a rough plan for the coming months. Clearly he would have to focus on Ross first. Once he started going after those in the Army, everyone's guard, including hers, would be raised up. It would be such a waste having to end her life prematurely.

Spangler looked up at the rearview mirror, smiling when he saw nothing behind him. Then he looked at the hard, rugged looking reflection that stared back at him. It was a badass look and it was growing on him.

Would she like it? he wondered. *Did that even really matter?*

CHAPTER FIFTY-EIGHT

New York Hospital, Flushing, Queens, N.Y.
Monday, December 30th, 2013 – 5:29 p.m.

Melody glanced up as the door opened, watching as Maguire quietly walked through. Immediately she could sense that something was wrong.

"James, what's wrong?"

Maguire knelt down in front of them, taking Mary's hand in his.

"Mary,..."

Melody's eyes went wide and she let out a gasp, as Mary broke down and began sobbing. Maguire leaned over and took Mary into his arms, holding her tightly, as she buried her face against his chest.

"Oh God, no, James," Melody pleaded, "there has to be a mistake."

"No, Mel," Maguire said softly, "he's gone."

Mary's muffled screams filled the room, as she beat her hands against Maguire's back.

"No...., No....., that can't be right," Melody said in a confused voice, as she stood up and began walking toward the door.

Maguire looked over at O'Connor who quickly moved to intercept Melody and ushered her back over to the chair.

"I'm so sorry, Mary, I don't know what to say," Maguire said softly, as he held her close to him.

She had gone limp in his arms and all he could feel now was her body trembling uncontrollably.

Maguire couldn't begin to fathom what was going through her mind and he knew there were no words that could make this better. She had just lost her husband and he had lost his best friend. Perhaps the only thing was to be there for each other.

Out in the hallway the Mayor and Dr. DuBois had both offered to be the one to break the news, but Rich was his best friend and the two of them were the closest thing he had to family. It was his job to tell her and, for the moment, he had to set aside his own feelings of pain and grief, as he tended to Mary.

As the moments slowly ticked by, he felt her sobbing begin to lessen. The flood of unbridled emotion had slowed to a trickle, as she slowly came to terms with the reality that he was gone.

Maguire could hear O'Connor speaking to Melody in that gentle, country priest tone that seemed to make even the most life-altering situations a bit more palatable. He was good at that.

He felt Mary pull away; watching as she slowly looked up at him. Her tear stained face was streaked with mascara and her eyes were red and swollen.

"Mary, I'm..." he began, but she held her finger up to his lips.

"There's nothing to say, James," Mary said softly, but with a fixed resolve. "I want to see him."

Maguire looked over at Peter May who nodded and stepped out of the room. A moment later he stepped back inside.

"Luke's taking care of everything, Boss."

"Thank you," Maguire said, as he sat down next to Mary.

"Where are the girls?" Mary asked.

"They're with Gen," he replied.

"I'm going to need to speak with them alone."

"Once we are done here I'll have them fly you out to the house."

"Thank you," Mary said softly.

There was a gentle, but firm, knock. Peter May opened the door then looked back at Maguire. "They're ready, Boss."

Maguire stood up and extended his arm to Mary, who used it to steady herself as she got up. Melody got up and met them at the doorway.

"Do you want me to come with you?" Melody asked.

Mary smiled, wiping away the tear that fell down Melody's cheek.

"No, but I'll need you more than ever when I get back."

Melody's jaw clenched as she fought back the tears.

"I'm not going anywhere, hon."

"I know," Mary said, then turned to face the door.

Peter May opened the door and Maguire led her out into the hallway.

As they emerged, the officers gathered outside snapped to attention, rendering a salute as they walked down the corridor. Just outside the room, Alan McMasters stood with several of his deputy mayors. As they drew near he stepped forward, taking Mary's hand in his.

"I am so sorry Mary," McMasters said. "Rich truly was an amazing person. He will always be remembered as a hero by this city and the NYPD."

"Thank you, Mr. Mayor," Mary replied. "My husband was deeply honored that you picked him to be your police commissioner."

"This city will never forget his sacrifice, Mary. We will never forget the debt that we owe to you and your daughters."

Mary smiled and swallowed hard, choking back the tears.

Maguire led her away, watching as two uniformed officers opened the door to the operating room.

The interior of the room was dimly lit now, befitting the solemnity of the moment. The large surgical lamps had been turned off and the room had been cleaned up as much as possible. Still, nothing could erase the metallic odor, mixed with hospital antiseptic, which hung in the air. A blanket covered Rich's body, hiding the visible brutality of the wound he had suffered, while his hands lay folded on top, one over the other.

Maguire's jaw clenched hard as he stared down at his friend. He could taste the saltiness of the blood as he bit his lip, barely containing the rage he felt inside. He had to hold it together for her, at least for the moment.

He stopped a few feet from the table, letting go of Mary's hand, as she continued. He expected her to break down, but she didn't. She walked around the table, staring down at Rich's face. Gently, she brushed an errant hair from his forehead.

"I always wondered how it would happen," she said softly. "The older you get the harder it is not to think about those things."

Maguire just listened, staring back and forth between the two of them.

"I suppose we all wish for the *'asleep in our bed at the age of ninety-eight'* method," Mary said with a slight chuckle, "but then I wonder, at ninety-eight would anyone even remember him?"

Mary looked down at Rich and took one of his hands in hers, caressing it gently. She closed her eyes and, for just a moment, imagined that he was just sleeping. That this was all some sort of crazy dream, but she couldn't keep her eyes closed forever.

"He might not have understood it before-hand, but Rich went out on his own terms," she said. "He died fighting for what he believed in, for what he loved."

"I should have done something more," Maguire said. "I should have talked him out of it."

Mary looked up at him, a flash of anger appearing on her face, "James Patrick, don't you dare."

"It wasn't his time," Maguire said defensively.

"Yes it was," Mary replied. "We might not understand the reason why, but it was."

"He didn't deserve this, Mary," Maguire said, fighting back the tears. "Rich was a great man who had more left to do in this world."

"Great men can die in obscurity," she replied, "but a hero who falls in battle is never forgotten. Don't second guess what happened today, it won't change anything, and don't let his name be forgotten."

"I won't," Maguire replied softly.

"Give me a minute alone with him, James."

Maguire nodded before turning and walking out of the room.

When he emerged, McMasters quickly pulled him aside.

"How is she?" he asked.

"Holding it together," Maguire replied.

"Listen, I know how close the two of you were. If there is anything Mary or his girls need, just let me know."

"I'll do that, Mr. Mayor."

"How are you doing?"

"Like I just lost my best friend," Maguire replied.

"I'm not even going to pretend that I know how you're feeling, James," McMasters said, "and I hope you understand that I am not trying to be insensitive."

"No, not at all."

"You're the First Deputy Commissioner, James," McMasters said. "I have to ask the question. Can you step in as acting police commissioner until we have a chance to appoint his replacement?"

"Yes," Maguire replied, "but when you appoint a new police commissioner I'll be stepping down. I think the next P.C. should have the opportunity to bring in his own people."

"Understood."

Just then the door to the operating room opened and Mary walked out.

Maguire moved in alongside her, taking her by the arm and led her down the hallway.

"James," she said, once they were out of earshot range of the others, "I want you to do me a favor."

"Anything," he said.

"I want you to kill the *sonofabitch* who did this to him."

"With pleasure."

CHAPTER FIFTY-NINE

Bowie, Maryland
Monday, December 30th, 2013 – 6:02 p.m.

The two men Mother had sent to Spangler's place stood in the middle of the office, their arms crossed in front of them, as they stared impassively at the FBI agents.

The Bureau's case had come to a grinding halt, after the man's declaration that the investigation was now a matter of national security; along with the threat of deadly physical force should the agents attempt to remove anything. Nothing in the demeanor of either man gave the agents any reason to believe they were joking.

The men had identified themselves as being with the Department of Homeland Security, and had produced valid ID's, but something didn't sit right with the Bureau folks and they were refusing to leave until they received an order from *their* superiors back in Baltimore, who at this very moment were burning up the phone lines to D.C.

"What the hell is going on?" Roy Gentry asked, as he walked into the office, "and why are they still here?"

"They say that they want an *official* order from Justice," one of the men said.

"And who are you?" Agent Wilson asked.

Mother turned around sharply and eyed the man.

"That's above your pay grade, junior," Gentry said dismissively and turned back to face his men. "Clear them out, *now.*"

"We're not going anywhere," Mason chimed in, as she joined her partner. "Not without orders from our boss or the Attorney General."

Gentry's jaw clenched firmly, as he turned around and stared at the two agents. The man's steely gaze caused both agents to feel a bit uncomfortable, as if they were being sized up by a predator.

"Young lady, I'm going to try and keep this professional," he said, in a low voice. "This is no longer a crime scene, but a national security investigation."

"Yeah, yeah," Wilson objected, "that's what *they* said, but the FBI investigates national security matters."

"*Not this one*," Gentry said sternly. "Thank you for your cooperation, but it's time for you to leave."

"That's all well and fine," Mason said, "but you're not my boss and until someone I know says that *you're in charge*, I guess you could say we have us a Mexican standoff."

"Can't say you weren't warned," Gentry replied, removing the cell from his jacket pocket and dialing a number.

Mason and Wilson looked at each other, and then back at the man.

"Sorry to bother you, but there seems to be a bit of a problem here, sir," Gentry said into the phone. "I have two FBI agents who refuse to surrender the scene until someone they *know* authorizes it."

Gentry listened for a moment then held out the phone.

Mason reached out cautiously and took the phone.

"This is Special Agent Sheila Mason," she said. "Who am I speaking to?"

Almost immediately the woman's eyes went wide.

"Yes, sir," she said, her voice cracking slightly. "No, sir... Yes,... I understand completely, sir. Good...."

The phone went dead.

"Night..." she said, the words trailing off.

She handed the phone back to Gentry, looking considerably shaken.

"We're sorry to have inconvenienced you, sir," she said to Gentry.

"Apology accepted," Gentry replied.

"Let's go, Larry."

"Who was that?" Wilson asked.

He was even more confused now than he had been. Wilson had never seen his partner act so strangely.

"Not now, Larry," she said, "It's time to go."

Mason turned around and addressed the technicians who were standing off to the side.

"Gather up your stuff, people, we're leaving."

Gentry watched as they left, closing the door behind them, then turned back toward the two men.

"Sweep the entire place," he said, "audio, visual, documents, all of it. I want to know everything that happened here in the last twenty-four hours. Once we know the answers to that, then I want to know the last forty-eight, then the last seventy-two, and so forth. Nothing is inconsequential. I want to know every interaction that Max Spangler had with his nephew."

"What about Project Bright Star, sir?" one of the men asked.

"The boss believes Bright Star has been compromised and he has shut it down," Gentry said. "If you find anything bag it and burn it."

"Yes, sir," the two men said in precise military unison and immediately went about their assigned task.

Gentry walked over to the desk and sat down, taking in the trappings of Spangler's office. It felt intimately familiar.

He reached over, opening the top of the cherry wood humidor that sat on the edge, and removed a Bolivar *Belicoso Fino* cigar. He clipped the end and lit it, taking several puffs until the tip glowed.

"Not bad, Max," he said approvingly, as he looked over at the man's body.

Soon the room was filled with an earthy aroma of cocoa and coffee bean, which did a wonderful job in countering the other smell.

Gentry leaned back in the leather executive chair and stared at the desktop. He'd have to go through it all, from top to bottom.

That was always the tough part, he thought, *finding the one, seemingly innocuous, item which proved to be the key to solving the whole puzzle.*

Sometimes those pieces were right in front of you and other times it felt like you were never going to stop searching.

Gentry took a puff and then laid the cigar in the ash tray.

The answers were here, somewhere.

"The only easy day was yesterday," he said softly, before opening one of the drawers and commencing his search.

●●●

Wilson and Mason walked back to their car in silence. As Mason walked over to talk with one of the technicians, Wilson got in the car and started it up, turning up the heat to chase away the evening chill.

He still wasn't sure what had happened back in the house, but obviously something had changed to cause his partner to do a complete 180 degree shift. If he was being completely honest, he'd have to admit that he was happy to be away from those other guys.

Not too many things bothered him and he certainly didn't fear any man. He'd seen them all, the white collar criminals and the blue collar ones. People who stole millions of dollars through electronic manipulation and others who'd slit your throat for a quick buck. In his career he'd chased down the worst of the worst and a few of them still haunted his nightmares, but these guys were completely different, especially the older one. That one looked like a ruthless professional. He was the kind of person who would kill you while you ate your dinner and then finish it for you.

Hell he didn't even really know who *they* were. He didn't care what the credentials said, they weren't DHS agents.

Spooks, he thought. *They had to be spooks.*

He'd done several cases with them in the past and despite the typical BS about being on the *same team*, he never felt comfortable around them. Spooks always seemed to have a different agenda and he was never quite sure just how far they would actually go.

One thing was for certain, they were encumbered by things like *probable cause* and *Miranda warnings*.

He heard the sound of the door opening and glanced over as Mason entered the vehicle.

"You alright?" he asked.

"Yeah," she replied, but it was obvious that she was still shaken.

"Are you trying to convince me or yourself?"

"I'm fine, Larry."

"So who was on the other end of the phone?"

Mason stared out the window.

It was snowing now. She watched as the intricate flakes landed on the glass and then quickly melted.

So beautiful, she thought, *and yet so fragile. Just like careers.*

"Sheila," Wilson said, snapping her back from her thoughts. "Who was on the phone?"

She turned and looked over at her partner.

"The President, Larry," she replied.

"*The* President?" he asked. "Of the United States?"

"Yeah, *him*," she said.

"What did he say?"

"He asked me if I knew who he was and if I wanted to be transferred to the embassy in Kazakhstan," she said. "Then he said that we were impeding a national security investigation and to leave immediately."

"You've got to be shitting me," Wilson replied.

"Can we go now?"

Wilson dropped the shift into reverse and looked over his shoulder, as the car backed down the driveway.

"Fucking spooks," he said.

CHAPTER SIXTY

Dalzell Canyon, South Dakota
Thursday, January 2nd, 2014 – 6:19 a.m.

The desolate canyon was still cloaked in darkness, save for a sliver of ambient light which peered out through a tiny crack in one of the cabin's shutters. Occasionally the light would briefly *flicker* as something passed in front of it.

Had the average person wandered along this part of the mountain, it was highly doubtful that they would have even noticed the flickering light, but the two men lying prone along the ridge line were not your average persons.

"Condor, this is Kestral One, we have interior movement," the observer said softly, the message relayed to the recipient via the throat mic the man wore.

"Copy, Kestral One, this is Condor, do you have target confirmation?"

"Negative, no target ID, no exterior movement."

"Copy, advise when you have target confirmation."

"Affirmative, relocating to the south."

"Copy, Crystal telemetry shows green, you're clear to proceed."

The two man sniper team had cautiously made its way to their current position the day before. It had been a long, four mile trek through the rugged mountainous terrain. They knew the threat that Spangler and his drone posed, so they were especially careful in their approach; an approach made a bit easier by the *state-of-the-*

art ground panoramic night vision goggles each man wore. The four optical tubes, which protruded outward, gave the wearer an almost insect-like appearance, but it also provided the ability to see a much wider field of view than that of conventional night vision goggles. They also had the benefit of the unblinking Keyhole-12 (Crystal) satellite which was providing real-time feed from two hundred miles above them.

"Time to do some skull dragging,"

Sixteen hundred miles away, a group of men stared at the flat panel video display and watched, as the two men slowly began to creep south along the ridgeline.

"You certain we have the right place?" Maguire asked softly.

Mother looked up, watching as one of the men seated at the table got up and walked into one of the *private* rooms to make a call.

"We won't be certain till we have eyes on the target," Mother said, in a hushed tone, "but these were the coordinates that were *imprinted* into the blank notepad we found. The land is owned by Sattem bin Nayef. He's a minor player in the royal family, but he holds sway among the senior members of the Saudi military. Bin Nayef has been tight with Max Spangler since he started up Aequitas."

"How tight?" Maguire asked.

"He used him to do some serious lobbying recently and pried loose about eight billion in arms from the *Boss*," Mother replied, nodding in the direction of the private room.

Maguire casually glanced over, noting that the office's glass window was now opaque, keeping both the user, as well as his conversation, from any potential prying eyes and lip readers.

"Everyone gets their back scratched," Maguire said sarcastically.

"Some days I take two showers when I get home," Mother replied.

"How long do we have the satellite telemetry for?" Maguire asked.

"Probably another hour, maybe an hour and half, then we'll go *dark* for a bit."

"I don't do well waiting," Maguire said. "I'd rather be on the ground."

"You and me both, Paddy, but it's a young man's game now."

Maguire leaned back in the leather chair, watching as the two figures crept silently along on the monitor.

Had it really been that long since I'd been out there? he thought.

As much as he didn't want to admit it, the man was right. They were old warriors.

No, he admonished himself, *Mother was old, and he was just old-ish*.

Still, of all the exotic places he had ever waged a military operation from, the White House Situation Room had them all beat, hands down.

The Situation Room, officially known as the John F. Kennedy Conference Room, was a five thousand square-foot dedicated room, in the basement of the West Wing of the White House, which was run by the National Security Council. It had been created in 1961, by then President John F. Kennedy, after the dismal failure of the Bay of Pigs invasion, which had been attributed to a lack of real-time information.

Over the decades the room had changed considerably from its austere beginnings. The current room resembled one that could easily be found in a Fortune 500 business, but unlike its civilian counterpart, this room had been built to keep secrets. In addition to the classified stuff, a number of technological improvements had been instituted, which allowed the watch teams to monitor global events, in real-time, in order to provide intelligence and support to the NSC staff, the National Security Advisor, and the President. Over the years the room had been used to oversee every major event from the Vietnam War to the September 11th attacks.

"More coffee?" Maguire asked.

"Sure," Mother replied.

Maguire picked up the cup and made his way over to where the silver metal carafes were lined up on a mahogany side table and refilled the two containers.

He glanced down at the gold embossed stars and eagle motif on the side.

Is there anything they don't mark? he wondered. *This place has more souvenir crap than Disney.*

"Movement!" a voice cried out over the speakers.

Immediately everyone scrambled back to their seats.

"Kestral One this is Condor Actual, have you acquired the target?"

"Copy, Actual, we have possible target in sight."

"What have we got, people?" The President said, as he took his place at the head of the table.

"A figure just walked out of the cabin, Sir," an Air Force Colonel replied.

"Is it our guy?"

"Kestral One, do you have confirmation ID?"

"Negative, Actual, his back is to us."

The group of men examined the image on the screen of a dark figure standing along a tree line.

"What is he doing?" the President asked.

"Kestral One, can you see what the target is doing?"

"I think he's peeing," the man replied.

Several members of the group stifled laughs.

"Advise when you have confirmed ID, Kestral One."

"Copy that."

Maguire knew exactly what was going on up on that mountain ridge. Right now, the men were working together to range the target, read the wind, and adjust for any other variables that might affect the shot. Once they were dialed-in, the spotter's role would shift to protecting the shooter. While a sniper rifle was critical in making those long distance shots, it wasn't worth much when the enemy came creeping in your back door.

The relationship between a sniper and his spotter was an intimate one. Sniper teams worked in the *no-man's-land* between, and even behind, battle lines, often with little or no support. First and foremost, the two depended on each other for survival.

A moment later the silence of the room was broken.

"Target acquired, target confirmed, what is your order?"

The Air Force colonel looked over at the President, who turned and looked at Maguire.

"Rich was your friend, James, you make the call."

"Send it," Maguire said without hesitation.

The President nodded to the colonel.

"Kestral One, you have a green light."

Sixteen hundred miles away a finger slowly squeezed the rifle's trigger, sending the 190 grain .300 Winchester Magnum bullet hurtling down range toward its intended target.

As a group, the nine men gathered in the room held their collective breath, as they awaited the outcome.

"Condor, hit confirmed, target down," a voice said a moment later.

"Kestral One, copy, target down, awaiting video confirmation."

There was no outburst from those gathered in the room, no cheers for vanquishing the foe, just a few professional nods and handshakes.

Maguire got up and turned toward the President, extending his hand.

"Thank you, sir."

"No need to thank me, James," the man replied, shaking Maguire's hand. "I owed you one, remember?"

"No you didn't," Maguire replied.

"I'm really sorry about, Rich," he said. "I wanted to come to the funeral, but I felt you already had a lot to deal with and you didn't need me screwing things up any more than they already were."

"I appreciate that."

"I'm leaving to go to a NATO summit in Poland tomorrow, but when I return I would like you and Rich's family to come back down for a memorial service at the Secret Service academy. We are going to do a re-naming ceremony in his honor."

"That would be nice," Maguire said. "I'll let Mary know."

"I'll have my secretary coordinate with your office."

"Thank you, sir."

Maguire watched as the man left the room.

"I thought you didn't like politicians," Mother whispered.

"I don't," Maguire replied. "They're a bunch of shifty bastards."

"Well, he certainly seems to like you."

"They all love you; just as long as they think they can use you to increase their polling numbers."

"He won't get a bounce out of this op," Mother said, "This one was totally off the books."

"No, he's looking at the long game," Maguire replied. "He knows that his numbers aren't that good right now and he is going to be in a tough battle when Cook tosses her hat into the ring. New York is a big market and he is going to want the key players close to him to leverage votes."

"I'll leave the *politicking* to you young guys. I'm getting too old for that bullshit."

"I hate to break the news to you, but I don't recall you ever being young."

"Asshole," Mother said sharply.

The two men made their way out of the room, stopping off to collect their cell phones from the lead lined cabinet near the reception area, before making their way upstairs. They paused outside the West Wing lobby to button-up their jackets.

"I suppose you need a ride?" Mother asked.

"That would be nice," Maguire replied, as the two men made their way to the parking area adjacent to the Old Executive Office Building. "Considering the fact that I'm not even supposed to be here."

"We do operate in a very odd little world, don't we, Paddy?"

"It beats a nine-to-five cubicle with fluorescent lighting, I suppose."

"I suppose it does," Mother said, as he got into the waiting car.

CHAPTER SIXTY-ONE

St. Patrick's Cathedral, Manhattan, N.Y.
Friday, January 3rd, 2014 – 9:59 a.m.

The limousine carrying Mary Stargold and her daughters came to a rolling stop behind the hearse that held the body of her husband. It was on loan from the Secret Service's New York Office, the very same office that Rich had left to take over the NYPD.

There hadn't been any credible threat to warrant the use of the armored limousine, it was more of a private sign of respect for the family of their fallen comrade. Immediately behind the limo was the Suburban which now carried acting Police Commissioner Maguire, a role which he found more difficult to accept with each passing moment. In the seat next to him sat Melody, staring out at the Cathedral's cold grey marble exterior.

Each of them was lost in their own thoughts, but all of them shared a similar reality. As much as they wanted to fight it, with each passing second they were that much closer to saying their final goodbyes to someone they loved.

Up above, dark foreboding clouds blanketed the sky above Fifth Avenue, as a cold rain gently fell to the earth. It was as if Heaven itself was mourning, shedding its tears for the fallen warrior.

"They're ready, sir," Amanda Massi said.

Maguire nodded, watching as she exited the vehicle and opened the passenger door. He stepped out of the truck, pausing to take Melody's hand and help her out. Then they walked, hand in hand, over toward the limo, waiting at the curb until the door was opened. Off in the distance they could hear the plaintive sound of drums from the Emerald Society.

Mary stepped out, followed by Emily who held onto Sophie's hand. Maguire walked up and held out his arm, which she took hold of, clasping her hand tightly over his.

"It all seems so real now, James," Mary said, looking up at him through bloodshot eyes.

Mary always had toughness about her, an impenetrable façade that made her seem much stronger than she actually was, but as Maguire watched, he could make out the cracks beginning to appear. He reached over, gently wiping away an errant tear that ran slowly down her cheek. Her face had a puffiness to it that belied the nights spent crying.

"I know it does, Mary," he replied.

"I just want to run away," she said. "If I run away this all ends and I can pretend it never happened. That Rich is just on one of those overseas protection assignments I hated so much. God, what I wouldn't give for that to be true. Maybe, if I hadn't complained, if I had just been happy and supported him, he would have stayed with the Secret Service and he would still be here."

Maguire took her in his arms, holding her tightly and shielded her face away from the throng of photographers who stood off to the side, their cameras recording the moment for all eternity.

"Don't do that to yourself, Mary," he said. "You complained like all spouses do, but you always supported him and he knew that. Rich did what he did because that is who he was, he was a sheepdog and nothing would ever change that."

He held her for a moment, feeling her body tremble in his arms, could hear the gentle crying, as the pain broke through.

An honor guard from the Ceremonial Unit stood on either side of them, at a distance. They formed a path, from the curb to the cathedral's front entrance, where his eminence, Cardinal Francisco Rinaldi, the Archbishop of New York, stood waiting for them, alongside Monsignor O'Connor.

"Have them close ranks, Amanda," Maguire said.

Amanda walked over and talked to the unit's C.O. A moment later both rows of uniformed officers closed in, creating a tighter phalanx around them, shutting them off from the prying eyes that looked on.

"You take all the time you need, Mary," he said, holding her tightly.

This was the unspoken bond that they all shared, the understanding that if one of them were to fall, that the others would be there to pick-up the pieces. It was also the one thing that no one ever wanted to talk about, because, in doing so, it stripped away the fantasy that they were all superheroes and recognized their own mortality. It was the reason why so many wore shirts emblazoned with a big red S under their uniforms or intimidating skulls decorating their body armor.

They were the modern day equivalent of King Leonidas' Spartan warriors, leaving behind those they loved, just to go forward and put themselves in harm's way to protect them. It was at times like this that he remembered the old saying attributed to Spartan mothers who sent their sons off to battle.

Come back with your shield, or on it, he thought, as he watched the back doors of the hearse open up and the pall bearers began removing Rich's casket from the back.

"I'm okay, James."

He looked down at Mary, who'd managed to get ahold of herself, finding the strength within to put the façade back in place.

"You sure?"

"Yes," she replied stoically.

Maguire took her hand and led her down the corridor, created by the honor guard, with Melody and the girls following just behind them. As they reached the top of the stairs, Cardinal Rinaldi stepped forward and took Mary's hand.

"I am so sorry for your loss, Mary," the man said. "I only had the chance to meet Rich on a few occasions, but he struck me as a deeply compassionate man. His love for the city and her people was clearly evident. Please understand that if there is anything that you, or your children, ever need, the full resources of the church are at your disposal."

Mary smiled and nodded.

She wanted Rich back, not the sermon on the merits of theology, but her husband. She wanted to feel him in her arms one more time, to hear his stupid laugh, or to listen as he screamed at the television like a lunatic, as his beloved Giants made him work for yet another victory. She wanted to listen to him snore and do all the trivial things that she had always taken for granted, but would never happen again.

She felt James gently squeeze her hand.

"Thank you, your eminence," she replied, as Maguire led her toward the door.

Monsignor O'Connor then led them into the cathedral.

Maguire felt Mary grip his hand tightly, as they walked inside the church. It was filled beyond capacity, as people from every walk of life took time out to pay their respects to the fallen warrior.

Maguire leaned down and whispered in Mary's ear, "Are you okay?"

"I have to be," she said somberly.

They walked up the middle of the nave, all eyes on them, as their footsteps echoed loudly on the marble flooring in the eerily silent church. Their eyes darted back and forth as they walked down the aisle, picking out familiar faces and exchanging forlorn glances. A few rows back from the front he spotted Alex, standing next to a uniformed officer from her department.

"Thank you," he whispered, reaching out his hand to hers and squeezing it gently, as they walked by.

The hundred foot plus walk had seemed like an eternity and they were both thankful when they had finally reached the end and took their place in the front pew, watching as Cardinal Rinaldi led the procession of Rich's casket to the altar.

Funeral services were always a somber affair, and this one was no different. He sat listening to the organist playing its dirges, and the mournful songs of the choir. Then he closed his eyes, doing his best to pretend that he was listening, as they went through the opening prayer, the first reading, the second reading, and finally the gospel.

Halfway through he heard Melody whisper in his ear, "No one prays that hard."

It wasn't that Maguire was irreverent; he understood that people grieved differently. It was just that as a SEAL he learned to mourn in a much different way.

"This is the Gospel of the Lord," Cardinal Rinaldi said.

"All praise to you, Lord Jesus Christ," came the response from the congregation.

"You're up," Mary said with a smile, the first one to cross her lips since the shooting.

"I know," Maguire said, standing up, "don't use fuck as a noun."

Mary fought to contain the slight chuckle, as Maguire passed in front of her and stepped out into the aisle.

He made his way up the steps, feeling the eyes of everyone on him, and walked over to the podium. On the table was a leather clad folder embossed with a gold police commissioner's badge. The mayor had tried to give it to him, but he had turned it down, saying that he was only a placeholder until the next P.C. was appointed. He opened it up and stared down at the prepared speech.

He read the opening line: *We gather here today to mourn the death of Police Commissioner Richard Stargold, a man who dedicated his life to the pursuit of justice and heeded the calling to serve his fellow man.*

He closed the folder.

"My sincere apologies to those who wrote my speech," he said, "but I'll be going off script today. Let's hope I don't get fired."

In the front row Melody squirmed in her seat, as Mary grinned.

"First I would like to address an issue which I find personally offensive. Since Rich's death, I have read a number of articles, and watched several news reports, by some of New York's most illustrious pundits and politicians, talking about how Rich would have been alive today if he had just allowed the *professionals* to do their jobs. I'm sorry, but I call bullshit. In addition to being my friend, Richard Stargold was one of the most professional law enforcement officers I have ever had the pleasure of knowing. He might not have known much about writing articles from the safety of a news room, but he certainly knew all about the issues pertaining to life and death."

The silence that had gripped the church now turned to nervous fidgeting and sideways looks, as the congregation tried to process what was being said.

"Not to take away anything from our vaunted media or enlightened politicians, but you folks have no clue as to what it is like to put yourself in harm's way for something greater than yourself. You're like peace-time royalty, strutting around in your shining armor, looking down your noses at those knights who bear the scars and damages from endless campaigns. You ridicule their unsightly appearance until the enemy is at the gate. Rich Stargold was such a knight. He knew what it was like to sacrifice himself and the choices he made were done, not with his safety in mind, but with yours. That is what a hero is and what a hero does."

Maguire paused, looking over to where Sophie and Emily sat next to Mary and Melody.

"Sophie, Em, I know it hurts and I wish I could take that hurt away from you girls, but never forget that your dad is a hero. Never ever forget that."

Sophie reached over, taking her mother's hand in hers. It was like watching the rebellious teenager in her disappear and a young woman emerge. Emily climbed up on Melody's lap and wrapped her arms around her neck, burying her face into her shoulder, as if she was hiding from the world.

"To all you cops out there, both the rookies as well as the veterans, pay attention, because I'm talking to you. If you wish to be successful, Richard Stargold, *your* police commissioner, left you a legacy that you must embrace. It is best defined by the words of the Apostle John in 15:13: *'Greater love hath no man than this, that a man lay down his life for his friends.'*"

Maguire gripped the sides of the podium, as he looked out over the assembled throng. As his eyes passed by Mary, he watched her nod approvingly.

"To the people of the City of New York, that is how Rich Stargold saw you, as his friends, and that was why he did what he did. Not because he was reckless, not because he wasn't professional enough to know better, but because he was professional. He knew the risks and put himself in harm's way, despite those risks. It is the same thing that the men and women of the NYPD, and law enforcement around the world, do every single day. Yet there are still some who seem to take enjoyment at Monday morning quarterbacking every decision, every action, made in a split second. I would like to tell you that this was some new creation, but it is not."

Maguire paused for a moment, as he made deliberate eye contact with all the traditional rabble rousers. The hypocrites, like the *Reverend* Archibald Jennings, who sought out every media bright light to castigate the police for their own benefit.

"A hundred plus years ago, Theodore Roosevelt, our 26th President, and the man who once sat in Rich's chair, said: *'It is not the critic who counts; not the man who points out how the strong man stumbles, or where the doer of deeds could have done them better. The credit belongs to the man who is actually in the arena, whose face is marred by dust and sweat and blood; who strives valiantly; who errs, who comes short again and again, because there is no effort without error and shortcoming; but who does actually strive to do the deeds; who knows great enthusiasms, the great devotions; who spends himself in a worthy cause; who at the best knows in the end the triumph of high achievement, and who at the worst, if he fails, at least fails while daring greatly, so that his place shall never be with those cold and timid souls who neither know victory nor defeat.'"*

"To the men and women of the NYPD, never forget that you are not one of those timid souls," he continued. "You are a sheepdog and the city of New York is your flock. That does not mean you will have an easy life, but it means that you are doing something most people will never have the courage to do. If you are in this for glory and accolades, you are in it for the wrong reasons. The sad reality is that no one loves the warrior until the enemy is at the gate. When that time comes, and you stand there ready to do your duty, I want you to remember this Spartan creed: *'This is my shield. I bear it before me into battle, but it is not mine alone. It protects my brother on my left. It protects my city. I will never let my brother out of its shadow, nor my city out of its shelter. I will die with my shield before me facing the enemy.'"*

"Today we do not mourn the death of our police commissioner, but we celebrate his bravery and courage in standing at the gate, facing the evil, for a purpose greater than himself. Richard Stargold will forever be known as the embodiment of the Department motto: *Fidelis Ad Mortem*, Faithful Unto Death. Today we bring him home, the warrior on his shield, and we stand ready to take his place."

Maguire stepped away from the lectern and moved down the steps, as the assemblage of uniformed and plain-clothed officers, gathered in the church, stood up and began clapping. He walked over to the flag draped coffin and pulled back the edging to reveal the hard wood. Then he reached into his suit pocket and removed his gold SEAL trident. He removed the safety clasps from the pins and laid it down on the casket. Then, with a closed fist, drove it into the wood with a resounding crack.

"Hooyah, brother," he whispered softly before taking his seat next to Mary.

She took his hand in hers and leaned over, whispering in his ear, "Thank you."

"For what?" he asked.

"For making his death not be in vain."

"It never was," he replied.

"To us, no, but they needed to hear it," Mary said, nodding toward the transept.

Maguire looked up, watching as two rows of uniformed officers came up from each side of the church and converged in the middle. A lieutenant came forward in an attempt to address this breech of protocol.

"I'll be back," Maguire replied.

The first uniformed officer was astride the casket now, and had one of his *collar brass*, denoting the command he was assigned to, removed from his uniform shirt.

"What's going on?" Maguire asked.

"Sir, this isn't..."

"What?" Maguire asked, cutting the man off. "Regulation?"

"Well, yes, it's not protocol, sir," the lieutenant replied.

Maguire looked the man over in his spit and polished uniform. Then he turned to the uniformed officer, taking in the rack of medals affixed over the man's shield. What he had done with his gesture was resonating with the rank and file officers in attendance. They needed this.

"We're changing the protocol today, lieutenant," Maguire said, then nodded at the officer. "Call it the warrior's send-off."

As they watched, the man laid the collar brass onto the casket and pounded it into the wood, next to Maguire's trident. Then he saluted the casket first and then Maguire, who shook the man's hand before sending him on his way. He stood there, repeating this for the next half hour, as one after another they came to pay their last respects. When they were done, the casket glistened with command insignia.

Maguire took his place next to Mary.

"They'll follow you to hell and back, James."

"Not me," he said, "but maybe the next guy."

Mary took his hand in hers and laid Rich's shield into it.

"No, there won't be a next guy, James. You're it."

"But McMasters will pick...."

"McMasters picked you," she replied with a smile, "with my blessing and support."

"Mary, I don't...." Maguire began to protest.

"We both know that this is what Rich would have wanted and this is what this Department needs," she replied. "You either truly believe in what you just said or...."

Mary let the words trail off, indicting him. She had him and he knew it.

"Why you?" he asked.

"Because Alan knew you wouldn't say no to me."

"That's so unfair," he said, staring down at the gold shield in his hand.

"All's fair in love and war," she replied. "You above all people should know better, Commissioner Maguire."

"After that speech, he just might want to reconsider his choice."

"After that speech, if he did he would lose his entire police department."

"I didn't do it for me, Mary, I did it for Rich."

"I know," she replied, "and so do they."

At the conclusion of the service, Maguire led them back down the aisle to the front of the church, following behind the casket. Outside they gathered with the Mayor and Cardinal Rinaldi, watching as the casket was reverently placed into the back of the waiting hearse.

Out on the street, a sea of blue uniforms lined either side of 5th Avenue, from Central Park in the north all the way down to 42nd Street to the south, before turning east toward the FDR Drive. Tens of thousands of officers from around the world, some from as far away as Japan, had descended upon the city to pay their final respects.

As they watched the door of the hearse close, Maguire leaned in to McMasters.

"Mary handed this to me," he said, showing the shield in his hand. "After my little speech, I wasn't sure if you wanted it back so that you could reconsider your options. I'm not the smart political choice."

"I don't need politicians, James," McMasters said, as the two men began to make their way toward their respective vehicles. "I want leaders. I wanted you before today and by God I want you even more after that eulogy."

"That might not go over well with some of the more politically correct folks," Maguire said.

"Don't you worry about that, *squid*," McMasters replied, as he turned and faced Maguire. "You let this old *jarhead* deal with them."

"Aye-Aye, sir," Maguire replied, shaking the man's hand.

"Glad to have you on-board, James," Masters said shaking his hand. "We'll talk on Monday and I will have my staff make arrangements for the formal swearing-in."

"What was all that about?" Melody asked, after he got into the Suburban.

"This," he replied, handing her the gold police commissioner's shield. "Mary gave it to me after the eulogy."

"What did you and McMasters talk about?" she asked, as she examined the shield.

"I asked him if he wanted to reconsider."

"You still have the badge," Melody said, handing it back to him. "I guess he still wants you."

Maguire turned in his seat and looked over at her, "You already knew, didn't you?"

"*Moi?*" Melody said, with a quizzical look.

"*Qui, vous, Angel,*" Maguire said.

"Why would you ever think something like that?"

"Because I originally turned him down," Maguire replied. "So McMasters asked Mary to do his dirty work, knowing I wouldn't say no to her, and she would never have done it without talking to you first."

"Rich wanted you to be his number two, because he knew that you were the best person to take the helm in the event something happened," she replied. "He may never have envisioned this, but that doesn't mean it's not true."

"I honestly don't know how I feel about it," Maguire replied, as he stared down at the shield.

"Isn't it a *no-brainer?*' she asked, using the very same words he'd used on Rich a few months earlier. "Consider yourself the caretaker of his legacy and just do the best damn job you can."

"Not to sound cocky," Maguire said, "but if Rich had me, who do I have?"

"I can't help you with that one, Cowboy," Melody replied, taking his hand in hers, "and my dance cards booked solid."

He stared out the window, watching as the sea of blue uniforms slowly passed by. Despite the somberness of the moment, it was always an impressive sight to see them in their wool reefer jackets with the double row of gold buttons. The uniform harkened back to a different age, when an officer on patrol was greeted as a welcome sight by residents and with fear by those inclined to do wrong. Now, it seemed as if the world had turned upside down. The good guys were being vilified and the bad guys were being treated as victims.

What the hell did you get yourself into? he wondered.

CHAPTER SIXTY-TWO

Waldorf Astoria Hotel, Manhattan, N.Y.
Saturday, January 4ᵗʰ, 2014 – 9:23 p.m.

"I'm so sorry I couldn't stay to talk, James," Alex said over the phone, "but I'm in the middle of an investigation, one of my cops is out sick and I just lost another to a training course for a week, so we are running thin up here."

"Don't worry about it, Alex," he replied. "The fact that you came down was all that mattered."

"How could I not?" she asked. "I didn't know him nearly as well as you, but in the short time that I did, I found him to be a genuinely nice man."

"I appreciate that," Maguire replied.

"So what's going to happen next?" she asked. "Have you heard any rumor as to who they might bring in to fill the spot?"

"Actually yes, I spoke to the mayor about it yesterday."

"Did he go outside the Department? Please don't tell me it's that asshole from the state police."

"Nope, he's making the move from within."

"God, I hope for your sake it's not some self-important, pretentious asshole," she replied. "You and I know the job is filled with them."

Maguire stifled the laugh.

"I don't know," he replied, "the guy McMasters tapped for the spot does have his moments."

"No shit?" Alex replied. "Who is it?"

"Me," he replied.

"Are you fucking kidding me?" she said, her voice a mix of shock and excitement. "My old partner the fucking P.C.? Isn't that some shit."

"It's something alright."

"I don't want to sound too happy, considering the circumstances," Alex said, "but I am happy for you and I know the job is in good hands."

"I'm glad you're so sure," he said, "I'm not so certain I share your enthusiasm."

"Bullshit, you'll do fine and you know it."

"We'll see," he replied. "I've got big shoes to fill."

"Not to take anything away from your friend, but you know the ins and outs of the job better than anyone. Hell it's not like you haven't been doing the job already, you're just changing chairs."

"You make it seem so easy."

"Hey, you survived working with me in the Seven-Three," Alex said with a laugh, "everything else after that is a walk in the park."

"You do have a point there," he replied.

"Is this official?"

"No, still acting," he replied. "Probably won't have the official swearing-in till later in the week."

"I want to come down for that."

"You don't have to," he replied.

"Are you shitting me?" she asked incredulously. "This might be the first and last time I will ever be in a police commissioner's office and *not* be in trouble, of course I will be there!"

"Hey, don't downplay your job," he said. "You're a chief of police in your own right."

"Yeah, of the Penobscot Police Department," she said with a laugh. "Give me a break, James. It was a nice gesture, but my entire department is nothing more than an over-glorified day tour shift in a 'B' house back in New York."

"Do you like your job?"

Alex took a drag on her cigarette and thought about the question for a moment.

"I do," she replied. "Not the small town politics, but I do like the job and my people."

"Doesn't matter if it's a big city or a small town, the politics will always be there," Maguire replied, "but if you like your job, and have good people, that's all that matters."

"Well?" she asked.

"Well what?" he replied.

"Do you like your job?"

Maguire stared out the window at the motorcade positioned inside the hotel's parking well, watching as a flurry of uniformed officers moved about.

He'd given everything for the job, including his blood, sweat and tears. Now he was poised to take over the reins of the nation's largest police department. Criticizing the departmental hierarchy was much easier when you were a member of the rank and file, but things took a different turn when you reached the upper echelons. When you were responsible for more than just yourself and the person next to you. That being said, it didn't mean that just because you had successfully climbed the promotional ladder, that you were somehow better. He had always viewed his job as the First Deputy as that of a facilitator; someone who made the job better for those who were doing it.

Maybe that was the difference, he thought. *You never climbed the ladder, you got parachuted in.*

"Hey, are you still with me, rookie?"

"Yeah, I'm here," Maguire replied, "and to answer your question, yes, I do love my job."

"Well, then go *kick ass and take names.*"

"Will do, Chief," Maguire replied with a laugh.

Suddenly there was a knock on the passenger window.

"Hold on, Alex," he said, as he lowered the window.

"Sorry to bother you, Commissioner," Luke Jackson said.

He was standing next to another man who wore a security pin on his lapel, a member of Eliza Cook's private security detail.

"No problem, Luke, what's going on?"

"Sir," the other man chimed in, "Secretary Cook is wrapping up her visit. She would appreciate it if you would accompany her to the airport in her vehicle."

"Okay," Maguire replied. "Give me just one minute."

"Yes, sir," the man replied. "Thank you."

Maguire raised the window and returned to the call.

"Hey, Chief *Hellraiser*, I have to go."

"I heard," Alex replied. "Try not to drool all over yourself with *Cruella*."

"Don't worry yourself, you're the only devil I drool over," Maguire replied.

"I wonder if I can get the NSA to send me a recording of that for later."

"Bye, Alex."

"Ta-Ta, James."

Maguire ended the call and exited the Suburban.

"Lead the way," he said to Cook's security man.

"Eagle Advance, to Eagle One," the man said into the covert mic at his wrist. "Notify Eagle Actual that Sailor is in route."

Maguire smiled at the radio call sign he'd been given.

"You former DSS?" he asked.

"Yes, sir," the man replied. "A few of us left the State Department when the Secretary did to continue providing protection for her."

"I bet the pay is a lot better in the private sector," Maguire said.

"There are some *additional* perks," the man replied.

"I bet there are," he replied.

Eliza Cook may have come from humble beginnings, but she didn't stay there long. Hard work had gotten her a law degree from a prestigious Ivy League school and her good looks had gotten her a job at an equally prestigious D.C. law firm. She parlayed the two into a series of highly successful personal and professional ventures. The little girl from Bitter End, Tennessee, whose parents never had more than a couple of bucks to their name, was now one of the most powerful women in America, backed up by a nine figure checking account.

They approached the vehicle just as Eagle was arriving, a security man holding open the door to the waiting Suburban.

"Good evening, Madam Secretary," Maguire said.

"Ah, Commissioner Maguire," the woman replied with a smile, extending her hand out to him. "I'm so glad that you could join me."

Even into her late 60's, Eliza Cook was still an incredibly attractive woman and it was something which she took full advantage of. Despite her formidable reputation for being cut-throat, in both the public and private sectors, many men still fell for her beguiling charm and good looks. She was like a modern day Sophia Loren. Even her designer dresses were specifically chosen to accentuate her rather *ample* attributes. One thing was for certain, Eliza Cook wasn't above using anything to aid in the furtherance of her political ambitions.

"The pleasures all mine, Madam Secretary," he said, shaking her hand.

It wasn't the soft, feminine handshake that he had expected, but rather a strong, assertive one.

"Please, call me Eliza, James," she replied, as she released his hand and then proceeded to get into the back of the SUV.

"This way, Commissioner," the security man said, motioning toward the driver's side of the vehicle.

Maguire followed him around and got into the back of the vehicle. A moment later the motorcade pulled out of the well, onto E 50th Street, with sirens and strobe lights announcing their departure.

"Allow me to extend my sincere condolences on the loss of your friend," Cook said. "I know this must be a very difficult time for you and your agency."

"Thank you, that means a lot."

"I was actually concerned about my visit here," she said. "What with all the executions, but then I realized that the NYPD was under your stewardship now and I knew I had nothing to worry about."

"I appreciate that."

"It made me wonder, do you like to hunt, James?"

Maguire was taken aback by the question. He'd done some small game hunting up in the Adirondacks, when he was younger, but once he'd gone into the teams he'd discovered that another type of hunting appealed to him more.

"No, ma'am," he replied. "Not anymore."

"That's too bad," she replied.

Maguire watched as she reached over and pressed a button, raising up a glass partition that separated them from the driver and her primary security man.

"I heard there was excellent predator hunting in South Dakota this time of year."

Maguire glanced out the window and swallowed hard. If she was trying to establish how *connected* she was, it had worked. Suddenly he felt her hand tap his leg.

"Oh look at me, talking about silly things while you have the weight of the world on your shoulders," Cook said.

"No, it's okay," he replied, looking back over at her. "I've often thought about taking it back up. As I recall, it was a very peaceful time."

"For the hunter, maybe," Cook remarked, "probably not so true for the hunted, but, then again, they rarely have a tale to tell."

"You are right about that," he replied, "but some prey shouldn't have peace."

"You'll make an excellent police commissioner, James."

"There's been no official decision," Maguire replied, looking to see just how plugged in she was.

"Really?" Cook said, with a quizzical look.

Maguire watched as she crossed one leg over the other, her dress sliding up just enough to showcase her well-toned thigh. "I could have sworn Alan told me that you were his man. Am I wrong?"

"No, I just meant that there hasn't been any *official* announcement."

"Nothing we talk about tonight is official, James," Cook said with a smile. "You know, back when Commissioner Stargold first mentioned you for the number two spot, Alan called to ask me what I thought about you. I told him that you weren't a *yes* man, but that you were extremely proficient, very professional and had impeccable discretion. I'm glad to see my assessment holds up."

"That's very nice of you to say," Maguire replied, "but I would think that a woman who just announced her candidacy for President of the United States might have other issues, unrelated to New York City, on her mind."

Cook smiled that killer smile of hers. While most men would melt, Maguire immediately felt his defenses kick in.

Here it comes, he thought.

"You are good," she said, rubbing his leg, "and you are right. As much as I would love to discuss you, and I really would, there is someone else in your house I would like to talk to you about."

"Melody," he replied.

"Yes, Ms. Anderson, although I understand she won't be a Ms. for too much longer."

"Yes, we just got engaged."

"What an amazing couple you two will make," Cook replied. "Good looks, money, power,.... Why it almost makes me nervous."

Almost, he thought.

"I want her, James," Cook said matter-of-factly. "Let's be honest, unless I have a heart attack, which my doctors assure me won't happen and my critics say couldn't happen, since I don't possess a heart, I will win the election. As much as I would like to believe I can control everything, I can't. So I need the best and the brightest by my side and your soon-to-be wife is at the top of my list."

"What list would that be?" he asked.

"Cabinet Secretary," Cook replied.

"Which one?" Maguire asked, taken aback by her statement.

"Good question," Cook replied. "The diverse capabilities of your lady doesn't make that very easy. The short list is Treasury or my old job. I really need someone to make sense of this mess we have gotten ourselves into, but I also need someone with looks and diplomatic savvy to straighten the feathers that this idiot has managed to ruffle. Either way, with her connections on the Hill, she is a fast-track nomination."

Maguire looked out the window, as the motorcade made its way over the Queensboro Bridge, processing what he was being told.

"You might have a tougher sell with her than McMasters had with me," he said. "I don't think she is a big fan of politics or politicians."

"Why do you think you are here with me right now?" Cook asked. "I know full well that I need your help. If I were in her shoes, I'd be damned if I would give up my life for government service."

"What makes you think she'll say yes to me?"

Cook laughed. Not a phony politician's laugh, but a genuine one, which made it even more disconcerting.

He felt her hand pat his thigh playfully. It was a game and he knew it. More importantly, he was willing to play it, to see where it went.

"Did she agree to marry you?" Cook asked.

"Yes," Maguire replied, doing his best to maintain his decorum, "but still...."

"Ah, my dear James, you still have a lot to learn about women," she replied. "When the time comes, I will make the offer, all I need you to do is be the voice of reason."

"That's all?" Maguire said skeptically.

"I make it my business to know people, James," Cook said with a serious tone. "Just like I know you, I know Melody. She's not driven by power, in fact she loathes it. She is strong enough in herself that she would gladly give it all away. I'm sure you have seen examples of that with your own eyes."

Maguire had to admit that she was right. Melody had continually sought out the right people, elevating them beyond their own capability and empowering them in ways that they could never have imagined. Even with Gen, who now, as a co-owner of GDL, was incredibly wealthy by her own right, yet remained as loyal as you could possibly imagine.

"Melody sees herself as a champion of the people," Cook continued. "She has achieved success and now she wants to give that back. She is the epitome of 'a rising tide raises all boats.' I need her to be that tide, James. More importantly her country needs her to be that tide and that is why I want her in my Cabinet."

"I'll do my best, Madam Secretary," he said.

Cook smiled. "You can't let it go, can you, James?"

"What's that?" he asked.

"The professionalism," she replied.

"You're the former Secretary of State, ma'am, and by all accounts, the next President of the United States. It's not my place..."

"To what?" she asked. "Reject my advances or act on them?"

"Ma'am?"

"I knew you were a rare commodity, James Maguire," Cook said, removing her hand from his leg. "If I did that to half the men who'd ever sat next to me I'd have them on their knees, drooling at my feet."

"And the other half?" Maguire asked.

"The other half is interested in the same thing as I am," she said with a knowing smile, "but I'd venture to say that even half of them would still *take one for the team*, if it meant getting access to power."

"And you want me to offer up Melody to you?"

"I want you to support me," Cook said. "I'm not asking you to like the game, I'm asking you to help me change the rules."

"We're not even on the same political team," he said.

"Does that really matter, James?" she asked. "The reality is that if we don't get the right people into office, there won't be a system left to vilify."

"You mean the right people, like Senator Mays?" he said, showing her that he was equally plugged-in.

Eliza Cook leaned into the corner of the seat, her back against the body of the car, shifting herself so that she could face him.

"Oh, you're good, James," she said in a low, sultry voice. "Perhaps I misjudged you."

"I doubt that," Maguire replied, "but information is always a two-way street."

"What do you want?"

"The same thing you want," he said, as the motorcade pulled onto the tarmac at LaGuardia Airport. "Information. You and I both know the threat to this city isn't over. I want access. Not what they think, but what they know, in real time."

"I thought you already had it after 9/11?" Cook replied.

"Bullshit," Maguire said. "You and I both know that isn't true. Intelligence is still treated as a rare commodity in Washington. While the brown-nosers and yes-men are scoring political points, the rest of us here in the streets are worrying about what is coming next."

"I'll see what I can do," Cook replied.

"Give me your word you will improve it," Maguire said.

"Okay, you have my word," Cook said, holding out her hand.

Maguire took it, feeling her hand tighten around his.

"You have my word," she said, "but do I have yours?"

"Yes," he replied.

"Good," Cook said, as she gripped his hand firmly and leaned in closer, whispering into his ear, "but I will warn you, James Maguire, don't get too comfortable here in in New York. I have a feeling your services will be needed elsewhere."

"And just what *services* would that be?" Maguire asked.

Eliza cook smiled seductively, as she knocked on the window.

"Anything that your president asks, sailor," she replied, as the door opened.

"Yes, ma'am," Maguire said.

"Good, I'll be in touch," she replied and then exited the vehicle, heading toward the waiting private jet.

Maguire waited for a moment and then opened the door. He stepped outside and came face to face with Dean Oliver. Immediately he felt his jaw clench tightly and the hair on the back of his neck stand up.

"Good evening, Commissioner," the man said, his voice low and even.

Maguire backed up, putting some distance between himself and the man.

"I understand that congratulations are in order for your promotion. I guess even death has a silver lining."

"I would have thought you, of all people, would have stayed in government service," Maguire said. "They usually frown on aiding terrorists and body snatching in the private sector."

"What's the old saying?" Oliver asked, "for King and Country?"

"Shouldn't that be *Queen*?" Maguire asked, ignoring the man's misuse of the quote.

"You say tomato, I say fuck you," the man said, with a feigned smile, his cold blue eyes cutting through the darkness.

"Good to see you haven't lost any of your *charm*."

"Politics can be a rough business," the man said, "but that doesn't mean we should hold onto personal grudges."

"My grudges with you aren't personal, Agent Oliver," Maguire replied, "I wouldn't put that much thought into it, but they are professional."

"I do the job I'm paid to do, Commissioner," Oliver said, "if that bothers you, that's your problem. Although word is that we'll be playing on the same team soon."

"We might be on the same team one day, but I highly doubt you and I will ever be teammates."

"*C'est dommage*," Oliver said, "but we'll be just fine, as long as you keep your nose out of my business."

"Don't do anything stupid and I won't need to."

"Commissioner."

Maguire turned around to see Luke Jackson standing a few feet away.

"Sorry, I'd love to stay and chat, but I have a city to protect," Maguire said before turning and walking away.

"*Au revoir*, Mr. Policeman," Oliver said with a laugh.

"What is it, Luke?"

"There's someone here asking to see you, Boss."

"Here? Who?" Maguire asked, looking around the tarmac, "Where?"

"Over there," Jackson replied, pointing to where a dark colored vehicle was parked, on the other side of the chain link perimeter fence.

As Maguire watched a lone figure emerged. Even in the relative darkness he recognized her instantly. It was Tzviya Harel.

CHAPTER SIXTY-THREE

LaGuardia Airport, Queens, N.Y.
Saturday, January 4th, 2014 – 10:57 p.m.

Maguire walked toward the opening in the chain link fence, his eyes fixated on the figure just beyond. As he drew closer he could feel his heart racing. She was still as beautiful as the last time he had seen her. Her long, shiny black hair was pulled back into a pony tail

"Zee," he said, quickly jogging the last few steps toward her, as she came to him, catching her in an embrace.

For a moment the world stopped and nothing else mattered, as he held her tightly in his arms. Her scent filled the air around him. He closed his eyes, as the memories came flooding back, both the good ones and the bad. The last time he had held her this way was the day she had said goodbye.

"God I've missed you, Zee," he said softly.

"I know, James," she replied. "So have I."

Reluctantly he released her, watching as her body shifted and she turned to face him. Nothing had changed since he had last seen her. Their embrace had told him she was still as strong as ever. In fact she was one of the few people, outside the teams, who had ever been able to keep up with him in terms of physical fitness. She was also one of the deadliest people he had ever known and he knew a lot of people. She held an E3 level in Krav Maga and when it came to actual fighting, she was an artist.

"I'm sorry about Rich," she said. "I was at the church."

"I knew you were," he replied.

"Oh yeah," she said coyly. "How did you know?"

He had missed her accent.

"I felt you there," he replied.

She was about to protest his *feeling*, but stopped abruptly when he added, "Just like I felt you at the hospital, after I got shot."

"You should never have gone running blindly into that subway station," she said, a tinge of anger in her voice. "You were reckless. You could have gotten yourself killed."

"If memory serves me, that thought had crossed my mind," he replied. "As I recall, it had been a rough couple of months."

"Don't say that," Tzviya said, "even if it's true."

"So are we just going to stand here and pretend?" he asked.

Behind them, the engines on Cook's jet throttled up, filling the air with a loud roar and causing them to halt their conversation as it began to taxi away. Tzviya hiked up the collar on the black wool coat she was wearing, covering her neck, as she stared at him, her jaw fixed and her eyes penetrating deep into his soul.

She still had the most amazing green eyes. One minute they could be warm and inviting and the next, cold and lethal. He had wondered how often those eyes were the last thing a person saw, just before she killed them.

"I never wanted to hurt you," she said, when the plane was sufficiently out of range.

"Then why did you, Zee?" he asked, in an almost pained and tortured tone. "I loved you and I thought you loved me."

"I did," she said, her eyes welling up with tears. "I do."

"Then I don't understand and I want to," Maguire replied. "Saying we can't be together anymore and walking out of my life, after everything we shared, doesn't exactly scream 'I love you, James.'"

"You don't think I understand that?" Tzviya said angrily. "Do you think it was any easier for me? That I was able to just walk away from you, as if you hadn't meant everything to me."

"I don't know, Zee," Maguire said, "I wasn't the one who walked away."

"This was stupid," she said, turning to walk back toward the car.

Maguire reached out, grabbing her by the arm, and pulled her back toward him. He knew better, but he wasn't about to let her get away again. Tzviya reacted to the perceived threat, spinning around in the opposite direction and coming back at him, her hand driving up toward his face. He'd been anticipating it and he moved aside, raising his arm up and blocking her strike with his forearm. She then spun around angrily, trying to leg-sweep him, but he'd moved back to quickly. When she came around he could see the fury in her eyes, but instinctually he knew it wasn't directed at him. He just happened to be the only one around to bear the brunt of it.

Maguire heard the sound of footfalls and glanced over, as Luke Jackson and Peter May came running toward him. He held up his hand quickly, to stop them.

"I'm fine," he said.

"Are you sure, Boss?" Jackson asked.

"Yes, just go back to the truck."

Then he turned back to Tzviya and raised up both his hands.

"Do you remember what happened the last time we fought like this?" Maguire asked.

He watched as the look on her face went from one of anger, to confusion and then to a knowing smile.

"I do," she replied, the tension easing away from her body. "Do you think you could still handle it?"

"They probably have a few rules against something like that on Port Authority property."

"Weren't you the one who said rules were meant to be broken?"

"I was," Maguire replied, "but then you couldn't break the rule when it mattered."

The playful looked drained from Tzviya's face.

"That was different," she replied.

"Stop carrying this around, Zee," he said. "I just want the truth. Don't I deserve that much for the price I paid?"

"I paid the same price, James."

"I didn't say that you didn't, but you at least got to look at the bill. That's all I am asking for."

Tzviya walked over to the chain link fence and leaned back against it, allowing her body to collapse to the ground. Maguire waked over and sat down next to her.

"I know your father was involved in this," he said. "I just need to know the truth. It can't be worse than the stories I've made up in my mind."

She laughed, then leaned over and rested her head on his shoulder. "You really think so?"

"Try me."

"You're right," she said. "My father was involved. Someone saw us that night at the Sheraton and reported it. They put us under observation and when he knew what was going on I got called back to answer for it."

"Jesus Christ, we were both adults, what was so wrong?"

"My father feared that with your background in the Navy that you were interested in more than my body," she said.

"Are you serious?"

"Very much so," she replied. "That's why he ordered me to stop seeing you."

"You could have said no," Maguire said. "Told him that you were an adult and you'd see who you wanted to."

"I did."

"And?"

"My father said that if that was my choice that I should enjoy the days I had left with you."

"Days?" Maguire asked "What the fuck were they going to do, kill me?"

Silence hung in the air, as the truth Maguire was searching for took hold.

"*Sonofabitch*," he muttered.

"My guess is that if I had refused, a *Kidon* team would have been sent to address the problem."

Maguire looked out over the East River, staring at the lights on Riker's Island, and processed what she had just said.

The Kidon was the name of the department within the Mossad that was responsible for assignations. They were the best of the best, masters of their trade: espionage, torture, murder, nothing was off-limits. They possessed talents and abilities most spy agencies could only dream of. Need a man in Pakistan? No problem. Need a man in Pakistan that not only speaks the language, but the native dialect to a particular region? Got you covered. The men and women of the Kidon even studied under medical examiners, learning how to avoid killing someone and leaving even the slightest tell-tale mark or bruise.

They were well versed in all types of weapons: from poisons to knives, to piano wire and any manner of explosives. They also had an arsenal of firearms at their disposal, from easily concealed handguns to sniper rifles which had a killing range of a mile plus. Even sex was used if it furthered the mission.

Maguire knew that if they had sent a team out for him, despite all his training and capabilities, there was no doubt in his mind that he would be dead. You couldn't fight an enemy you never saw coming.

"When I heard you had been shot, my first thought was that he had lied to me," she said. "That's why I went to the hospital. I needed to know you were still alive."

"Then what did you do?"

"I told my father that I would adhere to his order," she said, "but that if anything happened to you that I would come after him."

"So that's why you disappeared."

"I couldn't run the risk, James. I loved you too much to let anything happen to you."

Maguire wrapped his arm around her shoulder, feeling her lean in close to him, her head pressing against his chest. It had been more than four years since he had last held her in his arms and at this very moment it was as if nothing had ever changed.

No, that wasn't true, he thought, as he stared out across the river. *Everything had changed.*

Rich was gone and next week he would have to officially take over the helm of the New York City Police Department. Not to mention the fact that the woman he was engaged to was being vetted for a Cabinet position. All while he sat on this cold airport tarmac with a foreign spy.

Everything in him told him that this was a bad idea; that he should just get up and walk away. He had his answer and nothing was going to change their situation. He leaned over and gently kissed Tzviya's head, feeling her wrap her arms tightly around him.

She felt it to, he thought.

He closed his eyes and the rest of the world just faded away.

Fuck it, he thought. *Rules were meant to be broken.*

EPILOGUE

Westmore, Vermont
Thursday, January 9th, 2014 – 1:02 p.m.

The afternoon silence was shattered by the loud *crack* of the rifle's report, the echo carrying for a time as it bounced off the cliffs surrounding the southern edge of Lake Willoughby.

"I'm just saying that I don't understand this obsession you have with him." Susan said, as she looked down the spotter scope at the small, paper target that was tacked onto a tree a half mile away.

"9," Susan called out, "upper right quadrant."

"It's not an obsession, my dear," Tatiana said, as she made a minor adjustment on the scope. "It's a game."

"You have to admit that you're pushing the envelope a bit."

"How so?" Tatiana asked, as she set her cheek back down against the rifles stock.

"You don't think that last play was a bit *reckless*?"

Tatiana took a breath and then squeezed the trigger slowly, following through until she felt the recoil against her shoulder and the loud report, as the 175 grain .308 Winchester round headed down range.

Susan looked through the lens, "10."

"I wouldn't call it reckless," Tatiana replied. "I saw an opportunity and I took it. Like they always say: *carpe diem*."

"I'm all for seizing the day, Tee, but you killed the friggin' New York City Police Commissioner."

"Isn't that what we do, love?" Tatiana ask, as she began packing the sniper rifle back up in its hard case. "Kill people?"

"Yes," Susan replied, rolling up the shooting mat, and I would like to keep on doing it."

Tatiana closed the rifle case and locked it. "And they aren't looking for us."

Much to Susan's amazement, the shooting was being pinned on the Army flunky who'd been linked to the other murders.

"Yet," Susan replied, "but what happens when they catch the guy and he has an alibi for that one?"

Tatiana loaded the case into the back of the SUV and sat on the rear tailgate, looking at Susan.

"You assume that they will bring him in alive," Tatiana said. "Let's not forget that the man has been linked to the deaths of four cops. Maybe I'm wrong, but I'm guessing they aren't going to be feeling all warm and fuzzy when they finally knock on his door."

"All I'm saying is that, unless we want this little *Thelma & Louise* ride to come to the same brutal end, we need to be more careful."

Tatiana hated to admit it, but Susan was right. She'd allowed herself to have a moment of stupidity, not about the shooting, but about the little gift she had left behind. While she was methodical in making sure there was nothing to link back to her, in the form of DNA or prints, she had still left a piece of evidence behind.

It could have been worse, she thought. Her original idea had been to email him a taunt, but at the last second she changed her mind.

Maybe it was time to take a break from the game she was playing with him and get back to the random fun that they enjoyed.

"You're right," she said.

Susan laid the mat into the back of the truck and turned toward the woman with a surprised look on her face. "I'm what?"

Tatiana smiled and grabbed the girl, pulling her close and kissed her.

"You're right. There, I said it again, are you happy?"

"Shocked, but delighted," Susan replied.

Tatiana wrapped her legs around Susan's waist, holding her playfully. "Let's pack up and go have some fun."

"Really?"

"Yeah, your call," Tatiana replied. "We'll go and do whatever your little heart desires."

Susan wrapped her arms around Tatiana's neck. "My little heart desires a lot, Tee."

"Name it?"

Susan closed her eyes and thought about it for a moment.

Over the course of the last few months they had been all over the East Coast picking and choosing their victims on a whim. It had kept things interesting, but at the same time it was all so impersonal, so detached. It was safety, but without the satisfaction. There was a lot to be said about looking into the eyes of someone you knew while the life slowly drained out of them. They had the most pitiful look, as they realized you were their personal grim reaper.

In a way she envied the fact that Tatiana was still playing her game, getting even with those who had wronged her. She had started out that way, but had let it go, opting to follow Tatiana's lead. It just seemed so hypocritical to want that, after she had just chastised her.

"Oh c'mon, sweetie, it can't be that hard," Tatiana said. "Do you want an acquaintance or stranger?"

"Acquaintance," Susan replied, as she opened her eyes and stared at Tatiana.

"There, that wasn't hard," Tatiana said. "Who?"

"Mr. Goodridge, my algebra teacher."

"Ooh, tell me more."

"I sat in the back of his class," Susan replied. "He'd walk around during class, while he was giving a lecture, and always ended up behind me. I'd feel him put his hand on my shoulder and rub it."

"You think he wanted you?"

"Oh yeah," Susan replied, "he was definitely a perv. He made the seating assignments at the beginning of the year and his favorites in every class always ended up in the back row."

"Did you want him?"

"I don't know, maybe," Susan said. "Probably to get even. You know, in some fucked up *'my daddy didn't love me'* sort of way."

"Was he good looking?" Tatiana asked.

"He was cute, but kinda creepy," she replied. "I'm sure he could have gotten any woman he wanted, but he seemed to be more interested in young girls."

"I think we've all had those teachers."

"You did?"

"Yeah, my senior year I had, Mr. Roberts for my AP History class. He sat all the girls that had big boobs in the front row. It became this big joke and we'd all take turns wearing the tightest shirts we could. "

"Guess they're all over," Susan said with a laugh.

"How do you want to do it?"

"I wouldn't mind sending him out with a bang," Susan replied.

"Well then, it looks like we're heading home," Tatiana said.

"You're so good to me," Susan replied.

She leaned forward and kissed Tatiana deeply, feeling the warmth of the woman's lips against her own.

Susan had never questioned her relationship with Tatiana. They were like best friends, *with benefits*. Neither woman had any qualms about their relationship or their sexuality. They routinely used sex, with both men and women, as a weapon to achieve their goals, but it never interfered with the pleasure they derived. In fact, in many ways it seemed to enhance it. There wasn't anything better than a post-murder romp, when the adrenaline was at its highest.

"Do you think it's a good idea?"

"We'll get in and get out before anyone knows we were even there," Tatiana replied. "Then we'll head southwest and enjoy the sun for a few months."

"Mmmmm, good," Susan replied. "I need to work on my tan."

"And you know how much I like to watch you work on that tan," Tatiana said.

"Let's do this," Susan said with a mischievous look, her voice giddy with anticipation.

"Okay," Tatiana replied, as she unwrapped her legs from Susan's waist and got up, closing the SUV's back hatch.

Penobscot was a quaint little town. In many ways it reminded her of the place that she had grown up in. It appealed to her because she could enjoy the town's familiar ambiance without having to worry about being recognized.

That's not entirely true, she thought, as she climbed into the SUV.

Tatiana shuddered at the thought, as if a surge of electricity had gone down through her body into her lap.

She gasped.

"You okay?" Susan asked.

"Huh?" Tatiana replied, as she started up the vehicle. "Oh yeah, just got a chill."

Susan reached over and turned up the heat. "That should help."

Tatiana put the SUV in gear and headed down the rough path, her thoughts on the idyllic little town a hundred miles away.

There was one person in Penobscot who knew her; one person who posed not only a threat, but a tantalizing target as well.

One day, she thought, as she bit her lower lip. *One day.*

About the Author

Andrew Nelson spent twenty-two years in law enforcement, including twenty years with the New York City Police Department. During his tenure with the NYPD he served as a detective in the elite Intelligence Division, conducting investigations and providing dignitary protection to numerous world leaders. He achieved the rank of sergeant before retiring in 2005. He is also a graduate of the State University of New York. He and his wife have four children and reside in central Illinois with their Irish Wolfhound.

For more information please visit:

http://andrewgnelson.blogspot.com/

Like us on Facebook:

https://www.facebook.com/pages/Andrew-Nelson/168310343376572

ANDREW G.
NELSON

Made in United States
North Haven, CT
15 April 2022

18254082R00241